CW00742462

Bella's Countryside Christmas

Claire Huston

Copyright © Claire Huston 2024

The moral right of Claire Huston to be identified as the author of this work has been asserted in accordance with the Copyright, Designs and Patents Act 1988.

No part of this publication may be reproduced, stored in a retrieval system, or transmitted in any form or by any means without the prior permission in writing of the publisher. Nor be otherwise circulated in any form of binding or cover other than that in which it is published and without a similar condition including this condition being imposed on the subsequent purchaser.

This book is a work of fiction. All characters and events, other than those clearly in the public domain, are fictitious. Any resemblance to real persons, living or dead, is entirely coincidental and not intended by the author.

All rights reserved.

Published by Goldcrest Books International Ltd
www.goldcrestbooks.com
publish@goldcrestbooks.com

ISBN: 978-1-911505-35-8

For Hester
x

Chapter 1

Perched on a bench against the back wall of St Stephen's, Bella realized it had been years since she had visited anywhere brimming with such festive magic. Above her, the twin colonnades on either side of the nave were draped with garlands of holly and ivy. A wreath of bright red poinsettias adorned the end of every pew. On the window ledges, tall creamy candles trimmed with gold ribbon shimmered, and the cool air around her carried faint aromas of clove and orange. Acoustic versions of Christmas carols floated from hidden speakers and echoed off the vaulted ceiling. And, at the front of the north aisle, a tall fir tree stood bedecked in white lights, glittering tinsel and colourful baubles.

Bella shivered as her gaze slid down from the single bright star at the top of the tree. When she had first tiptoed into the church, the warm candlelight and thick stone walls had offered welcome shelter from the icy wind howling through the gloomy graveyard outside. But, having sat motionless for goodness knows how long while her thoughts wandered, a wintry draught—which was drifting around the floor like a restless spirit—had wrapped itself around her ankles.

Bella pushed to standing, the movement as sluggish and reluctant as the realization slouching its way to the front of her mind: St Stephen's was undeniably beautiful. Dammit. And, to add insult to injury, the place was packed with history too. The little church in the Cotswolds village of Haileybrook had been home to centuries of events which had each left their mark, creating an indescribable feeling that would bring a touch of priceless charm to any occasion. Double dammit.

Bella sighed as she shuffled up the side aisle towards the tree. It would have been quicker to stroll up the main aisle, but she didn't dare. Her treacherous imagination might place her dad at her side, his chest puffed out, the proud father of the bride. And worse, if her gaze landed on the space in front of the altar, she might see Ethan waiting there, his eyes brimming with tears of joy above a wide smile. A smile she would probably never see again. A thought which delivered yet another blow to her dented heart.

Stop dithering! her inner voice chided and, checking the time on her phone, Bella had to concede it had a point. She should head back before anyone noticed she had left the hotel. Her colleagues had been quick to accept a fictional headache as a reason to miss the afternoon sessions, but it was nearly half past four and she should leave soon if she was going to be on time for pre-dinner drinks.

Ugh! Another night of wearing a tight smile and nodding politely while pretending to listen to people she would happily shove off the end of a pier was likely to bring on a real headache. No amount of cheap house wine would be enough to make it bearable, something Bella knew from experience.

She sighed again as she wandered up the aisle, her gaze falling on a far more recent addition to the church's décor: on a low table to the left of the fir tree sat a nativity scene. No doubt made by local children—or their unwilling parents—the Holy Family, visiting Magi and attendant animals appeared to have been clumsily constructed from cardboard, tinfoil and felt. They were painted in bold primary colours which seemed too strident for their humble stable, which Bella suspected had once been a shoebox.

She was about to take a closer look when a noise made her freeze. It appeared to come from behind the fir tree and sounded like a woman's voice. Bella glanced over her shoulder in the direction of the door as her pulse accelerated. She could have sworn the church was empty. The last thing she wanted was to bump into anyone. She couldn't cope with answering any tricky questions or—

Bella's worries were silenced by a squeal of hinges and a shrill voice. 'I don't care! Honestly, Jack. Why are you always so useless?'

Bella ducked behind the nearest pillar as the woman continued, her pitch rising to a yell, 'If you can't help me, Jack, then find someone who can. Go on. Piss off!'

Bella tugged at the collar of her heavy wool coat and flinched as the door slammed shut. She really should go. Sneak out while she still could.

Peering around the pillar, Bella caught a glimpse of a tall man pacing the line below the shallow step where the nave met the chancel. The useless Jack, she presumed. He had short dark hair, lightly tanned fair skin and was wearing a charcoal-grey suit. She guessed he was roughly the same age as her, although perhaps a little closer to forty. His jacket was unbuttoned, revealing an embroidered ivory waistcoat and emerald-green tie. He had a cream rose pinned to his lapel—

Bella's breath hitched, an invisible hand seizing her throat. There were few reasons a man would be wearing a morning suit and a buttonhole in a church. Oh God. This could not be happening.

Her gaze flicked to the exit once more then back to Jack. He was staring down at his phone as he wandered, probably wouldn't look up until he heard the outer door open and by then she would be safely out in the freezing air, on her way back to the conference centre.

Her heart thudding, Bella inched backwards, keeping her gaze trained on the man before her as if he were a grizzly bear she'd encountered in a dark wood. After a few successfully silent steps, her spirits were lifting when Jack tapped his phone screen, completed a sharp turn, tripped up the step behind him and lurched into the fir tree.

Oh no. The nativity scene!

The tree tottered as Bella darted forwards, her high heels thudding off the stone flooring. An urgent need to save the fragile nativity from being flattened by a seven-foot evergreen overwhelmed her inner monologue which was screaming that this was the perfect opportunity to make a clean escape. What did she think she was playing at?

Arms spread wide, she skidded to a halt by the table and had a split second to whip her face to one side before the tree fell into her embrace.

Chapter 2

Oof. Heavy *and* delightfully spiky. Well that certainly hadn't been one of her better ideas.

Huffing a breath out the side of her mouth to shoo a strand of red tinsel away from her eye, Bella glanced down to where the tip of one of the tree's lower branches brushed the side of the nativity stable. If she hadn't been wearing one of her favourite pairs of four-inch stilettos the tree would have squashed the manger and its precious contents.

'Er, hello?' said a deep voice from the other side of the tree.

'Yeah, hi,' Bella managed to grit out, her lungs squeezed by the weight of the tree and a fear of being garrotted by a string of fairy lights. 'D'you think you could you get this off me?'

'God, sorry. Of course. Hold on.'

A few low grunts and a good deal of rustling accompanied Jack's efforts as he lifted the tree away from Bella. The relief on her burning arms and grumbling lower back was intense, but Bella didn't move away from her backstop position immediately. 'Have you got it?'

'Yes, you can let go. I'll just get it steady.'

Bella took a step to her right and brushed a few stray fir needles from her coat while watching Jack settling the tree into its previous position. Hmn. He clearly wasn't as useless as the shouty woman claimed. And he was no weakling either: Bella would have bet there were some impressive biceps and pecs hidden under his suit.

Jack stepped back, his hands outstretched and gaze trained on the tree as if daring it to wobble. 'And I think'—he said, dropping his arms to his sides—'we're safe.' He smiled and turned to face Bella. 'Thank you again.'

Bella's lips parted as their gazes collided. *Wow*. She was sure Jack would be forgiven all sorts of accidental damage if he flashed that smile about. Its dazzling work was supported by a pair of deep brown eyes which glittered in the dim light. She blinked, taking in the waves in his hair whose shine hinted at curls partially restrained by product. His jawline was strong and straight, a contrast to his nose, which was slightly crooked, possibly the product of an old injury—

'That was a lucky escape. I can't thank you enough.'

Bella blinked again, making an effort to focus on what Jack was saying.

He continued, 'I mean, if the tree had hit the stable'—he gestured towards the nativity scene and shuddered—'I'd have run the risk of being struck down.'

'I doubt it.' Bella shrugged, attempting to look as nonchalant as possible and ignore the swooping sensation in her tummy. 'I'm not an expert on divine punishments, but smiting seems harsh for a first offence.'

Jack's lips quirked into a lopsided smile and he dropped his voice to a murmur. 'Who says it's my first offence?'

Bella laughed, her pulse kicking in delight at Jack's joke and the mischievous glint in his eye. 'So, you're a serial, rather than a casual, destroyer of nativity scenes?'

'Yep. You got me. I spend the entire festive season roaming village churches, stumbling into mangers.'

'Scattering angels.'

'Sending little donkeys flying.'

Bella pressed her lips into a serious line to contain a giggle and nodded. 'Good to know.'

'Forewarned is forearmed.' Jack chuckled but he seemed distracted, his gaze flicking upwards to above Bella's head.

Bella glanced over her shoulder. 'Is something wrong?'

'Oh no, sorry.' He lowered his gaze. 'It's … I think you have some tree in your hair.'

Oh great. Bella's hands flew up to her head. She had fixed her long blonde hair into a high bun before leaving the hotel, but now the smooth updo felt a lot less polished.

Jack reached out towards Bella's hair. 'There are just a few—' He paused and whipped his hand back. 'Sorry. I should have— Would you like me to help?'

'Go for it.' Having a stranger picking fir tree needles from her hair wasn't exactly ideal, but it was preferable to walking about looking like she was wearing a bird's nest. 'Thank you.'

'No problem,' said Jack, taking a step closer and gently pulling a piece of greenery from the right side of Bella's head. 'It's my fault after all.'

Jack was so absorbed in his task, it gave Bella complete freedom to stare up at his face. Up and up and up. How flipping tall was he anyway? Her eyes weren't even level with the knot of his tie, so he had to be at least a good foot taller than—

'You'll tell me if I hurt you?' Jack glanced down and Bella rapidly averted her gaze.

'Sure,' she muttered and inhaled slowly to calm her racing heart, inadvertently drawing in a long drag of Jack's aftershave which was a light, fresh fragrance with hints of spice and musk running underneath. It was … Bella searched for the right word while taking another sneaky sniff. *Alluring.* That was it. And very, well … *manly.*

It left her a little light-headed.

'Almost done. This last bit's being stubborn.' Jack's brow furrowed in concentration but his touch was gentle and so welcome that Bella struggled not to let her eyes drift shut so she could better revel in it. Oh Lord, how long had it been since a man had touched her? On purpose, mind. The ones who barged into her on the Underground didn't count. Besides, they usually stank of rank body odour. Ugh.

'Are you OK?'

Bella glanced up. Oh drat. Her downturn in mood must have shown on her face because Jack was staring at her, his eyes filled with concern. His hand had stilled by the side of her head, his touch a warm whisper against her hair. Bella held his gaze, and the swooping feeling in her belly returned, only this time it was more like the alternating rise and fall of a roller coaster.

'I should have asked if you'd like to sit down.' Jack withdrew his hand. 'That was stupid of me.'

'No, really,' Bella said, not wanting him to mistake her

for some weak maiden in distress. But his interest in her well-being had pricked her wounded heart and ludicrous tears welled in her eyes. She blinked and swallowed hard. 'I'm fine. The last few days have been—'

'Jack? Jack! Where the bloody hell are you?'

Jack whipped round towards the chancel and the strident voice—which appeared to be coming from behind a door to the left of the altar—and his expression twisted into a wince.

'A friend of yours?' asked Bella.

'One of my oldest friends.' Jack paused, staring at Bella as if seeing her for the first time. 'Are you *not* here for Ashley's wedding?'

'No. I was ...' Bella floundered. Why was lying always such a struggle? 'I was in the area and a friend of mine was thinking of getting married here'—she swallowed, the half truth sticking in her throat—'so I thought I'd take the opportunity to pop in. See what's so great about the place.'

'Ah. Well, to tell you the truth, you're probably better off not being part of today's festivities.'

'Things aren't going to plan?'

'How did you know?'

Bella shrugged. In this case, putting two and two together was easy. And she had always been good at maths. 'The shrieking from the on-edge bride was a giveaway. You're not the groom, are you?'

'No!' Jack's barked response came so swiftly that Bella startled and Jack seemed equally surprised by the vehemence of his reaction. He cleared his throat, his brows settling as he continued, in a more measured tone, 'No. Ashley and I did date, for a while, but today I'm just an usher. I was told to get here well in advance in case any guests arrived early.'

'And needed to be ushed?'

'Exactly. Ashley was supposed to be here with someone from the bridal party to help her with her dress—the vicar said she could use the vestry—but there's been some sort of crisis with their hair or make-up'—Jack let out a huff of exasperation—'and they're late. The wedding's supposed to start in half an hour and Ashley can't fasten her dress. There are loads of fiddly clasp things and tiny slippery buttons.' Jack held up his hands. 'And apparently my "huge clumsy man hands" aren't up to the job.'

The door to the vestry opened a couple of inches, allowing Ashley's voice to sail out unimpeded. 'Jack? Are you there?'

'I'm coming,' said Jack. 'Just a minute.'

Bella gazed at Jack's pinched, harried expression, and a tingling sensation slowly filled her limbs. A sure sign she was on the verge of doing something impulsive and probably stupid.

Oh no. Do not get involved, her inner voice warned. *You were leaving, remember?*

'Could your plus-one not help the bride with her dress?' asked Bella.

'No. I …' Jack dropped his gaze to the floor. 'My date couldn't make it. She cancelled this morning.'

'Oh dear. Is she ill?'

Jack's shoulders hunched and his voice was barely audible as he said, 'She messaged me to say she had a date with someone else.'

Ouch. Jack had been abandoned, left to attend his ex-girlfriend's wedding alone. And Bella had thought she was having a bad day.

The vestry door opened another couple of inches and Ashley hissed, 'Hurry up, Jack!'

'I should get back to Ashley,' said Jack. 'Thank you again for your help—'

'I can sort out her dress.' The words rushed out before Bella's inner voice had a chance to object. She held up her hands. 'Tiny nimble woman hands, see?'

Jack's lips parted and he stuttered before saying, 'I couldn't possibly ask you to—'

'No trouble,' said Bella, ignoring her inner monologue, which was calling her a meddling busybody and a prize idiot. 'It'll only take a minute, then I'll be on my way.'

Jack opened his mouth again, but it was Ashley's voice that leapt into the silence. 'Jack! Get in here or I'll never speak to you again!'

Bella took in Jack's slack-jawed expression and decided to take charge.

Being a pushy, interfering cow and stepping in where you're not wanted isn't the same as taking charge, Bella.

Bella straightened, shrugging off her critical inner voice. 'Don't worry,' she called towards the vestry door, 'we're coming,' and strode past the still-stuttering Jack into the chancel.

Chapter 3

The vestry door was made of thick planks of ancient wood overlaid with the curled black flourishes of a pair of iron strap hinges. Even so, it opened easily in response to Bella's touch to reveal a cramped room with a single slit window high up in the north wall. Unlike the rest of the church, it was bare of any festive decorations and the sole furnishings were to the left of the door: a tall wardrobe and two filing cabinets. The right wardrobe door, which housed a full-length mirror, was open. In front of it stood a tall woman, her black hair twisted up in an elaborate coiffeur fixed by delicate pearl pins. Bella tilted her head to better appreciate the woman's slender, well-proportioned figure. Statuesque. That was the proper word for her.

The trouble-making dress, which gaped at the back, was a dramatic ivory ballgown in an iridescent fabric Bella guessed was satin. The wide off-the-shoulder straps created a plunging neckline which showcased the bride's long neck, toned arms and flawless light brown skin.

Bella struggled to contain a gasp of longing. The poofy

skirt and plunging top was one of the dress styles she had hankered after but was forced to reject after some characteristically honest feedback from Summer. During her first visit to the bridal boutique, Bella had waltzed out of the fitting room, near ecstatic in a meringue-like cloud of tulle and lace, only to be greeted by her little sister's hooting laugh. And while Summer's voice on the video call was distorted, when she told Bella the dress made her look like a 'dumpy pale pepper pot', Bella got the message.

'Oh!' Ashley spun to face Bella, revealing a face to match her goddess figure: large dark eyes, perfectly arched brows and a glowing complexion. 'Who the hell are you? Where's—'

'I'm here, I'm here,' Jack said, rushing over the threshold.

'Finally!' Ashley glared at Jack, cast a quick glance at Bella and drew in a long breath.

Bella decided to jump in before the bride could get into full flow. 'Jack said you needed help and I have the small hands you require.' Bella waggled her fingers like a magician encouraging a rabbit out of a hat.

Bella followed Ashley's incredulous gaze down to her wiggling fingers. What the hell was she doing? She wouldn't be surprised if Ashley threw her out.

But Ashley's thunderous expression softened. 'Oh! You must be Jack's mysterious Helen.' She thrust out a hand, grabbed Bella's into a shake and then hit Bella with a dazzling smile that only added to her confusion.

'Uh, actually—' Jack made a valiant attempt to interrupt, but the bride was not to be stopped.

'You know,' Ashley said, her voice a series of clipped

vowels and consonants which, to Bella's ear, spoke of inherited wealth or excellent elocution lessons, 'some people had started to wonder if Jack had made you up!' Her gaze cut to Jack and she rushed to add, 'Not me, of course.'

Bella was certain her face must have been a picture of befuddlement, but perhaps the stunning Ashley was used to having that effect of people. She leant closer to Bella and murmured, 'Bets have been placed on whether you'd show up today. I'm a few quid up. Thank you.'

'Actually, Ashley—' Jack began again, his cheeks dashed with darkening strips of crimson.

'And the people who didn't think Jack would invent a woman, thought he must be hiding you because you were hideous!' Ashley continued blithely, as if every word that slipped from between her glossed lips wasn't compounding Jack's obvious horror—his eyes were as wide as saucers and his jaw slack—and Bella's growing dislike of her breezy disregard of her audience's feelings.

Bella swallowed, her throat burning with Ashley's lily-heavy perfume, as she formed a plan. She would introduce herself, button up the woman's sickeningly gorgeous dress and beat a hasty retreat.

'Jack's love life is something of a famous disaster,' Ashley said, chuckling. 'Since he and I split up, none of the new girls have hung around long enough to meet us. Imagine!'

Bella narrowed her eyes, her fingers balling into tight fists. Beside her, she could feel Jack deflating, his shoulders sinking under the weight of embarrassment. A sharp pang of sympathy stabbed her. She didn't know Jack, but no one deserved to be shamed for being unlucky in love.

And certainly not by an ex-girlfriend on her wedding day. Obviously this day would always have been difficult for him as Ashley's ex, but when everyone found out his date had cancelled on him at the last minute …

Unless.

Don't, said her inner voice. *This has nothing to do with you. And it's a bit soon for you to be attending a wedding, isn't it? I know you'd all but sell a kidney to avoid going back to the conference, but—even by your standards—this is a truly terrible idea.*

Bella smiled. She could walk away from a bad idea. But a truly terrible one? Irresistible.

Training a wide grin at Ashley, Bella curled her left arm around Jack's right. 'Well, their loss is certainly my gain. I hope you'll all think I was worth waiting for.'

Jack cleared his throat and Bella looked up to meet his gaze. When their eyes met he raised his eyebrows a fraction, as if to say, '*You don't have to do this.*'

Bella squeezed his arm and was pleased to find his bicep was as impressive as she had guessed. Holding his dark stare, she lifted a single eyebrow in response to his unspoken plea before turning back to Ashley. 'I'm sure the rest of your guests will be arriving soon. Let's get this dress sorted.'

Chapter 4

Her dress securely fastened, Ashley swished out of the vestry to join the bridal party in the porch. Bella smiled as she closed the door and leant back against it, the tension in her shoulders melting away as the latch clicked into place.

Unfortunately, Jack didn't seem to share her relief. He paced the vestry like a caged animal, raking his hands through his hair. Uf! Much more of that and the man would make her dizzy.

'Are you all right?' Bella asked.

'I can't believe you did that!' Jack threw his hands up. 'What are we going to do now?'

'Perhaps start with calming down? Stand still for a second?'

Jack came to an abrupt halt. 'How are you so calm?'

Bella took a slow breath in and a moment to check in on herself. Her pulse beat a slow regular rhythm and her hands were steady. He was right. Despite having launched herself into the middle of a situation which was possibly unwise for her mental health and apparently terrible for

Jack's stress levels, she wasn't so much as breaking a sweat. Probably because the congregation gathering on the other side of the door weren't her friends.

And not because it's easier to solve someone else's problem than deal with your own? whispered her inner voice, which Bella was beginning to resent for being an overly clever, sarcastic cow.

Jack ran a hand along his jaw. 'I guess we should come up with an excuse for you to leave as soon as possible.'

'Oh?' Bella frowned, Jack's words leaving her feelings smarting. She had expected a little gratitude and co-operation. She might not be his mysterious—and no doubt amazing—Helen, but was the idea of spending an evening with her that awful? She swallowed her hurt and lifted her chin. 'Why?'

'Well, because ...' Jack gestured to Bella's outfit. 'You clearly have somewhere else to be tonight.'

Ah. Bella glanced down. She had slung her coat onto one of the filing cabinets before tackling the fiendish fastenings of Ashley's gown. Doing so had revealed her emerald velvet wrap dress. It had long sleeves, a deep V-neck and gathered at the waist before flaring out to fall to her knees. Bella loved how the cut flattered her curves and the colour complemented her pale complexion and white-blonde hair, although she was less confident about the large silver bow which was fixed to the deepest point of the neckline. On the upside, she was certain it would emphasize her impressive cleavage and draw attention away from her less favoured features. On the other hand, she worried it made her look like she was wearing gift wrapping. In general, Bella's tastes in clothes veered away from anything 'glittery' or 'cute'. But she was willing to make an exception for Christmas. After all, wasn't that what Christmas involved? Being a shinier, jollier version of yourself?

Bella raised her gaze to meet Jack's, but he quickly dropped his stare to the floor. 'I mean, obviously it's a very nice dress and a beautiful'—Jack spoke quickly and lifted his gaze, but his stare only reached the level of her chest before he dropped it to the ground again—'um, bow. The bow is ... striking. Glittery.'

A smile pulled at Bella's lips. Ha! The bow seemed to be exerting an attention-grabbing effect on Jack. Although, once his powers of speech returned to normal and the blush blooming in his cheeks subsided, some eye contact would be nice.

'Thank you. Actually I wear these shoes all the time.' Bella shrugged. Heels weren't optional when you barely scraped past the five-foot mark. 'But you're right about the rest. I'm staying at a hotel in the area for my company's annual conference.' She sighed loudly. The whole event was a gratuitous back-slapping exercise and a nauseating celebration of the savage pursuit of money without a care for the people behind the numbers—

'You're not exactly enjoying it, I take it?'

Bella released a shaky breath. She was glad Jack had interrupted her thoughts before she worked herself up to hyperventilating. And, as a bonus, he was now looking her straight in the eye. 'It's been horrendous,' she said. 'This is the fourth one I've been to and I didn't think it could be worse than previous years. But then my colleagues love beating records. A right bunch of prize knobheads.' She cringed as Jack's eyebrows shot up. How many times had Ethan told her that people didn't find her straight-talking charming? 'Sorry. I have this habit of calling a spade a spade. Er, let's just say they're not the nicest people.'

Jack barked a laugh. 'Don't apologise. Anyway, your aversion to your colleagues explains why you'd rather help me this evening than get back to …'

'The gala dinner.' Bella shuddered. 'The company's yearly celebration of greed as the greatest good.'

'I'm starting to feel a little better about roping you into this.'

'Hey, I walked into this myself. The question is, are *you* up for it?'

Jack's gaze settled on the door above Bella's head for a moment as he pondered her question. Gradually, he lowered his gaze to meet hers, the beginnings of a nervous smile at the corners of his mouth. 'I'm in. Let's do it.'

Bella grinned and pushed off the door, her pulse picking up. There was nothing quite like cooking up a plot. 'Right. I reckon we have fifteen minutes before the wedding kicks off. We use that time to get our origin story straight.'

'Origin story? We're not superheroes.'

'Speak for yourself.'

Jack snorted. 'All right, Wonder Woman. Carry on.'

Bella's smile stretched. That was one nickname she would like to stick. And she particularly enjoyed how it sounded in Jack's deep voice. 'How we met will be the first question everyone asks. We'll also need to know a bit about each other's backgrounds. Enough for us to pass ourselves off as a couple. And'—Bella held up a finger—'we should come up with what we're going to say—a sort of all-purpose get-out excuse—if we're asked something we should know, but don't.'

'Blimey.' Jack tilted his head to one side, appraising Bella anew. 'Have you done this before?'

Bella loosed a nervous laugh as a surge of adrenalin made her skin tingle. 'No. But I love a good plan. Does Helen love a good plan?'

'Uh …'

'I take it your relationship with Helen wasn't long-term?'

'We met online. Chatted for months. Messaged. But we only met in person once.'

And then she'd ditched him for someone else. Bella gave Jack a tight smile to hide her need to wince. 'OK. "Online" as in a dating site or an app?'

'App. Matched. Have you ever used it?'

'No, but some of the girls at work do.' And were always complaining about the rubbish men they met through it. It had made Bella grateful she'd been off the market for so long. 'So we matched, chatted for months, then our first date was a few weeks ago and we went to …'

'Three weeks ago. We met in Oxford for a drink then went to the cinema.'

'Because you and Helen both live in Oxford?'

'I live to the north of the city but Helen came across from London.'

'Fantastic.' Bella gave the air a small punch. 'I live in London. That will help. What did you see at the cinema?'

'There was a classic action season on at the art house. So we saw what was on that night.' Jack stuffed his hands in his pockets, his gaze returning to the floor. 'Which was *Predator*.'

'*Predator* as in Arnold Schwarzenegger fighting an invisible alien in the jungle?'

'Yes,' Jack said, his reply a mutter. 'I think that was my big mistake. I don't think she was thrilled. I should have looked into what was on before, but it was all very last minute and—'

'Don't be ridiculous!' Bella wouldn't allow Jack to feel bad about what was clearly an excellent decision. 'It's a classic of the action-suspense genre. If that's what drove Helen off you should be glad you haven't wasted time on someone who doesn't appreciate what is obviously a masterpiece.'

Jack looked up, a shy smile tugging at his lips. 'It is a good film. It may have dated badly in some ways—'

'No. It still holds up. That's the benefit of not overly relying on visual effects and—' Bella cut herself off. They didn't have time for this conversation now. Besides, Ethan used to say her enthusiasm for violent action films was worrying and spoke of anger issues. But Bella believed there was a deep satisfaction to be had from watching people who deserved it get punched square on the nose. 'Sorry,' she said, shaking her head to banish Ethan from her thoughts. 'I went off topic. So, we went to the cinema, bonded over our love of classic action films and voilà!' She gestured to herself. 'Here I am, on our second date. Next. Helen's surname is?'

'Snow.'

'Seriously?' Bella paused while Jack nodded. 'OK, I'll brace myself for the odd *Game of Thrones* or Christmas joke, but at least it's easy to remember. Does she have any siblings? Pets? Flatmates? Or is she a resilient loner who struggles to keep her single cactus alive?'

Jack laughed, his dark eyes shining with amusement. 'I believe she shares a house in London with friends. Only child, her parents live in Durham. She has an ancient, one-eyed cat called Smoky which I believe she would save from a fire before any of her housemates. She sent me many, many photos of that cat.'

'Right.' Bella nodded in understanding. She was convinced her own time living and working in London had made her increasingly misanthropic. Not helped by her most recent experience of having to share a cramped terraced house with four other people. The days she found all her milk had been used, yet again, she would happily have traded her housemates for a pet. 'I'm a cat lady in training. Her job?'

'Primary school teacher. She has a class of six- and seven-year-olds.'

'Amazing!'

'Don't tell me that's what you do too?'

Jack's left eyebrow was raised in an expression that spoke of total incredulity. Bella bristled. Did she not give out maternal teacher vibes? She could totally be a teacher! 'No, but my best friend is, so I have plenty to work with. What do you do?'

'I work in estate management.'

It was Bella's turn to raise an eyebrow. What the heck did that mean?

Her confusion must have shown on her face, because Jack continued, 'It's a family business. Although, that's not … It's not exactly … It's more that I work with family property.'

Hmn. Well that clarified precisely nothing. Bella had opened her mouth to ask for more details when the door behind her swung open and a stocky man in a morning suit which matched Jack's ducked across the threshold. He tossed his head, sending his long fringe of sandy hair away from his face only for it to settle back low over his eyes a second later. 'There you are, Smithy! And you must be the lovely Helen.' He grabbed Bella's hand and pumped it up and down with alarming enthusiasm. 'Terrific to meet you.'

'Hi Simon, good to see you,' said Jack. 'Is everything OK out there?'

'The bridal party are in the west tower entrance. Lots of fussing and clucking. You know what females can be like! I made myself scarce as soon as I could.' He shuddered and Bella—glancing down at his left hand—was unsurprised to find it bare of a wedding ring.

Jack nodded. 'And David and Ethan?'

'The groom and best man are in position and the congregation are piling in. I can understand why you'd rather be in here'—he leered openly at Bella, his gaze roving over every part of her except her face—'but I could do with a hand with the ushering.'

'Of course. Sorry. I'll be out in a minute.'

'No problem, Smithy. Can't say I blame you.' Simon grinned and, licking his lips, dropped his gaze to Bella's cleavage. 'If you get bored with this loser, Helen, come find me later, eh?' Simon chuckled. 'I'll take care of you.'

Bella wrinkled her nose as if she'd had the misfortune to stumble across a horrific stench and said, 'No thanks, Simon. Frankly, I'd rather die.'

Jack's jaw dropped and his wide gaze flicked to Simon, but his friend threw his head back and guffawed. 'A girl with spirit too. Excellent!'

Frowning, Jack seized Simon's arm and manoeuvred him, rather roughly, over to the door. Ignoring Simon's grunts of protest, he said, in a commanding tone which brooked no argument, 'Two minutes, Si,' and—using a fluid, powerful movement—shoved Simon over the threshold and slammed the door behind him.

Bella nodded. That was the way to deal with guys like Simon. Nicely done, Jack.

Sadly, Jack didn't seem to be as impressed with his performance. His head dropped forwards and he was shaking it as he turned back to Bella. 'I'm sorry. Simon can be …' He tailed off, struggling for the right words.

Bella had no such problems. 'A leery, sexist arsehole?'

'Yes. I'm afraid that's pretty accurate.' Jack's frown lifted as a happier thought came to him. 'But, on the bright side, I don't think we have to worry about convincing Simon we're on a date.'

'No,' said Bella. 'He'll be too busy looking at my boobs to care who I am. Unfortunately I doubt everyone will be so easily distracted. So'—Bella clapped her hands, returning to information-gathering mode—'from the "Smithy" thing, I take it your surname is Smith?'

'Yes, I've always gone by Smith.'

Bella narrowed her eyes. What did *that* mean? Did Jack have a secret identity? Intrigued, but short on time, Bella shelved her questions for later. 'OK. I think I know enough for now. And you're needed out there. Let's go.'

'Wait. Here.' Jack swooped on Bella's coat and with an efficient swish worthy of an experienced bullfighter, swung it round ready for her to slip into.

'Thank you,' said Bella, quietly impressed at the

decisiveness and precision of his movements. Not to mention his attempts at chivalry. She spun to face him, keen to confirm a final detail which had been niggling her since Simon mentioned it. 'Is the best man called Ethan?'

'Yes. He's David's—the groom's—younger brother. Why?'

Bella shrugged, feigning indifference while trying to shake off her unease. The best man sharing a name with her ex was a coincidence, not a bad omen. Ethan was a fairly common name, after all. 'Oh, no reason,' Bella lied. 'Just checking I had my facts straight. Let's go.'

Jack nodded and reached for the iron door pull. His fingers had wrapped around it when a tightness in Bella's chest propelled her forwards and she slapped her hand onto the door next to his, blocking his progress.

His eyebrows lifting in surprise, Jack stared down at her as she slowly raised her gaze up to meet his. Bella took a deep breath and focused on slowing her booming pulse. But then the growing hubbub of chatter on the other side of the door was joined by organ music—a piece by Handel which had been on Bella's own list—and a new squeeze gripped her lungs, making her light-headed. What had she signed up for? Perhaps this was the first bad idea she'd had that was too terrible to see through?

'Are you OK?' asked Jack, his voice a soft murmur. 'You don't have to do this. It's very kind of you, but I'll survive—'

'No. I'm all right.' Bella inhaled slowly, and Jack's clean spicy scent helped revive her. No matter how difficult the next hour might be, she wouldn't abandon him. It wasn't in her to leave anyone high and dry. Perhaps there was a middle way through this? 'Would you mind if I didn't sit through the ceremony? If I waited out in the porch?'

Oh Lord, she thought, struggling to hold Jack's gaze, he must think I'm crazy. But how to explain her sudden aversion to watching the happy couple tie the knot? 'It's just that …' Bella paused. A half truth would be better than an outright lie. 'I always cry at weddings and I don't have the kit I need in my car to completely redo this face.' She held her palms up to either side of her face and pouted playfully.

Jack smiled. 'No problem. In fact, if you don't mind the company, I was thinking of doing the same thing, at least for the crucial vows.' His smile fell away, his lips pulling into a tense line. 'I suspect there are a few people running another book on me breaking down.'

What? Were all Jack's 'friends' insensitive jerks? 'No problem.' Bella pushed her shoulders back, resolute. Jack and she were a team now, and she wouldn't leave him alone at his ex's wedding to face the scrutiny of Ashley's awful guests. 'Shall we?'

Bella gripped the top of the door handle, but Jack didn't move. His posture was rigid, his expression tense, the image of a man peering over the edge of a cliff into the abyss below. 'Are *you* OK?' she asked.

'Yeah.' The reply came out as a whisper. Jack cleared his throat. 'Sure. How do I look?'

Bella let her gaze sweep over him slowly as she came up with a response that would be equal parts honest, reassuring and—ideally—funny. 'Gorgeous. I'd say you'll have to watch out for wandering hands if you're going to be walking about looking that … *usherable*.'

Jack laughed, the tension vanishing from his posture. 'Thank you. I'll be on my guard.' He held out his free hand. 'Ready?'

Bella eyed his large palm and long, strong fingers, and a shot of anticipation fizzed in her belly. She grinned and clasped his outstretched hand. 'Ready when you are.'

Chapter 5

The porch under the west tower was thankfully an enclosed vestibule. An angel had installed a small heater underneath the bench against the north wall and Bella wiggled her feet in delight as the warm air tickled her calves. She tipped her head back, gazed up at the large ivy wreath topped with sprigs of holly on the opposite wall and wondered what the hell she was playing at.

On the other side of the heavy interior doors, the congregation were finishing a rousing performance of 'O Come, All Ye Faithful'. Bella had joined in with a brave attempt at the descant part on the last verse, her struggle with the highest notes only partly explaining why her eyes had filled with tears. She blinked rapidly and sniffed. Get a grip, she told herself. It was a terrific crowd-pleasing song which would ring out in millions of church ceremonies this time of year. Just because it had also been on *her* list for *her* ceremony, didn't mean the universe was taunting her. At least, not any more than usual.

Her phone buzzed in her coat pocket. Bella cleared her

throat as she retrieved it, her shoulders slumping as she saw the name on the screen: *Dad*.

She swallowed and, mindful that the congregation next door had fallen silent, put on a quiet version of her brightest voice. 'Hi, Dad! How are you?'

'Fine, love. Eleven days till Christmas. Have you packed yet?'

In eight days Bella would be flying to join her dad and stepmum at their villa on the southern Spanish coast. She smiled, imagining the balmy Mediterranean sunshine in the depth of winter, one of two things which had persuaded her against sitting alone in her poky room on Christmas Day, weeping while watching *It's a Wonderful Life* and wondering how her life had gone so wrong. The other clincher had been her stepsister, Lucinda, who had confirmed she and her boyfriend Alex would also be jetting to the Costa del Sol to act as a buffer between their parents' well-meaning questions and Bella's pain.

'I have to get this conference done first, Dad. When do Lucinda and Alex arrive?'

'A few hours before you do.'

Bella clenched her fist and mouthed 'yes', but her delight meant she missed something her dad had said about Summer. 'Sorry, Dad. Did you say Summer is coming too?' Bella's voice rose to a squeak of incredulity.

'No, love. She'll be in Marrakesh. Or was it Alexandria? It's hard to keep track.'

'The point is, she's not coming.'

'You know what your sister's like.' Her dad chuckled and Bella's fist tightened. She wished Dad would tell Summer not to be so monumentally selfish. It was bad enough she'd failed to show up for Dad's wedding two and a half years ago. But now she was turning down an invitation to a family Christmas gathering, one at which she could finally meet their stepmother and awesome stepsister in person instead of over video chat. Ugh! Bella gritted her teeth as she listened to her dad continue to excuse her sister's behaviour, 'Summer's a free spirit. You never know, she could still drop in. That would be a nice surprise.'

Oh yes, the return of the prodigal daughter. Bella rolled her eyes. She should end the call before she said something that would no doubt be held against her forever because, unlike Summer, she never got a free pass. 'Yes, Dad. Sorry, but I have to go. The conference—'

'Of course. Don't let me hold you back. I know they can't do without you.'

Bella bit her bottom lip. It was lovely that Dad was so proud of each of her recent promotions and bonuses, but it also made it impossible to tell him the truth: that she hated almost every second she was at work and had dreams of quitting in dramatic style, burning the place to the ground after wiping the database and millions off the company share value in the process. He was so happy in his retirement, he would struggle to imagine it. 'Thanks Dad.'

'Oh, there was just one more thing.'

Bella closed her eyes and dropped her head forwards. It would be Summer. It was always Summer. 'Yes?'

'Your sister hasn't asked you for any money, has she?'

Bella pinched her brow ridge. She hated lying. Especially to her dad. 'Not lately,' she said, hoping she sounded breezy rather than shifty. 'Why? Has she said something?'

'No, she hasn't. I'm probably fretting over nothing. This latest job of hers must pay better.'

It didn't. Bella had sent Summer money three times in the past nine months, receiving empty promises about future repayments in return. She sometimes wondered if *not* sending Summer money might teach her to be more responsible with her spending. But then Summer would ask their dad for help, which would worry him when he was supposed to be taking it easy and enjoying his retirement.

Bella lifted her gaze to the decorations draped around the porch. She should end the call before she had to lie further. 'Dad, I'm sorry, I have to go now.'

'No problem, love. You get on.'

Bella swallowed the sour ball of guilt in her throat. 'Speak soon and love to Marion.'

'She'd say the same. Bye, love.'

A squeak of hinges echoed over her father's parting words, drawing Bella's gaze to one of the doors to the nave which opened just enough for Jack to slip into the vestibule. Bella's smile widened, her blood humming in response to Jack's grin and nod of acknowledgement. But her smile froze when a second figure followed him into the porch.

She was one of the bridesmaids. Though Bella had abandoned the nave when the bridal procession was halfway up the aisle, she'd had the chance to take in the forest-green sheath dresses and burgundy shrugs sported by the five women preceding Ashley towards the altar. Though her outfit lacked the stunning elegance of Ashley's ivory gown, the newcomer—who was slender and a good eight inches taller than Bella—carried her festive frock well. Her long brown hair cascaded over her shoulders in an elegant curtain of loose curls and her flawless dark brown complexion glowed despite the dim lighting in the porch.

'Hello, I'm Dinah,' she said in a stage whisper as she closed the door and came forwards to shake Bella's hand. 'I'm delighted to meet you, Helen. The wedding chat groups have been buzzing about you!'

Bella smiled awkwardly and tilted her chin up to meet Dinah's gaze. Were all the women in the bridal party amazons? Was being catwalk-model height or above a requirement to enter Ashley's friendship group?

'Dinah's one of Ashley's cousins,' said Jack.

'Right ...' Bella stared at Jack and widened her eyes slightly, giving him silent encouragement to give a better explanation for the woman's presence in the vestibule.

'And she was sitting at the end of my pew,' Jack continued. 'When I got up to leave, to see how you were, she decided to come too.'

'I couldn't miss the opportunity to meet you before the others!' Dinah beamed and wrapped her left arm around Jack's right. 'It was also stuffy in there so when Jack made to sneak out, I jumped at the chance to keep him company.'

Dinah gazed up at Jack's profile, her stare turning doe-like. Ah, thought Bella, as Dinah swayed into Jack, bringing them hip to hip. The bridesmaid had followed Jack because she had a huge crush on him and wanted to check out the competition. Fair play to her.

'Have you known Jack for long?' asked Bella, seeking to test her theory.

'Oh, forever!' Dinah flicked another adoring gaze to Jack. 'Everyone in there'—she waved over her shoulder in the direction of the nave—'we've all been friends for ages. I think I met him at one of my aunt's garden parties when I was about sixteen, so he would have been … um, I guess twenty-one or thereabouts.'

Bella smiled. Dinah was doing a good job of feigning vague recollection, but Bella was certain the bridesmaid knew how old Jack had been to the day when she had first laid heart-shaped eyes on him.

'So that must be—' Dinah puffed her cheeks out, pretending to consider—'nearly twenty years ago. Amazing.'

Dinah beamed at Jack once again, but he gave her a tight smile and gently eased her hand from his arm. Bella, sensing he might appreciate a little support in his efforts to escape Dinah's enthusiastic clutches, stepped closer to him and took his hand. 'It's lovely that you've all known each other for so long,' said Bella, straightening as Jack squeezed her fingers in what she took to be a silent thank you.

'Yes.' Dinah's gaze dipped to Jack's and Bella's joined hands and her smile slipped for a moment. 'At one time everyone thought it would be Ashley and Jack at the altar, but I guess she wasn't the one for him.'

Wow. Bella's gaze flew to the crease which had appeared between Jack's brows. While she admired those who knew what they wanted—and Dinah was certainly making her target clear—she wasn't a fan of anyone who pursued their desires in a way that trampled on the feelings of others. Dinah might have been mooning over Jack for the best part of twenty years, but today her thoughtless words had wounded him and she needed to back off.

'Oh well,' said Bella, sliding her hand out of Jack's grasp and wrapping it around his waist. 'Who knows? The one for him could be right here.'

'Indeed,' said Dinah, her tone hardening as she glared at Bella. 'She could. She could be right under his nose.'

As she held Dinah's gaze, now glacial and unwavering, Bella's blood thrummed. There was something irresistible and stimulating about competition. Rationally, she knew this was the absent Helen Snow's fight, not hers. But as Dinah tilted her doll-like face to one side and treated Bella to a reptilian grin, Bella met it with a knife-sharp one of her own.

'Erm.' Jack eyed the two women warily, took a step towards the doors to the nave and startled when applause and whooping erupted on the other side of the dark wood. He lifted a hand to his chest and released a breath. 'I think that's Ashley and David married.' He exchanged a glance with Bella and, as the muted clapping in the church subsided and the organ struck up again, Bella could have sworn the muscles in Jack's jaw relaxed and his shoulders dropped a quarter of an inch.

Jack turned to Dinah. 'They'll be signing the register now, Di. Perhaps you should go back before Ashley misses you?'

'Oh Jack.' Dinah bounced over to Jack and patted him on the shoulder. 'You should stop worrying about Ashley. That's David's job now.'

Dinah fluttered her eyelashes at Jack, the picture of friendly concern, but Bella could practically hear the voices in the bridesmaid's head screaming '*Me, me, me! I'm right here! Pick me!*'

Dinah sighed. 'But you're right. She'll probably want a photo with us standing behind her and David.' She gave Jack's arm a playful punch, cracked open the door to the church and slithered into the nave.

Jack checked the door was shut before turning to Bella. 'Sorry about that. Di can be defensive of her friends.'

'I can see that.' Bella considered Jack's words and scanned his face. He had no clue about Dinah's feelings, did he? Ugh! Men could be so oblivious. Shaking her head, she said, 'Tell me, do I have to prepare myself for all the women here being in love with you or is it just Dinah?'

'Wh— What? No!' Jack spluttered. 'Di's not ... she's ... she's—'

'Like a sister?' asked Bella, her tone containing both pity and sarcasm. 'Wake up! She's fancied you since she was sixteen and now her cousin is safely married off she's ready to make her move. Even if that involves shoving Helen Snow under a snowplough. I'll have to watch my back.'

'No.' Jack shook his head, refusing to see the obvious. 'You don't know her. I've never—'

Jack's denials were interrupted by the door opening again and Dinah poking her head through the gap. 'Jack! Ashley's demanding you appear in one of the photos. But don't worry'—she gave his bicep a squeeze and fluttered her lashes—'I've saved you a space next to me. Oh, and Helen?' She paused to check she had Bella's attention. 'Ashley's arranged for a tonne of photos of the wedding party here after the ceremony, so you should go on to the reception. There's no point in you hanging about in a draughty church when you could be drinking champagne. Don't worry about Jack, he can squeeze in the back of the bridesmaids' car next to me.'

And with a triumphant grin, Dinah vanished back into the church leaving Jack staring after her, open-mouthed. His eyes flickered left and right, and Bella could imagine the pennies dropping into neat stacks in his mind as he took a whirlwind tour back through his interactions with Dinah over the years.

'Oh God,' he said, scraping a hand through his hair. 'I think you might be right.'

Bella shrugged. 'It's an annoying habit of mine.'

'You can still leave,' said Jack, closing the space between them in two strides. He stared down into Bella's eyes, his own gaze wide with urgency and possibly a little fear. 'You don't have to come to the reception. Honestly. I'll say you had a family emergency.'

For a moment, Bella was tempted. But then she remembered the uninterrupted awfulness of the evening awaiting her back at the conference centre and shuddered. The wedding reception could turn out to be dreadful but there would probably be some fun moments to break up any tricky spots. Not all of Jack's friends could be as leery as Simon or as keen as Dinah, surely? Also, the thought of Jack squirming through the wedding breakfast while Dinah wrapped herself around him like a famished cobra sent a twinge of unease through Bella, making her stomach queasy.

'No. I'm staying.' Bella adjusted one of her pendant earrings and the resulting throb in her earlobe chased away the unpleasant feeling in her tummy. Jack's beaming smile, which made his dark eyes glitter, might also have helped. Her lips curled in response to his grin and she continued, 'She may be a misanthropic cat lady in training, but I'll have you know that Helen Snow never runs away from a fight.'

Chapter 6

'With all due respect, Helen, you're wrong. The first film is undoubtedly the best.'

'Oh, Drew.' Bella sighed dramatically, loud enough to make sure the sound carried through the chatter around them. 'And I thought we could be friends.'

Drew guffawed, the pale skin of his cheeks flushing a wine-tinged purple. 'Drat. A beautiful friendship ruined by James Cameron.'

'You can't pin this on him. All he did was make a better film the second time around.'

'I'm not going to get you to see the light, am I? I lost a similar struggle with Pete when we started dating.' He cast a fond glance to his left, where his husband was absorbed in conversation with the guest on his other side. Drew reached for the bottle of red on the table in front of them. 'Would you like some wine?'

'No, thanks.'

Drew eyed Bella's spotless wine glasses. 'Is wine not your thing? Pete would sympathise, it gives him dreadful headaches.'

'I have no objection to wine, but I'm driving, so I reached my limit with the glass of champagne for the toasts.'

'Good Lord, you're doing this whole evening sober!' Drew grimaced as he poured himself a generous glass of red. 'You're a hero.'

'Well you're mine.' Bella's tone was light as she shared a sly smile with Drew and clinked her water tumbler against his wine glass, but her words were sincere. Having arrived at the reception before most of the guests, Bella had groaned when a hunt for the seating chart revealed that Jack and 'Helen' would be sharing a table with the delightful Dinah. Predictably, Dinah had slid into the seat on the other side of Jack before his bottom had hit his chair and proceeded to monopolize his attention. Bella had resigned herself to spending the next couple of hours being largely ignored when Drew and Pete had swooped down on the two free seats to her left like a pair of merry, middle-aged guardian angels.

'If you want to treat this hero,' said Bella, giving Drew a sweet smile, 'you could donate the rest of your dessert to her.'

Drew followed Bella's gaze down to his plate where half of his serving of fondant chocolate pudding perched next to the remains of a scoop of vanilla-and-honey ice cream.

'Ha!' Drew took a large spoonful of his dessert and popped it into his mouth. While chewing, he muttered, 'You're definitely a hero, but I wouldn't share this with Pete and he's the love of my life.'

'Fair enough. I can't say I—' A knock to Bella's elbow interrupted her begrudging acceptance.

His face fixed on Dinah, Jack was doing a good job of appearing to give the bridesmaid his attention, even with a sheen of boredom in his dark eyes. But his left hand was sliding his dessert plate—which held a good two-thirds of his chocolate pudding—towards Bella.

Bella's mouth watered. She couldn't take the man's dessert, could she? Surely he would need the sugar to get him through listening to another of Dinah's bridesmaid horror stories?

Bella reached out and pushed the pudding back towards its rightful owner but Jack's hand flew to the side of the plate, blocking its advance. Without moving his head he gave it a sharp shove towards Bella and then tapped the tabletop next to it. Twice.

Well. That was her told. For all she knew it was morse code for 'eat it', 'go ahead' or 'I don't like chocolate pudding anyway'. And who was she to argue with the man?

Grinning, Bella grabbed her spoon and laid into the mound of gooey chocolatey perfection before Jack came to his senses. Humming as she savoured the heavenly warm combination of textures, she laid her fingers on Jack's wrist and gave it a squeeze of appreciation.

Jack's gaze flicked to Bella and the side of his mouth quirked upwards. The tiny movement caused the warmth in Bella's tummy to spread down to her toes, which curled in her shoes. She parted her lips to say thank you, but Jack had already returned his gaze to Dinah and was moving his hand to lift his wine glass to his lips. He tilted his head back to take a small sip of his drink, allowing Bella to admire his strong jawline at the same time as his restraint. If she'd been listening to Dinah for the past couple of hours, she'd have struggled to resist the urge to chug down an entire bottle to take the edge off the experience.

Drew tapped Bella's left wrist. 'So when you're not driving, what's your poison? Gin? Rum? Whiskey?'

'Um ...' Bella blinked, wondering how to varnish the truth: that ever since her first promotion—nearly three years ago—she had been steadily drinking more in the evenings. It had started with the odd glass of wine, but had gradually escalated as her dread of returning to the office the next day had grown. And after her breakup and moving into the shared house with a group of rarely seen, slovenly milk thieves, there was rarely anything left in the bottle before she fell into bed and passed out. 'Actually,' she said, taking a sip of water, 'I've been meaning to cut down on the booze.'

'Haven't we all?' said Drew. 'But a wedding is hardly the place to start.'

'Hmn.' Bella frowned as she polished off the last of Jack's dessert. A few hours ago she would have agreed with Drew without hesitation. Drinking had become an essential, unquestioned way of enjoying any social event. Heck, at her own father's wedding she had polished off at least two bottles of wine before the cutting of the cake. But today, powered almost exclusively by water, with Jack by her side and Drew's stories to keep her entertained, she was enjoying herself while completely sober.

Huh. Surely that wasn't that unusual? Bella fidgeted in her seat, casting her mind back over the past year. Nope. She couldn't remember the last time she'd laughed this much. Or drank so much water. Which was having inevitable consequences.

'I'm popping to the ladies',' said Bella.

Drew nodded. 'Don't be long. I'll be dying with boredom without you.'

Bella pushed her chair back but, as she rose, Jack grabbed hold of her hand. 'Everything OK?' he asked, his stare freezing Bella in a half crouch.

Bella glanced over his head, her gaze finding Dinah's, who was glaring at her in open hostility. Shooting Dinah her breeziest smile, Bella swayed forwards, bringing her lips close to Jack's ear to mutter, 'I'm just going to the loo.'

She straightened, but Jack didn't release her hand. 'Please don't climb out the window,' he said, his gaze openly imploring.

Bella laughed, slipped her hand from his and used it to hit him playfully on the shoulder. He'd barely spoken to her throughout dinner, so she doubted Jack was worried about missing out on her sparkling repartee. Holding his gaze, she examined the sincerity in his dark eyes. Perhaps he feared Dinah might go for broke and climb into his lap without 'Helen' there to act as a deterrent?

'I'll be back in a minute.' She grinned and added, jokingly, 'Missing you already!'

Jack laughed and, his dark eyes reflecting the spark of mischief in Bella's own, replied, 'I'll be counting the seconds to your return.'

Bella's chest swelled with happiness. She'd forgotten the terrific buzz that came from being wanted. Even if only as some kind of defensive buffer. And, as she wandered across the room—under the twinkle of the fairy lights wrapped around the exposed oak beams running the length of the ceiling—a spring entered her step and she rolled her shoulders. To her surprise, they felt looser and lighter, as if the weight of the cloak of gloom which had been wrapped around her since the disaster of last Christmas was finally beginning to ease.

Chapter 7

Bella's spirits had also been lifted by getting out of the church, which had been haunted by too many ghosts of a life that could have been. Unlike St Stephen's, Coopers' Farm was a feature of Haileybrook she'd never heard of before and home to a stunningly beautiful reception venue. The eighteenth-century barn on the outskirts of the village had recently been fully renovated, and the owners had had the sense to preserve as much of its original appearance as possible by rebuilding the walls with a warm creamy shade of local stone and the roof in traditional grey slate.

The wedding's festive theme was reflected in the décor in a way that was understated and tasteful, without a scrap of tinsel, plastic bauble or Santa hat. The tables were covered in white linen cloths with centrepieces made of crystal bowls, ruby-red candles and sprigs of holly. When they arrived at their place, each guest had found a dark green napkin folded skilfully into a cloth Christmas tree. Next to it nestled the wedding favour: a small box wrapped in shiny gold paper and a silver bow which matched the ribbon on the front of Bella's dress. And the whole room was perfumed with cosy notes of cinnamon, vanilla and nutmeg.

A one-storey extension on the east side of the barn housed a spacious entrance porch and the kitchens. It was also home to a large Christmas tree, which Bella eyed warily and gave a wide berth. She did not need to have two trees fall on her in one day. Or ever, for that matter.

She was entering the porch when her phone rang. And even though she had been expecting the call, a ball of dread solidified in the pit of Bella's stomach on seeing the name on the screen.

'Hi Jared,' Bella said, making sure to use her best strangled *'I'm ill'* voice.

'Bella, I got your message about missing the gala dinner,' Jared said in his trademark bored drawl. Honestly, for an event organizer, he was amazingly blasé about everything.

'Yes. Sorry. My migraine hasn't lifted so I thought—'

'That's fine. This is a courtesy call to confirm I got your message.'

'Oh. Right. Thank you?' Bella struggled to keep her tone listless. Sick people shouldn't have the energy for retaliatory sarcasm. But really, could he not at least fake concern for her well-being?

'And I have to remind you that checkout is before 10 a.m. tomorrow.'

'Sure. Well thank you for—'

'Goodnight.'

Bella blew out a huff of air and glared at the phone screen. Charming. A bus could hit her and the company would replace her in five seconds without a tear being shed no matter how much they professed to celebrate her achievements.

A sour taste on her tongue drove Bella to rummage in her handbag for a mint. She popped one in her mouth and, looking up from her bag, her gaze landed on the other side of the porch where a couple was absorbed in a low and—judging by their hand gestures—rather tense conversation. The woman's long buttery-blonde hair was tied back in a ponytail. Her black top and trousers added little volume to her body which was lean and angular, the only curve in her silhouette created by the baby carrier on her front which contained a whining child with a head of unruly blonde curls. Bella's gaze snagged on the woman's feet which were in a pair of glossy ruby slippers. They could have been stolen directly from the movie of *The Wizard of Oz* and made Bella think of Kate, her best friend, who would have loved to add them to her colourful wardrobe.

Bella frowned as she strode into the bathroom and entered the first stall. She should call Kate. This time last year they'd been in almost daily contact, but since last Christmas it had been increasingly difficult for Bella to witness her friend's loved-up delirium. Sensitive to Bella's misery, Kate had done her best not to directly mention how happy she and her boyfriend Max were, but her joy seeped into her tone until every conversation became a painful reminder to Bella of how disastrous her own love life had become.

Bella grimaced. She was a terrible friend. Kate had been nothing but supportive of Bella's wedding planning, even when her friend was going through a nasty breakup. Why did Bella struggle to be equally magnanimous? To be fair,

Kate had always been a bit of a saint. But Bella had recently saved a nativity scene from disaster and surely that had to count for something?

Bella was about to reach for the flush when the sound of the bathroom door opening was followed by a pair of voices.

'Oh my God,' said one of them, her voice slightly obscured by the sound of handbags unzipping, 'have you seen Dinah?' She snorted. 'Could she be any more obvious?'

The snap of a lipstick tube prefaced a nasal reply, 'I know. In Jack's place I wouldn't have come today. It must be hard enough just being here without having to fight Dinah off.'

'And it's not as if he's even on his own. He has a date.'

'Who exists!' The nasal voice escalated into a shrill whine. 'He didn't make her up after all.'

'I told you.' Another snort. 'Jack's no Casanova, but he's a good-looking guy. I don't get why so many of you thought he invented this Helen woman.'

'Because he was so vague and evasive about her.' The woman with the nasal voice paused, and Bella could make out sounds of rummaging in a handbag. 'She doesn't seem like his usual type, does she?'

Hidden in the cubicle, Bella breathed as shallowly as possible, hoping to stay concealed long enough to hear their verdict on Helen. She also found herself weirdly fascinated by what Jack's usual type was. Perhaps if Ashley was any indication, he had a minimum height requirement?

'I couldn't say. I don't think I've seen him with anyone apart from Ashley.'

'Hmn. I don't remember any blondes before. Do you

think it's her natural colour? And she's rather petite and on the chubby side.'

'She's voluptuous! And did you see her shoes? Fabulous.'

'True.'

Bella smiled. The women might be dreadful gossips, but their excellent taste in footwear took the edge off their critique of her appearance.

'Do you think he's invited her on the skiing trip?' asked the snorter.

'No! They've just started going out. Besides, I doubt Jack's going this year. Ashley and David will be off on honeymoon and Jack's only ever been invited on the trip because he's Ashley's friend.'

'But he must have been on the trip every year now for'—the snorter paused to do the maths—'twenty years, surely?'

'It's bizarre. I've wondered if Ashley keeps him around as a sort of emotional support animal,' said nasal voice. 'Plus he's always willing to go on supply runs and tidy up.'

Inside the cubicle, Bella startled at a sudden pain in the palm of her right hand. She relaxed her fingers, which she had curled into a tight first, revealing a row of deep nail marks in the fleshy mound next to her thumb. Ashley's behaviour towards Jack in the church had been far from pleasant, but Bella had been prepared to give the bride the benefit of the doubt. After all, she was incredibly stressed out, and the best people could turn into bossy monsters when under enough pressure. But every word nasal voice said was chipping away at Bella's limited stores of goodwill.

The snorter, who seemed to have a greater capacity for empathy than her friend, said, 'Poor Jack. It's not as if he has the option to spend a jolly Christmas at home with his family. We all know the situation there.'

The two women exchanged grunts of understanding which further fanned the flames of Bella's curiosity.

The snorter continued, 'Perhaps he'll spend Christmas with Helen.'

'Ha! Fat chance. You know since Ashley none of the women he's dated have hung around.'

'I know. Jack does have bad luck. He's sweet.'

'He's not sweet. He's *nice*. That's his problem.'

Bella frowned. The nasal woman had said 'nice' as if it were a fatal character flaw.

As if she were channelling Bella's thoughts, the snorter asked, 'What's wrong with nice?'

'Well, no woman wants nice, do they? Nice guys finish last. There's a reason that's a saying.'

Inside the stall, Bella opened and closed her mouth, her pulse pounding at the utter codswallop the woman was spouting. All Bella had ever wanted was a nice guy. And for a while she'd had one and wanted to be with him forever. A dull ache in her side made her wince as she pictured Ethan's smiling face. She had chosen him. It was just a shame that, when it came down to it, he hadn't chosen her.

Oblivious to Bella's presence or pain, the nasal woman continued, 'Look, I'm not saying women want to date arseholes, but bland isn't attractive. You want a guy to have a touch of mystery about him. Jack's so straightforward and … *decent*. Ugh! It's dull.'

Unable to refrain any longer—there was only so much tripe her ears could withstand—Bella pushed the flush and stepped out of the cubicle.

The two women were, to Bella's best guess, in their mid-thirties. They were facing a row of mirrors above a long sink which was essentially a stylish trough made of a creamy-coloured stone containing a subtle glitter. The woman on the right, who had pale skin and a sleek bob of red hair, saw Bella first. She froze with the applicator wand of her berry lip gloss in the middle of her lower lip.

'What?' the woman on the left asked in her nasal whine before she too noticed the eavesdropper and her hands, which had been busy teasing the caramel highlights in her long hazel hair, stilled.

'Hi!' said Bella.

'Oh my God,' said nasal voice, whirling to face Bella, her light brown skin darkening along her high cheekbones. 'You're—'

'Helen with natural blonde hair and fab shoes. My boobs are real too, in case you were wondering.' Bella grinned at their wide eyes and flicked her gaze to the floor: the redhead was wearing a pair of Louboutin gold mules while the brunette was sporting a pair of black patent Jimmy Choos. Bella made a fine adjustment to her initial appraisal of the women: they not only had good taste in shoes, but the money to back it up. Perhaps they would be willing to share their secrets with a fellow connoisseur of the high heel? 'You obviously know everyone here well,' said Bella, reasoning that it could never hurt to appeal to someone's vanity. 'So I was hoping you could answer a couple of questions.'

The redhead turned away from the mirrors and exchanged a glance with her friend. The brunette shrugged and swiped her hair off her shoulder. 'OK. What do you want to know?'

Bella pushed on. She didn't know how long their love of gossip would overwhelm any desire to close ranks against a group outsider. 'Were Ashley and Jack together a long time?'

'Uf! Forever.' The redhead pressed her lips together, transferring her lip gloss to her upper lip. 'They were childhood sweethearts.'

Bella nodded. 'And they split up …'

'About ten years ago,' said the brunette.

'Do you know why?' Bella asked.

'Sure.' The brunette patted her hair. 'Ashley found a guy who was more her speed.'

'Her speed?'

'You know,' said the redhead. 'Ashley's into go-getters, high-flyers, business owners.'

The brunette chuckled. 'And they've all had at least three luxury cars or a yacht.'

Bella frowned, her not-so-sunny first impression of Ashley darkening into a bottomless pit of dislike, as she returned to her line of questioning. 'But given that Jack and Ashley broke up so long ago, I don't see how it's still such a big deal—'

'Ah, well'—the redhead's shiny lips curled as she got to dish out the juicy stuff—'Ashley got together with David a couple of years ago after a string of guys who never lasted more than six months. Everyone thought she'd have her fun with her millionaires and go back to sensible old Jack eventually.'

'And that Jack, predictably *nice* as he is, would be waiting for her,' said the brunette.

'Hmn.' Bella approached the sink to wash her hands,

forcing the other women to shuffle further apart to give her space. 'And I take it Jack and his family don't get on?'

Bella glanced up at her reflection and caught the women exchanging a look of incredulity behind her back.

'You don't know?' asked the brunette.

'Hasn't Jack told you about them?' added the redhead, her pencil-line eyebrows drawn together in suspicion.

Crap. Jack would probably have told Helen something about his family, wouldn't he? Especially as he worked in the family business.

Bella shook her hands and strutted to the paper towel dispenser, buying herself time to think. 'Oh, you know,' she said, drying her hands, 'this is only our second date. If the stuff with his family is dramatic, he probably doesn't want to scare me off.'

The redhead snorted and said, 'Fair enough,' quickly accepting Bella's excuse.

But the brunette narrowed her eyes, leaving the whites barely visible between her thick lines of false lashes. 'He's told you nothing about his family? That's odd isn't it, when you've been messaging each other for months?'

'Oh yes,' said Bella, keeping her tone as breezy as possible while a string of curses flashed through her mind. The sodding messages. Of course they'd probably have said something to each other about their families. What else could they have been talking about?

Bella threw her used paper towel into the bin, a desperate and slightly wicked idea forming. They thought Jack was bland and lacked mystery. So perhaps this was Bella's opportunity to spice up his image a little. 'You're right. We did message loads. But, you know, a lot of that time was taken up with sexting. And clearly family doesn't get mentioned in *that* unless you're seriously warped!'

The redhead's jaw dropped, a strangled sound emerging from between her berry-pink lips. Her friend's perfectly filled brows shot skywards, but she recovered quickly. 'Sorry. We are talking about *Jack*, right?'

A shot of defensive fire sparked inside Bella. Why did all these people—who were supposed to be his *friends*— treat Jack so dismissively? True, she'd only known him for a few hours, but all she'd seen suggested he was a smart, thoughtful, generous guy. So why the sniffiness towards him from everyone else?

A ghostly hand squeezed Bella's heart. She knew what it felt like to be rejected and unfairly maligned. And she wasn't about to let these people belittle Jack for being a decent person whose main fault seemed to be that he wasn't rich.

The redhead snorted. 'I can't imagine Jack would have been—'

'*You* may not be able to imagine it, but I am very happy to say that there's nothing wrong with *his* imagination.' Bella stepped close enough to the redhead to smell the strawberry scent of her lip gloss and lowered her voice to a salacious drawl. 'He really knows what he's doing.' Bella swallowed hard, battling a burst of laughter swelling in her chest, and her voice came out even gruffer than she had planned. 'I'm talking the highest quality, hottest filth you've ever read.' She rolled her eyes and sighed as if the mere recollection of the fictional messages was orgasmic. 'I don't know about you two'—Bella laid a hand on the redhead's wrist and flicked her gaze to the brunette—'but in my experience, the quiet ones are the most surprising. Still waters and all that.'

Bella gave her reflection a cursory inspection, noticing the red flush stealing up her neck. She never could lie without her pale complexion giving her away. Time to leave.

Three strides took her to the exit. She grabbed the door handle and turned back to the women. The redhead's eyes were as round as saucers and her jaw slack. A muscle next to the brunette's left eye ticked, making her look like a robot glitching.

Bella grinned even as her cheeks burned. She'd have to hope they'd believe her sudden flush was another response to remembering Jack's supposedly legendary dirty talk. 'It was nice chatting,' she said. 'But I should get back to Jack. Like you say, Dinah's keen and I wouldn't want her trying to make off with him. And certainly not before I get him into the bedroom.' She winked at the women and dashed across the threshold, the laughter in her chest exploding past her lips in a rush of air she was barely able to disguise by shouting 'Ciao!' over her shoulder.

Chapter 8

Keen to make a clean getaway from the scene of her lie, and a part of her hoping that her absence would free the redhead and brunette to spread her tall tales to their friends, Bella crossed the lobby and slipped out through the glass doors at the front of the annex.

A few hours earlier, the paved space outside the barn had hosted pre-reception drinks under the bright overhead lights fixed to the eaves of the roof. Silent waiters had sailed between the cocktail tables offering champagne and orange juice. The growing winter chill was kept in check by gas flames roaring in a series of stainless-steel patio heaters. A string quartet, wrapped in so many layers of wool that only their eyes and fingertips were exposed, crouched in the far corner of the terrace playing a repertoire of solemn, tasteful Christmas carols. Though beautiful and haunting, the stately music did little to create a party atmosphere and when they struck up a portentous rendition of 'In the Bleak Midwinter', Bella had considered slipping them a tenner and begging them to break into 'Jingle Bells'.

Now it was almost 9 p.m. and, with all the guests inside getting ready for tea and cake, it would have been reasonable to expect the outdoor area to be a place of quiet refuge. But instead of peace, Bella found pandemonium.

'Get him!'

'Give it back!'

'Pass it, Timone!'

The children moved so swiftly, Bella had difficulty counting them, but guessed there were between six and twelve, which was also a good estimate of their age range. Several of them wore Santa hats decorated with snowflake-shaped lights which added a festive note to the anarchic rugby-style game they were playing.

Amid a crescendo of noise, the ball whizzed past Bella and one of the larger boys dived for it. He missed the ball, but collided with the edge of one of the freestanding cocktail tables which wobbled before righting itself.

'Careful, kids!' A musical voice carrying a rasp of concern came from Bella's right. Following it to the corner of the patio, Bella's gaze settled on the blonde woman with the ruby slippers she had seen earlier. Her stare was fixed on the progress of the game as she bounced on the spot to keep warm. 'Be careful!' she shouted again, wrapping her arms around her slender frame before adding, 'We don't want anyone to get hurt.'

Her voice wavered over the last few words, making Bella doubt her heart was entirely in the statement. 'Hi,' said Bella, dodging two children to approach the woman. 'How did you get lumbered with this lot?'

'I've been asking myself the same question.' The woman managed a thin smile, her gaze darting to Bella before returning to the children. She shivered and resumed bouncing, a gentle back-and-forth movement made by shifting one of her hips.

Bella had thought the movement was an attempt to keep out the winter chill but, as her gaze fell on the empty baby carrier dangling from the woman's shoulders, she realized the motion was one particular to carers of young children. 'I see you managed to find someone to look after your baby,' she said.

'Yes, there is that, I suppose.' The woman put her hands to the empty carrier and sniffed, her eyes filling with tears.

'Oh I'm sorry,' said Bella, stepping forwards. 'I didn't mean to upset you.'

'No, it's not you,' said the woman, waving her right hand as she wiped at her tears with her left. 'It's just, tonight has been rather … *challenging*.' She sniffed. 'Oh God, I shouldn't be telling you this, you're a guest—'

'Not really,' said Bella, who was flooded with a strange yearning to help the fragile-looking woman. It was probably because those ruby shoes had made her think of Kate. If anyone hurt Bella's best friend, Bella felt Kate's wounds in her own flesh. Or at least she did eventually, after she'd got over the initial urge to inflict significant pain on whoever had upset her friend in the first place.

'I'm not a proper guest,' Bella explained. 'I'm more an emergency, last-minute plus-one. I don't know these people. Or their'—she broke off and gestured to the pack of screaming children—'charming offspring.'

The woman huffed a laugh. Encouraged, Bella continued, 'I take it you run this place?'

'Yes! I do! Thank you.' The woman gave Bella a nod of appreciation. 'You're the first guest not to assume

I'm a waitress, cleaner, and today, childcare assistant. I wouldn't mind, but do they have to be so rude? I had to give Danielle'—her hands flew to the empty baby carrier—'to Seth to take back to the house because she was getting upset and this horrible woman cornered me to shout at me that my daughter was making a tiny bit of noise and then said that the childcare arrangements here were awful and she was in mind to complain about it to the owners. But we are the bloody owners!'

Bella gave a grunt of understanding and support, guessing the woman's rant was much needed and as therapeutic as it was impressive. At the same time, she flexed her toes inside her shoes, preparing to slip one off and run inside to throw it at the head of the foul guest who had thought herself important enough to yell at a woman holding a baby.

The blonde woman tucked her golden hair behind her ears, revealing a pair of enamel snowman earrings. Bella smiled as she examined the snowmen's black top hats and red scarves. Perhaps she should get Kate a pair like that for Christmas to add to her existing collection.

'Sorry to go on at you,' the woman said, wiping away a final tear.

'Not at all. I'm Bella by the way,' said Bella, before adding in a rush, 'but people here know me as Helen. But I'm actually Bella. It's a long story.'

'I'm Lucy.' She smiled and shook Bella's outstretched hand. 'Nice to meet you.'

'Do you want to go inside?' Bella's gaze roved over the gooseflesh on Lucy's arms and her slender frame. Without any natural padding, she must be freezing.

'The only place I want to go is the farmhouse,' Lucy said. 'Danielle won't settle without me, and Seth—that's my husband, I don't think I said—he needs to come back here to wrap up with the caterers. And now I'm stuck here making sure this lot don't kill each other.'

As if to illustrate Lucy's point, three of the children crashed into each other and collapsed in a roaring heap next to the women, making Bella jump. 'Did the childcare person for this evening not show up?' asked Bella.

'There wasn't one booked!' said Lucy, throwing her hands up in despair. 'It's something we're more than happy to arrange and I mentioned it twice to the wedding planner but they said it wouldn't be necessary.'

'Hmn.' Bella raised an eyebrow, waiting for Lucy to continue.

'And when I tried to explain there's no dedicated childcare service today, none of these children's parents wanted to listen!' Lucy gasped, her breath leaving trails of white steam in the icy air. 'Sorry. I'm not usually like this. But we only opened this place last April and Seth has all these other plans for the farm and if this doesn't work out we won't have the money.'

Bella nodded sympathetically. She had worked with the owners of dozens of small start-ups before she moved to London and the story was a familiar one.

'Seth always says that the first couple of years of any business is crucial and in hospitality good reviews are everything to ensure long-term success. But now I have to stay here.' Lucy gestured to the whooping kids. 'I can't leave these kids alone, and all so that rude woman won't go online and slate us. I know running about is keeping them warm, but we'll have to go inside soon and then I'll be back to square one.'

Bella lifted the back of her hand to the numb tip of her nose. Lucy was right: they should all get back inside rather than risk hypothermia. But where could they stash a muddle of noisy kids?

Don't get involved, Bella's inner voice chided. *You're not supposed to be at this wedding, remember? You've already made yourself memorable to those women in the loos with your tales of Jack's sexting prowess and now you want to save the day for Lucy? For goodness' sake! That Wonder Woman comment of Jack's has gone to your head.*

Bella hugged herself as she watched the children cheer another goal. The thought of running inside to a steaming cup of tea was alluring. After all, this was Lucy's business and none of hers. She should summon the heartless version of herself that her bosses loved so much they kept feeding it with promotions and bonuses, say goodnight to Lucy and get herself a large slice of wedding cake.

Lucy shivered, a full-body tremor ending in a rapid shake of her head which caused the bright light from the lamps on the side of the barn to catch the silver sheen of her snowman earrings. Bella blinked against the sudden flash and a sharp memory of Kate the previous year, wearing her similar reindeer earrings, came into her mind's eye. Bella's heart squeezed. Her best friend wouldn't leave Lucy to struggle. Kate would round the kids up and suggest an inventive way of keeping them out of trouble.

You're not Kate. Go inside and enjoy the cake. Lucy will be fine.

Bella dropped her head forwards and caught another

glimpse of Lucy's sparkly shoes. Kate really would love those. And she would want Bella to try to help.

Tea and cake would have to wait.

'How many of them are there?' asked Bella, struggling to complete a head count while ignoring the voice in her head telling her she was a blithering idiot. 'Twelve?'

'Eight.'

'Seriously? Blimey, they've certainly mastered the art of taking up space.' Bella turned to stare through the glass doors of the annex into the lobby and main dining area beyond. 'Could you stash them in the kitchen?'

'The caterer would flip. And it would probably be even more dangerous than whatever it is they're playing now.'

Bella shut her eyes to better picture the inside of the venue. With the kitchen out, the only other spaces apart from the main reception room were the toilets, the lobby and …

'There's a mezzanine,' said Bella, opening her eyes. 'On one side of the dining space. The safety rail's decorated with fairy lights. What's up there?'

'That was one of Seth's ideas to make the most of the height of the barn while creating a unique area which might offer added value to corporate clients.' Lucy took in Bella's raised eyebrows and laughed. 'You can tell I'm quoting him, can't you? Apparently it's a convenient "breakout space".'

'I think that means you're legally obliged to have at least two beanbags up there,' said Bella, who was no stranger to corporate away days and their jargon.

'Ha!' Lucy smiled. 'We've got six. It hasn't had much use yet as most of our bookings have been weddings, anniversaries and christenings. But it's a useful place to store the audiovisual equipment. And I've had a couple of brides drop their bouquets from the balcony and—'

'Wait, wait. Sorry to interrupt.' Bella held up a hand. Something Lucy had said had triggered the fragile beginnings of an idea. 'You said audiovisual equipment. Does that involve a TV?'

'Sure. A large flat-screen. A couple of events have used it to show celebration films.'

'Do you have Wi-Fi in there?'

'Of course. Seth says a hospitality space without Wi-Fi is doomed.'

'In that case, I have a suggestion.' Bella grinned. She hoped a sunny expression would fool Lucy into thinking she was as confident in her idea as she appeared. 'Why don't I explain inside before we all freeze?'

'Terrific.' Lucy beamed at Bella, her blue eyes shining with hope. 'OK everyone,' she called to the children, clapping her hands for attention. 'Guys! We're going inside now.'

Rather than responding to Lucy's gentle calls, the children continued their game, shrieking about unfair play or shouting to teammates for assists.

'Oh dear,' said Lucy, biting her bottom lip. 'I'm rather out of practice.'

Bella harrumphed, sending a fine cloud of white mist into the freezing air. She shook some of the freezing numbness out of her right hand, slotted the tips of her thumb and index finger between her lips and sent out an ear-piercing whistle which brought the game to an instant stop. 'Oi! You lot!' Bella waited for all eyes to fall on her.

She dropped her voice to a low growl and jerked a thumb over her shoulder. 'Inside. Now.' The children exchanged glances, most of them seemingly waiting to see what the oldest kids—a couple of lanky almost-teenagers who were annoyingly already taller than Bella—would do. Bella sighed and played her ace. 'There's cake in there.'

The tallest kids moved first and the others scrambled after them, giving Bella a second to grab the handle of the nearest door and stand back to allow the children to flow past her into the lobby.

'Wow.' Lucy's wide eyes glittered with admiration as she ducked past Bella. 'You're not a teacher are you? Or some sort of wild animal wrangler?'

'Me? Nah.' Bella chuckled as she followed Lucy inside. 'I'm just an accountant.'

Chapter 9

'I'm not watching any Disney princess rubbish!'

'You shut up! It's not rubbish.'

'Woah, guys. Stop!' Bella held out her hands. 'Please. I'm sure we can find something everyone wants to watch.' Her gaze shuttled between cousins Timone and Zara, who were currently engaged in a staring contest. At thirteen and six years old they were the eldest and youngest members of the group and also, it turned out, those with the most entrenched views on what constituted great cinema. And though Zara was over a foot shorter than her cousin and her movement was restricted by the countless layers of aqua tulle in the skirt of her iridescent princess dress, Bella would have put money on her winning if the conflict escalated to a physical fight. The girl's eyes spoke of murder and zero qualms about resorting to dirty tactics. She had quickly earned Bella's respect.

Determined to remain a neutral arbiter, Bella cast her gaze wider, taking in all the kids. They were watching the cousins' grudge match from the comfort of a number of large beanbags arranged in loose semicircles in front of the television. 'Does anyone else have any other suggestions that everyone can enjoy?'

A hand went up from a pale, freckly child to Bella's left who was still wearing a Santa hat. 'What about *Wreck-It Ralph*?'

Sadly, the perfectly sensible suggestion only served to reignite the debate, setting off a squeal of frustration from Zara which sliced through Bella's head, making her teeth vibrate.

Bella cast a longing glance over the railing down to the hive of tables below. Was it too late to grab the strings of fairy lights wound around the banister rail and rappel over the side of the balcony?

At her table, Drew and Pete sat shoulder to shoulder, laughing and tipping back wine. However, Jack was missing, leaving Dinah no other option but to speak to the man sitting on the other side of her. Perhaps Jack couldn't take any more of Dinah's attentions and was currently squeezing his broad shoulders through the tiny bathroom window. Smart guy.

She raised a hand to her ear as another squeal pierced her skull and her gaze shifted from Jack's empty chair to her own place setting where a sliver of wedding cake waited for her. Bella frowned. Was that what Ashley and David believed qualified as a decent piece of cake? And where was her cup of tea?

Bella stifled a sigh and returned to scrolling through the list of films on the TV screen. Lucy had given Bella her passwords to accounts on several streaming services and Bella had browsed a couple of them, hoping the right film would leap out at her.

The simple act of scrolling down the grid of thumbnail images engulfed Bella in a wave of nostalgia. Bella and Ethan used to enjoy discovering new programmes together and bingeing on the latest releases. But lately Bella hadn't had the energy to invest in a groundbreaking drama or twisty thriller. Most evenings she would crawl into bed with her laptop and watch old favourites until her eyelids closed themselves. The familiar voices, faces and scenarios of action-adventure movies—particularly favoured if they featured low to zero romance—became a much-needed comfort blanket.

'Ouch!'

'It was a cushion!'

'You threw it at me!'

'It didn't even hit you, Timone!'

As the pitch of the juvenile voices climbed once more, Bella's fingers twitched. If this carried on much longer she would hurl the television remote at Timone and probably end up getting arrested. Perhaps she should nip down to the kitchen and see she could snag a few of those miserably slender pieces of cake for the kids? They might distract them for a few minutes and chewing cake would make it harder for them to shout at each other.

'OK, guys.' Bella held up her hands. 'I'm going to see if I can get you—'

'Does anyone want some popcorn?'

Bella followed the deep voice to the top of the stairs, where Jack stood holding a huge wicker basket brimming with cone-shaped plastic bags stuffed with popcorn and tied with red ribbons. He grinned, his smile staying in place as the kids squealed and fell upon him in a greedy avalanche.

'Woah!' He chuckled and lifted the basket out of their reach. 'We'll start with one each.' He shuffled past two of the taller children, set the basket down against the wall and retreated a safe distance from the ensuing frenzy.

'Hi,' said Jack, treating Bella to a dazzling smile.

'Hey,' Bella said, aiming for a casual tone which in no way conveyed how Jack's smile had made her knees a little wobbly. 'Is that entire thing full of popcorn?' she asked, eyeing the enormous basket suspiciously.

'I've been told there are some blankets in the bottom. Some of the younger ones might fall asleep if made comfy enough.'

'I see. And I'm guessing you didn't stumble across a basket of popcorn and decide to bring it up here?'

'No.' Jack shook his head. 'I was looking for you, actually.'

'Oh, Jack.' Bella swayed into Jack and batted her eyelashes playfully. 'Could you not carry on without me?'

Jack rocked into Bella, returning her gentle nudge. 'Honestly, life had begun to lose all meaning without you by my side.'

Bella laughed. 'Had you convinced yourself I'd done a runner?'

'I was worried I might have given you a bad idea when I asked you not to climb out the loo window, but then I bumped into this guy called Seth in the lobby. He asked if I knew a blonde woman called Helen who his wife said was wearing a dress with a fabulous silver bow on the front.'

Bella glanced down at the bow in question, glad—but not entirely surprised given her glittery ballet shoes—that Lucy had liked it. 'And Seth gave you the basket and directions,' she said.

Jack nodded. 'They had a wedding here last weekend that involved a popcorn machine and these are the leftovers.'

'Wow.' Bella had been partial to the idea of a reception featuring a candyfloss machine and—at her most adventurous—a fish and chip van. But Ethan had hated the idea. In fact, they hadn't seen eye-to-eye on much to do with the wedding. Perhaps she should have seen that as a sign, but at the time she'd been so loopy about him—her own happiness so tied up in his—she had got into the habit of giving way just to see him smile.

'Not your sort of thing?'

'Hmn?' Bella snapped her attention back to Jack, who had apparently taken her vacant expression as a sign of her firm disapproval of popcorn machines. 'No. I mean, yes. That is, I think it's a great idea. Different. And sensible if your guests are the sort of people who'd get hungry and grumpy while waiting for dinner or even after dinner.'

'That sounds like a lot of people I know,' said Jack. 'OK, so with a popcorn maker as one option, what else would you have at your wedding reception? And don't tell me you've never thought about it. Anyone who's ever been to a wedding has thought about what they'd do the same or differently.'

Bella smiled in response, but it was merely a polite effort. Thinking back over her and Ethan's plans brought back a carousel of bittersweet memories. He had wanted a church wedding and a small, quiet reception at a nearby hotel. But Bella had favoured holding the ceremony and reception in one place so the guests wouldn't have to shuttle between locations and could relax. Also, while Ethan had been fixated on a winter wedding, Bella had always pictured a warm, sunny day with tables and even picnic blankets outdoors, a sweet stall, candyfloss maker, and games for the adults and children. She sighed. 'Basically, I think I'd want a mini summer funfair,' said Bella.

Bella braced herself for a snort of scorn, but Jack nodded and narrowed his eyes, pondering her vision. 'Would this include a bouncy castle?'

'Obviously.'

'Helter-skelter? Bumper cars?'

'Oh my God. Possibly beyond my budget, but that would be amazing!'

'Sounds great.' Jack beamed. 'I'm in. By any chance would you consider a live band and then, when it gets late and everyone's hungry from dancing in the moonlight, a chip van?'

'Yes!' Bella punched Jack's arm to express her surprise and delight. Who'd have thought Jack would turn out to be her ideal wedding guest?

A small voice, muffled by a mouthful of popcorn, asked, 'Ice cream truck?'

Bella and Jack turned as one to look down at Zara, who stuffed another handful of popcorn between her lips while staring at them, awaiting an answer.

'Well I think that's the best idea yet. Don't you, Jack?'

'Absolutely.'

'Cool!' Zara paused her chewing. 'Can I come?'

Bella frowned. 'To what, sweetie?'

Zara rolled her eyes. 'To your wedding. Duh.'

Bella glanced at Jack, whose lips had parted in a reflection of her own stunned expression. She spluttered,

'Oh, we're not, you know …' Bella smiled at Zara, hoping the child would help her out, but the girl continued to stare, her expression a patient demand for a better answer. Bella swallowed, her mouth suddenly dry. 'Jack and I, we're not getting married.'

'Right!' Jack laughed nervously, the deep blush rising up his neck beginning to redden his cheeks. 'We're just, um …'

'Friends!' said Bella, a tad too loudly. Blimey, that had sounded weird. And desperate.

'Right again!' said Jack, his voice overbright, a note of strain at the edge of his jovial tone.

Zara narrowed her eyes and tilted her head, her unblinking gaze shuttling between the faces of the adults above her. The skin at the back of her neck prickling, Bella repressed the urge to shudder and reach for Jack's hand. How did kids manage to snap from cute to creepy so quickly?

Zara blinked—thank goodness!—and said to Bella, slowly, as if she was testing her theory as she voiced it, 'Are you deciding if he's a frog or a prince?'

Bella's lips fell open. 'I … um … that is …'

'Are we going to watch a film or what?' asked Jack, his gaze roving over the kids, who were still happily munching popcorn.

Bella laid a hand on Jack's back and almost sagged with relief. A total change of subject. Excellent. Good thinking, Jack. 'Yes, we should hurry and choose something before the music starts downstairs.' Bella cast a glance over the balcony to the dining space below where the tables were being cleared. 'Maybe something Christmassy?'

'*The Grinch*?' called a boy squatting on a red beanbag next to the television, his suggestions setting off a string of others.

'*The Polar Express*!'

'*The Muppet Christmas Carol.*'

'*Elf*!'

'All good suggestions,' said Jack. He bent down so his lips were close to Bella's ear and muttered, 'What do you think?'

'*Die Hard.*' Bella grinned, her thumb hovering over the remote while on the TV screen a thumbnail of a bloodied Bruce Willis in John McClane's iconic white vest appeared.

Jack chuckled, the low rumble of his laughter warming Bella's cheek. 'One of my favourite Christmas movies. But it's not exactly age appropriate for this audience.'

Bella sighed, making a mental note to watch the movie one evening the following week—perhaps while packing for her upcoming trip to Spain—and pressed a couple of buttons on the remote to return to a list of child-friendly options. 'So, having reluctantly ruled out anything with machine guns and detonators, I guess we're going for *The Muppet Christmas Carol*?'

'A cinematic classic based on a literary classic,' said Jack, nodding in approval.

'One could argue it's educational,' said Bella, her tone joking, 'It is a timeless morality tale.'

'Indeed it is,' said Jack, his lips twitching as he struggled to keep a straight face. 'With Muppets. And Sir Michael Caine.'

'OK. If you could hand out more popcorn and the blankets, I'll sort this.' Bella turned to face the television and, after a brief wrestle with the labyrinthine menu options, the film title card appeared. 'Thank goodness for that. For a second there I thought we might have to act the thing out for—'

Bella froze and stared at the empty space behind her. The space where Jack had been standing a moment ago. She glanced about the mezzanine but her search was fruitless.

Ugh. Typical. Just when she'd begun to think she and Jack were a team, he'd left her to take care of everything on her own. She kicked herself for her naivety. That's what she got for forgetting her mantra: if you want something done, do it yourself. She gave the remote a vicious prod, her skin prickling with irritation at her own stupidity. She could be downstairs, stuffing her face with cake and laughing with Drew. Instead she was stuck babysitting, alone, and all while disturbingly sober. The Christmas spirit was probably to blame as well. You relaxed and let a speck of goodwill to all men get under your skin and you were in danger of being exploited like a total doormat. How had this—

'Here you go!' Jack cleared the final couple of steps to the mezzanine. In one hand he held a teacup and in the other a small plate. 'Sorry,' he said, coming to a halt in front of Bella, 'I was going to bring them earlier, but I needed both hands for the basket.'

Oh. Dumbfounded, Bella reached out to take the teacup with her left hand while she inspected the cleanly cut wedge of wedding cake in the centre of the plate. It had to be at least three times the size of the miserable crumb she'd seen waiting for her at the table downstairs. A pristine ivory layer of buttercream, decorated with white chocolate snowflakes, encased two layers of fluffy golden sponge, sandwiched together with another creamy layer of icing. From the menu card, Bella knew it was lemon drizzle. One of her favourites.

'I went to the kitchen and asked them to cut you a decent slice as they seemed a bit mean to me,' said Jack, lifting his gaze from the plate. 'I hope you like lemon cake. I think there was a plan to have a traditional Christmas cake at some point, but Ashley's not a fan.'

Bella nodded, words continuing to fail her. It was so rare that anyone gave her such a pleasant surprise, she wasn't sure how to respond. 'Thank you,' she mumbled.

Jack pointed at the remote control she was cradling in her right hand. 'Do you want me to take that and get the film going while you enjoy this?' He held out the plate.

'Great,' said Bella, handing over the remote so eagerly it almost fell to the floor. But Jack had quick reflexes in addition to good instincts regarding her cake needs and—with a lightning move worthy of Spider-Man—he snatched the tumbling remote out of the air. Bella raised an eyebrow. He might have called her Wonder Woman but, as he had come to her rescue once more, Bella started to wonder if there was something of the superhero in Jack as well.

Apparently not seeing anything remarkable in his miracle save, Jack smiled at Bella and passed her the cake. 'That was close,' he said, turning his attention to the remote control safely gripped in his hand. 'Give me a sec and I'll get this going.'

Bella closed her mouth. The tangy, sweet citrus scent of the cake had begun to make it water and she was in danger of drooling. She took a bite of cake and closed her eyes to better savour the taste. Oh wow. Some genius had put a hint of raspberry flavour in the buttercream.

Bella opened her eyes and sighed as she set about demolishing the rest of the slice. The cake was wonderful, but her enjoyment of it was probably enhanced by the sight of Jack stepping in front of the television and calling the kids to order with a single clap of his hands. His audience fell silent as one, entranced by the tall man with glittering eyes and a warm smile.

Her gaze fixed on Jack introducing the movie with an impressive degree of festive enthusiasm, Bella ran a fingertip over her plate to scoop up a stray speck of icing and popped it into her mouth. Mmm. Delicious.

But while her senses were mostly focused on enjoying the cake, her mind refused to stray from the ongoing surprise that was Jack. And, as he pressed play and gestured for her to join him on the small sofa in the back row of their makeshift cinema, Bella's swirling thoughts settled into a single question: why was Jack single? Had Ashley hurt him so deeply that the wound hadn't healed? And, if that were the case, rather than an inconsiderate, last-minute no-show, was the mysterious Helen Snow actually a woman with fine intuition who'd had a lucky escape?

Chapter 10

Bella woke gradually, like surfacing from a deep dive. Her limbs heavy, she was filled with warmth and cosiness, and was only vaguely aware of the soft brush of a blanket against her neck and the faint glow of twinkling lights at the edges of her blurred vision.

Her lips curled into a lazy smile as she was hit with a long-forgotten memory of a Christmas when she was little. She remembered being wedged between her parents on the sofa on Christmas Day. Stuffed with dinner—the whole house smelled of roast turkey—and half the chocolate bars from her selection box, Bella had been lulled into a doze by the Queen's speech, the glistening strings of lights on the tree and the afternoon family film. She had rested her head against the sofa cushions and, her belly and heart full, had drifted off to sleep feeling safe and loved. That was back when home was a place free of worries, a place where everything could be fixed and Bella's greatest worry was baby Summer chewing her favourite toys. Back before everything was broken.

Reluctant to return to the present, Bella shifted slightly, luxuriating in how marvellous the cushion under her head and shoulder felt. Her right hand was wrapped around it and she took the opportunity to give it a squeeze. *Mmm.* It was firm but yielding, warm and soft. She hummed and snuggled deeper into it. *Ah*, so comfy. Even if it was moving.

Wait. *What?*

Blinking rapidly, she turned her head in to the cushion, which appeared to be a tube covered in fine white cotton. Cotton on which there was a circular shadow where she had drooled in her sleep. Oh crap.

A nasty suspicion slithering down her spine, Bella lowered her foggy gaze to the end of the 'cushion' where, as she had feared, there was a hand.

Slowly, carefully, clinging to a shred of hope that her cushion might also be asleep, Bella inched upright. Perhaps, if she was lucky, he wouldn't even know she'd passed out on him.

'Oh hello, you're back.' Jack smiled down at her as she righted herself, allowing him to retrieve his arm. His brown eyes shone with amusement and the lopsided curve of his lips suggested he found Bella having drooled on him funny rather than annoying. Nonetheless, Bella was thankful the tea and cake had removed her lipstick or she'd be offering to dry-clean his, no doubt expensive, shirt.

Bella glanced at the audience around them. The smaller children had followed her example and were fast asleep, with Zara's snoring audible even over the music coming from the dance floor downstairs. The older kids were staring at the television, entranced as Scrooge was confronted by a spooky Ghost of Christmas Yet to Come.

'You missed the Ghosts of Christmas Past and Present,' said Jack, rolling his shoulder which was no doubt stiff after supporting Bella's dead weight for half an hour. 'But so did most of the kids. It's the inevitable post-cake energy dip.'

Grateful to Jack for not having needled her for giving him a dead arm and ruining his shirt, Bella smiled at him, gazing at the strong, handsome contours of his face. She sighed. If Ashley did dump Jack because he wasn't a millionaire, she was more deserving of Bella's pity than disdain. But Bella would give her both anyway. She was generous like that.

'If you don't mind,' Jack said, shuffling to the edge of the sofa, 'I should go downstairs for a while. In case there are some more ushering duties I'm skiving by being up here.'

Bella frowned. Had Jack been waiting for her to wake up to leave? Oh Lord, this was embarrassing. 'Uh, sure. Of course.' Bella fidgeted with the neckline of her dress, the skin of her decolletage heating with shame. Not a fan of being held back by anyone, the idea she'd been keeping Jack stuck on the mezzanine, pinned to the sofa under a drooling lump while longing to escape ... *Ugh!* Not a pleasant thought. 'I'll be fine.'

Jack pushed to standing in a fluid, graceful movement. 'I'll see if I can find someone to come up here and relieve you,' he said. 'If you'd like the chance to dance, that is. Besides, this really wasn't your job.'

Bella shrugged. 'That's OK. I got a cheeky kip out of it.' She shoved herself up to standing in as graceful a move as she could manage and motioned to Jack's left sleeve. 'Sorry about creasing you.'

'Don't worry about it. I'm amazed I didn't fall asleep too.'

A patter of fast-climbing footsteps sounded on the stairs, heralding the arrival of a wiry man with pale skin, delicate features and short blond hair. He was wearing a plain black suit, although a bright crystal snowflake was pinned to his lapel in a nod to the season. Bella recognized him from the lobby, where he had been engaged in a hushed conversation with Lucy, and assumed he was Seth, Lucy's husband and business partner. 'The cavalry's here!' he announced with a wide smile.

'Hi Seth,' said Jack. 'Did you get everything sorted with the caterers?'

'I did, thanks. Were you heading downstairs?' He jerked a thumb over his shoulder. 'A guy called Simon was looking for you a minute ago.'

'I was. Have you come to take over from us?'

'Yes.' Seth frowned. 'I'm so sorry you've both missed out on the party to do this.'

'Don't worry about it,' said Jack, moving past Seth to the top of the stairs. 'I should find Simon. I'll see you both later.'

Seth watched Jack disappear down the stairs and turned back to Bella. 'I can't thank you enough for helping Lucy.' He beamed at Bella, the crinkle between his eyebrows vanishing as he mentioned his wife. 'It's been a stressful time. Some of the guests the past couple of months have been … challenging. So thank you.'

'Like Jack said, don't worry about it. But'—Bella raised an eyebrow and added, in a teasing tone—'if I ever need a venue in Haileybrook with an awesome breakout space, I hope I can expect a discount.'

Seth laughed. 'You've more than earned one. We'd be delighted. Now'—he clapped his hands together—'what do I need to know?'

'You'll need the remote.' Bella turned to search in the folds of the heaped blanket on the sofa for the control. 'You have about twenty-five minutes left of this film. If you need another, you might want to take their suggestions and go to a vote, but I would advocate running this place more as a benign dictatorship than a democracy if you want to get anywhere.'

Seth laughed again, his blue eyes sparkling. 'Got it. Thanks.'

'Here you go,' Bella held the remote out to Seth. She glanced about the room, a dull ache settling in the centre of her chest as she realized her work here was done. And though she wouldn't have predicted it, she'd loved her time up on the mezzanine with Jack and the kids in their— eventually—peaceful Christmas cocoon. Bella's gaze settled on Zara, still sleeping on a moss-green beanbag, serene and angelic in her iridescent dress, even though the volume of her snoring could rival that of the guy who had fallen asleep in one of the post-lunch conference sessions the previous afternoon. Bella blinked at the memory, the world of work seeming a distant thing. One she hadn't thought about for hours.

'Uh'—Seth cleared his throat—'are you going to let go of that?'

Bella looked down to where her fingers were wrapped tightly around the end of the remote control. 'Sorry!' She released it and rubbed the back of her neck, hoping to wipe away some of the awkwardness making her skin itch. 'What time is it?'

81

'About half past ten.'

Oh. Icy dread pooled in Bella's stomach. It was later than she'd thought and she would have to drive back to the conference centre soon. Her brief stop in Haileybrook had been an adventure, but her time moonlighting as Helen Snow had to come to an end. The unending joys of reality beckoned.

She summoned up a half smile for Seth. 'Thanks. And good luck.'

Bella had reached the top of the stairs and laid her hand on the rail when Seth called after her, 'Lucy would like to talk to you before you leave. I think she wanted to thank you again.'

'Sure.' Bella did her best to mirror Seth's relaxed smile before turning to trudge down the stairs, her spirits falling further with each slow step.

Chapter 11

Bella retrieved her coat from the standing rail. The heavy wool wrapped her in its comforting embrace as she wriggled into the sleeves and fastened the shiny maroon buttons. She brushed her fingertips over the soft fabric and smiled, pleased that she had bought the coat rather than making do with her rather worn old grey number. It had been Kate who had persuaded Bella to treat herself, and had provided the necessary reassurance that the dark-green-and-red tartan with a subtle gold thread stripe was smart and discreetly festive and did not—as Bella had feared—make her look as though she was wrapped in a picnic blanket.

Her heels clicking off the slate flooring, Bella strolled towards the glass doors, dipping her hands into the coat's fabulously deep pockets—another selling point—for her gloves and hat. Behind her, the music of the reception formed a booming wall of noise, but outside the moon was bright and the clouds drifting past it were tinted an eerie steel blue.

'Snow.'

Bella squeaked and startled.

'Sorry.' Lucy—whose footsteps had been masked by the blaring brass section of 'Mambo No. 5'—gave Bella an apologetic smile. 'Toby, my brother-in-law, always says clouds that colour mean snow is on the way.'

'He's a meteorologist?' asked Bella.

'Pretty much.' Lucy grinned. 'He's a farmer.'

'Ah.' Bella nodded. She pointed to Lucy's shoulders, which were baby-carrier free. 'Is the weather expert also watching the baby?'

'He's partly in charge. Danielle is asleep up at the house with Toby, my father-in-law and Seth's nan. They'll call if she wakes up.' Lucy dropped her gaze to Bella's hands, which were clutching her gloves and hat. 'You're leaving already?'

'I think it's for the best. I was never supposed to be here and if I stay much longer I risk leaving more of an impression than is wise.'

Lucy frowned. 'I don't suppose there's any chance you live locally? You've been a lifesaver and I think Seth would like to offer you a job and'—she carried on over Bella's chuckling—'invite you to dinner as a thank you.'

'That would be lovely but I'm staying at a hotel. In fact, I have nearly an hour's drive back to it, another reason I should be on my way. And then tomorrow it'll be back to London'—Bella paused to sigh, an exhalation so deep it dragged the corners of her mouth down with it—'where I live and work.'

'You don't seem too thrilled about that,' said Lucy. 'My best friend Elle raves about London and she's only been a couple of times. She makes it sound so glamorous and exciting. Is it not?'

'It can be.' Bella lifted her gaze back to the moon and the silently drifting clouds. 'But I'm not from a big city and sometimes ...' She paused. How could she explain it? 'OK, this is random, but stick with me.'

'Sounds great. Carry on.'

'A couple of weeks ago, I came up the stairs out of the Underground with the usual stampede of commuters. That's when you have to keep your eyes on the pavement in front of you so you don't trip over something or someone. Anyway, once the crush thinned out, up ahead on the pavement, I thought I saw an earthworm. The poor thing was stranded on a city pavement far from any grass or soil. But then, as I got up close, I realized it was a shoelace.' Bella snorted. 'A random brown shoelace.'

The memory of the non-worm had haunted Bella. The sight of it had filled her with a gnawing sorrow, a nostalgia for an irretrievable something she couldn't put a name to. It had taken her a couple of days to realize that she had identified with the worm, a creature out of its natural habitat struggling to get by and in constant danger of being trampled by the uncaring masses. But she doubted Lucy would get all of that from her daft story.

Lucy nodded, her expression solemn. 'I get it.'

Bella's eyebrows flew up in surprise. Blimey. Was Lucy a psychoanalyst as well as a mother and small-business owner? 'You do?'

'Sure.' Lucy shrugged. 'My friend Elle, she can't wait to get out of here. She always describes Haileybrook as some lost corner of England, a speck in the middle of nowhere where nothing ever happens. But it's never felt like that to me. I was born here. I've lived here my whole life. For me, it's where everything worth knowing about or being involved in happens. I love it and couldn't imagine being anywhere else. I wouldn't want to live surrounded by concrete in a place where even a worm turns out to be a discarded shoelace.' She turned her gaze to the moon. 'Everything here is so beautiful, I've been spoilt and I couldn't live without it. Of course we do shuffle along at a slower pace than people in the city. And you won't find much that you could call "high culture" around here. No opera or gallery openings, no movie stars and film premieres. But it's peaceful. Properly peaceful. And I find a happiness in that I don't believe I could find in the hustle and bustle of a big town or city.'

Bella followed Lucy's gaze up to the sky. The two women stood in silent contemplation for a moment and Bella swore that she felt a whisper of the peace Lucy had described stealing under her skin. She closed her eyes to better appreciate the sensation and, when she opened them, a speck of white danced into her field of vision, drifting down from the sky and floating towards the glass door in front of them. It was quickly followed by a troupe of larger snowflakes which fell steadily through the dim quiet outside and settled on the patio in a powdery carpet.

Bella stared, unwilling to miss a second of the arrival of the first winter snow. There was a spark of magic in the moment and she wanted to linger in it if she could.

'Would you look at that?' said Lucy, breaking the spell. 'Toby was right.' She glanced at Bella. 'I don't suppose you see snow that often in London?'

'No,' said Bella, the word sounding more doleful than she had intended.

'There's a walled gazebo over there with a bench.' Lucy pointed to a small wooden structure which reminded Bella of a rural bus shelter. 'It's supposed to be for the smokers. Seth insists we leave a heater in there for them.'

Lucy's last comment was delivered with a firm note of disapproval. Bella glanced at Lucy, guessing the blonde was made of tougher stuff than her willowy frame suggested. Her glittery shoes probably concealed steel toecaps. 'Seth insists,' Bella said, 'but *you* would happily let the smokers freeze while they're poisoning themselves?'

Lucy laughed, the tightness around her eyes and mouth relaxing. 'Guilty as charged. God, does that make me an awful person? It's just that it's expensive to run the heater and there's gum and patches to curb the cravings, right?'

'Don't apologize to me.' Second-hand cigarette smoke made Bella's throat feel as if it had been grated and prolonged exposure made her nauseous. 'I have about as much sympathy for them as you do.' Bella eyed Lucy askance, reassessing her. She guessed she was in her mid-twenties, and yet she was married, had a baby and was running her own company. And apparently happily so. What was her secret? 'If you don't mind my asking,' said Bella, 'how old are you?

'Twenty-six,' said Lucy. 'For another three weeks. My birthday's in early January.'

Bella struggled not to wince. She would be thirty-six in March, so there was practically a decade between them. And yet what did Bella have to show for her ten-year head start? She was single, working a job she loathed, often so stressed she could barely function without some weapons-grade migraine medication and the best fun she'd had in ages had been at a wedding she wasn't even invited to while impersonating someone else's date!

Lucy continued, 'Although there have been days when Danielle's hardly slept that I've felt ninety-six.'

'I think you look fabulous.'

'Thank you,' said Lucy. Her smile fell and her tone turned serious. 'But honestly, there have been more than a few rough patches since June. If we hadn't had the help of friends and family, I don't know how we'd have managed. My parents, the Coopers, Elle and her parents have all pitched in. Even Mr Fletcher at the pub babysat one time. And Cath made most of our meals for the first three months …'

Bella nodded as she listened to Lucy ramble through the long list of people around her who had carried her through the second half of the year. A close, local network providing unconditional and often unsolicited help. Bella knew nothing like it. She had been sixteen when she'd learned the only person she could ever truly rely on was herself. Although, she relented, over the past couple of years both Kate and her stepsister, Lucinda, had been brilliant at lifting her up when she was low.

Seemingly unaware she had lost Bella's undivided attention, Lucy continued, '… and even Mrs Harman offered to help, but of course Rose said that over her dead body would Grace Harman be looking after her great-grandchild.' Lucy paused to take a deep breath. 'Sorry, you should have stopped me. I'm holding you back.' Lucy opened the door while Bella pulled her hat down over her ears. 'Thank you again, Bella. You may not have supposed to have been here, but I'm glad you were.'

Bella mirrored Lucy's warm smile. It was impossible not to. Lucy's entire manner was so effortlessly amiable, she could have drawn a genuine grin from the Grinch. And Bella had been more than happy to listen to her enthusiastic babbling because it had allowed her to delay her departure. The moment she would have to return to the heavy chill of her own life and leave Jack, Haileybook and the warm bubble of wedding festivities behind, never to return.

Chapter 12

Lucy might not have been thrilled about providing an outdoor heater for smokers, but Bella was soon glad Seth had got his way.

She shivered and shuffled along the bench, closer to the heater. Her coat was thick but her ankles would be the first part of her to freeze if she sat in the gazebo much longer. But every time she told herself it was time to go, her gaze would slide back to the falling snow and she became hypnotized by its beauty.

Obviously she had to leave. But did it have to be forever? Bella narrowed her eyes, turning the idea over. Perhaps she could come back to Haileybrook for a short stay in the future. Drew had mentioned that the bridal party were staying in accommodation on Coopers' Farm. Apparently the stables conversion was stunning with no expense spared on the fittings and finishing touches. And it would be nice to see Lucy again, spending some time surrounded by greenery in a place where real worms and all sorts of other animals—other than giant rats and urban foxes—thrived. Her schedule was crazy for the next couple of months, but perhaps, if she put in some extra hours, she could escape the office in March—

A fluttering of wings broke Bella's concentration and a solitary robin alighted on one of the cocktail tables on the patio. Its round black eyes shone as it stared at her and tilted its head. *'What are you doing out here all alone?'* it seemed to be asking.

Good question, thought Bella.

A blast of 'All I Want for Christmas Is You' burst out of the barn as one of the glass doors opened. The explosion of sound made Bella jump and the robin launch into flight, disappearing into the black-blue sky.

'Lucy said I'd find you here,' said Jack as he approached.

He had to duck to enter the gazebo and, even then, the dark hairs at the back of his head brushed against one of the many garlands of holly and ivy leaves decorating the edges of the roof.

'Here.' Bella scooted along the bench, leaving space for Jack next to the heater. Her ankles might be tingling with cold, but she was wrapped in a coat, hat and gloves. Jack had ventured outside without any additional layers and she doubted his suit provided much insulation.

'Oh no, I couldn't.' Jack hovered, chivalrous distress furrowing his forehead. 'You were here first, you should sit nearer the heater—'

'For God's sake, sit!' Bella said, thumping the wood next to her in case Jack had any doubt from her snappy tone how much she wasn't in the mood for a polite argument.

'Yes, ma'am.' Jack's lips curled into a sly smile of amusement and he took the space on the bench. 'You seemed pensive, out here staring at the snow.'

'I was just wondering if it's deep enough to lie in and make snow angels.'

Jack chuckled. 'I don't think it's quite there yet.'

'I agree.' Bella smiled at him and gestured towards the barn. 'So what am I missing in there?'

'Drew's been asking after you. Said if I'd done something to make you run away, he'd never forgive me.'

Bella grinned. 'From the brief time I've spent with Drew, that sounds about right.'

Jack twisted towards Bella, his long legs extending past the tips of her shoes, which barely reached the ground. 'You two seemed to be having an animated debate over dinner. What was that about?'

'We were trying to settle a matter of great, possibly cosmic importance.'

'I never doubted it for a second. What was it?'

'Which is better: *The Terminator* or *Terminator 2*?'

Jack sucked in air through his teeth, his expression a playful grimace. 'That is a tough one. But I'm going to guess ...' His gaze locked on to Bella's and he narrowed his eyes as if he were trying to read her mind. 'You favour the second film?'

'Of course.' Bella shrugged as if Jack's answer were the only possible one. But she was quietly pleased he had got it right.

'Does the liquid-metal terminator and Arnie playing the good guy swing it for you?'

'Those are important factors. But the greatest thing about that movie is what they did with Sarah Connor.'

'You mean that she's spent her time since the first film becoming a total badass who can do a million chin-ups without breaking a sweat?'

'Absolutely. And not just because her arms are amazing, but because it makes complete sense. Her whole world came to an end in the first movie. She had to start from scratch. I mean, if you'd been hunted by a killing machine and knew nuclear apocalypse was coming, you'd want to give yourself the greatest chance of survival. It's excellent character development.'

Bella swallowed and sniffed, realising that her eyes had filled with tears. The sudden onset of sniffles was likely due to the cold. But more than that, Bella had also been through the wringer over the past year. Obviously her situation wasn't quite as dramatic as Sarah Connor's but, compared to Sarah's, Bella's response to the upheaval in her life had been weak.

Outside the gazebo, the robin swooped over the patio and up to the barn roof. Bella's gaze followed the bird's cheerful red breast, but her thoughts continued to circle. Maybe it was time to seize her own destiny rather than sleepwalking along the gloomy rut fate had carved for her. It wasn't an impossible task. Look at her dad! He'd wallowed for almost twenty years after her mum left. But since retiring, selling up and moving to Spain he'd never been happier. And now he had a new wife, a fabulous stepdaughter and was the local bridge champion.

Bella tracked the robin as it completed another dive down to the patio, her heart fluttering like its pale brown wings. That was it. She needed a Sarah-Connor-style life makeover. Without the guns. That seemed excessive. She'd probably skip the chin-ups too. There was no sense in overdoing it and—

'So,' said Jack, the single word dropping into the silence

like a large rock into a still pool, jolting Bella from her reverie, 'what you're saying is, you appreciate the movie for the depth of the characterization. And not at all for the car chases and explosions?'

Bella laughed and Jack's serious expression relaxed into a wide grin. 'Those are also pretty cool,' said Bella, swaying into Jack in a playful nudge. 'But obviously I take car chases very seriously too.'

Jack returned the nudge, the movement bringing him close enough for Bella to lean against his shoulder. 'As is right and proper. And, speaking of serious things, were you leaving without saying goodbye?'

'No,' Bella responded quickly but, when she pondered her actions, she wasn't sure she'd spoken the truth. Had she planned to go back to see Jack after getting her coat? Or had Lucy opening the door enabled a desire to slip away unnoticed? 'But I do need to be going soon. I have to drive back to the hotel and it'll probably take an hour now it's snowing.'

'Some of those country roads could be dicey in this weather. You should probably go soon before it gets heavier.'

'Yes. You're right.'

They continued to sit side by side, motionless, staring out at the snow. Bella had forgotten about the risk of frostbite to her ankles, so warm was Jack's company and the gentle press of his arm against her own.

'Snow can be treacherous stuff,' said Jack. 'But it's so beautiful.'

Bella sighed and allowed a little more of her weight to rest against Jack's shoulder as she gazed at the unbroken sheet of snow in front of them. And just when she thought the scene couldn't be any more picture perfect, the robin returned, landing on the table closest to the gazebo, close enough for Bella to appreciate the details of his sharp beak, colourful plumage and intelligent stare.

'Oh, look!' she breathed, squeezing Jack's arm in delight. A wide smile on her lips, she turned to face him, but her breath hitched when she discovered that, rather than looking at the robin, Jack's gaze was trained directly on her.

The light from the lamps on the side of the barn reflected off the falling snow, casting Jack's face in a glow which made his dark eyes appear larger. Bella found herself mesmerized as Jack continued to hold her gaze for longer than was merely friendly, or even polite. Her heartbeat accelerating, Bella ran her tongue over her lips and dropped her gaze to Jack's mouth before returning it to meet his deep, steady stare.

'I'll never be able to thank you enough for stepping in at the last minute and coming here today,' said Jack, his low, confidential tone making Bella shiver. 'Actually'—he dropped his gaze for a moment, his brow furrowing—'I have something to ask you.'

Chapter 13

Bella's heart thudded against her ribcage. Oh Lord, was Jack going to ask her out? He seemed to be a great guy, and he was certainly handsome, but she wasn't ready to date anyone seriously yet. And she wouldn't want to mess Jack about given he'd already suffered being strung along by Ashley. In fact, would she want to date someone who was possibly still hung up on their ex? But anyway, she had a lot of work to do on herself. Sarah Connor didn't get those arms overnight—

Jack cleared his throat, bumping Bella from her whirling thoughts. She swallowed, her mouth dry with apprehension as Jack asked, 'Do you know why I've had five women give me their phone numbers since dinner?'

Bella blinked, needing a second to dismiss her feared imaginary scenario, absorb Jack's actual question, and for the penny to drop. She snorted, trying to resist the pressure of the giggles building in her throat. 'I have an idea.'

'Go on.'

'A couple of women were suspicious about why I didn't

know certain things about you if we'd supposedly been exchanging messages for months.'

'I see.'

'I had to come up with an excuse on the spot. Something which would kill off any further questions.'

'All right.'

'So I told them we'd spent most of our message exchanges sexting.'

Jack's lips parted and he blinked. 'You told them—'

'And I may have given them the impression that you're basically the Shakespeare of the erotic text message. Hence why so many women are suddenly giving you their numbers.'

'Oh my God.' Jack sprang off the bench and, his face towards the snow, scraped his hand through his hair. 'I don't believe it.'

Bella stared at his hand, which stopped at the back of his neck and pinched the skin above his collar. Oh heck, she thought as the skin at Jack's nape reddened, she'd gone too far this time. Ethan had often told her she should think more before she spoke.

Bella inhaled deeply and released the breath slowly, the edges of it turning misty in the chill air. Jack's tall silhouette stretched up to the gazebo roof, a dark line against the bright snow. It began to vibrate slightly as Bella stared at it. Crap. He had to be furious. Bella winced and braced herself to be shouted at. Which, when she thought about it—her defensive instincts kicking in as usual—didn't seem entirely fair. Did Jack have decent grounds to be angry with her? After all, she'd found herself in a bind and had only been doing her best to get out of it. And she could have come up with a worse excuse—

Jack bent forwards and rested his hands on his thighs, his shoulders shaking.

Oh bloody hell, thought Bella, the spark of self-defence extinguished as swiftly as it had ignited. Now she'd done it. She'd made the man cry.

'Jack?' Bella pushed off the bench, her voice thickened by a lump of guilt in her throat. 'Are you all right?'

Jack gulped as he straightened and turned towards Bella. The twin tracks of tears on his cheeks confirmed her fears, and she was preparing to make a rare apology, when he drew in a ragged breath and managed to wheeze, 'The Shakespeare of—' before descending into another burst of silent laughter which rocked his torso and robbed him of the power of speech. He dragged in another breath and made another valiant attempt. 'That's the funniest—I can't—'

Bella giggled, her laughter motivated as much by relief as amusement. It would have been impossible to watch Jack, so seized with mirth that he had to fight to stay upright, and not join in. And as Jack pushed a hand to his belly and panted, 'Oh, it hurts,' Bella's giggles swelled into what Kate liked to call her 'trademark cackle'.

Jack leant against the side of the gazebo, clutching his midriff and taking a series of deliberate breaths to tame his laughter into a roll of rumbling chuckles. Bella grinned as he used the side of his hand to wipe the last of the tears from his face. Their shared amusement had filled her with a pleasant warmth which had made it down to her chilled ankles. 'You scared me for a second there,' she said.

Jack slapped a hand to his chest and, between gasps, replied, 'Sorry. I was so worried about today. But of all the things I could have imagined would happen …'

'Come on, Jack! You didn't have "gaining a reputation as the Wordsworth of dirty talk" on your wedding bingo card?'

'Does that mean our fictional sexting involved mentions of daffodils?'

Bella threw back her head and hooted with laughter. 'Oh man, I wish I'd thought of that! It's not too late though.' She gestured towards the barn. 'I can go back in and add all the lurid floral details you want.'

Jack grinned. 'Thank you, but you've done more than enough. I can't tell you how many of the men have been slapping me on the back.'

'Ah, of course.' Bella nodded. Men could be such simple creatures. 'Why do guys find that sort of stuff so impressive?'

'I think in this case it's because I'm the last person they expected it from.'

Jack's smile slipped and, before any feelings of self-doubt could ruin the unrestrained jollity of their moment, Bella rushed on. 'Well perhaps this will teach them not to underestimate you.'

'I hope so. I'd hate for your good work to go to waste.'

'That makes two of us.'

Jack's smile returned and he stepped forwards, closing the gap between them. Gently, he placed his hands on Bella's shoulders and, holding her gaze, said, 'Thank you.'

'You're welcome.'

'May I give you a hug?'

Bella tilted her head from side to side, pretending to consider. 'I think I can allow it.'

'I'm honoured,' said Jack, as he folded his arms around

Bella, bringing the side of her face to lie against his broad chest.

Bella slid her arms around Jack's waist. 'Too right,' she said.

Jack chuckled, loosening his grip on Bella enough for her to pull back and rest her hands on his forearms as she looked up at his face. Up and up and up. Uf! She'd never get over how tall the man was. It was ridiculous. His head was almost brushing against the ceiling of the gazeb— *Oh*.

Directly above them, nestled among the twists of holly and ivy running around the gazebo roof, was a sprig of mistletoe.

Bella's pulse picked up again as she stared at the cluster of white berries. Oh God, what if Jack felt obliged to kiss her when he'd been trying to keep it strictly platonic with a hug? Ugh. Awkward.

Calm down, she told herself. It's just a daft plant. It didn't have supernatural powers to force people to kiss each other. Besides, if she didn't say anything, Jack probably wouldn't even notice it.

'What?' Jack followed Bella's gaze upwards.

Bella silently cursed herself. Dang it, she been staring right at the bloody mistletoe like an idiot. She might as well have pointed at it.

Jack lifted his chin until the white berries almost hit his nose. 'Ah,' he said. 'I see.' He lowered his gaze to meet hers. Holding her stare, he asked, in a low tone barely more than a whisper, 'So what do we do now?'

As Bella scanned Jack's face for signs he wanted to escape, the corner of his mouth quirked and a glimmer of amusement shone in his eyes. He inched a little closer to her and Bella slid her hands up his arms to rest on his biceps where they took on a life of their own and gave the firm muscles they found there a squeeze. *Mmm*. What was it that was so attractive about a man with nice arms?

She dragged her stare from Jack's dark gaze back up to the mistletoe. It was an ancient tradition, she told herself. If they didn't kiss they'd probably be cursed to be unlucky in love forever or something.

I thought it was a daft plant with no supernatural powers? her inner voice quipped.

Oh shut up, thought Bella as she wrapped her fingers around Jack's necktie and gave it a gentle tug to encourage him towards her, rose to the tips of her toes and pressed her lips to his.

Jack froze for a moment before tightening his grip on Bella's waist. Tilting his head, he swiftly responded to her brief peck with a deeper kiss delivered at an expert, magic angle which made Bella's heart thud in delighted surprise. A wonderful heat raced through her, stretching all the way down to her toes which tingled and curled inside her shoes. The hot, shimmering feeling made her light-headed and soon she wasn't sure if her feet were even touching the ground.

Time seemed to slow and stretch, as if the gazebo existed in a bubble outside reality, and Bella was left unable to tell if the dull booming in her ears came from the wedding disco or her heart. And the moment became even more unreal when the booming was joined by the sound of bells. Blimey, that was a first.

Jack gave a low groan of frustration. Blinking, possibly to chase away his rather dopey smile, Jack pulled back from Bella and checked his jacket pockets. 'Sorry, that's my phone. It's here somewhere.' Eventually he retrieved the phone from his back trouser pocket. He stared down at the screen and let out a long sigh. 'It's Simon. Probably another ushering emergency. I'd better duck inside.' Jack shoved his phone into his pocket, grabbed Bella's hands and, as he rubbed his thumbs tenderly over the back of her fingers, Bella wished she could rip her gloves off so she could feel his skin against hers. 'Wait for me here, I'll be one minute. Don't go anywhere. Remember, we still have to make those snow angels.'

Bella laughed and rolled her eyes. 'OK, if you insist.'

'I do.' Jack beamed, his eyes shining as if his face had been lit from within. He gave Bella's hands a quick squeeze and bounded towards the barn, glancing back to call out, 'One minute!' before slipping inside.

Chapter 14

Bella stared after Jack, then closed her eyes, taking a few seconds to bask in the lingering glow of their kiss. Inside her chest, her heart was skipping as merrily as the latest Christmas hit blaring out of the barn. Wow. The world would be a better place if doctors could prescribe kisses like that.

Smiling to herself, Bella glanced at the clock on her phone. A minute had already passed since Jack had gone inside. She sidled closer to the heater and marched on the spot, wiggling her freezing feet. The magical warming effects of the kiss appeared to have a limited duration and her toes were going numb.

The snow rained down in a denser thicket of flakes, settling silently on the patio tiles and tables. It wouldn't be long until there was a white carpet deep enough for snow angels, although—Bella frowned at the thought—that also meant the narrow country roads to the hotel would be getting treacherous.

Bella glanced at the barn door and back to her phone.

Two minutes had passed since his departure and still no sign of Jack.

What was she doing? She needed to get back to the hotel and sneak back to her room before any of her colleagues caught her skulking in the corridor. And this would be the ideal time to leave. Her kiss with Jack had been the perfect end to a pretty perfect evening. The first time in ages that she had created a cache of memories she would be happy to revisit. Besides, the longer she hung around the reception, the more likely it was that the Helen Snow charade would become more complicated and awkward. Jack's friends—who would probably be extra friendly after a few drinks—were likely to ask to friend her on social media. She'd already had to dodge one request from Drew, who wanted to add her on Facebook.

But you told Jack you'd wait here for him, whispered her inner voice, which was unusually loud and crisp this evening. A definite downside to sobriety.

Bella shivered, a stab of guilt pricking her as she imagined Jack's expression when he found she had gone. He didn't deserve to be abandoned, especially after Helen had already let him down. But, ultimately, it would be better for him if she left. It would be beyond awful for their ruse to be uncovered. How embarrassing!

Fluffy flakes of snow stuck to Bella's cheeks as she stepped out of the gazebo. She pulled the neck of her coat closer to her tingling nose and stalked to the narrow path which led down to the car park. The smooth white trail of snow was lit on either side by a chain of orange lights and stretched off into the gloom underneath a row of pine trees. A trickle of doubt snaked down Bella's spine as she stared into the darkness ahead. She paused and turned back towards the bright glow surrounding the barn, her breath catching in her throat. What if she went back for a minute? Just long enough to get Jack's phone number and—

Her coat pocket vibrated as her phone buzzed to life, making Bella startle.

Oh. Bella frowned as she glared at the screen. Summer was calling. She forced her lips into a smile as she answered the phone. 'Hi Summer, what's up?'

'Bel? I don't have long. I need a favour.'

The ice in Bella's toes shot up to her heart. Her sister usually spoke in a bright, musical tone, but now her voice was low and urgent. 'Are you OK? Are you in trouble?'

'No, no. Short on cash, that's all. I get paid next week, but I have some things I have to pay for this weekend. Could you lend me some money?' The line went quiet but Bella thought she could hear her sister sigh before she added a muffled, 'Please.'

Bella clenched her jaw, grinding her teeth in frustration. She would love to lecture Summer on the benefits of budgeting, but this was not the time. She needed help, not a sermon. 'OK, sure. I'm out at the moment, but first thing tomorrow I'll—'

'I need it now.'

'Really? I don't see how it could be that urgent—'

'It is. It's super urgent.'

'But I'm kind of out in the middle of nowhere right now, Summer—'

'You could do it from your phone using the app I told you about last time, right?'

'Uh, well, it wasn't exactly secure.' Bella shuddered as she remembered the hassle she'd had after her last transfer to Summer. 'I'm pretty sure that's how my card details got cloned. I had to cancel the card and—'

'OK, do it however you want,' Summer replied, her tone brisk, 'but can you send the money within the next hour?'

Bella ran a trembling hand over her mouth. Blimey. This had to be an emergency. 'Um, yeah, if I can get back to the hotel. But I'd have to leave right now to make it and with the snow it might be—'

'That's fantastic. You're a lifesaver. Honestly. A total lifesaver. Hang on, I have to tell the guys the news.'

Summer voice turned muted and distant, but Bella could make out the words 'rent' and 'eviction', followed by some cheering which came, she assumed, from Summer's current housemates who must also be rubbish at budgeting.

'Bel, you there?'

'Yeah, always here,' said Bella, silently cursing while batting her palm against her forehead. Why, oh why was she such a pushover when it came to Summer?

'Thanks again. And, Bel?'

'Yeah?'

'Please don't tell Dad. He'll worry, you know he will.'

Bella dragged her hand down the side of her face. She knew all too well. 'You're right. I won't.'

'You're the best! Thanks again. You'll remember to do it in the next hour?'

Bella stared at the golden light around the barn and listened to the distant sounds of the merry gathering in full swing. A wistful smile lifted one side of her mouth.

Wherever he'd got to, whatever ushering duties were keeping him busy, she hoped Jack enjoyed the rest of his evening and capitalized on the kudos her lies had gifted him. And, though she didn't believe in Christmas wishes, she closed her eyes and wished his future would hold nothing but happiness.

'Bella?' Summer's voice rang out, a harsh note in the snowy silence, dragging Bella back to their conversation. 'What's going on?'

'I'm on it.' Bella spun towards the car park. 'I'll message you when I'm back at the hotel.'

'Thanks. Love you!'

'I love you too,' said Bella, but Summer had ended the call before she had a chance to finish her farewell. Bella shook her head, stuffed her phone back in her pocket and scurried down the dim path. There wasn't a minute to lose if she was going to come to Summer's rescue. She was now a Wonder Woman with a firm deadline and no time for wishful thinking.

But, despite her haste, as Bella neared the end of the path, she allowed herself one final glance over her shoulder and wistful sigh. 'Merry Christmas, Jack,' she whispered through the drifting snow and, hugging the bright memories of the evening close to her heart to fend off the worst of the winter chill, she faced the path ahead and strode towards her car.

Chapter 15

ALMOST ONE YEAR LATER

'You know, it's only an hour-and-a-half drive from our place to Haileybrook. If you wanted company next weekend, to help you settle in.'

Bella smiled as Kate's voice boomed out of the car speakers. She'd called her friend about half an hour earlier when she'd been forced to leave the motorway and navigate the smaller roads which criss-crossed the Cotswolds countryside. It was the first Sunday in December and, more than once, Bella found herself alone on the road. She was pleased to have Kate's cheerful tones for company.

'Thanks, babe,' Bella said, pausing the car at a junction leading from an unmarked narrow road bordered by fields to yet another narrow road bordered by fields. 'But unpacking will take me less than an hour.'

'Not unpacking. Settling in,' said Kate. 'We could go shopping for homely touches. Candles, cushions, the essentials.'

Bella rolled her eyes. Kate was a fan of the quirky and colourful. She had recently started renting a house with her boyfriend and in less than a fortnight Kate had covered every inch of the place with colourful throw rugs, canvas prints of inspirational quotes, and the various misshapen, well-intentioned creations her pupils had given her over the years.

'We could have a girls' night in,' continued Kate. 'Hot chocolate, face masks, a good movie.'

A few years ago, Kate's suggestion would have filled Bella with despair and serious concerns about the premature onset of middle age, but now it sounded terrific. A selfish, weak part of her was tempted to take Kate up on her offer. But she had leant on Kate for emotional support a lot over the past couple of years and this first step into her new life was something she wanted to do alone.

'We can have a girls' night in the new year when you're not so busy with school Christmas performances,' Bella said, pulling onto the grass verge to let an aggressive driver in a jeep zoom past her. 'But, speaking of movies, don't you have to be somewhere?'

'Thank you, Bella!' Max's voice came through the speakers, distant, but clear. 'We're going to be late.'

Kate and Max had an early Sunday afternoon date at their local art-house cinema which was showing a Hitchcock double bill of *Dial M for Murder* and *Rope*.

Kate clicked her tongue. 'The ads and trailers take twenty minutes, we'll be fine.'

'Go on,' said Bella. 'Or there'll be no time to get pick 'n' mix.'

'Oh, all right,' said Kate. 'But the best of luck for tomorrow. Knock 'em dead. Not literally, though. Unless they're evil to you, in which case, call me if you need an alibi.'

'Good luck, Bella!' Max called. Bella could picture him standing at the front door, shaking Kate's sparkly raincoat and rainbow-striped umbrella in a desperate bid to encourage her to leave.

'I'll let you know how it goes,' said Bella.

'You better or you'll find me on your doorstep. Seriously, if you need me—'

'I'll call.'

'Good or I'll have to threaten you with detention. I'll speak to you soon. Bye!'

'Enjoy the cinema!' Bella grinned as she ended the call. Kate's feisty side had reappeared since she'd got together with Max. He seemed to bring out the fighter in her and Bella was delighted by the re-emergence of scrappy Kate.

She turned up the radio and, humming along to the chorus of 'Do They Know It's Christmas?', glanced at the sat nav. It was coming up to five to one and she'd enter Haileybrook in about ten minutes. That would make her almost half an hour early to meet her new landlady, but she could always wander around the village for a while and get the lie of the land. Find the local shop at least. She'd need milk and teabags. And something for dinner. And lunch.

A rumble of hunger temporarily overwhelmed the fizzy cocktail of excitement and apprehension sloshing about in Bella's tummy. She should have packed something for lunch. Drat. What else had she forgotten? Why did she feel so underprepared?

Bella tightened her grip on the steering wheel. In the month since she'd accepted the job at Brookfield Park, she'd questioned her decision hundreds of times. Why on earth was she moving somewhere she'd only been once before? And on a fleeting visit. Today would be the first time she was seeing the village in daylight, for heaven's sake! Viewing pictures on Google Street View and reading a surprisingly detailed blog about local life didn't really count.

It's not too late to go back, whispered a voice in the back of her head. *They'd have you back at your old job in a heartbeat. This is going to be a disaster.*

No. Bella shook her head and gave the indicator lever a sharp jab. Her inner voice of doom was wrong and Kate was right. It was all going to be fine. She just needed to ignore her inner monologue and unhelpful comments from—

Her phone rang and the jaunty strains of 'Viva España' sent Bella's heart dropping to her toes. *Great.* The last person she needed to talk to right now.

Bella took a deep breath, smiled and answered the call. 'Hi, Dad.'

'Hello, love. Are you there yet?'

'Nearly,' said Bella through her rictus grin. 'A few more minutes.'

'That's good. All ready for work tomorrow?'

'As ready as I can be.'

'I'm sure it'll be a doddle for you. Compared to your last job it's hardly going to be rocket science.'

Bella bit down hard on the inside of her cheek. He meant well, she told herself. It was something she had been telling herself a lot over the past month. 'It'll be fine.'

'Yes, I'm sure. But ...'

Bella threw a glare at her phone. *Wait for it ...*

'Are you sure about this, love?'

Bella stared dead ahead and practised the meditation breathing techniques she'd been trying out lately. Anything to stop her shouting something she'd regret.

Blissfully unaware that his daughter was approaching boiling point, Bella's dad continued, 'We're all used to Summer being all over the place.' Her dad chuckled. 'That girl changes her location and job like you change your shoes. But you've always been so ... *sensible*. This isn't like you.'

Bella rounded her lips and exhaled slowly, attempted to expel her frustration in an imaginary column of scalding smoke. 'But I've explained, Dad,' she said, hating the high note of despair at the edge of her voice. 'The London job wasn't ever what I wanted to do.'

'And this is? There must be loads of jobs in Birmingham or Oxford, tonnes of accountancy firms that would bite your arm off if you applied to work there. Why do you have to move out to the sticks to work in a retirement community?'

'It's a beautiful place, Dad. And I'll have a lot more autonomy in my work.'

'But you were doing so well before. Climbing the corporate ladder.'

Bella rubbed a hand across her mouth to stop herself screaming, '*I was miserable, Dad! Why can't you see that?*' Instead she took another calming breath and said, 'I could be running the whole of Brookfield Park in a year. You never know.'

'Ha! Now that does sound like you.' He snorted. 'I suppose I can't understand why anyone would want to retire in the English countryside when they could retire abroad and get some sun.'

The day had been grey and overcast since dawn and, as another shower of rain drummed against her windscreen, Bella found it hard to argue with him. Far easier to end the call.

'Dad, I'm going to arrive in a few minutes so I'd better go.'

'OK, love. But if you need anything—'

'Thanks, Dad. I'll call you.'

'And look, if you change your mind about the whole thing—'

'Bye, Dad! Love you!'

Bella tapped the phone screen to hang up and sighed. Everything was fine. She could do this. She was in the right place, at the right time, doing the right thing.

Unfortunately for Bella, her guts weren't convinced by the power of positive affirmations. A stress ache, something Bella hadn't experienced since she'd left her job back in July, was developing low in her belly. Marvellous. When she'd unpacked she'd have to search for a podcast on how to tackle—

Woah! The silver saloon in front of Bella's car suddenly came to a near halt, causing Bella to brake so hard she was thrown forwards and back against her seat. She threw an urgent glance at her rear-view mirror but thankfully the road behind her was deserted. What in the world was going on?

Bella lifted her nose, craning to see past the car in front. On the grassy verge, a small red car had stopped at an awkward angle, its hazard lights flashing. Bella winced in sympathy. What a horrid place to break down. And she'd thought she was having a stressful day.

Bella crawled forwards and, as she drew level with the red car, she caught a glimpse of the driver's long blonde hair and refined features. Was that—? Oh my God, it was!

Checking her mirror before she stood on the brakes, Bella stopped and wound down the passenger window. She leant across the seat and shouted, 'Lucy? Are you all right?'

Chapter 16

Lucy's eyes widened. 'Bella?'

'Hold on.' Bella pulled over in front of Lucy's car. She grabbed her jacket from the passenger seat and, raising the hood, opened the door. 'Have you broken down?' she asked as she arrived next to Lucy's window.

'The engine cut out and now it won't start. Oh my gosh, you're getting soaked, get in!'

Bella scurried around the front of the car, slid into the passenger seat and slammed the door. The force of the closure sent the air freshener hanging from the rear-view mirror swinging. It was a common green tree-shaped freshener, but someone had gone to the trouble of adding miniature baubles and tiny strands of tinsel to it.

'Seth did that,' said Lucy.

Bella blinked. Oh dear, she must have been staring. 'I haven't even thought about Christmas decorations yet,' she said.

Lucy gave Bella a kind smile. 'You've got lots of time.'

Huh. Lucy certainly wasn't behind on getting into the

festive spirit. Her baby-blue raincoat was covered in a pattern of holly leaves and cartoon robins. The little birds brought a ghost of a smile to Bella's lips as she remembered her last visit to Haileybrook. There had been many days over the past year that meeting Jack in the church, agreeing to the Helen Snow charade, and all her shenanigans at the reception seemed like a dream. An overwhelmingly good, if often bizarre dream. One with a perfect ending, a Christmas kiss under the mistletoe with gorgeous Jack, the snow falling around them, his warm, strong arms wrapped around her—

'Bella? You hear that?'

Drat. Bella gave herself a shake. She'd wandered off into memories of Jack. And the kiss. *Again.*

'Sorry.' Bella focused on the grinding sound which came in response to Lucy turning the ignition key. Blimey. That wasn't good. 'Hmn. If you've done that a few times you might have flooded the engine,' said Bella. 'Your battery's probably dead. I'd try to jump-start you, but my leads are at the back of my boot behind boxes and suitcases. I assume you haven't run out of fuel?'

'I've got half a tank,' said Lucy. 'Are you a mechanic as well as an accountant?'

'No,' said Bella, impressed Lucy had remembered what she did for a living. 'I just like to know enough about my car that the garage doesn't think they can rip me off.' She lowered her hood and raised a finger towards her hair. 'They see the blonde and make assumptions.'

Lucy gave a weary nod of understanding, making the end of her golden ponytail shake. 'Yeah. Been there, done that.'

'Do you need a lift somewhere?'

'Don't worry. The farm's only a couple of minutes away. If it wasn't raining we could walk. But I'll call Seth and he can get us.'

'Us?'

Perhaps hearing herself mentioned, Danielle, who was safely strapped into her booster seat in the rear passenger seat behind Bella, began to whimper. 'Mama, home!' she cooed before returning to making grizzling noises.

'Oh my God, she's huge!' said Bella, staring at the chubby toddler while remembering the baby Lucy had attached to her the last time she'd seen mother and daughter.

Lucy laughed. 'You haven't seen her for almost a year. She's nearly seventeen months.'

'Mama, home!' Danielle said, rattling the set of colourful plastic keys grasped in her fist.

'And she can talk,' said Bella.

'And walk. And run.' Lucy sighed. 'She's a handful.'

'Mama, home. Now!' said Danielle, her lips contorting into a threatening pout.

'And she's assertive,' said Bella, eyeing Danielle with wary respect.

'She's a right bossy madam is what she is,' said Lucy, although she aimed a fond smile over her shoulder at the girl.

'Well so am I,' said Bella. 'And if that car seat comes out, you have to let me drive you both home.' Lucy opened her mouth to protest, but Bella rolled on, 'I'm not leaving you stranded out here in the rain.'

'Really, you don't have to—'

'Come on,' said Bella, lifting her hood and opening the door.

A few well-practised moves later and Lucy had transferred Danielle's seat to Bella's car while Bella shifted Lucy's shopping—nappies Lucy had popped to the nearby town of Norton to buy—from Lucy's car to her own.

'Thank you,' Lucy said as she closed the door and lowered her hood, sending a shower of droplets onto her shoulders. 'I wouldn't have minded waiting around for a rescue party if I'd been on my own, but with Danielle—'

'Home!' chimed in Danielle.

'Exactly,' said Lucy, fastening her seat belt. 'I only said I'd take her with me shopping because I hoped she'd fall asleep on the way. She's been up half the night. If we're lucky she might drop off now.'

'Fingers crossed.' Bella started the engine and pulled away. 'Tell me when I have to turn off the road.'

'You've got a couple of minutes yet.' Lucy wriggled back into her seat, flexing her toes in the warm air streaming from the heater. 'I'm so glad it's you. When Cath said that someone called Bella was renting her cottage—and she mentioned you were blonde and made a guess at your age—I hoped it was you.'

A trickle of unease followed a rogue raindrop down the back of Bella's neck. 'Cath Parks?'

'That's right. She'll be the best landlady ever. Her cottage is the cosiest place too. Right on the village green and it's so close to Brookfield. You could walk to work when the weather's nice. And you're seconds from the shop and pub and ...'

Bella stared dead ahead, only half listening as Lucy sang the praises of her new home. A home she hadn't set foot in yet. The rolling sensation of foreboding in her tummy returned. Lucy also seemed to know about her new job at Brookfield Park. Had Cath announced her upcoming arrival to the whole village? Were new residents of Haileybrook so rare that she should expect a welcoming committee? Should she have taken more care with her hair and make-up that morning? Was wearing her oldest pair of black jeans a mistake?

'Here's the turning.' Lucy jabbed a finger to the right. 'Once you're on the track, go straight on towards the house, ignore the road to the barns.'

The entrance to Coopers' Farm was clearly signed. A large brown board with bold white lettering and arrows pointed guests in the direction of the barns and stables. Bella steered the car straight but her thoughts circled. 'How do you know Cath?'

'She's my best friend Elle's aunt and, well, sort of her mum, I guess.' Lucy shrugged, apparently untroubled by her nonsensical statement. 'It's complicated. But Cath's marrying Elle's dad next year. Finally. They're your neighbours. You know that, right? Their cottage joins onto yours.'

Bella frowned. She'd known Cath lived in the cottage next door to the one she was renting to Bella. But Bella had been banking on village life being simpler. Free of drama, especially family drama. What sort of family weirdness was her landlady involved in? And would it spill through the adjoining wall into Bella's house?

'Here we are,' said Lucy as the farmhouse came into view. 'You can park behind the Land Rover.'

The rain slowed and the sun burst through the clouds as they entered the courtyard. The rectangular plot was home to three buildings: the house in the centre with a pair of long, low stone sheds on either side. The tiled roof of the one to the left sagged in several places and Bella suspected the one to the right had similar problems given that it was covered in scaffolding and plastic sheeting.

'Another of Seth's projects,' said Lucy, nodding towards the construction works. 'Now money is coming in from the guest suites, he's starting on these two sheds. We might use them to expand the education centre or for more furniture storage. Sorry you have to see the place in a state. Let's get into the house.'

The two-storey farmhouse was made from blocks of local Cotswolds stone whose recently rain-washed silvery veins glittered in the sunshine. It had white-framed windows and a cheerful postbox-red front door which was adored with a green-and-gold wreath.

In a landscape of browns and greens, squatting under a steely winter sky streaked with white and grey clouds, the house looked as if it had been part of its surroundings forever. Its apparent timelessness made Bella feel uneasy, an intrusive newcomer who hadn't even set foot in her own house before calling on others.

She swallowed the knot in her throat and twisted in her seat to speak to Lucy, who was unhooking Danielle's seat from the back of the car. The girl had fallen asleep and Lucy was manipulating the buckles as if trying not to detonate a bomb. Bella lowered her voice and said, 'I won't come in. I have to meet Cath at the cottage at half past one, so I should be on my way.'

Lucy grinned and, in a quiet, sing-song tone, no doubt designed to keep her daughter out for the count, said,

'Firstly, that's over twenty minutes from now and it'll take you three minutes to drive there. And secondly, that Mini over there belongs to Cath'—she pointed across the courtyard where a sage-green Mini Cooper was partially obscured from view by a yellow builder's skip—'so you might as well meet her now.'

Bella frowned, glancing down at the scuffs on her jeans and the flecks of mud she had picked up around the ankles when she'd dashed to Lucy's car. 'But I'm not dressed for any sort of social occasion—'

'Nonsense,' Lucy said, her tone brisk. 'This has been a working farm for three centuries. You think we care about what anyone's wearing?'

'But—'

'And it's only me and Seth at home anyway. Seth's nan, dad and brother are all in London until tonight. Toby and his girlfriend are taking the other two to see a show as a pre-Christmas treat.'

Bella opened her mouth to protest, but Lucy cut her off. 'I won't take "no" for an answer. You said you can be a bossy madam. Well so can I.' Lucy's lips curled up on one side, but her stare was level and unflinching.

Bella met Lucy's gaze and narrowed her eyes. Lucy narrowed hers in response. It was a look Bella had seen in the mirror enough times to know that the lady wasn't for turning. 'OK, fine,' said Bella, throwing her hands up in defeat. 'But let me change my shoes so Seth and Cath don't think I'm entirely uncivilized.'

Bella rummaged under the passenger seat and pulled out a pair of three-inch black stilettos. She kicked off her navy driving pumps and sighed as she slid her toes into the pointed fronts of her pair of emergency car-based heels. Ah, yes. Muddy jeans or not, *now* she felt dressed. Straightening, she tilted her head as she considered the farmhouse again. She was being daft. What was there to worry about? Lucy was inviting her in and perhaps it would be good to be introduced to Cath by Lucy, their mutual friend. They could have a quick chat, she would grab the cottage keys and be unpacking within the hour.

Lucy's eyes widened as she noticed Bella's change of footwear. 'The yard can be slippery after rain. Will you be all right in those?'

'Don't worry about me'—Bella grinned at Lucy as she opened the driver's door—'I could walk through fire in these. Let's go.'

Chapter 17

Bella followed Lucy into the hallway and waited by the kitchen entrance, hanging back as Lucy strode into the room.

'We're home!' Lucy set Danielle's car seat down by the door and skipped across the terracotta floor tiles to where Seth was standing, his hands immersed in a large Belfast sink, looking out the kitchen windows. She smiled at Bella and motioned for her to come into the room, then pecked Seth's cheek and said, 'You'll never believe what happened on the way back here—'

Bella took a tentative step forwards. Blimey. Now she knew why Lucy's car only had one Christmas decoration: the rest were in her kitchen. In the far-right corner a broad pine tree grazed the ceiling, its green needles almost hidden by an explosion of tinsel, baubles and lights. Next to the tree was a wide chimney alcove, which was home to a squat range cooker, a black iron monstrosity Bella suspected could be as old as the farm itself. Above the cooker, the chimney breast was covered in snowflakes hacked inexpertly from white paper. Similarly rustic paper chains, in a variety of bold colours, dangled in casual loops between the dark wood beams running across the ceiling. The panes of glass in the windows and the back door were dotted with bright vinyl stickers of snowmen, presents and reindeer which partially obscured the view to the garden beyond.

The merry melody of 'Rockin' Around the Christmas Tree' was playing at a low volume and the air carried a fantastic smell of roast beef. Bella closed her eyes and took a deep breath to better appreciate the aroma, making her mouth water.

'Bella!' A wide smile of greeting making his blue eyes shine, Seth crossed the kitchen, stopping in front of Bella after skirting around the end of an enormous oak dining table, which was more an architectural feature than a piece of furniture. 'It's terrific to see you again.'

'You too.' Bella shook Seth's outstretched hand and lifted her gaze to the paper chains overhead. 'It's impressively festive in here.'

'Oh, it's just a few bits and pieces. Most of which were made by the kids at the education centre. And Danielle picked the things for the tree.'

'Seth doesn't know when to stop when it comes to Christmas decorations,' said Lucy, strolling over to her husband's side. 'You should see the life-size Santa in the garden!'

Seth's smile fell. 'You said you liked it.'

Lucy slipped her arm around his waist. 'I do. And I'm forever grateful you didn't get the inflatable dinosaur wearing the Santa hat. Or the full set of reindeer.'

Seth's smile returned. 'There's always next year.' He

shifted his focus to Bella. 'Lucy tells me you've been riding to our rescue yet again, Bella.'

'It was nothing.' Bella shrugged. 'Anyone would have done the same.'

'But they didn't,' Lucy said, stepping over to Danielle's car seat and hoisting it up onto her arm. 'Bella, I'm going to leave you in Seth's capable hands while I take Danielle upstairs and try to get her into her cot without waking her up.'

Seth watched Lucy sweep out of the room before returning his attention to Bella. 'So, Bella. It *is* you. This is great! Lucy's been wondering for weeks what the odds were of someone else called Bella moving to Haileybrook. My nan and Toby didn't think it was you, but I was optimistic.'

Bella smiled at Seth's enthusiasm but unease tickled the back of her neck. She had been planning to ease herself into village life slowly. The plan had been to start work on Monday, find her feet and then perhaps reach out to reconnect with Lucy and meet some more of the locals. But if the farmhouse residents had been discussing the possibility of her arrival for weeks, did that extend to the rest of the village too? 'I was supposed to meet Cath Parks at her cottage but Lucy said she's here?'

'She's out in the herb garden collecting rosemary,' said Seth. 'Her partner is meeting some old work friends for lunch, so Cath offered to come over and cook for us. And, believe me, you should never turn down an offer of Cath's cooking. She's the best— Ah, here she is now.'

The back door opened and a short figure wearing a grey oilskin jacket, their face obscured by the hood, scurried into the kitchen. Before they closed the door behind them,

Bella caught a glimpse of a giant plastic statue of Santa on the lawn outside.

'Brr! The wind out there would cut you in two,' said Cath, throwing back the hood of the oilskin and shuddering. 'Oh!' She paused, her hand frozen on the jacket zip, and stared at Bella. 'Hello, Bella. What a lovely surprise.'

The glow of Cath's smile was welcome and soothing. It was good to see another familiar face, particularly when Bella's previous meeting with Cath had been virtual, a brief video chat to finalize the details of her tenancy.

Seth explained what had brought Bella up to the farmhouse while Bella took the chance to inspect her landlady. Cath was shorter than Bella had expected, roughly the same height as Bella without her heels. Her ash-grey hair was styled into a smart chin-length bob and her round pink cheeks were the prominent feature in her pale face. She was wearing an outfit in coordinating shades of purple: a knee-length corduroy skirt in plum, a cotton top in violet and a wide-collared cardigan in lavender.

'I'll hang your coat up in the hall,' said Seth, taking the damp oilskin from Cath.

'Thanks, Seth.' Cath patted his arm and turned to Bella. 'I was going to pop this'—she wiggled the sprigs of rosemary clutched in her right hand—'in with the potatoes, lower the heat under the beef and come to meet you at the cottage. But this is perfect. You can stay here for lunch and we'll go to the cottage afterwards.'

'Oh no, I couldn't,' Bella rushed to reply. 'You weren't expecting me.'

'If you're worried you'll be stealing someone's beef and Yorkshire puddings,' said Lucy, breezing back into the kitchen, 'you needn't be. Cath always cooks enough for an army.'

'There is plenty,' said Cath, clearly taking Lucy's comment as a compliment. 'Where's Danielle?'

'Asleep in her cot,' said Lucy. 'It was touch and go for a moment, but I managed to sneak out without waking her. I might actually get to eat my food while it's hot for once. You'll stay, won't you, Bella?'

'Um, that would be nice ...' Bella chuckled nervously. Staying at the farm for lunch would eat into the time she had planned to use for unpacking, getting in essential supplies and re-reading the welcome pack her new employer had sent her. On the other hand, the beef smelled divine and her tummy was rumbling. 'But I should go. I was hoping to get to the village shop to buy some essentials before it closes, and I'm not sure when that is on a Sunday.'

'I've left you milk, eggs and butter in the cottage fridge,' said Cath. 'And a loaf of bread, some jam and honey. Oh, and a portion of the lasagne I made yesterday.'

'You're in luck,' said Seth. 'Cath's lasagne is amazing.'

'That's very kind,' said Bella. 'But you shouldn't have—'

'Don't worry,' said Lucy. 'Cath loves to mother people. And feeding others is her mission in life.'

Cath laughed. 'It's true. I can't stand to see anyone go hungry. Oh, that reminds me, I made you a tin of shortbread, Bella. As a welcome present.'

'Wow.' Seth's eyes grew wide. 'You *are* lucky. Please, if you need any help eating it, call me—'

'Us!' said Lucy. 'Call *us*.'

'Call us,' said Seth, mirroring his wife's sly smile. 'Any time. Day or night.'

Bella joined in the collective chuckling, but her laugher was a little forced. Navigating your way through another family's in-jokes and particular humour was always tricky. And she was out of practice. It had been a long time since she'd been in the middle of any good-natured family banter. And it had been even longer since anyone had attempted to mother her. It wasn't something her own mother had ever been keen on. Even before she left.

Perhaps sensing Bella's lingering misgivings, Lucy reached out to take her hand. She gave it gentle shake and said, 'Please stay for lunch.'

Bella frowned. 'I don't want to intrude—'

'You're not!' Lucy squeezed Bella's hand. 'You rescued me from the roadside and we still haven't thanked you properly for stepping in with the kids at the reception last Christmas.'

'Besides,' said Seth, 'if Cath chose you to mind her house, that means you're practically family.'

'Um, well …' Bella's mind whirled. Since when was being a paying tenant 'minding' someone's house? What was she getting into? 'If you're sure.'

'Wonderful! Take a seat,' said Seth, gesturing to the end of one of the oak benches which ran the length of the monumental dining table. 'I'll finish setting the table.'

'I'd better get back to the potatoes,' said Cath, whirling towards the range.

'OK. Thank you.' Bella sank onto the bench, allowing her growing hunger pangs—it had been a long time since her rushed breakfast—overrule her misgivings. It was just lunch, she told herself. If it tasted as good as it smelled, any awkwardness would be worth it. Besides, her hosts were clearly all lovely people and—

Out in the hallway, the front door slammed and a woman's voice called, 'You should think about locking your door!'

Lucy snapped her head towards Seth and hissed, 'You said you'd tell her not to come!'

'I tried.' Seth set a handful of cutlery down on the table. 'But you know what she's like.'

'Yes, I do! She invited herself to lunch because she knows you're too polite to tell her not to come.'

'I'll take my coat off myself then, shall I?' Sailing in from the hall, the voice of the unwanted guest now carried a clear note of disapproval which caused Lucy to lift her hands to her head in a show of despair.

'How about I pop out to greet our guest?' said Seth. 'Come on, Luce.' He squeezed his wife's elbow as he passed her. 'She's not that bad.'

'No.' Lucy lowered her voice to a mutter. 'She's mostly awful.'

Seth gave Bella an apologetic smile as he shuffled past her and out the door. The cheery grin was probably intended to reassure her. It failed. Bella rubbed the uncomfortable prickling at the back of her neck. She had been worried about feeling out of her element in such a tiny country community. But her arrival in Haileybrook—and she hadn't even made it into the village yet!—had made her feel like a fish stranded on a sandbank, gasping for water. Her last visit to Coopers' Farm had involved subterfuge, misleading snobby wedding guests and wrangling restless kids. And now, as Bella took in Lucy's thunderous expression, she could only wonder what kind of drama she'd blundered into this time.

Chapter 18

A stout woman barrelled into the kitchen. Bella guessed she was in her late seventies, but—in her matching brown-and-green tweed jacket and skirt, a maroon scarf tied at her throat and ruddy cheeks—she could have slipped through a time portal from an early twentieth century hunting party. 'When are the builders going to be finished out there, Seth?' she said. 'We suffered years of construction vehicles and workmen disrupting the village while they were building the commune, and now you seem determined to prolong our agony.' She paused to sniff and reposition her grip on the black umbrella clasped in her left hand. 'It's one thing after another around here. I'm amazed your father allows it.'

'Oh, hello Mrs Harman,' said Lucy. 'So you have come for lunch after all.'

'Mrs Harman,' said Seth, ignoring his wife's chilly welcome. 'Please let me take your umbrella.'

Mrs Harman harrumphed, her prickliness temporarily calmed by Seth's bulletproof cheerfulness and hosting skills. 'Very well,' she said and, as she passed her umbrella to Seth, her gaze fell on Bella. Her small dark eyes, which were set close to her pointed nose, narrowed and she peered at Bella like someone inspecting a museum exhibit. 'And who are you?' she said. 'Has Toby tired of that flighty city girl and got himself a new model?'

Bella stuttered, stunned by Mrs Harman's rudeness. Fortunately, she was saved from having to respond by Lucy. 'Serena and Toby are still very happy together, Mrs Harman.' Her tone of voice had grown more menacing with every word. 'I'll be sure to tell them both you were asking after them.'

Still doing his best to smooth over the bumps in conversation, Seth chuckled and said, 'This is Bella, she's—'

'The girl who's moving into Cath's cottage!' Mrs Harman, apparently having shaken off Lucy's rebuke, returned her attention to Bella. 'And you'll be working at Brookfield Park, you poor dear.' The tweed-clad menace shook her head. 'Perhaps you can bring some order to the place. Those people run amok. They've been here barely five minutes and they think they own the village.'

Bella frowned, the rumbles of hunger in her stomach joined by a sting of concern. Mrs Harman made it sound as though Brookfield Park had opened yesterday rather than over two years ago. Everything Bella had seen and read about it had made the place seem like a harmonious, tranquil environment populated by under a hundred retirees, but Mrs Harman would have first-hand experience of the residence and made it sound chaotic. Was Bella's impression wrong? Should she be worried?

'Don't listen to a thing Grace says,' said Cath, turning her back to the oven and brandishing a wooden spoon towards Bella. 'She's just upset because some of the Brookfield's residents have been asking questions and giving her competition on the village council.'

Mrs Harman stepped closer to the oven, facing down Cath and her spoon. 'You know I don't mind *healthy* competition, Cath. But these people have tried to steamroller over those of us who've been here for years. And Lavender Williams has appointed herself to run the Christmas Fair. Ha! That woman's memory is shocking and getting worse. She shouldn't be in charge of anything. It's intolerable. I have been head of the council for twenty years without receiving a single complaint, and now they're proposing elections of all things.'

'Yes, democracy.' Cath tapped her spoon against the side of a bubbling pot. 'Whatever next?'

'But we've always done things our way and they think they know better—'

Bella was so absorbed in listening to the two women trade barbs that the thud of a glass of water striking the table in front of her made her jump. 'Cath's made the mistake of setting Mrs Harman off on one of her favourite topics.' Lucy's voice was little more than a whisper as she lowered herself onto the bench opposite Bella. 'I'm sorry. I'm sure you were looking forward to a quiet lunch. But, in a way, I suppose it's good that you've met Mrs Harman today.'

Bella frowned as, over by the cooker, Mrs Harman's voice rose and her hand gestures became boisterous. 'Why do you say that?'

'Because forewarned is forearmed.' Lucy sighed. 'You'll know what she's like and you may decide it's a good idea to stay well away from any serious village council business.'

'Village council business?' Bella asked.

Seth chuckled as he took a seat next to his wife. 'It mostly revolves around cracking down on littering and making sure listed buildings aren't altered.'

Lucy muttered, 'God help anyone who tries to put a conservatory on the back of a house in Haileybrook.'

'And of course there are events like the Spring Fayre.' Seth held up a finger. 'Fayre spelled with a *y*, by the way. That's very important.'

'Oh, I think I know about that,' said Bella. When researching Haileybrook, she had kept returning to a website run by a local woman who documented developments in the village. It featured lots of great photos. 'I saw some pictures online. There was a coconut shy, tombola and a tea tent. Bunting everywhere.' She smiled, the photos had brought back happy childhood memories of the fun she'd had at similar summer fairs at school. 'The website made it look great.'

Seth and Lucy exchanged a glance and a small smile. Seth said, 'That'll probably have been on our friend Elle's blog. The pictures from last year were terrific, it was a lovely sunny day. It's the big event on the village social calendar. Although'—Seth cast a glance towards Mrs Harman before continuing—'this year a group of Brookfield's residents managed to persuade the council that a Christmas fair—'

'Very deliberately spelled without a *y*,' said Lucy.

Seth raised his voice to continue over his wife's interruption. 'That a Christmas fair would be a good idea.'

'Shh!' Lucy nudged Seth in the ribs, making her husband wince. 'Keep your voice down.'

Bella leant forwards. 'Why are we whispering?'

Rubbing his side, Seth glanced at Lucy before explaining, 'Lucy has been trying to avoid getting roped into helping out with the Fair.'

'No thanks to you!'

'I only said that if we could help, we would be—'

'We have a wedding reception in the barn that day, Seth! We're spread thinly enough as it is. If I hadn't put my foot down, you'd be spending the afternoon in a grotto dressed as Santa, while I'd be up here alone trying to juggle guests, caterers, musicians and a toddler.'

Seth chuckled, wrapped his arm around Lucy's waist and twisted to stare into her eyes. 'You know I'd never abandon you. Even to be Santa for the afternoon.'

Lucy rolled her eyes, but her frown melted away as Seth drew her closer and planted a kiss on her forehead.

A wistful smile crept onto Bella's lips in response. Lucy and Seth were clearly a good team and lucky to have found each other. Although, as heart-warming as their partnership was, the sight of it also came with a whisper of loneliness. It would be so nice to have someone in her corner again.

As Lucy pecked Seth on the cheek, Bella bit her lip, allowing the nip of pain to refocus her thoughts. She had moved to Haileybrook to concentrate on herself. She would start her job tomorrow. Settle in and eventually make some friends, perhaps get a little involved in the local community. Romance was the last thing she had planned. Although, she thought as her gaze drifted back to Seth and Lucy exchanging adoring stares, perhaps she could consider the possibility of dating again in the new year?

Bella tapped the tabletop, dismissing her wistful thoughts to return to practicalities. 'When is the Fair?'

'Saturday after next,' Lucy said. 'In the old school building.'

'It's the community hub now,' said Seth.'

'Sorry, yes,' said Lucy. 'I'm still getting used to the name change. Anyway, Bella, I don't know how involved you wanted to get with village events, but if you don't want to jump straight in with both feet …'

'I should make sure I have something else to do the Saturday after next?' Bella asked.

Lucy nodded. 'I wouldn't normally warn you off. I help out every year with the Spring Fayre and, apart from being bossed about by certain people'—she tipped her head in the direction of Mrs Harman—'it's great fun. But the Christmas Fair is a new thing and I worry it might lead to a showdown between the Brookfield's residents and Mrs Harman. They can't agree on anything and apparently they've had to use council votes to overrule her—'

'Are you talking about the Christmas Fair?' Mrs Harman's shrill voice cut across the kitchen like a scythe. 'It's ageing me, trying to keep the thing on track.' Mrs Harman illustrated her point by dragging a hand across her brow as she strolled towards the table. 'Those Brookfield Park women are impossible to work with. They keep refusing my help when I know they're short of hands …' She trailed off, her bird-like stare alighting on Bella. She tilted her head and narrowed her eyes, giving her the unfortunate appearance of a chicken. A mean one. Bella shuddered. 'You could help though,' Mrs Harman said, jabbing a finger in Bella's direction.

Frozen under Mrs Harman's glare, Bella needed a light tap to her foot to rouse her. She glanced across the table to find Lucy staring at her and shaking her head. 'Um, well,' said Bella, her mouth suddenly dry. 'I don't know about that. I've just got here.'

'There'd be no better way to settle into the village,' Mrs Harman said, warming to her own idea. 'You could keep me updated on those women's schemes. You're likely to see them every day. They do live where you work.'

'Bella is not going to be your mole, Grace,' said Cath. 'Leave her be.'

Thank God for Cath, thought Bella, giving her a grateful smile. The last thing she needed was to be anyone's spy. She had enough to worry about already.

'No one is asking anyone to be a mole,' said Mrs Harman. 'I'm merely suggesting she consider getting involved. It is raising money for an exceptionally good cause.'

Across the table from Bella, Lucy's eyes widened. She shook her head a fraction and mouthed, *'Don't ask.'*

Bella had always been nosey and Lucy's reaction only made her more curious. And so, with a sinking feeling in the pit of her stomach, Bella swallowed and asked, 'What good cause?'

'Hmn?' Mrs Harman blinked, doing her best to look the picture of innocence and not at all like the manipulative witch Bella suspected she really was. 'The Christmas Fair is raising funds for Norton Children's Hospice, dear.'

Oh. Well then. That was that. Who could say 'no' to helping unwell children?

'So can I put your name down on the list of volunteers?' asked Mrs Harman, her tone sugary and smug.

'Uh, I …' Bella floundered.

'I'm sure Bella will think about it,' said Cath. 'Now, take a seat, Grace. Lunch is ready.'

'I will think about it,' said Bella, giving more silent thanks for Cath as her landlady bustled to the foot of the table bearing an earthenware dish piled high with steaming roast potatoes. 'Ooo, that looks fantastic.' Bella's enthusiastic response was both a convenient way of changing the subject and genuine: a reflection of both her hunger and relief.

But though the food was delicious, and kept everyone too busy to pressure her into volunteer work, Bella struggled to enjoy the meal. Whenever her gaze wandered down the table, she found Mrs Harman giving her the sort of look a fox would give a wounded rabbit and—under the weight of such a predatory stare—Cath's perfect Yorkshire puddings left a bitter aftertaste on Bella's tongue. Her quiet life in the country hadn't got off to the serene start she had expected and, the more she found out about life in Haileybrook, the more she wondered if she hadn't bitten off more than she could chew.

Chapter 19

'I know it doesn't look like much at the moment,' said Cath. 'But when the wisteria's in bloom, it's gorgeous.'

Bella couldn't stop grinning. Having escaped Coopers' Farm with a full belly and without having made any unbreakable promises to Mrs Harman, she was finally standing in front of her new home. She pressed her palms together, holding in a squeal of glee. The photos hadn't done the cottage justice. Built from fudge-coloured Cotswolds stone and topped with traditional thatch, the three-hundred-year-old house had white window frames and a smart admiral-blue door. The wisteria Cath referred to was merely a skeleton of brown branches climbing up the wall and over the doorway, although someone had gone to the trouble of winding strings of Christmas lights around the dormant plant. From the photos she had seen, Bella knew the purple blooms of the wisteria would be beautiful but, as the afternoon light dimmed, the pale blue lights— which fell in fine strands like icicles—had a welcoming magic of their own.

'It's lovely,' said Bella.

Cath pointed at the façade. 'Malcolm did a good job with the lights. I normally have a wreath on the door, but I didn't know if you'd want one. And you should be able to decorate it in your own way.' She frowned. 'As long as you don't go overboard. I doubt you'll be surprised to hear that Grace Harman has complained about some of the neighbours' decorations in the past.'

'So I should abandon any plans to borrow Seth's giant Santa to put on the roof?' asked Bella with a wry smile.

Cath chuckled. 'I'm glad to see you've got Grace's measure. And please don't worry about the things she said about Brookfield. All the people from there I've met have been very friendly.'

'I'm sure,' said Bella, although a niggle of doubt still troubled her. Twenty-four hours from now she'd have nearly completed a full day in her new job. A thought which simultaneously made her bounce with excitement and want to crawl under a blanket and curl up into a ball.

Cath shivered. 'I think we'll have a frost tonight. Come on, let's get you inside.' Bella followed Cath through the garden gate and down the short path to the front door. 'I would warn you to watch your head, but I don't think the low ceilings will be a problem for you. They never have been for me either.' Cath smiled as she unlocked the door. 'I'll give you the grand tour and get out of your hair.'

The tour took under five minutes. Downstairs consisted of the living room and kitchen, all filled with a faint, pleasant scent of lavender. Upstairs were two bedrooms, the bathroom and the airing cupboard, the last housing a clunking boiler which, though noisy, seemed to be doing a good job of keeping the cottage warm.

'The heating can be noisy,' said Cath, closing the cupboard door on the gurgling sounds coming from the pipework. 'If it gives you any trouble, please call or drop round.'

'Thanks,' said Bella, trailing Cath back to the top of the stairs. 'Woah!' Bella placed her foot where the floor should be, only for it to meet air, causing her to stumble into the wall.

'Oh yes, the floors are uneven.' Cath patted Bella's arm. 'You'll get used to it, like finding your sea legs. This corridor is probably the worst, but the living room floor has a dip in it too.'

'Noted.' Bella gripped the handrail tightly as she descended the stairs. It would be fine, she told herself. She'd get used to it. A minor inconvenience compared to finding a housemate had stolen her food or used all the toilet paper.

Cath paused between the foot of the stairs and the front door. 'I'm sorry the decoration isn't more exciting.' Her gaze roved the magnolia walls, white skirting boards and oatmeal carpet which—with help from the large mirror over the fireplace, floor lamp in the corner and cream knitted throw blankets covering the sofa and armchair— were doing an excellent job of bringing light and the illusion of space to a dim, cramped room. 'But Seth said plain decoration was best so as not to put anyone off and he does know what he's doing when it comes to interior design. And I'm happy for you to put your own pictures up to add some colour.'

Bella gave Cath a reassuring smile. 'It's fine. I'll get some Christmas decorations soon anyway.'

Cath mirrored Bella's smile. 'Just the kitchen to go.'

Cath strode through the archway into the kitchen, her smile broadening as she trailed her fingertips over one of the beech countertops. Her gaze travelled across the white cupboard fronts and pale yellow tiles to the double window over the sink on the back wall of the cottage which looked out onto the garden and gave the room a natural brightness.

From the wistful glances Cath was casting about the room, Bella knew this was the one she'd miss the most. If the lunch she'd devoured at the farm was Cath's usual standard, her landlady must have spent countless happy hours in the kitchen. Perhaps this was the place Bella could rediscover the joy of cooking? It had been a long time since she'd made food. Takeaways, defrosting and reheating didn't really count. And she used to enjoy baking when she was younger, seeing Summer's face light up when she produced a tray of brownies or cupcakes.

Cath crossed the kitchen to the tall fridge standing next to the back door. She tugged at the handle and, bathed in the glow of the light from within, ran a hand up and down in front of the contents as if modelling a range of game show prizes. 'The lasagne is in the covered dish. Then there's milk, eggs and butter. There's a loaf over there in the bread bin. You'll find tea and other bits and bobs in the cupboard. Oh'—she removed a dark green bottle from the fridge door—'and this is a welcome gift. Some fizz for your new home.'

'Thank you, that's lovely,' said Bella, not having the heart to tell Cath that she hadn't drunk any alcohol since August and didn't plan to start again any time soon.

Cath closed the fridge door. 'Do you need any help bringing your things in? Malcolm said he'd be happy to lend a hand.'

'Thank you, but I'll be OK. I only have a few boxes and cases. Actually, I'll come out and get the first one now.' Bella made for the front door, hoping Cath would follow her. It was kind of her landlady to offer to help, but now Bella was minutes away from being able to get on with unpacking, her pulse had picked up in anticipation of crossing some tasks off her to-do list, leaving her jittery and restless.

'I think that's everything,' said Cath as Bella opened the door. She passed the house keys to Bella. 'But if you need anything, you have my number. And when you've settled in, you should come round for dinner one evening.'

'I wouldn't want to be a bother,' said Bella, following Cath down the garden path towards her car.

'We'd love to have you. Since Elle, our daughter, went off on her travels earlier this year, we've missed having a younger person around the place.'

'Is she coming home for Christmas?' asked Bella and immediately regretted the question when Cath's expression turned glum.

'We don't know. She's in India at the moment and isn't sure of her plans. Plane tickets aren't cheap.'

Bella nodded as she opened her car boot and slid out a packing box. 'My sister's constantly on the move. Travelling all over the place.' As far as Bella knew, this Christmas would be another that Summer would be too busy to drop in on Bella or their dad. But there was no reason to assume Elle was equally indifferent to her family's feelings. 'Hopefully Elle will be able to come back for a visit.'

'Fingers crossed,' said Cath. 'It would be the first year we haven't all been together and it would be so strange.' Cath shivered. 'I'd best get inside. You too. It'll be dark soon.' Cath opened the garden gate to the cottage next door and turned back to say, 'See you soon, Bella. Welcome to Haileybrook.'

Bella waited until her landlady's front door slammed before slumping forwards, her hands resting on the floor of the boot. Why was polite small talk so exhausting? Cath was clearly a lovely person, but after the early start to her day and the unexpectedly sociable lunch at Coopers', all Bella wanted was to be able to click her fingers and find her stuff transported indoors, put away and herself curled up on the sofa with an enormous cup of tea and a crime drama on the television.

Not having a team of house elves, it took Bella a few runs back and forth to the car to shift her lifetime possessions to the living room. She folded her arms and glared at the small pile, wondering—not for the first time—how she had got here. Surely her meagre luggage was a poor show for someone thirty-seven years of age?

The sound of a car rumbling through the village drew her attention to the window and the fast-fading light. A shiver crept down her spine as the engine's growl grew distant and vanished into a total hush. Gosh it was quiet. Back in her room in London, as she had struggled to sleep amid the screams of yet another car alarm and the bellows of drunken late-night revellers staggering home, she had fantasized about this sort of peace. But now, as she wrapped her arms around herself and shuddered, she wondered if the cacophony of city noises had been an unappreciated companion.

A creak upstairs made her startle. Slowly, her gaze rose to the ceiling, arriving at the light fitting in the centre of the room as another creak upstairs was accompanied by a clang. An icy weight sunk its claws into Bella's chest as she stared upwards, listening for more signs of monsters lurking in the airing cupboard or under the beds. Perhaps she should take Cath or Lucy up on their offer of some help? Or maybe she should call Kate or Lucinda? Or maybe even Dad—

Ugh! Bella gave her head and shoulders a rough shake to chase away the creations of her overactive imagination. She was being ridiculous! She'd been taking care of herself since she was sixteen. She wasn't a trembling maiden in need of rescue.

Bella scoffed, yanked the lid off the nearest box and lifted out one of her favourite shoes: a four-inch platform peep-toe sandal in black suede. She wrapped her fingers around the toe of the shoe and brandished the stiletto, taking a few practice swings. Ha! There was nothing to be frightened of. If anything, any monsters hiding in the corners of the house would learn to fear *her*. Ethan had always said he pitied anyone who dared to rile her when she had one of her shoes to hand—

Bella's smile froze on her lips. *Ethan.* It had been over sixteen months since they had split up. So why did he continue to hang around the corners of her mind and sneak out when she least expected? Sighing, Bella removed two more pairs of shoes from the box. On the bright side, at least Ethan's surprise appearances no longer made her ache with a sadness which seemed to dwell deep inside her bones. Now, when the memories came, they were accompanied by a whisper of regret, embarrassment and more than touch of anger. Although, to her credit, Bella had been working on the last one. Meditation and affirmations were helping. As was cutting out alcohol. But clearing the red mist clouding the memories of their break-up was slow going. After all, rage had been Bella's default reaction to most irritants or setbacks since she was a teenager. Being angry was far easier than being sad.

Bella was reaching for another pair of shoes when her gaze snagged on an unfamiliar shimmer of silver in the lower corner of the box. What was that? Frowning, she grabbed the mysterious item: a make-your-own gingerbread house kit with a pink Post-it note stuck to the upper-right corner of the box. The note carried a short message in Kate's neat handwriting:

To Bella,
A house for your new home!
Lots of love,
Kate and Lucinda xx

The picture on the box showed a cute biscuit house, its windows, door frames and roof tiles picked out in white icing and decorated with chocolate drops in colourful shells. The yard contained gingerbread trees, candy canes and a cookie Santa while a dusting of powdered sugar completed the sweet, glistening scene. Bella smiled at the gift from her friends. It appeared she would be getting back into baking sooner than she had imagined.

Hugging the box to the spark of warmth glowing in her chest, Bella closed her eyes and took a deep breath. *I can overcome anything I need to*, she told herself. She gripped the edges of the box until the cardboard dug into her palms. *What's happened has happened and I choose to move forwards.*

Bella opened her eyes. Right. Time to get on with it.

Resolving to send Kate and Lucinda thank you messages later, she carried the box into the kitchen and left it on the counter next to the kettle. Kate must have sneaked the box into her luggage when she had helped Bella pack. And it was likely to have been Lucinda who had sourced the present: a caterer would know the best place to get a baking gift.

The kettle rumbled. Watching the steam emerging from the spout, Bella smiled. Everything was going to be fine. She'd make some tea, fire up her Christmas playlist and let Mariah Carey and Wham! keep her company while she unpacked. Humming along to the opening bars of 'Last Christmas', she retrieved the milk from the fridge and, swaying in time to the music, danced back to the kettle. What had she been worrying about? Her entrance to Haileybrook might have involved an unplanned detour, but now she was back on track. Tea, unpack, a quiet evening, an early night and she would be refreshed and ready to impress her new colleagues in the morning. Really, she'd been daft to let herself stress. She'd barely had a minor setback and—

The lights went out, leaving Bella squinting into the grey gloom of the late afternoon. Somewhere in the near distance a burglar alarm wailed and a dog barked as the power cut swept across the village.

Bella huffed a laugh and set the milk down on the counter with a thud. Great. Unpacking in the dark was yet another thing she hadn't had on her 'a great start to my new life' bingo card. She could only hope that her luck would turn tomorrow and her first day at work would be nothing but sunshine and rainbows.

Chapter 20

By eleven o'clock the next morning, Bella was praying for another power cut. Any excuse to get a break from the computer filing system she had inherited from her predecessor. Although to go so far as to call it a system would be a mistake: it lacked any order or logic. And unfortunately her line manager appeared to have no idea of the mess Bella had been left.

'Harriet was wonderful. So careful and diligent. She'd been with the company thirty years and worked here at Brookfield Park since we opened. She will be missed.' Linda Chan—who had loosely grasped the tips of Bella's fingers upon greeting her and told Bella she was welcome to call her 'Ms Chan'—sniffed and glanced askance at Bella, as if she had already weighed Bella's relative merit against that of the marvellous Harriet and wanted Bella to know she had been found wanting.

'I'm sure,' said Bella, doing her best to smile while meeting Ms Chan's disapproving stare. Blimey, it was difficult to look the woman in the eye. Bella guessed she was in her late fifties, but her straight-backed intimidating poise and smooth pale skin made it hard to be sure. She had a kind of glacial beauty, with her fine bone structure, wide-set eyes, high forehead and jet-black hair making a striking impression. She reminded Bella of Michelle Yeoh and, like the movie star, Bella was pretty sure Ms Chan could have felled anyone who crossed her with a single blow.

'Hmn.' Ms Chan glanced at the gold watch circling her slender wrist. 'I have a meeting with a contractor in five minutes. I've arranged for you to meet some of the residents—the charity committee ladies—at eleven thirty in the lounge. That's in the Pavilion. I trust you'll be able to find your own way there? You remember where it is from your tour?'

'Um, yes?' said Bella, cursing herself for sounding so unsure, but my God, Ms Chan's stare could have made a champion sprinter forget how to walk. The tour was the first item on the induction day programme Ms Chan had drawn up for her. It had been brisk and thorough. Rather like Ms Chan herself.

Bella pointed at the other desk in the office. 'When will I meet the estate manager, Mr ...' Bella trailed off, the name of her office companion escaping her. It was something ridiculously double barrelled, wasn't it?

'Mr Trentham-Whitley Smythe had planned to be here when you arrived.' Ms Chan sniffed, and Bella took heart at this small sign that she wasn't the sole member of staff who had yet to win the approval of Brookfield Park's general manager. 'But the power cut yesterday caused several unforeseen tasks which he had to prioritize for the welfare of our residents.'

'Right.' Bella nodded. The power cut had only lasted about thirty minutes, and though Cath had called her immediately to offer assistance, Bella had been fine with the help of her phone torch. What sort of problems could the failure in the power supply have caused at Brookfield? Something else she had to learn. 'I'm sure I'll meet him later.'

Ms Chan gave Bella a curt nod. 'Good. I'll see you at one thirty to visit the records room so you can see where Harriet kept all the financial paperwork.'

Paperwork? Bella's jaw dropped. She had assumed all records were digitized and stashed somewhere in her predecessor's maze of a computer filing system. But if there were mountains of paper as well, the Lord only knew what other devilish knots Harriet had left her to untangle.

Ms Chan smoothed the sides of her pencil skirt as she glided out of the office, the teal carpet muffling the sound of her heels. Bella waited for the footsteps to fade entirely into the distance before she slumped into the cushioned embrace of her office chair and thumped her head against the backrest. Uf! Hopefully once she'd settled in Ms Chan would dial her scrutiny down a few notches. If not she would be regularly exhausted by lunchtime and might not make it to the end of her three-month probation period. A period during which she could be fired on the spot.

Slowly swaying her chair from side to side, Bella ran a thumb along the tight band of muscle to the side of her neck as her gaze wandered around the open-plan office. At least there was no chance of the office décor bringing on a migraine. The desks, cabinets, shelves and drawers were all in a matching light beech. A cream emulsion covered the walls, broken occasionally by an inoffensive watercolour landscape in a predictably beech frame. In the corner were a sink, fridge, microwave and kettle, although Bella couldn't imagine Ms Chan would take kindly to employees heating up leftover curry for lunch. In fact, when her manager had told Bella she was welcome to eat in the residents' restaurant, her tone had made it sound more like an instruction than an invitation.

Stop distracting yourself and get back to Harriet's mind-bending digital hodgepodge, hissed her inner voice, which had been mercifully silent in Ms Chan's presence. It seemed even it was scared of her.

Bella flicked to a clean page in her notebook, drawing satisfaction from running her fingers over the fresh sheet and drinking in the crisp scent of paper. With the file directory open on the screen in front of her, Bella made notes on the bonkers places Harriet had hidden the most important files. Honestly, if the woman hadn't been retiring, she ought to have been reprimanded.

She quickly became so engrossed that when a voice said, 'Hello,' she jumped and her pen slipped from her fingers, clattering onto the desk.

'Sorry. Didn't mean to scare you.' The man standing in the office doorway was giving her an apologetic smile. From his thick grey hair and the deep lines in his tanned forehead, Bella would have put his age in the mid- to late sixties. 'I'm Trevor Webster. I'm a fairly new resident. You must be the new Harriet.' He crossed the office and extended his hand over the top of Bella's screen. 'Nice to meet you.'

Bella took Trevor's hand and used his grip to help her to standing. 'I'm Bella Hughes. Nice to meet you too, Mr Webster.'

'Oh no, please call me Trevor. Everyone does.' Trevor's straight white smile slipped, he glanced over his shoulder and lowered his voice to say, 'Except the formidable Ms Chan.'

Bella chuckled. 'In that case, please call me Bella.' Trevor's smile stretched into a grin and Bella was struck by thoughts of another film star. With the twinkle in his dark brown eyes, Trevor had an air of George Clooney about him. Although his black trousers, light blue shirt and navy blue blazer revealed an incredibly lean silhouette, so perhaps he could be George's thinner, distant cousin? 'Did you want to see Ms Chan?' asked Bella.

'What? Good gracious, no. I came to find our estate manager, young John.'

'John? Oh! Mr Tren, Tren—' Bella shook her head, annoyed with herself but also with John for having a triple-barrelled surname. 'Sorry. His surname won't stick in my memory.'

'I suppose Trentham-Whitley Smythe is a lot to remember. I was hoping to have a quick word with him. You see, I'm expecting a delivery later this week and I expect I'll need some help getting it up to my apartment. It's not strictly his job, but John's usually very kind and helpful with things like that.'

'Sorry, apparently the power cut has given him a lot of extra work.'

'Ah, I should have thought of that. I myself had one or two of the single ladies asking for my company yesterday afternoon.'

I bet you did, thought Bella, sneaking a glance at Trevor's ringless left hand.

'I shan't keep you back. I'm sure you have a lot to do, what with being in control of the purse strings.' Trevor's lips curled up on one side. 'In many ways, you're the most powerful person in Brookfield.'

Bella locked her gaze on the twinkle in Trevor's eye and matched his lopsided smile. 'Are you trying to charm me, Trevor?'

'Why? Is it working?' Trevor laughed and Bella joined him, delighted to be having a conversation with someone friendly. 'No, I mean it. Finance manager is a post that comes with great responsibility. I think it became too much for dear Harriet in the end. I've only been here since March, but even I could see she was frazzled in the last couple of months before taking retirement. We used to have tea together a couple of times a week and she cried once.'

'I had no idea,' said Bella, a punch of guilt landing heavily in the centre of her chest. She knew what it was like to be miserable in a job and shouldn't have rushed to judge Harriet. 'I hope she's enjoying her retirement.'

'She is! Last I heard she was on a cruise around the Med. Living the high life.'

'Good on her.'

'You know, you and I should have tea sometime,' said Trevor.

'That would be nice.' Bella glanced at the clock on the computer. 'And that reminds me. I'm supposed to be meeting some of the residents down in the Pavilion at half past.' Bella reached for her notebook, pen and phone. 'I should get going.'

'That's on my way,' Trevor said, beaming. 'Allow me to escort you.'

'Thank you,' said Bella, making her way towards the door past Trevor's outstretched hand.

'Oh, Bella, wait a minute!'

Bella turned back as Trevor retrieved her handbag from the side of the desk and held it out to her.

'I wouldn't leave this sitting around.'

Bella frowned. She hadn't thought of the office as the sort of place she'd need to be keeping her wallet under lock and key. 'Have there been problems with thefts here?'

'Goodness no.' Trevor smiled. 'But one can never be too careful. Better safe than sorry.'

'OK.' Bella slung the bag over her shoulder. 'Thank you.'

'Who are you meeting?' asked Trevor as they strolled down the stairs to the ground floor.

'I was told to ask for Lavender Williams, the head of the charity committee.'

'Ah.'

Bella whipped her gaze to Trevor's face. His 'ah' had been full of dark significance. 'Should I be worried?'

'Not at all.'

Trevor's tone was breezy and confident, but failed to reassure. 'Really?' she asked.

'Really and truly. Lavender is a terrific lady. A wonderful organizer.' He turned his dazzling smile to Bella as he opened the outer door. 'Look! You brought the sun with you.'

The heavy smoky clouds of the previous day had vanished overnight, leaving behind a bright blue sky streaked with the occasional whisp of white. In the sunshine, the garden at the centre of the Brookfield development glittered, as the light caught on the remaining raindrops and reflected off the sand-coloured paving.

'It's rather drab now,' Trevor said, gesturing to the flower beds on either side of the wide path. 'But in summer it's beautiful.'

'Oh, I don't know,' said Bella. 'I think it looks great.'

Clusters of pink and purple heather brought colour to the otherwise green and brown flower beds, with the yellow tones of Mexican orange blossom glinting gold in the sunshine. At regular intervals along the path, box hedging had been carefully shaped into a variety of cones, spirals, balls and, in the corner of the garden nearest the Pavilion, someone skilled in topiary had created the outline of a small bird, possibly a robin.

'My apartment is there on the top floor,' said Trevor, pointing up to their left.

Trevor's apartment was one of a number of one- and two-bedroom homes housed in a series of three-storey buildings on either side of the garden. Bella knew from Ms Chan's whistle-stop tour of the premises that the blond-toned bricks and the grey tile roofs had been chosen to better echo the materials used in local traditional architecture. But their slender balconies with black metal railings gave the apartments a Parisian air. All the railings were wrapped in gold and silver tinsel, and each balcony was cheered by the ruby flowers of a potted poinsettia. At ground level, small Christmas trees were visible through many of the apartment windows.

The community also had a series of detached cottages, each with charming names such as Starview and Oak Hollow, which were further from the central complex of communal buildings. Bella had lagged behind Ms Chan as much as she dared during her early tour to read their names, which were displayed on wooden plaques next to their duck egg-blue doors.

'You didn't go for a cottage then?' asked Bella.

'No.' Trevor shook his head. 'Rather beyond my price range, I'm afraid. Anyway, a one-bed suits me and my bachelor ways. I don't spend much time in there anyway. I can usually be found in the Retreat or here, at the Pavilion.'

The Pavilion was a large, single-storey construction made of the same creamy toned bricks as the apartments. However, unlike the residential buildings, the front façade of the communal complex was made of glass panels. They gave passers-by a clear view of the towering Christmas tree in the entrance lobby. Beyond the lobby were the lounge, restaurant, library and games room. As its name suggested, the Retreat—which had a similar design to the Pavilion and was tucked away behind the apartment blocks—contained a pool and spa, treatment rooms, gym and café.

Trevor and Bella strolled side by side to the Pavilion entrance and came to a halt under the broad apex roof canopy over the porch. Taking a deep breath of the crisp air, Bella smiled as she turned to face her companion. The walk and Trevor's relaxed cheerful company had lifted her spirits. Perhaps today wasn't going to be a complete disaster after all.

'Bella, it has been lovely meeting you,' said Trevor. 'But I'd best let you go. You mustn't keep Lavender and her ladies waiting.'

Bella remembered Trevor's earlier reaction when she had mentioned Lavender's name and a wave of uneasiness made her shudder. Something about Lavender having her own 'ladies' made her wonder if she was about to wander into a coven.

Her anxiety must have shown on her face, because Trevor said, 'You honestly don't have anything to worry about. They're a friendly bunch. And ... well, do you like Christmas?'

The question caught Bella off guard. 'Uh, yes. Actually I was thinking the office could do with some decorations.'

Trevor's dazzling grin returned. 'Then you should be fine. Lavender's group are currently preoccupied with a Christmas fair they're holding in the village on Saturday week.'

Oh, thought Bella, the muscles in her shoulders relaxing. They were *those* women. The ones Grace Harman had been railing against yesterday at the farm and had wanted Bella to spy on. Uf! And here she was letting herself get carried away worrying unnecessarily. Bella smiled at her own foolishness. She'd been worrying about having a cup of tea and a chat with a harmless group of older women as if she were about to walk into a nest of vampires!

Trevor patted her on the arm. 'You've nothing to worry about. I have a feeling they won't be able to get enough of you.' He leant forwards, his smile disappearing as he whispered, 'They're always hungry for young, fresh blood.'

Chapter 21

'Thank you, Sanghita. You've done brilliantly getting so many raffle donations from local businesses. And it's wonderful that tickets are selling like hot cakes. Now, let's turn to Santa's grotto. Wendy: where are we at?'

Lavender Williams wasn't a vampire, whatever her fair skin and crimson-slicked lips might suggest. Holding a relaxed stance in front of a loose horseshoe arrangement of eight spectators and backlit by a shaft of sunlight, Lavender—who Bella guessed was in her mid-seventies—was a tall, broad woman with her thick white hair styled in a pixie cut which flattered her oval face. She wore black ankle boots, slim-fitting olive-toned trousers, and a cream tunic.

Lavender listened patiently as Wendy, a rather mousey, freckled lady in her late sixties who spoke in barely more than a whisper, gave an update on her progress in tailoring a made-to-measure Santa suit for the occupier of the Fair's grotto, all without raising her gaze from the floor. Bella was sympathetic. With her no-nonsense tone and the menacing way she was wielding a telescopic pointer, Lavender was an intimidating figure. She stood next to a freestanding whiteboard on which someone had drawn a floor plan for the Christmas Fair. However, Lavender emitted such a towering aura of authority, Bella wouldn't have been surprised if the committee leader had spun the board to reveal a ten-point plan for world domination.

'Marvellous, Wendy. Let us know if you need any help. Given how tall our Santa is, we're lucky you're such a whizz with the sewing machine.' Lavender directed a kind, if condescending, smile at Wendy. 'Bella!'

'Hmn?' Bella snapped her gaze to Lavender and away from the plate of mince pies on the coffee table in front of her. It had been a long time since breakfast and the pastries looked homemade. But, no matter how much her mouth watered at the thought of the buttery, flaky cases and their sweet filling, she was determined to restrain herself. The last thing she needed was to drop mince pie down her front. She could only imagine Ms Chan's expression of disgust if she returned from lunch with a brown stain on her blouse.

'Are you all right?' asked Lavender. 'You looked miles away. Is something troubling you or were you just admiring Wendy's mince pies?'

Bella gave Lavender a nervous smile. Under the skin-crawling scrutiny of Lavender's stare, it was tempting to blame her distraction entirely on Wendy's baking. But Bella's attention had also been captured by something Wendy had said about the grotto. 'Um, well actually …' Bella checked herself. She'd just arrived. It was unlikely that Lavender and her troops would appreciate a newcomer blundering in and giving them notes. 'Never mind. It's nothing.'

'Out with it!' said Lavender, swishing the pointer towards Bella's nose. 'All contributions are welcome here. It's how we come up with our best ideas.'

Bella chuckled, doing her best to ignore a suspicion that Lavender wasn't always as open to suggestions as she was making out. 'It's probably nothing, but'—she turned her gaze to Wendy—'did you say the grotto is going to be free to visit?'

'That's right.' Wendy nodded. 'The gifts are being donated after all.'

Bella sighed. She should leave well alone. It wasn't up to her to tell anyone how to run—

'You think we should charge, don't you?' said Lavender, her gaze narrowing further.

'I don't mean to sound mercenary,' said Bella. 'But people will expect to pay. You don't have to charge the earth, but I'm sure you could ask around and see what other local fairs have been charging. And with the money going to charity, I don't think anyone will mind.' Bella's gaze drifted down to the table in front of her. 'And you should definitely sell those mince pies. They look amazing.'

'For goodness' sake, try one!' Lavender whipped the pointer stick towards the table, causing the woman sitting nearest to her to shrink back defensively. 'You've been staring at them since you got here.'

'Oh no.' Bella shook her head. 'It's fine, I—'

'It's Wendy's secret recipe.' Lavender strode forwards, grabbed the plate and shoved it under Bella's nose. 'They're delicious. All the ingredients are locally sourced.'

'I'm sure.' Bella swallowed as her nose filled with the scent of sugar and spice. 'Honestly, you could pack them into little trays to sell.' Bella swayed back as Lavender pushed the plate even closer to her face. 'You'd make a fortune—'

'Back off, Lavender.' Iris Chapman, who was sitting to Bella's right, leant forwards to wave the plate away. 'Don't shove them down the poor girl's throat.'

Bella twisted to give Iris a sneaky smile of thanks. The only member of the Christmas Fair group who didn't seem daunted by Lavender, Iris was in her late sixties. In contrast to Lavender's muted neutral clothing, Iris wore a cashmere jersey in vivid scarlet and an ankle-length skirt covered in a kaleidoscopic primary-coloured print. As if her outfit weren't eye-catching enough, she also wore a large brooch over her heart. It was in the shape of a Christmas wreath and Bella suspected the green and white stones in the circular gold setting were emeralds and diamonds.

Despite the differences in the women's appearance, Iris seemed to share Lavender's penchant for red lipstick, with her own lips coated in a ruby shade which complemented her dark brown skin and hazel eyes.

'I was merely offering her some hospitality.' Lavender put the plate back on the table and glared at Iris. 'She is our guest.'

'Yes she is.' Iris patted Bella on the knee. 'All the more reason not to terrorize her with baked goods.'

Lavender inhaled slowly through her nose and, before she could breathe out fire, Bella jumped in. 'I don't want to spoil my lunch so why don't I take one for later?' Bella stepped between the two women, reached for a holly-patterned napkin from the top of the pile next to the plate and used it to wrap a mince pie in a neat paper parcel.

Lavender's lips curled into a bright smile as a general murmur of approval passed around the group. 'That's a great idea, Bella. I can see why they hired you.' Lavender swiped the pointer stick towards Bella, narrowly missing her face. 'You're clearly a natural problem-solver.'

'Oh, I don't know about that.' Bella shrugged as she returned to her chair, Lavender's praise sitting uncomfortably on her shoulders.

'Take the compliment.' Iris swayed into Bella, nudging her shoulder. 'You've only just got here and you've come up with two suggestions for how we could make more money at the Fair. We're thrilled to have you on board.'

'Ah, well, I'm not …' Bella stammered as she glanced at the expectant faces to her left and right, Lucy's warning about getting involved in the Fair ringing in her ears. Oh, Lord, they'd caught her. Why could she never keep her mouth shut? She'd thrown out a couple of easy ways they could raise a few extra pounds and in doing so she'd walked straight into their trap like a blithering idiot. But maybe, she thought, pressing a hand to a growing tightness in her chest, there was a way to minimize her involvement. 'I'm sure the Fair will be a huge success. But I've only just got here, as you said. And I'll be so busy with work for the next few weeks until I've learned the ropes, so I'm not sure I'm the best person—'

'You can't be any worse than your predecessor, that's for sure,' said Lavender, her comment raising another chorus of murmurs from the group.

'Oh?' Bella's curiosity overcame her desire to slip the noose. 'Do you mean Harriet?'

'That woman!' Lavender harrumphed. 'She's responsible

for the loss of part of the funds we raised at the summer garden party.'

Her mind whirring, Bella asked, 'Some of the money went missing?'

Before Lavender could reply, Iris said, 'Personally, I think it was an unfortunate mix-up. Harriet was so upset. Genuinely devastated. She even offered to put in the money that went astray from her own pocket. But some people'—her gaze flicked to Lavender—'have gone as far as to suggest that Harriet may have put her hand in the till, so to speak.'

Bella's jaw dropped. Just when she'd started having some sympathy for Harriet, Iris was hitting her with the suggestion the woman had embezzled charity funds? 'If you don't mind me asking, how much money are we talking about?'

'Almost five hundred pounds!' Lavender's voice rose to an indignant squeak.

'Out of a total of?'

'Nearly two and a half thousand.'

Wow. If it had been a few tens of pounds, Bella might have believed Iris's miscounting theory. But a fifth of the money raised going astray? That was definitely suspicious.

'Wow is right, dear,' said Lavender, giving Bella a nod of approval.

Oh, crap. Bella rubbed a hand over her mouth. Had she said that out loud?

'We'll be keeping and counting all the monies from the Christmas Fair ourselves, won't we, ladies?' said Lavender, glaring at her audience until they were nodding like a row of dashboard ornaments.

While she was almost overwhelmed with relief that there was zero chance of her being asked to keep the Christmas Fair books—it would be idiotic to set herself up for being subject to the same suspicions that had befallen Harriet—Bella's inquisitiveness about the creator of the nightmare filing system awaiting her in the office drove her to ask, 'Do you think the money going missing is why she was sometimes upset towards the end of her time here?'

Lavender's blue stare narrowed. 'Who told you about that?'

'Trevor. Mr Webster.'

Trevor's name, like the sun breaking through the clouds, instantly cleared the stormy expression from Lavender's face. 'Oh, Trevor's such a dear. He took pity on Harriet.' Lavender beamed, her eyes glowing. 'He's such a kind soul.'

A ripple of agreement passed around the circle and the same glow stole into all the ladies' eyes as they exchanged conspiratorial glances and smirks.

Ah. Bella allowed herself her own smirk of satisfaction. She'd been right about Trevor's Clooneyesque charms.

'You're absolutely right, Lavender,' said Iris. 'Yesterday, during the power cut, Trevor came to check on me. He does worry.'

For a second, Lavender's smile froze and her gaze narrowed. But the fractional tightening of her expression vanished as quickly as it had appeared, and she chuckled. 'Yes, well, he knows that some of us are less capable than others. He is inclined to be charitable.'

Bella's eyes widened. Oh dear. Her gaze shuttling between Iris and Lavender, who were engaged in a terrifying staring match, she realized that Trevor wasn't only a source of entertainment for the female residents. He was a source of conflict.

Wendy cleared her throat, causing Iris and Lavender to blink and refocus their attention on the unassuming figure at the edge of the semicircle. 'Trevor was calling on me when the power went out. He was keen to stay but I told him he should check on others if he felt they might be in need.'

Bella bit her lower lip to hold in a burst of laughter. Good on Wendy for throwing her hat into the ring. She looked like a timid freckled mouse, but she clearly had game.

Unfortunately, Iris and Lavender didn't find Wendy's revelations amusing. And given the poisonous glares directed at Wendy from a couple of the ladies to Bella's left, Trevor's fan club membership was numerous. Blimey. Were men so thin on the ground at Brookfield that they were fought over?

Bella glanced over her shoulder at the rest of the lounge. There were a few other residents, sitting in padded armchairs in front of the small Christmas tree in the corner, reading or chatting over tea. But they were all women. 'Aren't any men helping with the Christmas Fair?' asked Bella.

Iris was the first to blink. She followed Bella's gaze to the other side of the room. 'I see you've noticed how far women outnumber men here. We've a fair few widows you see.' She shrugged. 'And then those with husbands—like Ruth and Sanghita'—she nodded across the circle—'like coming to our meetings to get away from them.' She chuckled and the rest of the ladies joined in.

'John has been marvellous, of course,' said Lavender.

Bella took a deep breath, determined to get it right this time. 'You mean Mr Trentham-Whitley Smythe.' Ha! She'd finally got it. Take that, triple-barrelled posh surname nonsense.

'Yes,' said Lavender. 'He's such a helpful young man.' Lavender's opinion of John received a loud murmur of agreement from the rest of the group. 'He's only been here since September but he's made such a difference. He always goes above and beyond.'

'Exactly. According to Ms Chan he's supposed to spend most of his time in the office dealing with suppliers,' Iris said. 'But, as John says, it's often quicker and cheaper for him to do the odd job himself.'

'And he's right, of course,' said Lavender. 'I mean, you could call in someone to change a light bulb, but we all know what sort of charges those cowboys try to hit you with.'

'And I'd much rather have John in my apartment than some strange man with dirty hands and terrible manners,' said Iris, reinforcing her point with a haughty sniff.

Bella nodded to cover her confusion. If everyone found John to be such a helpful delight—not to mention someone who saved Brookfield money—why did Ms Chan seem to disapprove of him?

'He worked so late last night, trying to sort everything out after the power cut. And he was in early this morning dealing with the alarm company and trying to get all our burglar and fire alarms reset and sorted.'

Ah. As understanding dawned about how the power cut had caused John to miss his meeting with her earlier that morning, Bella felt a burst of hope. Perhaps, daft surname aside, this John guy could be an ally? An understanding person to offload to about Ms Chan's Medusa-like glare?

'Do you have a young man, dear?' Lavender asked Bella, and Bella stiffened as the undivided attention of every other woman in the horseshoe shifted to her face.

'Oh, uh, well …' Bella stammered, her face heating.

'Or a woman, of course,' added Iris, giving Bella an encouraging smile.

'No, not at the moment. And I'm not looking for anyone right now,' said Bella, parroting the same speech she'd given to every well-meaning friend of her father's during her summer in Spain. Although today the words rang a little hollow. Since witnessing Seth and Lucy's happy partnership at the farm, a tiny part of Bella had begun to wonder if, perhaps, dipping a toe back into the dating pond wouldn't be such a terrible idea. But there was no need to tell the committee ladies that. 'I've just moved here,' she continued, 'and I want to settle into my job and—'

'Is John single at the moment?' Ignoring Bella's attempts at deflection, Iris turned to Lavender for confirmation.

'I'm not sure,' said Lavender. 'He did mention a girl once. Deirdra? Diana? Or was it Dinah? Anyway, he's never said he's attached. And Bella here is definitely single.' Lavender stared at Bella, her eyes shining with the prospect of a matchmaking project.

Bella's pulse accelerated. She needed to nip this in the bud before they had arranged her marriage to a guy she'd never even met. 'Honestly, I'm not—'

'Speak of the devil! Here he is.' Lavender waved her

arm in a wide arc as if she were signalling a plane to land. 'John! Come and meet Bella.'

Bella dropped her head forwards, fighting the urge to hide her reddening face with her hands. She supposed it could have been worse. At least Lavender hadn't announced she was single to the whole lounge.

A deep voice behind Bella said, 'Good afternoon, ladies. How are your plans going?'

'Very well, thank you, John,' said Iris. 'Have you got everything sorted after the power cut?'

'Yes, thanks.' Although it was prefaced by a tired sigh, the rumbling voice contained a smile. 'The alarm contractor just left. But if you have any more trouble, let me know.'

Hang on a minute. Bella straightened as the fine hairs at the back of her neck stood on end. She knew that voice.

'We've been filling Bella in on our progress,' said Lavender. 'Bella, this is John.'

Her heart thudding in anticipation, Bella twisted in her seat. Her gaze landed on a tool-laden utility belt slung around a trim waist before travelling up and up and up, skimming past a black T-shirt stretched across a broad chest, until it reached John's face. A face which, though it was covered in more stubble than the last time she'd seen it, contained a familiar pair of gorgeous brown eyes and kissable lips.

The heat in Bella's cheeks flared and her jaw dropped, the shock of recognition striking her dumb. A warm glitter of delight swept over her skin as her mind buzzed with a single question.

What on earth was *Jack* doing here?

Chapter 22

Jack's stunned expression—the parted lips and wide brown eyes—was the same one he'd worn almost a year ago when she'd strode past him into the vestry to answer Ashley's distress call. He clearly hadn't been expecting to see her back in Haileybrook either.

A touch light-headed, Bella tightened her grip on the back of her chair as a shy smile tugged at her lips. She hadn't realized how much she had needed to see a friendly face until now. And Jack's face—in fact, the rest of his body too—looked extremely good. She should have known the man would be able to rock a pair of work boots, dark jeans and a T-shirt just as well as a morning suit. He had been clean-shaven the last time they met, but his current light dusting of stubble emphasized his strong jaw. And the utility belt around his hips was hitting all the right notes. Blimey, had the lounge got hotter all of a sudden? Bella allowed her gaze to flicker down to the string of tools one final time before training her focus on Jack's face, wishing she could fan her burning cheeks. What was it about people who knew how to fix things? Why did competence with a hammer and wrench make someone suddenly a hundred per cent more attractive?

You're staring, her inner voice prompted. *Say something!*

Bella cleared her throat and, her voice a hoarse wheeze, said, 'Hi.'

Oh, brilliant, Bella. Genius. Well done.

Jack blinked and closed his mouth, but seemed to have lost his voice.

'Do you two know each other?' Iris's gaze shuttled between Bella and Jack, the keen stare of a cat who had caught the scent of a mouse.

'Um. Well ...' Bella stuttered, unsure of how to reply. Her gaze searched Jack's face, desperate for clues as to how he would like to answer. Would Jack want to admit they already knew each other if that meant he'd have to explain *how* they met? The committee ladies would probably love the story, but Ms Chan was unlikely to be delighted to discover that her two newest employees were already acquainted. And that they'd fraternized. Conspired. Kissed.

The blush burning in Bella's face travelled down her neck until she was certain her complexion must be nothing but an unattractive rash of pink smudges. She didn't want to flat-out deny having met Jack before. That would be rude and she would never want him to think she wasn't pleased to see him. But she didn't want to get him into trouble with Ms Chan either. Oh heck. She had to say *something*. Perhaps there was a way to fudge it? To be deliberately vague or—

'No,' said Jack. 'No, we've never met.' He looked down

at Bella, but his eyes failed to meet hers, his gaze hovering around her shoulder. 'You're the new finance manager?'

Jack's eyes were cold, missing the warm shine Bella had so admired during the brief time they'd spent together last year. A heaviness pooling in her stomach, Bella stared at him, the lump which had formed in her throat stopping her from answering his question.

Lavender, not one to leave a silence unfilled, jumped in. 'Yes, Bella started this morning.'

'Wonderful,' Jack said, although his tone made the word ring hollow. 'I'm sure she's having a busy day, so I should let her get on. And I should get back to it too. I was just dropping by to let Iris know her alarm's sorted.'

Iris smiled at him. 'Thank you, John, dear.'

'Right, then.' Jack nodded, his gaze sliding quickly around the group. 'See you later, ladies.'

A few strides took him to the lounge door and a moment later he was gone, leaving Bella staring after him. What in the world was going on?

'Huh.' Lavender tapped her index finger against her top lip. 'John seemed in an awful hurry. It's not like him to be so brusque.'

Iris shrugged. 'He's had a stressful couple of days. I'm sure it's nothing.'

Was it nothing? Was Jack OK? Bella frowned and directed her stare down to her feet which were stubbornly frozen to the carpet. What was she doing? Why was she sitting here when the only person who could answer her questions had left?

Bella pushed to standing so quickly, her head swam. 'I better get back to the office,' she said as she backed out of the semicircle. 'It was lovely to meet you all and best of luck with the Christmas Fair.'

Bella whirled towards the door, her retreat accompanied by a chorus of 'You too, dear' and a particularly loud 'But we haven't put you down to mind a stall yet!' from Lavender which only made Bella double her pace.

Her legs grew steadier as the crossed the lobby but her thoughts swarmed like angry bees. Jack couldn't have failed to recognize her, could he?

After barging through the outside doors, Bella was forced to pause for a moment to allow her eyes to adjust to the bright sunlight. She raised her hand to shield her gaze and, as she scurried down the path to the garden, a tall silhouette in the distance caught her eye.

Eager to catch up with Jack, Bella upped her pace to a trot and, fuelled by decades of consuming detective dramas, her mind filled with a series of increasingly unlikely explanations for Jack's behaviour. He had been in a car accident and the consequent amnesia had wiped all memories of the past year. John was Jack's evil twin, come to Haileybrook to launch a dastardly scheme using a job at the local retirement community as the perfect cover. Jack had witnessed a mafia killing and been given a new identity and relocated to a sleepy village in the middle of nowhere for his own protection.

'Jack!' She raised her voice when she was sure she would be within earshot. 'Jack! Wait!'

Jack paused, allowing Bella to catch up. She halted a few steps from his back and drew in a series of deep breaths, recovering from her run. A smile stole onto her lips as her gaze roved across his broad shoulders. It was so good to see him. Actually, she needed to tell him that. But it was probably best to start with an apology.

'I'm sorry about that,' she said. 'I was so surprised to see you, I didn't know what to say. I wasn't sure if you'd want me to tell your fan club back there that we'd already met or—'

'Surprised? How can you possibly be surprised?' Jack's voice was low, but loud enough for Bella to notice how it trembled. And when he turned to face her there was a fiery intensity in his gaze which made her take a step back. 'You'd been told I worked here. You knew my name.'

'But I didn't. I mean, I was told your name, but ...' Bella floundered, Jack's glare making her thoughts scatter. Pull it together, she told herself. He can't really be mad because you're unfamiliar with how his name appears on his passport. 'To me, you're Jack.' She smiled, trying to inject some much-needed levity into the conversation. 'Since when is that short for John?'

Jack spluttered, two pink dashes appearing on his cheeks. 'Since hundreds of years ago! That's when!'

Bella took another step back, retreating from the sudden blast of heat in Jack's voice. Her lips parted as her mind reeled, but another part of her bristled with indignation. What was his problem? 'Well excuse me for not knowing everything,' said Bella. She spoke slowly, making a deliberate effort to keep her voice low. It was her first day in a new job and she would not be goaded into a slanging match in a public space. Besides, surely her not having recognized his name was a small issue? She'd already apologized. Couldn't they both see the funny side and move forwards? 'But I think I have a case for not immediately connecting you with Trentham-Whitley Smythe when you said your name was Smith.'

Jack opened and closed his mouth, apparently stumped. Ha! She'd got him there.

Holding Bella's stare, Jack planted his hands on his hips and the air between them seemed to thicken as the awkward silence stretched. Bella narrowed her eyes. If he thought she would blink first, he was very much mistaken. She had stared down much more intimidating—although not taller, she'd give him that—opposition in her time and she was damned if she was giving ground today.

Eventually, Jack let out a slow breath and some of the rigidity in his posture loosened. 'I said I *went by* Smith,' he said, his voice muffled and a little sad. His gaze slid to the ground. 'You would too if you'd been lumbered with a surname like Trentham-Whitley Smythe.'

Bella nodded, her bubbling irritation calming for a moment. The man had a point. Although it still didn't explain why he was so annoyed with her. 'OK. I can understand that. I just … I honestly didn't join the dots with your name. But I don't see why that has upset you—'

'You vanished. At the wedding.' Jack lifted his gaze and, when it collided with Bella's, his brown eyes were glassy. 'I looked everywhere for you. I couldn't believe you'd leave after we'd …' He scrubbed a hand across his face as if he was trying to wipe away the same vivid memory which had filled Bella's mind: the two of them cosied together in the gazebo, laughing as the snow fell around them. 'And I kept looking for you, but you didn't tell me your name so I kept coming up against all these dead ends.' Jack spoke faster now, a growl of frustration bleeding in at the edges of his voice. 'And after a few months, I had to give up before it drove me mad.'

Bloody hell. Bella rubbed the itch tickling her neck. She had imagined that, when he'd found her gone, Jack would have shrugged, returned to the party, made up some excuse for why 'Helen' had had to leave, and then enjoyed the rest of his evening, basking in all the positive female attention Bella's tall tales had won for him. Now, hearing that he'd been so affected by her departure, her tummy flipped and a bitter taste filled her mouth. Rather than quickly forgetting her, he'd looked for her for a *few months?* Wow. Maybe this wasn't a situation which could be easily fixed after all.

Jack threw out a hand in the direction they had come from. 'And then I walk into the Pavilion, after having got hardly any sleep last night because of the bloody power cut making the alarm systems go haywire, and there you are! You're just sitting there in the residents' lounge with the Christmas Fair ladies like, like you'd always been there and I hadn't noticed you until now. Honestly'—he huffed a mirthless laugh and lifted his gaze to the sky—'I thought I was hallucinating.'

At a loss as to what to say, Bella tried to fall back on levity. She smiled. 'The Christmas Fair ladies can have that effect on you.'

Jack didn't return her smile. Instead he stared at her, blinking slowly as if he were still struggling to believe she was real.

A white cloud ringed with grey passed in front of the sun and, as its shadow fell across the garden, Bella shivered. There had to be a way to rescue the situation. After all, Jack and she had to work together now. Perhaps they could start over?

'I'm real. And I'm here to stay,' she said, wincing as her comment made Jack grimace. 'At least for my probation period or until Harriet's filing system kills me.' She forced a half-hearted chuckle. 'So, why don't we treat today as square one?' She extended a hand towards him. 'Hello, I'm Bella Hughes. It's lovely to meet you and I look forward to working together. Perhaps we can watch each other's backs when it comes to Ms Chan?'

The corner of Jack's mouth twitched at the mention of Ms Chan, and a corresponding spark of hope flared in Bella's heart. Perhaps she'd found a chink in his armour?

But the ghost of a smile on Jack's lips vanished as quickly as it had appeared. His gaze fell onto her hand and the muscles in his jaw and around his eyes tightened, as if he were flinching away from a cobra poised to strike. He shook his head. 'No, sorry. I can't. I can't do this again. Look, I think it'd be best if we try to stay out of each other's way.' He glanced at Bella's face—just long enough for her to see the sheen of sadness in his eyes—turned and strode away.

'Jack?' Bella lowered her hand, staring at Jack's back. *'Wait!'* she wanted to scream. *'We can't leave it like that! We have to sort this out!'* 'Jack!' Her shout carried across the garden, but failed to knock Jack off course. He ploughed ahead, turned left onto one of the side paths and disappeared behind an apartment block.

Bella raised her fingers to her throbbing temples. The memory of Jack's face as he'd contemplated touching her hand—the way he'd practically recoiled in disgust— cut like a sharp blade. It was such a contrast to another memory, a favourite she had revisited many times over the past year: the warmth of Jack's strong hands on her waist and his dark gaze as he held her close in the gazebo.

Her chest tight, Bella drew in a jagged breath. The dull pain at the sides of her head began to creep down behind her ears. Oh fantastic. She hadn't had so much as a headache since she quit her last job, let alone a migraine. Moving to Haileybrook and taking the job at Brookfield was supposed to be the beginning of a more relaxed life, not a source of more stress.

Bella stared at the shadowy space where Jack had stood. There had to be a way she could fix this. Perhaps when her head wasn't pounding, she could come up with—

'Bella!' Iris barrelled down the path from the Pavilion, the speed of her movements making the multicoloured pattern on her skirt shudder and vibrate in ways that didn't help Bella's incipient headache. 'Bella! You forgot your handbag, notebook and the mince pie.'

Bella smiled at Iris, but her heart plummeted to her toes. She'd been so consumed with the need to speak to Jack, she'd left all her things behind with the Christmas Fair group. Great. Now the residents would think she was forgetful and flighty. And—even better—Iris must have witnessed her yelling after Jack. Now all she needed was for these bits of gossip to get back to Ms Chan before five o'clock and her ideal first day would be complete.

'I'm so sorry,' said Bella, giving Iris her most charming smile. 'I needed to ask Ja— I mean, John, a couple of questions.'

Iris handed over Bella's belongings, while giving Bella a sympathetic smile. 'Of course you did.' She raised an eyebrow and lowered her voice. 'Not one of us would blame you, you know. He's a lovely young man. And I do think he's single, even if he did mention a Diana or Dinah a couple of times.'

Dinah. Dinah! Bella had forgotten about Jack's greatest admirer. Perhaps, after spending Ashley's wedding throwing herself at Jack, Dinah had finally got her man.

Bella blinked at Iris, doing her best to ignore the way her heart seemed to seize at the thought of Dinah coiling herself around Jack. 'Um, well'—Bella took a run at replying to Iris, but the expectation behind the woman's sly smile and raised eyebrow made it hard to think clearly—'I don't think—'

'Don't worry, love.' Iris patted her upper arm, the twinkle in her eye brighter than the diamonds in her brooch. 'If these things are meant to happen, they will. Although'—she chuckled—'that won't stop Lavender interfering. You've been warned.'

'Thanks. I'll keep that in mind.'

A loud growl came from Iris's stomach. She clapped a hand to her belly and said, 'Dear me, it must be lunchtime. Trevor is coming to my place.' Her smile contained a trace of smugness at this victory in the competition for Trevor's affections. 'But the others are sure you'd be eating in the restaurant. Should I ask them to save a place for you?'

It was a kind offer and if Bella's appetite hadn't deserted her she'd probably have taken Iris up on it. 'That's OK, thanks. I'll get something later.'

'All right. But remember to eat. I'm pleased I slipped an extra mince pie in there.' She nodded towards the parcel of napkins Bella was balancing on top of her notebook. 'You need to keep your strength up. Especially as you'll be working with Ms Chan.'

And, having delivered two dark warnings in as many minutes, Iris turned and strolled back to the Pavilion. Watching her go, Bella slung her bag over her shoulder and crossed her arms. Though the clouds had drifted by and the garden was once again bathed in sunshine, she shivered. Time to get back inside.

Bella slouched her way back up to the office. What a morning! Her boss disliked her, her predecessor had left her a huge mess and her colleague wanted nothing to do with her. The only upside to the whole situation was that she was now looking forward to being shown the records room. If avoiding Jack was to become an ongoing feature of this new stage in her career, at least a small filing room would be an ideal place to hide.

Chapter 23

'Please tell me you're not thinking of quitting. You've barely been there a week!'

Bella rolled her eyes, pleased that Lucinda couldn't see her exasperation. Although, to be fair, if her caterer stepsister could have seen her—standing in the cottage kitchen transferring perfectly baked gingerbread house components to a cooling rack—she would probably have been delighted. 'I've worked nine full days, thank you very much,' she said in the direction of her phone, which was perched on the counter next to a mixing bowl. 'Eleven if you count the extra hours I put in at the weekend. But no. You know I won't quit that easily. My probation period is three months and that's the initial lease I've taken out on this place, so I'll suffer through that at least.'

'Is it getting any better?' Lucinda raised her voice above background noises of hissing steam, clanging and chopping. It might have been 8 p.m. on a Thursday, but Lucinda was busy overseeing a kitchen as usual. Her team were catering for a Christmas party at Compton Hall, a stately home not far from Lucinda's house. 'You must be making progress on some front, surely?'

'I think I'm close to cracking Harriet's filing system. It only took working the weekend and my evenings every night until today.'

'And you're using your first free evening to make a gingerbread house? Shouldn't you be in front of the TV with your feet up?'

Bella glanced through the archway to the front room and the sofa. It had taken considerable willpower not to sink into its warm, cushiony embrace after dinner. Although the spicy aroma of the freshly baked gingerbread made her glad she'd made the effort. 'A break would be nice,' said Bella, casting another longing glance at the sofa, 'but I feel like I'm behind on Christmas.'

Lucinda laughed. 'I don't think you can be behind on Christmas!'

'I didn't either, but I popped over to the shop on the High Street after work and every building is decked out in lights and has their window displays stuffed with candy canes, baubles and tinsel. The cherry trees on the green are covered in a fine web of fairy lights and, when you thought it couldn't get any better, someone has fitted a festive topper to the postbox. You know, one of those fab knitted ones that Kate loves.'

'Oh my God, I love those too. Why haven't you sent me a photo?'

'Sorry, I will. It's Santa's upturned legs and boots sticking out of a chimney pot with presents scattered about on the snowy rooftop. All knitted. It must have taken someone ages.'

'It sounds like the citizens of Haileybrook are full of the joy of the season.'

'Exactly. And I haven't a single decoration up. I worry that if the locals find out how bare it is in here they'll assembly a pitchfork-wielding mob and chase me out of town.'

'Relax. From the photos you have sent me, the outside of the cottage looks terrific.'

'That's all thanks to Cath and her partner. Perhaps I should ask them to drop into the office. It's a beige wilderness.'

'Getting back to the subject of the office'—Lucinda's tone turned serious again—'have you made any progress with your colleagues?'

Bella closed the cupboard in front of her with a swift push. It was the sort of shove she had visualized giving Ms Chan more than once over the past eleven days. 'Ms Chan seemed a little impressed with me putting in overtime during my first week. I think. It's impossible to tell what's going on in her head. Her two facial expressions are underwhelmed and unimpressed.'

Lucinda snorted. 'We've all worked for people like that. What about Jack? Is a reconciliation in sight?'

'I've barely laid eyes on him.' Bella dropped a spoonful of icing sugar into the mixing bowl and coughed as a cloud of sweet dust exploded towards her face. 'And the few times we've been in the same space, he's all but run away. Like he's allergic to me or something.'

Lucinda must have detected the note of dejection in Bella's tone. 'You still like the guy though, right? Because, to be honest with you, his behaviour is making me think he's a bit of a knob.'

'I don't think he's being malicious.'

'Maybe not, but it's hardly mature behaviour, is it? You have to work together. He should get over himself and speak to you.'

'You have a point. But we've both been busy. Honestly, I could have tried to corner him for a chat, but I haven't had the time.'

'But why should this be down to you to fix? You already offered an olive branch.' Lucinda fell silent as the noise of clanging on her side of the line intensified. 'You told me this guy was handsome, right?'

Though Bella was in the middle of the tricky procedure of transferring another loaded spoonful of icing sugar from the packet to the mixing bowl, Lucinda's question made her freeze. That was an interesting shift in topic. Why did Lucinda want to know what Jack looked like? 'Uh, yeah. He looks a bit like Henry Cavill. I mean, he doesn't have the chin dimple or anything, but the jawline is there and he has a great smile. Like a light-up-a-room sort of smile. He's not quite Man of Steel muscular—which isn't my thing anyway—but he's strong. Probably all the DIY. I told you about how good he is at fixing things, didn't I?' Bella sighed, her heart skipping as she pictured the utility belt around Jack's hips. 'And the stubble seems to have been a temporary feature. He's been clean-shaven all the other times I've caught a glimpse of him.' Bella paused, realising her rambling had left her slightly breathless. On the other end of the phone line, Lucinda remained quiet behind the hubbub of the kitchen. 'Hello?'

'I'm here. Just listening.' Lucinda's tone was light, but Bella could have sworn there was a note of insinuation in her voice. 'When you first met Jack, back at that wedding, nothing happened between you two, did it?'

Drat! The spoon slipped from Bella's fingers and the icing sugar plummeted into the bowl, sending up another cloud. Bella waved her hand in front of her face while kicking herself for only telling Lucinda an edited version of the truth when she had seen her in Spain last Christmas. But for some reason, she wanted to keep her and Jack's kiss to herself. 'No!' Bella rubbed her fingers across her brow, probably leaving tracks in the icing sugar behind. She shouldn't have shouted. Now Lucinda would be even more suspicious. 'No, it was like I said. A good dinner, spreading sexting gossip among the guests and then watching a movie with some kids.'

'All right. If you say so,' said Lucinda, sounding entirely unconvinced. 'How's it going with the Christmas Fair masterminds? Have you been roped in to minding the money yet?'

'No. Spending days in the records room meant Lavender and Iris weren't able to pin me down. And by the time they found me, Lucy had come to the rescue.'

'How did she do that?'

Bella frowned. Hadn't she already told Lucinda about the nativity play? Or had she told Kate? Or Dad? Blimey. She needed a break from the numbers and some time in human company. 'The hall roof at one of the local schools sprung a leak meaning they'd have to cancel their nativity play. Lucy offered to let them use the barn conversion. And so that's how I'm spending tomorrow evening. Raving away my Friday night, stone-cold sober, shaking a donation box, trying to persuade proud parents and grandparents to give money to fix a school roof.'

'They're not going to use real animals from the farm, are they?'

'I believe Seth floated the idea, but Lucy shot it down.'

'Sounds like a sensible woman. Children are tough enough to herd. No point adding sheep, goats and a donkey into the mix.'

'Speaking of mixing.' Bella filled a cup with water and placed it next to the bowl of icing sugar. 'I'm about to make the icing glue for the gingerbread house. Any tips?'

'Add a teaspoon of water at a time. Don't rush it or it'll end up too thin. And don't try to do it while speaking to me.'

Bella shook her head as she followed Lucinda's instructions. She wasn't sure she'd ever get used to having a bossy older stepsister. Was this what it was like for Summer? Which reminded her—the thought coming with a pinch of guilt—she should message Summer. Her sister had sent her a single message asking about Bella's first day at Brookfield—a message Bella suspected had been the result of their dad's prompting—but she had heard nothing from Summer since. Then again, it wasn't unusual for Summer to go silent for weeks if she was off to a new destination.

'Is that your way of telling me to stop distracting you at work?' Bella asked.

'No.' Lucinda's reply was emphatic. 'You need to concentrate or your gingerbread dream home will turn into a shack. And ...'

A loud rustling came out of the phone, followed by the sound of two muffled voices. No doubt a customer with an important catering-related enquiry. She should let Lucinda go.

'Bella? Sorry about that,' Lucinda's voice was clear, but quieter than before. 'My friend Becky's just brought a small issue to my attention. I'd better go and help her.'

'Don't let me keep you. Go work your culinary miracles or whatever it is you do.'

'Thanks. Good luck with the nativity tomorrow. Oh! And don't miss the *Napier* Christmas special. It's next Friday.'

'As if I would,' said Bella smoothly, hoping that her tone covered the fact she had forgotten about the show. Lucinda's partner, the actor Alex Fraser, played one of the main characters in the increasingly popular detective drama. It wouldn't be wise to confess to her stepsister— Alex's greatest cheerleader—that the much-anticipated Christmas edition of *Napier* had slipped her mind. 'I'm looking forward to it and I'm sure Alex will be as brilliant as ever.'

'You're right, he will be. But, as you know, he's never a hundred per cent happy with his—' Lucinda broke off for a moment before returning, her voice a breathless rush. 'I'm sorry, Bella, I do have to go. Keep me updated on how you're getting on.'

'No worries. Love you and give my love to Alex.'

Lucinda answered immediately, but Bella could tell her mind was already elsewhere. 'Will do. Love you, bye!'

Bella sighed and turned her head towards the kitchen window. The weather forecast had predicted the first snowfall of the winter would arrive earlier that afternoon, but Bella had been disappointed by blue-grey skies which promised much but brought nothing. And it seemed from the uninterrupted darkness beyond the glass that the evening skies would also fail to deliver. Oh well. Bella shrugged and returned her attention to her gingerbread project. She'd have to settle for making her own snowy scene for now.

Despite a moment's struggle with a slippery piping bag, making the icing and using it to glue the parts of the house together only involved short bursts of breath-holding and swearing. Bella stepped back and a bubble of pride swelled in her chest as she admired the progress of her creation. If someone had told her a year ago that she would soon be capable of having such a calm, productive evening—with a serene background soundtrack of Michael Bublé's festive crooning—she would have scoffed in disbelief. During her London life, by half past eight on a weekday—on the few nights she would have been home from work—she'd have opened a bottle of wine before she removed her shoes and spent the scarce hours before bed drowning her misery in a pool of Beaujolais.

But she shouldn't let her success go to her head. The dexterity she would need to complete the fiddly icing decorations on the sides and roof of the biscuit house might prove her undoing. Hmn. Bella frowned as she examined the picture on the box. Perhaps she should simplify the design?

Bella glared at the cute snowy scene on the box, willing inspiration to strike. But the only thing that came to mind was the memory of bright snow dancing down from an inky night sky, a surprising sprig of mistletoe on a gazebo roof beam and the warm, toe-tingling embrace of a gorgeous guy beneath it.

Gah! Bella scrubbed her hand over her eyes to dismiss

the memory, but thoughts of Jack refused to be banished so easily. During her first couple of days at Brookfield, she had decided to focus on her tasks and leave him to brood. With time he'd mellow towards her, right? But, the more she replayed their conversation and the longer she considered what he believed to be her unforgiveable actions, the less sympathy she had for his position. Did she really deserve the silent treatment forever?

Bella pouted and grabbed the icing bag, giving the top of the plastic cone a vicious twist. How was she supposed to have known that Jack would care so much about her leaving? They'd known each other for only a few hours when Summer's pleas for cash had sent Bella rushing back to her hotel, so why would Bella have assumed Jack had developed an attachment to her? And—she gave the bag another twist—if he'd truly been that into her, why hadn't he—

The doorbell chimed, shocking Bella out of another fruitless spiral of Jack-related questions and saving the icing bag from a catastrophic split.

Ugh! Bella gave a grunt of annoyance and dropped the icing bag on the counter, but her pulse kicked in pleasure at the prospect of a distraction. Could it be carol singers? She loved carol singers! Even the bad ones. Although, she reasoned as she left the kitchen, it was a little early for them. But maybe—and her spirits lifted further at the idea—it was Cath. Her landlady had told Bella the other day that she was making a huge batch of iced festive cookies for the cake stall at the Christmas Fair. Cath could probably tutor Bella on how to ice her gingerbread house like a true pro.

A smile of excitement on her lips, Bella yanked open the front door, ready to greet whoever was waiting outside.

Oh.

The snow had started to fall. But, although she had been longing to see it, Bella hardly noticed the fluffy flakes settling on the garden path. Instead, her wide-eyed gaze was fixed on the blonde woman in front of her. Her naturally pale skin was a light tan and her small pointed nose and round cheeks—a copy of Bella's own—were covered in a dusting of freckles. Her outfit—a light rain jacket, cotton top, denim shorts and canvas sneakers—sent a sympathetic shiver through Bella. The woman was accessorising her unseasonal clothing with an enormous backpack which towered above her head. Its weight forced her to bow forwards, bringing her eyes to the same level as Bella's.

'Surprise!' The woman held up her dainty hands and shook them either side of her bright smile.

Bella opened and closed her mouth, but no sound came out. Why was Summer on her doorstep? How did her sister even know her address? What in the actual flip was going on?

Summer returned her hands to the straps of her pack and shifted her weight from foot to foot. 'Um, are you going to invite me in, Bel? I'm freezing my bits off out here. In case you haven't noticed, it's ruddy snowing.'

Chapter 24

Summer dropped her rucksack onto the living room floor with a thud. She planted her hands on her hips and scanned her surroundings. 'Oh my God, this place is just as cute as the photos.' She bounded over to Bella and wrapped her arms around her, holding her close long enough for Bella's nostrils to fill with the vanilla notes of Summer's favourite perfume and wonder if her sister had less flesh on her bones than the last time she'd hugged her. It had been so long, she couldn't be sure.

Bella shivered in the remnants of the icy draught Summer had brought across the threshold with her, the shudder finally returning her ability to speak. 'What are you doing here?'

Summer laughed. 'Hey, Summer! It's so great to see you. How's it going?'

Bella pinched the bridge of her nose. 'Yes, sorry. All of that. This is ...' Bella drew in a painful breath, her chest having tightened since opening the door. 'It's such a surprise. I thought you were halfway round the world.'

'I was.' Summer's expression turned serious. 'I was in Cambodia teaching at the best school. The people were great, the food amazing and the weather was a lot warmer.'

Bella's gaze flicked down to her sister's bare legs and she shivered again. Summer had always hated the cold and, even in August, would complain that her fingers and toes were freezing. Bella had often sent her to school with an extra scarf and, on the worst days of winter, a hot-water bottle. It would have taken a lot to bring Summer back to England in winter. Had something terrible happened to her? Had someone hurt her? Did Bella need to get on a plane and break someone's legs? 'So what brings you here?' Bella asked, scanning Summer for injuries. 'Are you OK?'

Summer chuckled. 'I'm fine. Like I said, *I* was having a great time in Cambodia. I'm here to check on *you*.'

What? Bella shook her head, hoping to dislodge the low buzzing noise in the back of her brain. 'Why?'

'In a word? Dad.'

Bella rubbed her forehead. That made even less sense. 'What has Dad—'

'He kept bugging me about you!' Summer stomped towards the kitchen and rested her back on the wall next to the archway. 'He kept calling me and leaving voice messages and then sending messages too, asking if I'd heard from you, asking me to check in on you.' She released a weary sigh, as if their father's concern was a heavy burden she had been carrying for a long time. 'He's never done that before. And, honestly Bel, after a few weeks of it, he started to freak me out. And I guess I was thinking about moving on anyway and a couple of guys at the school mentioned this unbelievable place they were going to in Brazil, and England was in the middle of my route, sort of, and this place'—she pointed towards the window and the village beyond—'is kinda famous in the travel community thanks to Elle Bea's blog. Have you seen it?'

'Uh … yes.' Preoccupied with making a mental note to call her father as soon as possible, Bella needed a moment to remember the website she had used to research the village. 'The writer is my landlady's daughter.'

'That's amazing!' Summer grinned, the shine returning to her eyes. 'She's updating it now while she's travelling. Her pictures and stories from India are unreal. Anyway'— Summer shrugged—'the stuff she put on there about Haileybrook has made it a destination. You know, as a quintessential English village with thatched cottages, green, little church, and the pub has some amazing reviews. So I thought, why not? I could pop in, check you haven't totally lost your mind and stop Dad hassling me.'

The buzzing in Bella's head shifted into a ringing throb in her temples. Had Dad told Summer that he feared Bella had lost it? What else had he said? Bella winced, narrowing her eyes. Had the light in the living room got brighter?

Oblivious to Bella's discomfort, Summer had leant over the threshold to the kitchen to further her inspection of the cottage. 'Oh my God, this place is tiny! Is upstairs like this too?' Summer strode for the stairs but, unaware of the drunken floor, stumbled. Acting on protective reflex, Bella shot forwards to break her fall, but Summer managed to right herself and held a hand out to halt Bella's advance. 'I'm OK.' Summer glared down at the hidden dip in the floor. 'That'll take some getting used to.'

Though Bella's mind was sluggish, dulled by the high-pitched whining in her ears, her attention snagged on 'used to'. Was Summer planning to stay with her for a long time? Without any warning? The guest bed wasn't even made up!

Bella took a deep breath. Since quitting her last job, she had been making a conscious effort not to blurt out her first reaction to situations. Following Kate's advice, she was trying to dial her responses down from a ten to a less confrontational six or seven. This seemed like another perfect opportunity to practise. So, instead of yelling, 'Bloody hell, Summer! You can't show up out of the blue and assume it's fine to move in,' she said, 'Uh, Summer?' and waited for her sister—who was hoisting her enormous pack onto her shoulders—to glance at her before continuing, in a soft voice, 'When you say "pop in", what exactly did you mean?'

'That I'm going to stay here with you for a while, of course.' Summer slapped Bella on the top of her arm and spun round to scale the stairs, not looking back as she shouted, 'Which room is mine?'

Bella slumped against the wall at the foot of the stairs as the invisible vice which had encircled her lungs squeezed. She loved her sister. Deeply. Fiercely. And it was wonderful, if surreal, to see her in the flesh. But Summer had always been an agent of chaos and—as Bella let her head hang forwards and listened to her sister installing herself in Bella's countryside haven—her sister's heavy footsteps became the sound of Bella's fledgling hopes of experiencing something approaching tranquillity being trampled to dust.

Chapter 25

'I don't see why they couldn't have had at least one sheep.' Lavender tipped some coins through the slot in the collection box on the table in front of Bella. They clinked as they connected with the other donations inside the former shoebox which had been jazzed up with a string of green tinsel. 'What is the point of moving the performance to a real farm if you can't feature any of the animals?'

'The farm is doing the school a favour, Lavender.' Iris slid a folded ten-pound note into the collection box and gave Bella a wink. 'And are you volunteering to clear up the sheep's droppings or step in when it starts to chew the Virgin Mary's robe?'

'I just don't think it would have been that difficult,' said Lavender, directing her stare past Iris to inspect the inside of the barn. 'I must say, they've done a good job setting everything up. Although those decorations are rather amateurish.'

While it was usually home to various arrangements of circular dining tables, that evening the barn at Coopers'

Farm had a small wooden stage at the far end and the space between it and the lobby was filled with two blocks of audience seating in neat rows. All of the chairs were covered in crimson covers. The decorations Lavender was pointing at were a series of Christmas-themed paintings by the school children, which Lucy had fixed to dark green strings and hung between the ceiling beams. The bright pictures, featuring glittery stars, collage Magi and cotton wool snowmen, were adorable.

'Those pictures are by a group of four- and five-year-olds, Lavender,' said Iris. 'I think you may be asking too much.'

Lavender and Iris exchanged hostile stares. They towered over Bella, who was suddenly glad she was sitting safely behind a folding picnic table. Although, if the staring match became any more aggressive, Bella might have to climb over the table to put space between the combatants. 'Thank you for coming,' she said, her words causing the ladies to turn their sharp gazes down to her. Bella swallowed, her mouth dry. Time to turn on the charm. 'I hope you enjoy the play. The children have been working very hard on it.'

'Thank you, Bella,' said Lavender. 'And, as she's unlikely to tell you herself, you should know that Iris is out of sorts because she's misplaced a brooch.'

'Oh, I'm sorry,' said Bella, recalling the diamond and emerald piece Iris had been wearing on her first day at Brookfield. 'Is that the one in the shape of a Christmas wreath?'

Iris nodded and dropped her gaze, her expression shifting from murderous to despondent. 'Arthur, my late husband, gave it to me as a fortieth wedding anniversary present.'

'Were you wearing it when it went missing?' asked Bella.

'I don't believe so,' said Iris. 'I could swear I'd put it on my dresser, in the usual place, but—'

'It'll turn up in one of your safe places,' said Lavender. 'Honestly, you're always losing things. Remember the merry dance we went on to find your keys and they turned up in the tea caddy.'

Iris responded to Lavender's comments with a razor-sharp smile. 'Did you ever find those pearl earrings you were saying you hadn't seen in a while, Lavender? Or that gold chain? Perhaps you put those in a safe place.'

Lavender sniffed and tugged at the wide lapels of her wool coat, which was a striking cerulean blue. She was clearly preparing another volley for Iris—perhaps a suggestion as to where she could stick her jewellery—and Bella decided it was time to remove herself from the line of fire. An audience could only encourage them to prolong their argument. And if she hung around much longer they would surely soon ask for her opinion as to who was in the right, and she wasn't foolish enough to get drawn into that sort of lose-lose situation. 'Oh, look!' Bella leapt to her feet and rounded the table while staring at the other end of the barn and the staging area where Lucy was chatting to one of the teachers. 'I think Lucy needs me. Would you ladies please do me the favour of watching the desk and the donation pot?' She gave them a warm smile. 'I wouldn't trust anyone else with such an important job. And I promise I won't be long.'

'I'd love to!' said Iris. 'Take your time.'

'But be back before the show starts,' added Lavender. 'My grandniece is one of the angels and I wouldn't want to miss anything.'

'Of course,' said Bella, backing away from the desk and almost crashing into the Christmas tree on the other side of the lobby in her haste. 'Thank you.'

In the main body of the barn instrumental versions of Christmas carols played out of the speakers in the corners of the room, forming a layer of sound over the chatter of the many parents and carers who had already taken their seats. Bella scurried down the aisle and slipped behind the curtain which had been hung across the barn to create a backstage area shielded from the audience.

'Bella!' Lucy, who had crouched to straighten an angel's wings, sprang up as Bella approached. 'Who's watching the entrance?'

'Don't worry. Lavender and Iris are covering for me. I'm hoping giving them a task will stop them killing each other. A murder wouldn't exactly be in keeping with the "peace on earth and goodwill to all" message we're going for tonight.'

Lucy laughed. 'OK, well they'll probably triple our donations. You may have noticed they have stares which would frighten the tightest of people into opening their wallets.'

Bella gasped in mock outrage. 'Obviously I have no idea what you're talking about, but I think triple is conservative.' Bella glanced about at the thirty or so children packed into the backstage area. They were grouped into jittery clusters of shepherds, angels and wise men. In the middle of them all was the Holy Family: a yawning boy in a brown cloak hovering next to a brown-haired girl in blue who was clutching a plastic baby doll by its foot.

The sight of the miniature Mary and Joseph transported Bella back to a memory of another nativity scene and her dash to prevent it from being flattened. How Jack had smiled at her, his large brown eyes and his low voice full of warmth. How gently he had removed the stray pieces of tree from her hair— Gah! Bella planted her hands on her hips and refocused her gaze on Lucy. She really had to put Jack out of her mind.

'Can I do anything to help?' asked Bella.

'Thanks, but I think we've got it under control. Is it filling up out there?' Lucy bustled over to the curtain, the wide sleeves of her peacock-blue top swishing as she went, and peeked round it. 'Good. Lots of early birds. We should be able to start on time. Is your sister here yet?'

'She should be here any minute. I told her curtain-up was quarter to six and she said she'd get here before to lend a hand. Something must have kept her back.'

Bella smiled at Lucy, fighting the instinct to curl into a ball with shame. Bella had told Summer about the play the previous evening and asked her to attend and help out for less than an hour. In her most reasonable voice, she had explained that it was important to her to support Lucy and take part in a community event and she would appreciate Summer coming along. Summer had shrugged and said she'd try, but she had a lot to do. Apparently the village was so photogenic, she planned to spend the day taking snaps of the green, old school building and St Stephen's, then check out the Cross Keys pub. But when Bella had popped home at lunchtime, worried that all her messages to Summer had gone unread, she had found her sister in bed.

'It's snowing, Bel,' Summer had whined, pouting and tugging the duvet up to her chin. 'I'm freezing. I know you said your boiler was temperamental but I reckon you need it fixed. And I haven't been in these sort of temperatures for ages. I think it's some sort of shock. I'll try to build up to going out later.'

Bella loved her sister. But she often wondered if, in going above and beyond to shield Summer from the harshest consequences of their mother's departure, she had accidentally coddled her and made her into an ungrateful, selfish brat. But she did have a point about the boiler. She should call Cath and ask her to send someone over to take a look at—

'Ow!' Bella hollered as a miniature shepherd barrelled into the back of her legs, walloping her bottom with his crook.

'Justin!' Lucy stooped so her eyes were on a level with those of the small human cannonball. 'Take care to watch where you're going. This is the second time I've had to tell you. Let's not make it a third. Best behaviour, remember?'

Justin nodded. 'Yes, Mrs Cooper.'

'Good.' Lucy straightened. 'Now apologize to Miss Hughes and run along. You'd best grab one of those toy sheep quickly or you'll be left with the pig again.'

'Yes, Mrs Cooper.' The boy flicked a chastened gaze to Bella and muttered, 'Sorry,' before darting away.

Bella stared after him. Perhaps she could get Lucy to teach her how to use that tone and stare on Summer.

'It must be lovely to have your sister visiting.' Lucy gave

Bella a warm smile. 'I'm looking forward to meeting— Oh, look! There's Jack.'

'Really?' Bella tried to arrange her features to look interested, but not too interested. 'I didn't know he was coming tonight.'

'He helped set up the chairs. He can't stay for the performance.' Lucy grabbed Bella and tugged her over to the curtain, but when Bella glanced into the audience the only glimpse she got of Jack was a tall figure retreating into the lobby. Lucy nudged Bella and said, 'I can't believe he's been working at Brookfield since September and I found out when you told me! Did you know he moved into the village this week?'

Bella closed her eyes for a moment to prevent her eyebrows flying upwards. Casual. She was completely casual about all things Jack related. 'No, I didn't know where he was staying.'

'Seth says he was staying in Norton until he finished his probationary period at work. And now that's done he's renting one of the newer houses in a cul-de-sac on the edge of the village. Actually, it's Elle's place.'

'Elle as in Cath's daughter?'

'Yep.' Lucy laughed at what must have been an extremely non-casual expression on Bella's face. 'Don't be surprised. You'll soon learn this is typical village stuff. Everyone knows everyone and everything is connected.'

'Right.'

'Sorry, I don't mean to make it sound scary. It's actually great.'

'Right.' Bella did her best to inject some enthusiasm into the single syllable the second time, but her heart was heavy. Having spent the past two weeks having to watch Jack dash away every time she got near him at work, now she would have the opportunity to relive the same scenario in the village pub, shop and community centre. Heck, even stepping outside to take a walk around the green would be risky. Fantastic.

'You know, I heard a lot about Jack from Seth, after the wedding. But I didn't get the full story about you two. You were his last-minute plus-one, weren't you? What's the story?'

'That's a long, dull story,' said Bella, waving her hand dismissively as if the tale came with its own bad smell. 'Why don't I tell you about it some time when the Archangel Gabriel isn't about to choke one of the Magi with his halo?'

'Oh my goodness! Connor!' Lucy's cutting tone made a small demon in angel's clothing freeze and whisk his halo behind his back. 'Your costume isn't a toy! I'm coming over there.' She turned to Bella. 'Sorry. Duty calls.'

'I should return to my post too.' Bella pointed towards the lobby. 'I see Trevor has turned up, so—in the spirit of maintaining peace and goodwill—I'd better get over there before his arrival gives Lavender and Iris another reason to fight.'

Chapter 26

For her return trip, Bella slunk around the edge of the main room and slipped between the audience members gossiping in the lobby.

She grinned as she sneaked up behind Trevor, who was loitering by the welcome table, his back to her. Probably waiting for his latest date. 'Trevor!' Bella tapped him on the shoulder. 'What are you up to?'

Trevor startled, jumping and whirling to face Bella as if she'd jabbed him with a cattle prod. He kept a hand on the table next to the donation box to steady himself, his face a pale waxy mask of shock.

'I'm so sorry,' said Bella, her blood turning icy. Lord, had she given him a heart attack? 'Are you OK?' She reached out to touch the elbow of his grey herringbone coat. 'Do you need to sit down?'

'You gave me a turn.' Trevor clapped a hand to his heart. 'I'm all right, thank you.'

'Are you sure? God, I feel dreadful. I shouldn't have—'

'It's fine.'

Trevor chuckled, but Bella could have sworn she detected a hint of sneer in his tone and expression. But then, she deserved it. She could have killed the man. 'I didn't expect to see you here. Are you a long-time fan of youth theatre?'

'He's here because *I* invited him.' Lavender stepped into the space next to Trevor and slipped her arm through his. 'Did you drive over, Trevor?'

'Actually, I decided to walk.'

'In the dark with ice and snow on the pavements and lanes?' Lavender tutted in disapproval. 'You could have slipped and done yourself a mischief. Oh well, you're here now, that's all that matters. And I've saved you a seat,' she said, gazing adoringly into Trevor's eyes. 'We should sit down. It's going to start in a minute.'

'Right you are. Where are we sitting? Oh, I see. Iris is waving at us.' Trevor grinned and nodded towards the front section of the audience where Iris was drawing large semicircles in the air. 'Talk to you later, Bella. And jolly good job filling the donation box. I reckon the school will be able to fix their roof with a few quid to spare. Well done.'

'Thank you,' said Bella. 'But I can't take all the credit. Lavender and Iris have been in charge of the box too.'

'That doesn't surprise me. They're both excellent fundraisers.' Trevor took a step towards the audience. 'Are you coming, Lavender?'

'I'll be along in a minute.' Lavender smiled at Trevor. 'You go ahead.'

As she watched Trevor bowl down the aisle towards Iris, Lavender's smile twisted into a bitter pucker. But her expression softened when she turned her attention to the lobby entrance. She widened her eyes and said, in the fake-stunned tone used by someone arriving at a surprise birthday party they had planned themselves, 'Oh, look! There's Jack. I'd forgotten he'd mentioned he was helping here today. But that's so like him. It is truly remarkable that he's single.' She hummed and gave Bella a sly, pointed look. 'I think practically everyone's here,' Lavender said, scanning the audience. 'So if you wanted to talk to Jack, I don't think anyone would mind you abandoning your station.'

'I don't mind staying here,' said Bella. But while her words suggested her indifference, her treacherous gaze followed Lavender's to the two men—one dark, one fair—having a conversation on the other side of the glass doors. Jack and Seth stood in a pool of light, cast into the wintry darkness by the lights up on the eaves of the barn. Seth must have been treating Jack to some of his characteristic charm because Jack was smiling, his eyes shining with amusement. Bella sighed. She had forgotten how alluring Jack's smile was. It was almost as attractive as his laugh: a warm, deep chuckle which had been thrilling to draw out of him. And his hair … Bella ran her tongue over her lower lip while inspecting the short, unkempt curls. Mm. The tousled, bedhead look was likely a result of all his recent chair wrangling, but it also appeared as if some lucky person had been running their fingers through it and—

'Bella, dear?'

'Hmn?' Blinking, Bella returned her attention to Lavender who was contemplating her with her head tilted to one side. Drat. 'Sorry, I drifted off for a second. It's been a long day.'

Lavender nodded. 'You work so hard. All the more reason you and Jack should go for a well-earned drink.' Bella opened her mouth to protest, but Lavender grabbed Bella's coat from the back of the chair behind the welcome desk and—ignoring Bella's stuttering protests—slid its sleeves over her arms. 'I know, you're worried about the donation box, but don't fret.' She spun Bella to face her. 'I'll make sure it gets to Lucy. Quick now, off you go, Seth's leaving!'

Bella swallowed as Seth raised a hand in farewell and turned to leave. If she dawdled long enough in exiting the lobby, perhaps Jack would also leave and she'd just miss him.

'Don't dawdle, you'll miss him.' Loitering by the welcome desk, Lavender glared at her and made a shooing motion. Bella sighed. There was no way out of this. Although, perhaps this was a sign. A sign Lavender was an unspeakably pushy bat. But also that it was time for her to try a direct approach with Jack. To take another stab at clearing the air. And surely Christmas was the ideal time to let bygones be bygones?

Chapter 27

Jack had his back to the barn as Bella stepped onto the terrace. He was watching Seth hastening down the path but, at the squeak of the door closing behind him, he turned towards Bella. A shadow fell across his face and, as his smile vanished, Bella's heart sank. Was the mere sight of her that dreadful?

She half raised her hand in what she hoped was a non-threatening greeting. 'Hi,' she said, her mouth dry and tongue heavy. 'Could I talk to you for a minute?'

'Uh, actually ...' Jack shifted from foot to foot while his gaze shifted between the path and the building, as if he were evaluating his escape routes.

Her pulse accelerating, Bella took a couple of rushed steps forwards before Jack could make a run for it. It appeared there was no time for niceties. 'Are you planning on quitting your job?'

The words had rushed out, far louder than she had intended, but they had the desired effect. Jack's feet stilled and his gaze steadied, his eyes trained on her as his brow furrowed. 'What?'

'Do you have plans to resign from your job at Brookfield Park any time in the immediate future?'

'No!' Jack stuffed his hands into the pockets of his dark jeans, raising his shoulders into a defensive hunch. 'I only just finished my probation period.'

'That's what I thought.' Bella nodded. 'Whereas I'm at the start of my probation and plan to be here for the long haul. And so, as neither of us are going anywhere, I suggest you talk to me and stop legging it every time I come within a hundred yards of you.'

Jack dropped his gaze and his shoulders rose another inch. She'd unsettled him. Good. 'It's getting daft,' she said. 'Would it be so hard to say hello and exchange some small talk about the weather? We're British, for God's sake! Polite weather chat is baked into our DNA.'

Bella's breathing grew shallow as she waited for Jack's response. She could have sworn the corner of his mouth had twitched in response to her attempt at humour, but the rest of his expression remained stony. To her right, the gazebo lurked like the Ghost of Christmas Past, reminding her of a happier time. Did Jack keep glancing over there too? Would those memories help or hinder her call for a truce?

Eventually Jack drew in a long breath and said, 'I don't know.' His gaze flickered towards the gazebo again before returning to the snow at the edges of the recently cleared path. He shook his head. 'No, no. I … I can't.'

Bella had done so well for weeks. She'd followed the advice of her podcast meditation and wellness gurus by thinking before she spoke. Breathing away any hint of red mist. Positive affirmations rather than cathartic sweary rants and pillow punching. But Jack's refusal to try was the last straw on an already fragile camel's back.

'Can't *what*, Jack?' Bella had expected her tone to be pure venom, but her voice wobbled a little on Jack's name. Ridiculous. The situation was annoying. Irksome. Irritating in the extreme. Not upsetting, for heaven's sake. Blinking rapidly to discourage any tears from daring to collect, she planted her hands on her hips and glared up at him. 'Are you really that upset that I quietly left a party that I wasn't even supposed to attend? That my heinous, unforgiveable crime is not saying goodbye? You honestly think that's a good enough reason to shun me forever?'

Jack stammered and his expression softened. 'You don't understand. I thought we got on well.' His gaze shifted to his left, in the direction of the gazebo. 'Better than well. I thought we'd ... I thought our time together meant something. Because it did to me.' He cleared his throat and glanced at Bella before dropping his gaze and muttering, 'But it clearly didn't to you.'

What? Bella pressed her lips into a thin line of fury. No. Absolutely not. He was not getting away with that complete balderdash. She had done her best to keep her dial below ten, but this was one of those situations that called for eleven. 'Do you know how ridiculous you sound right now?' Bella paused until Jack glanced up and their gazes collided. 'If our time together meant nothing to me, I would never have kissed you! And have you taken a moment during all your "woe is me" wallowing sessions to consider that it would have been super-easy to find me if just once—just *one time* in the hours I was helping you cover your arse—you had asked me what my real name was?'

Jack's jaw dropped and Bella experienced a jolt of triumph at having landed a direct hit. 'But no, you didn't see fit to ask me what my name was, what I did for a living or if I had a family. Because why would you want to find out or cope with anything real or flawed about the woman who has shown up, who always shows up, the woman who is there to support you, the woman *you're with?* Why would you want to know when you have the option to ignore all of that and cling to the perfect fantasy version of her instead?'

Bella's sawing breath left a trail of steam in the darkness and her view of a truly flabbergasted Jack turned equally misty. Ah, dammit. In going to eleven she feared she had veered off topic. Not all of that had been about Jack. But—going by his dazed expression—at least she seemed to have made a dent in his armour. She sniffed and twitched her frozen nose. Crying in front of him would definitely lessen the impact of her words. It was time to get back inside where she would be able to blame her streaming nose and eyes on the change in temperature.

She swallowed and, channelling a familiar sense of exhaustion and defeat into her voice, said, 'Again, I'm sorry if I left without saying goodbye and hurt your feelings, Jack. If you must know, I was planning to go back into the reception and get your phone number but then a family emergency came up and I had to deal with it. Whatever you may think of me, I don't make a habit of leaving people I care about in the lurch.'

Bella backed towards the barn, yanked open the door and was struck by a blast of tuneless but exuberant infant carol singing. 'You know what'—clinging to the door handle, Bella held Jack's gaze, ignoring the leaden feeling in her guts—'if you don't want to talk to me ever again, Jack, then knock yourself out. In my last job—I'm an accountant by the way, thanks for asking—I survived while surrounded by a bunch of weapons-grade arseholes. In fact, I far outperformed all of the useless gits. So, ignore me all you want. After that experience, one *Jack*ass should be easy to handle.'

And with a caustic call of 'Merry Christmas!' as a final parting shot, Bella sailed into the welcoming heat of the barn, leaving an awestruck Jack on the frozen terrace.

Chapter 28

'And so Mary and Joseph went to Bethlehem.' The narrator nodded to add emphasis to her delivery. 'And 'cos Mary was tired—and my mummy says her ankles would have been fat and hurty—she sat on a donkey the whole trip.'

Having finished her lines, and award-worthy ad libs, the narrator beckoned to the angels and shepherds to get to their feet. The subsequent cacophony of grumbling, rustling and squeaking covered the audience's muffled laughter. A few introductory piano chords and the kids launched into an enthusiastic performance of 'Little Donkey'.

From her seat at the back of the room, Bella let her gaze wander over the performers, returning regularly to the loudest child—one of the taller angels on the left of the stage—who made up for in volume what he lacked in finesse. Bella smiled and let the fuzzy glow of the Christmas spirit wash over her, praying it might restore her inner calm. For though she'd come inside only fifteen minutes previously, she must have glanced over her shoulder a dozen times to check if Jack had followed her. But he hadn't.

She glanced over her shoulder again, but the lobby remained stubbornly empty and the only thing visible outside on the terrace was the steadily falling snow.

Oh for goodness' sake! Bella bit her lip and fixed her gaze on the singers in front of her. So what if Jack had left? It wasn't like she'd *wanted* him to follow her or anything. Why on earth would she want that? If he did come back, all apologetic and desperate to speak to her ... Well! She probably wouldn't even care and—

A light touch to her elbow made Bella flinch and, her heart pounding, she snapped her gaze upwards. But her pulse stuttered with disappointment when she found herself staring into a pair of blue, not brown eyes.

Summer stooped to bring her mouth closer to Bella's ear, 'Are you OK?'

Bella shook herself, recovering quickly. 'Fine, fine,' she said, drawing back to get a better look at her sister. She couldn't believe she had come. She was late, but she was actually here. Maybe Christmas miracles were a real thing?

'This is so cute,' said Summer, in an inappropriately booming voice. A dreamy smile drifted over her lips and her eyelids drooped as she swayed along to the final chorus.

Her eyes narrowing, Bella pulled her sister close and sniffed. An all-too-familiar scent made her recoil. Alcohol. Lots of it.

'Sooo adorable!' Summer accompanied her even louder opinion with a wave of her arm. The wide gesture unbalanced her, and Bella shot out of her seat to throw a steadying hand around her waist.

As the final notes of the song rang out, Bella used the applause as cover to hiss, 'Let's go. Come on,' manoeuvre

Summer into the corner of the lobby and lower her sister into a chair next to the large fir tree.

'Summer?' Bella crouched in front of her sister. 'Are you OK?'

'Never better.' Summer said, following her words with a dopey grin which made Bella's stomach fill with a painful combination of fondness, worry and irritation.

'You've been to the pub, I take it?'

'Yes!' Summer slapped Bella's arm, her eyes widening. 'How did you know? You always know things.'

Torn between joining in with Summer's giggling and shaking her sober, Bella's mind whirled. If Summer had been enjoying herself in the local pub enough to get tipsy, why leave to come to the nativity? Although, it wasn't so long ago that she herself would probably have wanted to have a couple of drinks before a social function like this one, if only to make it easier to mingle with relative strangers. And when Bella had been sozzled, lots of apparently illogical decisions had seemed leaps of genius.

Bella wrapped her fingers around Summer's and gave them a squeeze. 'So you were at the pub and you remembered that I'd invited you here? To the play?' Bella closed her eyes for a moment and pictured Summer stumbling alone along the grass verge next to the unlit country road which led from the pub to the farm. She shuddered. 'Did you walk here? You could have called me. I would have picked you up. I always came and got you, remember?'

'Pft! That was a long time ago.' Summer shook off Bella's hand. 'And no, I didn't walk here, it's freezing outside.' Summer shivered and pulled the sleeves of her light pink jacket down over her hands. The jacket was far too thin for the weather, but at least she had found a pair of dark trousers and black ankle boots somewhere in her enormous backpack to prevent her legs and feet freezing. 'I met these great people in the pub and we're going to a party. They're out in the car park. I told them to wait while I asked you if you wanted to come.'

Bella knew Summer was an independent twenty-nine-year-old. A seasoned globetrotter who didn't need her big sister to look after her. But the questions rushed out of her before she could stop them. 'Who are these people? What are their names? Where's the party?'

Summer snorted and, as she rolled her eyes, she looked more like the sulky seventeen-year-old Bella had regularly collected from outside clubs and pubs than a woman approaching thirty. 'God's sake, Bel. You're as bad as Dad. Chill out. It's a Friday night and I can take care of myself. Why the inquisition?'

'I'm just asking you for their names and a rough idea of where you're going.'

'Ugh! Fine.' Summer pouted. 'They're called Jess and Finley and it's a Christmas party at a big house which belongs to one of Finley's friends or his family or something. Anyway, it's about a half hour from here and it sounds cool. You know, food, music, dancing, fun? You remember fun, right?'

Bella remembered when what Summer was describing had sounded fantastic. But she had usually needed three drinks before feeling an urge to party. Lately Bella had been rediscovering the things she'd found fun before socializing had begun to revolve around alcohol. She was finding herself enjoying activities like staying at home making a gingerbread house or helping a friend at a nativity play.

'Come with us!' Summer said, breaking out of her sulk. 'You're not old yet, Bel. It'll be great.' Grabbing Bella's hands, she rose, pulling Bella with her. 'I've got to go, they're waiting for me. Come on, come with me.'

Staring at Summer's doe-eyed expression, Bella was tempted to give her what she wanted. A Christmas party could be the exact thing she needed. And following a nativity play, what better to get her into the festive spirit?

Summer shuffled towards the exit and gave Bella's arm a tug, making her heartstrings twang in response. This was how Summer ended up getting everything she ever wanted. She made her way sound like the best, easiest option. But, as much as the idea of a Christmas party appealed, Bella couldn't abandon Lucy or the kids, who were putting on a brilliant show. And—a tiny voice whispered deep in Bella's heart—Jack might come back. 'Sorry, Summer. I promised Lucy I'd help clear up after the show. They have a big wedding reception tomorrow and they need to take down the staging. And I need to get the donations back from Lavender and hand them over to one of the school staff and …' Bella noticed Summer's gaze misting over. Her sister was never one for details, particularly not when she'd been drinking. 'Look. Just promise you'll call me if you need a lift home or anything. And, when you get there, could you send me the address?'

'Sure.' Summer's pout returned, although her attempt at haughtiness would have been more effective if she hadn't been swaying on the spot. 'You know, Bel. I came here for you.' Summer stabbed a pointed finger against Bella's chest. 'I could be in Brazil right now. The least you could do is spend some time with me.'

'Well, if you wait until the play's finished, we could—'

'Don't bother. I wouldn't want to be a burden.' And with a final huff of disgust, Summer executed a woozy half turn and strutted out of the building.

Bella felt Summer's exit like a shower of icy water. It washed over her as the door to the terrace slammed, snuffing out the fragile flame of Christmas spirit which had been burning in Bella's belly. *Great.* Why, she wondered, was it often hardest to get along with the people she loved the most?

Her legs rubbery, Bella slouched back to her seat. And even though the play continued to be an enchanting display of innocent delight, Bella's mood stayed dark. Coming to Haileybrook was supposed to be a fresh start. But here she was in miserably familiar territory: incapable of doing anything right. First with Jack and now with Summer. Yet again, by trying to do the right thing, she had only succeeded in being a disappointment.

Chapter 29

By half past eight that evening, Bella was perched on her kitchen counter, staring at her completed gingerbread creation with tears in her eyes. Something about the smiling faces of the gingerbread family, posed in front of their perfect house, had made her well up. And she had thought giving up alcohol would stabilize her moods.

Bella's stomach rumbled. Lucy had invited her to a late dinner at the farmhouse, but the dark circles under her eyes told Bella that Lucy could do with an early night before another busy weekend. The last thing she needed was another guest to entertain.

She could have followed Summer to her new friends' party—Summer had stunned Bella by messaging her the address—but it would be after nine when she arrived and she didn't fancy turning up alone without an invitation.

So it would be another Friday evening alone, her brief interaction with the food delivery guy her only company and muttered threats at the water heater her only conversation.

As if urging her not to veer off track, Bella's tummy growled again, spurring her to grab her phone and scroll through dinner options. She should buy some vegetables. Think about eating the occasional salad. But then, with all the mince pies and chocolates the residents kept bringing to the office, perhaps that could wait for the new year—

Her phone vibrated and jangled and the name on the screen made Bella's heart clench. She swiped to accept the call and, taking a moment to steady her voice—no need to panic yet—she said, 'Summer? Everything OK?'

Ragged breathing was the only response. Bella pressed the phone closer to her ear, her own breathing turning shallow. 'Summer?'

'I don't feel well.' Her sister's voice was small and distant.

'I'm coming to get you.' Bella sprang off the counter and bustled to the front door. She hooked her phone under her chin as she grabbed her coat and pushed her feet into her boots. 'Is someone taking care of you? Are you somewhere safe? Are you still at the party?' Bella grimaced. That was a ridiculous number of questions to ask someone who was drunk and unwell. 'Sorry. Summer, are you still at the party?'

'Yes. Someone is looking after me.'

'Good.' Bella grabbed her keys, blood booming in her ears. 'If you have to, lock yourself in a bathroom. I'm coming.'

Later, Bella wouldn't be able to recall much about the drive to the address she tapped into her sat nav with trembling fingers except for snow and the hideous burning frustration of not being able to teleport to her sister's side.

She did her best to focus on the present, the road and her driving. But the least helpful part of her brain—the one containing her deepest, irrational fears—kept offering up nightmare scenarios in which Summer had been drugged, assaulted or was lying unconscious in critical need of medical attention.

By the time Bella pulled off a quiet country lane, made her way down a long drive lined with tall conifers and parked the car on the circular gravel driveway in front of a large, imposing house, every nerve in her body was a taut, vibrating bowstring. If she had been calmer, she might have taken in the symmetry and elegance of the three-storey, ivy-covered façade. She had come close to marrying an architect after all, and might have taken a moment to marvel that she had absorbed enough of Ethan's knowledge to recognize a Georgian manor house.

Instead, she barrelled up to the porch and, not seeing a bell, balled her fingers into a tight fist and pounded on the door, almost knocking off the pine-cone-and-red-berry wreath.

'Hey! Open the door!'

When her initial cries went unanswered, Bella returned to thumping the door and was contemplating going to look for a rear entrance when the door swung open. A squat, pasty-faced man stood on the threshold. Bella glared at him, prepared to argue her way into the house, but he stood to one side, grinned and said, 'Welcome. Come in, it's freezing out there.'

Bella darted inside before he could change his mind. Woah! The house was heaving with revellers. She'd only made it a couple of paces into the hall when her path was blocked by a wall of party guests. And any space above and between the crowd was filled with loud festive pop hits, the tinkle of glassware and boisterous chatter with the room's low ceiling and grey flagstones amplifying the festive cacophony. Bella put a hand on the wall to steady herself and dragged in a breath as she fought a rising tide of panic, despair and claustrophobia. How on earth was she supposed to find Summer in among this lot?

Loosening her scarf from her rapidly warming skin, Bella weighed her options. Shouldering through the crowd and asking every group she passed if they had seen Summer would be the least obtrusive plan. But it would be slow. Too slow. Perhaps if she could find where the music was coming from, she could hijack the sound system to get a message out to the whole house? She raked a hand through her hair. No. The source of the music could very well be on the other side of the building and could be harder to locate than Summer herself.

Her gaze darting frantically about her surroundings— God, had the owners of this place raided a Christmas bow factory? Were that many green, red and gold tartan bows on every frame and piece of furniture even legal?—Bella's attention snagged on the elegant curving staircase to her right. Only a few guests lay between her, higher ground and a better view. Plus, searching the upper floors for Summer, particularly the bathrooms, would probably be quick work.

Bella wove between revellers, narrowly missing getting showered with mulled wine, and bounded onto the staircase. Her cheeks flamed as she took the stairs two at a time. 'Please,' she prayed under her breath, 'please let her be OK.'

An extra spurt of energy took Bella towards the first-floor landing. Please let Summer be OK. Lord help her, but if anyone had hurt her little sister they would be sorry. She would burn this place to the ground, ugly stupid bows and— Oof!

With her thoughts fixed on vengeance and her gaze on her feet, Bella hadn't seen the person coming towards the top of the stairs. As she reached the landing she collided with them, the impact sending her staggering backwards.

Bella's stomach dropped as gravity reached out to drag her down to the ground floor. Wobbling on her heels, she windmilled her arms in a desperate attempt to right herself. Flailing, her lungs seized and heart stuttered but she refused to surrender to the inevitable. Gravity be damned. Summer needed her.

And, for once, it seemed the universe was listening. Bella's circling arms were gripped by pair of large, strong hands and, as suddenly as she had been struck off balance, Bella was firmly on her feet and being held against her reassuringly solid rescuer.

Her eyes squeezed closed, Bella listened to her rapid breathing as it intertwined with that of her saviour. Her heart slowing, Bella risked opening one eye and found herself staring at deep blue wool. She raised her gaze slowly, up over the broad chest to the turns of the roll-neck collar to the familiar square jawline above it.

A tingling sensation sparkled over her skin as she tilted her head back further until her gaze locked with Jack's.

'Bella?' Jack blinked and stepped back, relaxing his hold on Bella's arms but not letting go. 'What are you doing here?'

Chapter 30

'Summer, my sister. Have you seen her?' Bella's words flew out in a breathless rush. 'She's about five foot four. Long blonde hair, really pretty. Quite tipsy. She called me, said she was sick. I came straight here, but it was so busy down there I couldn't see. If anything's happened to her, I swear I will kill anyone who's touched a hair on her head—'

'Woah, woah. Slow down. Breathe.' His concerned gaze never leaving Bella's face, Jack rubbed gentle circles with his thumbs on her arms. 'Summer. You're her sister.' Jack huffed a laugh. 'I should have seen it. You have the same eyes.'

Bella's heart leapt with hope and she grabbed Jack's forearms. 'You've seen her? Where is she? Is she all right?'

'She's fine. A bit green around the gills, but she's resting now.'

'Take me to her.' Bella realized she was gripping Jack's arms tight enough to leave bruises. And barking orders at the man was hardly the way to convince him to help her. She slackened her hold on him and took a breath. 'Please.'

Jack's lips curved into a hint of a smile. 'Of course. Follow me.'

He led Bella down a long corridor lined with silver wallpaper and closed white doors. The minimalist colour scheme was interrupted by another generous smattering of festive bows, with each door bearing a large tartan bow at head height as if it were a wreath. A small part of Bella's mind pondered these further signs of a serious bow fetish—had a shop been giving the ribbon away?—but most of her brain was foggy, clouded by the surge of relief that had come upon discovering Summer to be safe. It had left Bella light-headed, a wooziness worsened by her heels sinking dangerously deep into the thick pile of the almond-coloured carpet.

Jack halted by the door on the left at the end of the corridor and raised his fist to knock. They waited for a few seconds, but the only sound was the muffled music from below them. Jack turned his head to glance at Bella, lifted a finger to his lips and opened the door.

A slender bed ran along the length of the left side of the room. To the right were a single wardrobe and a writing desk. The walls were a muted, tired blue, interrupted by a small window over the bed and two rows of empty shelving above the desk. The top of the desk held nothing but a jumble of dusty trophies and medals shoved into the corner next to the wardrobe.

On the nightstand, a single lamp cast a glow over the bed and its occupant. Lying on her side, Summer was sound asleep, her cheeks and lips flushed and her blonde hair fanned out around her head. She could have been mistaken for a princess in a fairy tale if it hadn't been for the bear-like roar of her snoring and the strategically placed wastepaper basket on the floor by her head.

Bella's knees turned rubbery at the sight of her sister and she was grateful when Jack placed his hand on the small of her back and steered her inside the room. She sank to the floor next to the bed and, as she ran her fingertips over Summer's hair, the feral thing that had been screaming and clawing inside her since receiving her sister's phone call finally fell silent.

Keeping her eyes on Summer, Bella waited for Jack to close the door and take a seat on the desk behind her before asking, 'What happened?'

'I stepped out of the kitchen to get some air and she was on the patio, sitting on the bench with her head in her hands.' Jack spoke quietly, his voice a deep murmur at Bella's back. 'She said her sister was coming for her, but she looked so ill I offered to help her find a bathroom. She was very sick, but she said she felt a lot better afterwards. I told her I'd fetch her some water and by the time I shoved my way through that lot downstairs and got back up here, she'd fallen asleep on the bathroom floor. So I carried her in here, put her on her side and the bin next to her, just in case.'

Bella's gaze rose from the bed to the strip of peeling blue paint above the window. This room had been neglected, its owner absent for some time. But the trophies in the corner of the desk belonged to someone. Perhaps someone comfortable enough with the manor house to know where the bathrooms were. The fine hairs at her nape prickling as her suspicions solidified, Bella turned her gaze to Jack. 'How did you know you could put her in here?'

Jack shifted his position on the desk, wrapping his fingers under the edge of the tabletop and clenching the wood so tightly his knuckles whitened. 'This is my old room.'

What? Bella flicked her gaze about the room, struggling to imagine a teenage Jack fitting in it. Surely his feet would have been off the bottom of the bed and his knees scraping the underside of the desktop? Why was he not moved to a bigger room as he grew? The house was enormous and there must have been a better space for a ludicrously tall person. Although—she conceded, returning her gaze to Jack—he looked less giant-like at the moment, perched on the desk with his shoulders hunched. It was as if the room had made him curl in on himself, like a hedgehog rolling into a defensive ball.

'This is your family home?' she asked.

'It's my dad's house. I moved out after university.'

'So this is your dad's Christmas party?'

A muscle in Jack's jaw twitched and he shook his head. 'My stepmother organizes it. It's her party. But my brothers always invite some people.' He gave a mirthless laugh. 'Too many people.'

Bella filed away a few more questions about Jack's family for another time. Right now her priority was her sister. 'Summer mentioned a Jess and a Finley. Do you know them?'

'They're my brother's friends.' Jack grimaced. 'Now I understand why she was alone outside. The last time I saw those two they were in the games room. Fin was standing on the pool table trying to recruit some other idiots to go for a midnight dip in the lake.'

Bella's fingers curled into fists so tight her nails dug into her palms. Some 'friends' they turned out to be, abandoning Summer when she was ill so they could muck about on some crazy scheme to go swim— Hang on. This house had grounds with a *lake?* Bella frowned as she turned her gaze back to Summer. Just how big was this place? And how rich was Jack's dad? Bloody hell, to have a lake didn't you have to be a lord or something? The thought caused a wave of uneasiness to flood her limbs, making her shudder. It was time to get out of here and back to her quiet tiny cottage with its dodgy heating and wonky floors.

'Well, whoever they are, they better pray they never cross my path. I'll have a few words to say to them for letting Summer wander off to get hypothermia.' Bella took a deep breath, releasing the angry tension in her jaw. 'Thank you for looking after her.'

Jack shrugged. 'Anyone would have done the same.'

'But they didn't. So thank you.' Jack shrugged again but didn't look away. After what she'd said to him before the nativity, she'd expected him to be evasive. Could his attitude towards her be changing? Or was she misinterpreting his goodwill towards Summer as a renewed warmth for her? Either way, he hadn't made a sprint for the door or told her he never wanted to speak to her again in the past ten minutes, so it was probably best not to push her luck. 'We should go. Let you get back to the party.' Bella gave Summer's shoulder a gentle shake. 'Summer,' she whispered, 'I'm here. It's time to go home.'

Summer snorted, but her eyes remained firmly closed and, though she fidgeted, she showed no signs of waking.

'Why not leave her a while longer?' said Jack. 'She'll

be fine here. Have you had dinner? There's tonnes of food downstairs if you'd like some.'

Bella opened her lips to refuse Jack's hospitality, but her stomach spoke first, growling loudly enough to be heard above the beat of the booming music coming up through the floor. Jack's lips quirked, although he was too polite to laugh. 'I was sorting out dinner when Summer called,' said Bella. 'But I don't want to be any trouble, I mean—'

'You're no trouble at all,' said Jack, pushing to standing. 'I meant it about there being a ridiculous amount of food going spare. It's the same every year. Everyone goes for the mulled wine and the food gets forgotten. You can leave your coat here.'

Jack opened the door and stood to one side, leaving space for Bella to pass him. She shrugged out of her coat, laid it next to her scarf at the foot of the bed and moved to the doorway. On the threshold, Bella paused and glanced back at Summer. 'She'll be fine,' said Jack. 'I promise. No one ever comes all the way back here. And she's not going to wake up in the next ten minutes.'

'You're right. I know you're right.' Bella sighed, wondering if and when she would ever stop worrying about her almost thirty-year-old sister. 'So,' she said as Jack closed the door and they strolled side by side back to the stairs, 'how come you're not downing vats of mulled wine along with everyone else?'

'Because I only drink with people I like,' said Jack, stepping in front of Bella to descend the stairs, leaving her to follow and ponder the implications of his words.

Chapter 31

While the front façade of the house had been large, Bella soon discovered it concealed at least two additional buildings. Perhaps more. After trailing Jack through half a dozen rooms packed with rowdy revellers, she lost count. She was usually better with numbers, but the adrenalin that had been fuelling her since Summer's phone call had worn off, leaving her distracted by a light head and hunger pangs.

Jack had been right about the food. The dining room was deserted. A long table covered in a maroon cloth ran along one side of the room. It was covered in an assortment of platters interspersed with thick white candles ringed with holly. Bella's gaze roved greedily over the dishes, many of which appeared untouched.

'I recommend the sausage rolls,' said Jack, handing Bella an enormous white plate. 'The samosas are pretty good too, if you don't mind spicy food.'

'Don't mind it at all,' said Bella, taking two of the triangular treats and putting them next to the three sausage rolls already on her plate.

Jack approached the row of glass bottles at the end of the table. 'Would you like some water?' he asked.

'Thank you,' Bella mumbled through a mouthful of buttery, flaky pastry. Good God, that was fantastic. She had never thought she'd find a caterer to rival Lucinda's brilliance, but whoever had made these could give her stepsister a run for her money. 'Still, please. Can't stand fizzy water.'

'Me neither,' said Jack. He handed Bella a glassful and poured himself another.

'Thanks.' Bella shared a small smile with Jack and took a sip of water. She deposited her glass on the edge of the buffet table and took a bite of her first samosa. Oh, *wow*. Blimey, that was terrific. Possibly better than the sausage roll. The rest of the guests were idiots. They should be queuing up for this stuff. If Bella had known what was on offer, she'd have brought a Tupperware container, filled it to bursting and then smuggled it out under her coat.

The atmosphere in the dining room was also perfect for anyone wanting to properly enjoy their food. The blaring pop tunes were a muted, distant pulse and the air was free of the obnoxious mixture of perfume and alcohol vapour which hung in the air around the guest-packed spaces. The ceiling was higher than in the rooms they had passed through, and the glittering geometric pattern in gold on the silver wallpaper and the light oak flooring gave the room a cool tranquillity.

The number of tartan bows was also comparatively minimal, although even a truckload of them wouldn't have been able to divert Bella's attention from the room's standout feature: an enormous abstract painting taking up half of the wall opposite the buffet table. Twice as long as it was tall, the oil painting was a swirling mix of blues. In the lower left corner a flush of red and pinks bloomed into the blue, making Bella think of a sunrise at sea. And though the paint whirled in dramatic strokes, so thick in places it stood off the canvas, there was something peaceful about the composition. Mesmeric.

'Do you like it?'

Bella blinked and turned towards Jack, realising as she did so that she had been frozen, staring at the painting with a samosa halfway to her mouth. How attractive. She dropped the samosa onto her plate. 'It's … I don't know. Peaceful? Like, this redness should be threatening, but the colours balance well and overall it's …'

'Harmonious.'

'Yes! That's it.' Bella grinned at Jack, mirroring his rather self-congratulatory smile. 'Wait a sec. This is your family home.' Bella frowned. 'You're not going to tell me you painted this when you were twelve or something, are you? Because that would be disgusting. I'm not sure it's legal to be that talented.'

Jack chuckled. 'No, you're safe. I've never had any artistic talent whatsoever. How about you?'

'My greatest artist achievement is recently completing a build-your-own gingerbread house kit.'

'Ah, right.' Jack's expression turned serious, although his dark eyes shone with amusement. 'So what you're telling me is that you're the Picasso of miniature edible buildings?'

Bella snorted. 'Too right I am.' Her fingers twitched, responding to her instinct to land a playful punch on Jack's arm. But she wasn't sure how far any thaw in his feelings towards her had progressed, and so didn't risk it. Far safer to exploit the current ceasefire to satisfy her curiosity. 'So if you're not an artist, what were those trophies and medals in your room for?'

'Skiing. Junior competitions during family holidays.' Jack shrugged. 'My dad used to enter me.'

'That's impressive. He must be very proud of you.'

'No, not really.' Jack shrugged again, leaving Bella unsure what to say next as Jack's comments chimed with her dim memory of the women in the toilets at Ashley's wedding insinuating that Jack and his family weren't close. And then they'd said something about an annual Christmas skiing holiday with friends, hadn't they?

Jack cleared his throat. 'Do you ski?'

Bella stared at Jack for a few seconds, trying to decide if he was mocking her. Not one thing about her wobbly thighs suggested she was a winter sports enthusiast. But his tone had conveyed genuine interest, so she decided to play along. 'No. I think I'd rather stay inside the ski lodge. Especially if it has a hot tub.' Bella closed her eyes as she pictured herself in the incongruous combination of a swimsuit and woolly bobble hat, immersed up to her shoulders in steaming, gently bubbling water, on the veranda of a chalet, enjoying an uninterrupted view of a snow-lined valley. 'And hot chocolate.'

'With some mini marshmallows on top?' asked Jack.

'Of course,' said Bella, a spark of delight warming her insides on finding that Jack shared something of her vision.

'You could make a few gingerbread houses while everyone else is skiing,' said Jack. 'Wow them with your fine art skills.'

'Nah. I doubt they could handle it. I wouldn't want to blow their minds.' Jack laughed again and, encouraged, Bella continued her line of questioning. 'Don't you go on an annual ski trip with your friends?'

Jack's eyebrows lifted. 'Uh, yes. I have done since my early twenties. How did you know about that?'

'A couple of guests at Ashley's wedding mentioned it. Did you go last year?'

Jack's gaze drifted upwards and he paused before answering. 'Yes. I did.'

The three short words came out as a string of slow, tortured sounds which—in combination with his thousand-yard stare—made Bella think that last year's trip hadn't been a joyous experience. 'Let me guess. Someone forgot to pack the mini marshmallows.'

Jack's frown lifted and the corner of his mouth twitched. 'Got it in one.'

'Damn I'm good.'

Jack smiled, one of his proper grins which made his eyes shine and Bella's breath hitch. He really was very handsome. Particularly when he was laughing at her jokes rather than scowling at her.

'Did Dinah go on the skiing trip last year?' Bella kicked herself as soon as the words left her mouth. That hadn't been smooth or subtle. She might as well have shouted *'Are you single?'* at the man. 'I mean, Dinah, Simon, Drew, any of the people I met last year. Do they usually go, did they go last year?' Bella pressed her lips into a tight smile to stop her babbling. She sounded deranged. She wouldn't blame Jack for escorting her to the exit and asking her to wait outside while he fetched Summer and her coat.

232

It was to Jack's credit that his answer was civil and untroubled. 'Dinah and Simon were there. It's a small group and they're mostly my brothers' friends. That's how we all met. Except for Drew. I met him at school and he became friends with Ashley through me.'

'Right,' said Bella, doing her best to appear as though Jack's comments had clarified the dynamics of his friendship groups and put to bed all her questions on the subject, while all she wanted to do was ask why he was friends with people he didn't seem to get along with and, more pressingly, would he and Dinah be going on the skiing trip this year?

'Bella?'

'Hmn?' Bella took in Jack's expression. A crinkle had appeared between his brows and his gaze had darkened. Oh heck, she thought. He's building up to something serious.

Jack took a deep breath, as if preparing to dive into a frozen pool. 'I wanted to talk to you about what you said earlier, back at the farm—'

'There you are, Jack!

A pale, slender woman bustled across the room towards them. Her glossy fair hair was styled in a low bun, which showed off her heart-shaped face and the diamond earrings swinging from her earlobes. She had striking green eyes set in a weirdly ageless face. But these points were secondary to Bella's two more important observations. One: she was wearing a cocktail dress in green-and-red tartan with a gold thread running through it. It had an enormous bow at the waist and two accompanying bows at the shoulders, acting as festive epaulettes. That solved the mystery of the ubiquitous bows. And two: as the woman's voice had cut across Jack's, every sinew of his body had drawn tight, like he had braced for impact.

'Honestly, I send you to get more champagne and you vanish.' The woman, who Bella guessed was Jack's stepmother, clicked her tongue against her teeth in reproval. 'I have thirsty guests waiting. I had to send one of your brothers.'

A shot of heat entered Bella's blood and she narrowed her eyes to glare at Jack's stepmother and her gaudy, clownish bows. Not only had this woman ignored her—wasn't she supposed to be the hostess of this party?—but she was speaking to Jack as if he were staff. In fact, even if he had been staff, it would have cost her nothing to be polite.

'Sorry,' said Jack. 'Something came up—'

'He was helping my sister,' said Bella. 'She was unwell and he was the only one who noticed or cared. I'm very grateful to him.'

For the first time, the woman swung her cool gaze to Bella. It dipped down to Bella's boots and slowly rose to her face, no doubt taking in the scuff marks on Bella's jeans from where she had helped haul furniture about the barn earlier in the evening, and pricing Bella's festive sweater—grey with three large snowflakes on a band of white across her chest—and its wearer as being too low value to be worthy of her notice. A millisecond nose wrinkle betrayed her disdain. 'And who are you?' she asked.

'Sorry,' said Jack, shifting into the space between the two women. 'Fee, this is Bella. Bella, this is Fiona, my father's wife.'

Fiona stared at Bella's outstretched hand for a moment, as if contemplating whether touching it would pollute her, before pinching the tips of Bella's fingers for a second and swiftly rubbing the contaminated hand against her dress. 'Nice to meet you,' she said, while her grimace of a smile said the opposite.

'Likewise,' said Bella, hoping her dead tone and absent smile spoke volumes.

'How do you two know each other?' Fiona asked, directing the question to Jack.

Jack and Bella shared a glance. Noticing a glint of something akin to panic in his eyes, Bella decided to give the less complicated answer. 'We work together.'

'I see.' Fiona's smile was smug, as if Bella had confirmed her suspicions. 'So I imagine you support Jack in his frankly inexplicable departure from the family business. Leaving to strike out on your own is one thing. But to leave us, to leave practically overseeing our stunning property portfolio to slope off to a nothing retirement home in some rural backwater. Well ...' Fiona trailed off, sighing and shaking her head, as if her profound disappointment at Jack's perceived step down in the world had robbed her of the power of speech.

Bella's blood, which had already been warmed by Fiona's opening remarks, began to boil. 'Everyone at Brookfield is glad he's a member of the team,' she said.

Fiona snorted. She scanned Bella anew and asked, 'And what is it you do? Do you assist Jack in changing light bulbs?'

A huff of exasperation escaped Jack. 'Fee, you know that's not what my job—' Jack pressed his lips together, probably telling himself it wasn't worth wasting his energy reminding his stepmother what his job entailed. 'Bella is an accountant. She's our finance manager.'

'Oh?' Fiona gave Bella a condescending smile. 'That must be riveting.'

'It is actually,' said Bella, her pulse skipping as she built up to a tiny lie. Well, a fairly large lie. But stuff it. Better to be inventive with the truth than strangle Fiona with one of her own stupid bows. 'In fact, before I moved to Brookfield I worked closely with the tax authorities investigating tax evasion by high net worth individuals.' Bella made a show of looking about at the antique furnishings in the room, levelled a steady stare at Fiona's no doubt priceless diamond earrings and enjoyed the sight of Fiona's face paling to a ghostly white before she continued, 'This painting is rather wonderful, isn't it?' Bella turned her gaze to the giant abstract canvas in front of them. 'It's a Handren, isn't it? It must have been incredibly expensive. I heard one of his canvases a fraction of this size went for a hundred thousand pounds not long ago. And sales tax on art can be steep. Did you purchase it yourself?'

Fiona stammered, her eyes flicking from side to side, like a trapped animal. 'I … uh, my husband bought it.'

'Hmn.' Bella nodded, composing her features into the sort of expression a detective might wear when asking a murder suspect why they had blood on their favourite gloves. 'Art is often a wise investment and also, by the by, a common method of money laundering. Did you know that, Fiona?'

'No!' Fiona's eyes widened as two dashes of vivid red appeared in her pale cheeks. 'Of course not!'

Ignoring Fiona's horror, Bella tapped Jack on his arm and asked, in a friendly, conversational tone, 'Did you know that, Jack?'

Jack was staring at the floor, one hand covering his mouth, the other wrapped across his torso. He lifted his gaze to meet Bella's for a second, but it was enough for her to see the laughter shining in his eyes. 'I did not,' he said, mumbling the words through his fingers.

'And you mentioned something about a property portfolio, Fiona?' said Bella. 'You'd be amazed at the cases my colleagues and I investigated involving wealthy property owners failing to make full and proper declarations regarding capital gains—'

'Lovely to meet you!' Fiona's voice was shrill and her smile a desperate grimace. 'But I'm afraid I must get back to my guests. I'm sure Jack's doing a fine job of taking care of you so I'll run along.' She wiggled her fingers in a weak wave as she backed towards the door and with a final, 'Bye!' all but sprinted out of the room.

'Nice to meet you too!' Bella shouted after her. She waited for a few seconds until she could be sure Fiona was out of earshot before saying to Jack, 'Do you think if we followed her we'd find her in her home office shredding papers and deleting emails?'

A smile lingering on his lips, Jack said, 'To be fair to them, while my dad and Fee may have a few flaws, I don't think they're tax dodgers.'

'You're probably right.' Bella smiled and nudged Jack playfully with her elbow. 'But I think you're being too kind.'

'Maybe. And thank you. For not rubbishing my job.'

'I told her the truth. Everyone at Brookfield thinks you're amazing. With the possible exception of Ms Chan, but then I don't think she finds anyone impressive.'

Jack nodded. 'True. But thank you anyway. And, speaking of impressive—' He pointed at the canvas hanging in front of them. 'You claim not to have any art skills, but knew this was a Handren. How come?'

Bella shrugged. 'My stepsister, Lucinda, she has a friend who's the partner of the artist. And I remember when Lucinda first mentioned Becky was dating Charlie, I looked up his work online.' She shrugged. 'I thought it looked a little familiar and then, while Fee was talking, Charlie's name came back to me. It's just a coincidence. And a result of me being nosey, as usual.'

'Well, I choose to remain impressed.'

Bella mirrored Jack's timid smile and, as she held his dark, unwavering gaze, a spark of attraction made her heart thud and goosebumps rise on her arms. The fizzy feeling flowing through her was similar to the buzz of anticipation from the long climb to the top of a roller coaster, knowing the thrill of the descent was near.

Jack glanced towards the door. 'We should probably get back to your sister.'

Summer! How could she have forgotten about Summer? 'Yes, absolutely,' Bella said. She popped the last piece of her sausage roll in her mouth and chewed while casting a forlorn glance at the buffet table. What a waste! Would wrapping some of the samosas in napkins and putting them in her coat pockets be a step too far?

Bella put her plate on the table and made for the door. 'You coming?' she asked Jack.

Jack looked up from the glass of water he was pouring. 'Yes, I was getting this for Summer. I was on my way to get her another drink earlier when I bumped into you.'

A fond, dreamy smile stole onto Bella's lips as she watched Jack finish his task. Being nice to her sister was an easy way to score a lot of points with Bella.

Stop it! her inner voice commanded. *The man will think something is wrong with you.*

But the smile refused to shift, staying put as Bella stepped back to let Jack cross the threshold first. 'After you,' she said. 'You cut a path through that lot'—she tipped her head towards the corridor which was stuffed with throngs of guests—'and I'll follow in your slipstream. How outlandishly tall are you anyway?'

'Six foot four. How outlandishly short are you?'

Bella planted her hands on her hips in a display of mock indignance. 'I'll have you know I'm a splendid five feet and a half.'

Jack's grin widened. 'That half inch is important to you, isn't it?'

'Now, now,' said Bella. 'It's not like a man to be dissing the importance of an extra half inch.'

Jack threw back his head and guffawed, sending Summer's water sloshing dangerously close to the rim of the glass. 'Oops! Better get this to Summer before I spill it. Come on.'

Bella and Jack edged their way back through the crowds, Bella tucked behind Jack to shelter in his wake. And though the revellers were as dense, raucous and unmoving as ever, Bella found the return trip seemed shorter than the outbound leg of their journey and over far too soon.

Chapter 32

The car engine purred and the frosty air in the car quickly warmed while the ice on the windscreen melted. As the front door of the manor house opened, Bella scrambled out of the driver's seat and opened the rear door, ready for her passenger.

Jack appeared on the threshold of the house, backlit by the glow of the party. Summer was curled in his arms, her cheek resting against the lapel of his black wool coat. As Jack and his cargo approached the car—his stride steady as if Summer's dead weight was nothing—Bella shuddered, moved by the chill night air and a curious mixture of emotions. There was a dash of envy at Summer's position, snuggled comfortably against Jack's broad chest. A pinch of gratitude in response to Jack's seemingly unending kindness. And, as a bolt of dark heat bloomed below her belly, Bella has to admit that her current cocktail of feelings contained a potent measure of lust.

She shivered again, the freezing breeze stirring her to stand aside and allow Jack to lower Summer into the car.

'I'll be back in a sec,' said Jack. 'I've got a couple of blankets for her inside.'

'Thanks,' said Bella, 'but only if it's not too much trouble …' She trailed off. Jack was already halfway to the house and wasn't to be deterred by her feeble protests.

A snore drew Bella's attention back to the car and her passenger. With renewed focus, Bella stooped and leant across Summer to fasten her sister's seat belt. She stabbed the buckle into the clip, but it refused to snap into place.

In her struggle, Bella's shoulder brushed Summer's cheek, bringing her sister out of her slumber. 'Where am I?' she asked, her voice a groggy slur.

'The back of my car. I'm taking you home.'

Summer blinked slowly, her gaze sliding up to the roof of the car and then past Bella to the heavy clouds in the night sky. 'It was snowing.'

'It's stopped. Let's get home before it starts again.'

'I was at a party in a big house. How'd I get in here?'

The glare Bella was giving the stubborn seat belt clip melted away as she replayed the memory of Jack scooping Summer up into his arms and carrying her carefully—as if he understood how precious she was—down the stairs and across the snow-covered driveway. 'Jack carried you. I did tell him we could wake you up, but he said there was no need to disturb you.'

'Who's Jack?'

Bella rolled her eyes. 'The man who helped you find the toilet and held your hair back while you were being sick.' Bella glanced at the crinkle of confusion above her sister's nose. 'Dark hair and eyes. Incredibly tall. If you squint he looks a bit like Superman.'

'Oh, him! He's nice.'

'*I know*.' Bella's answer came out more emphatically than intended, accompanied by a thrill of triumph as the unyielding seat belt clipped into place. The sound of footsteps on the gravel behind her made her smile and mutter, 'Speak of the devil ...'

Jack halted next to the car. He had a bundle of blankets tucked under his left arm and a small white cardboard box in his right hand. 'Here you go,' he said, passing the blankets to Bella. 'I got two in the end. I figured another one to go under her head would be a good idea.'

'Thanks,' said Bella, swiftly ducking into the car so Jack couldn't see the smile lighting up her face.

'Is that him?' Summer asked.

'Yes. He got you some blankets for the drive home.' Bella tucked the second blanket behind Summer's neck and head.

'Thank you, Jack!' Summer called. 'What's in the box?'

'A few things from the buffet. Mostly samosas. Bella seemed to like them and I thought you both might feel hungry later.' He offered the box to Bella. 'Or tomorrow when you're feeling better.'

'That's nice,' said Summer, her voice dreamy and distant. 'Isn't that nice, Bel? Bel? Bella!'

'Hmn?' Bella looked up from the box in her hands. She'd been staring at it, her mind occupied with thoughts of the delicious snacks inside and Jack's kindness. 'Oh, yes. Lovely, thank you,' she said to Jack. 'You've been very kind, but we'll get out of your way now and you can get back to the party.'

'Actually ...' Jack ran a hand over the back of his neck,

his gaze downcast and evasive. 'I don't suppose I could be cheeky and ask for a lift back to Haileybrook? I just moved into a place near the pub and—'

'We'd love to!' Summer rolled towards Jack as she made the offer, the seat belt preventing her from sliding out of the car into the snow. 'Wouldn't we, Bel?'

'Of course.' Though Bella meant them, the words came out from between gritted teeth as she heaved Summer back to an upright position.

'I don't want to be any trouble.' Jack cast a glance back towards the house. 'I was going to see if I could get a taxi to come out here but—'

'No, honestly.' Bella closed Summer's door. 'No trouble at all. Hop in.'

'Great, thank you.' Jack exhaled in a rush, his shoulders relaxing.

Bella slipped into the driver's seat. Jack found getting comfortable trickier, having to slide the passenger seat back as far as it would go. Mid-process, he glanced up and caught Bella staring at him. He smiled. 'Happens all the time.'

'I'm sure,' said Bella, reflecting on the contortions she'd had to go through in every car she'd driven to reach the pedals and see over the steering wheel properly. 'Um, you don't want to tell anyone you're leaving?' She tipped her head towards the house which, surrounded by the hush of the winter night, appeared to throb with light and music.

'Oh, no.' Jack shook his head. 'I doubt they'll notice I've gone.'

Jack's factual pronouncement of how little his family cared about his absence stung Bella. It was both sad and inexplicable. What was their problem?

Bella pressed her lips together as she rolled the car down the drive. The blunt Bella of a few months ago would have voiced that exact question, wading straight in with her pointiest-toed shoes. But she was aiming for greater delicacy in this new phase of her life and if Jack didn't want to elaborate, she shouldn't pry. And—as much as Bella longed to ask if Jack had got over her leaving Ashley's wedding without saying goodbye—with Summer in the back of the car, inebriated but with fully functioning hearing, it probably wasn't the best time to talk about that either.

So. Small talk it was then.

Bella glanced at Jack. Staring out at the layer of snow which sat on the hedgerows lining the road, he had relaxed back into his seat and, with the cardboard box balanced on his knees, was humming along to the radio which was playing the bouncy strains of 'Jingle Bell Rock'. He made such a contented picture, Bella was sorry to disturb him.

'You're not upset to be leaving the party early?' she asked. 'It's only ten o'clock.'

'No, honestly. Fee's parties are all the same. My role there is pretty much glorified waiter or cleaner. I'm much happier here.'

'OK. What is up with that? I mean, what is her problem? Apart from a terrifying fixation with tartan bows.' Bella winced, and if she hadn't been driving she'd have clapped both her hands to her mouth. Good job, Bella. Real restraint there. You held out for one whole minute before going for the jugular.

But Jack chuckled. 'She does love those bows. You should have seen it last year. White. That was the theme.

Every surface, decoration, platter and outfit in pristine ivory or cream. The party was like being trapped inside a nightmare snow globe.'

'I'm sorry.' Bella twisted her lips in regret. 'I shouldn't have asked. It's none of my business. It's just, your family ...' How could she say it in a way that didn't include any obscenities? 'They don't seem to ... appreciate you. Sorry. Forget I asked.'

'No, it's OK. That I'm something of the black sheep isn't a secret, if you want to know about it.' He chuckled again. 'And I'm guessing you do given you said you were nosey.'

Bella grinned, relieved she hadn't offended him. 'Olympic-level nosey. Always have been. You can ask Summer—'

As if on cue, a loud snore came from behind Bella. Jack looked over his shoulder. 'She's asleep again. I'll have to ask her for confirmation later.'

'She'll be happy to back me up. She'll also tell you I'm embarrassingly expert at blunt questions and comments.' Bella sighed. 'Although I've been trying to rein those in lately.'

'Why? I like that you're straightforward. You say what you're thinking. It makes a nice change.'

'Honestly?'

'Honestly. Most of the people say one thing to your face and another behind your back. It's not endearing.'

'OK, then ...' Though Jack had given her permission, Bella continued to be hesitant. 'What's the deal with your family?'

'I guess it all goes back to me being an afterthought.' Jack took in Bella's frown of confusion and continued,

'I'm almost ten years younger than the youngest of my three brothers.'

'Ah. I would call you a happy accident.'

'That's what my mum used to say.' Jack's lips curled weakly in a half-hearted smile. 'She died when I was eight.'

Bella's fingers tightened on the steering wheel. Sometimes she hated herself for being a nosey cow. 'Oh God, Jack. I'm so sorry.'

'It's OK.' Jack shrugged. 'I guess there'd always been some understandable distance between my brothers and me but the gap widened without Mum to fight my corner. I was away at prep school when she died, the same school my brothers attended before they went on to private boarding school. I stayed there after Mum died. I guess it was easier for Dad to follow what they'd done for my brothers and the idea was I'd go to the same school as them too. But the summer after I turned ten I came home for the holidays and my dad announced he'd got remarried and introduced me to Fee.'

Bella's jaw dropped. 'Just like that?'

'A whirlwind romance. They met while Dad was on business in the South of France—she was holidaying there—and they had a quiet ceremony. He was probably worried about how it would look, with her being the same age as his oldest son.'

'Ugh!' Bella shot Jack an apologetic wince. 'Sorry. I know we're talking about your dad, but ...'

'I know. A twenty-five-year age gap does seem creepy. But, despite all the sceptics they're together thirty-two years later, so you have to give them that. Fee does love Dad, I'm certain of it.'

'But not you?'

'If she does, she has an odd way of showing it. When she found out about the plan to send me to the same boarding school as my brothers, she pointed out there was a perfectly good state secondary in the nearest town. Why waste money on school fees for a fourth son? And my dad agreed with her.'

Bella's fingers had turned white against the wheel and her mouth had been open for so long her throat had dried. Swallowing the urge to shout something rude, she said, 'That's awful.' She frowned. So much about the differences between Jack and the people at Ashley's wedding suddenly made sense. 'Obviously, I don't mean going to a state school is awful. That's normal.'

'Agreed. And you know, I've thought about it a lot, and I'm glad. I got a good education—I mean the school didn't have its own golf course or anything crazy, but the facilities were fine and the teachers were mostly good—and my school friends are great people.'

'I think I'd be angrier with your dad than Fee,' said Bella. After all, it was too easy to blame a young wife for being manipulative, while pardoning the weak man who allowed himself to be played. And older brothers ... In Bella's experience—well, in her limited but disastrous experience of what had happened with Ethan's brother—they were trouble. 'And your brothers. Didn't they stick up for you?'

'They were all away at university when it happened. Somewhere I didn't go because Fee suggested it would be best for me to go straight into the business at eighteen. I got my degree at night school in my twenties.'

'They still should have said something. It was clearly unfair.'

'Yes it was. But I've been trying to let it all go lately.' Jack let the back of his head thump against the seat. 'I put up with a lot for a long time. Then, when I hit forty, it made me re-evaluate my relationship with my family and my role in the family business. I was basically managing properties owned by my dad's company, and doing a bloody good job, even if I do say so myself.'

'I don't doubt it.'

'Thanks. But I kept getting overlooked for promotions while my brothers were given fatter salaries for doing next to nothing. And when I questioned it, I was told I shouldn't be bitter, that it wasn't their fault I didn't measure up or didn't know the right people.'

A low growl rolled around the back of Bella's throat. 'Please tell me this is the moment you quit. Preferably after a long sweary rant telling them exactly what you thought of them, concluding with you putting on a pair of aviator sunglasses and driving off in a convertible which threw up dirt in their faces.'

Jack laughed. 'That would have been amazing. But no. I gave three months' notice and wrapped up my work to hand over. But even then, I don't think they thought I'd leave.'

'OK, no dramatic exit. But please tell me they're lost without you. Completely up a creek without a paddle.'

'It's only been four months but if my brothers' increasingly panicked messages are anything to go by, I think they're deep in the Amazon and the canoe is sinking. I suspect even Dad might have noticed the one person who did their job has gone.'

'Good. Could they tempt you back?'

'I don't know.' Jack ran a hand through his hair. 'I don't want the business to get in trouble, but I enjoy working at Brookfield. It's a nice place and I like the village too. And the people have been so welcoming.'

'Are we including Ms Chan in this? Because I have found her to be knowledgeable, efficient and mildly terrifying, but not *welcoming*.'

Jack smiled. 'She has her moments. And she's eased up on me since you arrived.'

'Ha! I'm pleased to hear I have my uses.'

Bella lowered her window a fraction, letting the sunny sound of Jack's laughter escape into the night. The temperature in the car had climbed and the sultry air was making Bella woozy. She took a deep breath of the icy breeze whistling along the deserted country road. Stay sharp, Bella. Any of the ice patches on the unlit country lanes could be treacherous. She couldn't let the pleasure of Jack's company, the rhythm of Summer's snoring and the jaunty Christmas tunes coming from the radio lull her into a dozy trance.

A pricking feeling on the side of her neck drew Bella's glance to Jack, who quickly shifted his gaze to the window and drummed his fingers on the lid of the takeaway box. Bella smiled. 'Out with it.'

'What?' Jack blinked, a wide-eyed picture of innocence.

'If you want to ask me something personal, go for it. It's only fair.'

'Are you sure? I don't want you to think I'm making a bid for your nosiness gold medal.'

'Ha! You haven't a hope of taking it, but you're welcome to try. Go for it.'

'OK.' Jack glanced over his shoulder to the back seat, where Summer snorted and wriggled but continued sleeping. 'I was hoping you could clear up something Summer said to me earlier. It's left me intrigued.'

Bella's pulse stuttered. Oh Lord. Which of her secrets had a drunk, rambling Summer spilled to Jack?

Chapter 33

Smiling to cover her sudden reluctance to tell Jack anything about her that he wanted to know, Bella said, 'Sure. What did Summer say?'

'When she said she'd called her sister, I asked her if she was sure she would come to get her and Summer was adamant her sister would show up. She said her sister had been looking after her since she was ten and I was wondering is that since you were ten or when Summer was ten or—'

'Summer was ten.' Bella's shoulders dropped as the tension seeped out of them. That was ancient history.

'Sorry.' An adorable crinkle appeared between Jack's eyebrows. 'I didn't mean to pry—'

'No. It's fine. Summer was ten, I was sixteen. When our mum left.' A dull throb of pain stirred in Bella's guts, but that would be it. Her mum had long since lost the power to hurt her.

'I'm sorry. Was she— I mean, did she—' Jack exhaled, pondering before speaking again. 'What happened?'

'She met a man who wasn't her husband, our dad. The other guy was rich. He came from a wealthy family and had never worked a day in his life. He didn't expect my mother to either and he didn't want the bother of children. So he gave her a choice: stay with her husband and children or go with him and live the high life. And she chose him.'

'That's— That's …' The furrow between Jack's brows was joined by a few creases on his forehead.

'Unbelievable? Total crap?'

'No. Sorry, yes, it is crap. But unbelievable?' Jack shook his head and his tone turned sorrowful. 'No. I'm sorry to say I can believe it.'

Bella glanced at Jack's downcast gaze, pondering his change in mood. Oh, of course! Ashley—by all accounts the love of his life—had ditched him for a guy with money.

Jack cleared his throat. 'But if your dad was still around, then why did Summer say you were taking care of her?'

'Mum leaving hit Dad hard.' Bella paused. This part of the story was tricky. The competing feelings of sympathy for and annoyance with her father always threatened to tear her in two. 'And he sort of checked out for a while. He managed to get up and go to work but that was pretty much it. We had to fend for ourselves and Summer was only ten, so I made sure she ate properly, washed, dressed, got to school and home again, did her homework. You name it.'

'Bel learned to French plait my hair after I whinged about it for days.'

Bella and Jack threw rapid glances towards the back seat and the source of the unexpected hairdressing story. Summer's eyes were closed and her voice dreamy as she continued, 'And then she didn't eat so I could have school dinners.'

'Pft! That was only a couple of times, Summer.' Casting a glance at Jack, Bella caught his horrified expression and quickly added, 'It turned out Dad's salary had been paying the bills, keeping a roof over our heads and *mostly* covering food. But Mum's salary had been doing the rest. So some belt tightening was needed.'

'And then that didn't work, so Bel got a job as well as doing her A levels,' said Summer.

'I worked a couple of hours, three evenings a week at the local corner shop. And weekends,' said Bella.

Summer giggled. 'Only took her a few months to take over the place.'

'Again, Summer exaggerates.' Bella raised an eyebrow in Jack's direction. 'I was stacking shelves, working the till, taking deliveries, and I noticed a few ways that the Howells—they owned the shop—could save money on their orders and improve their margins. Anyone would have spotted it.'

'But not everyone would have said something,' said Summer. 'And a couple of times she went ahead and did it without permission. "Do first, apologize later. Sometimes that's the only way to get things done," she'd say to me.'

'Yes, well. I'm trying to rein that in,' said Bella, her cheeks heating.

'Ha! Good luck with that.' Summer broke into another fit of the giggles. 'Anyway, if you hadn't done your thing you probably wouldn't have become an accountant. Tell Jack about that.'

'I think we've bored him enough, Summer.'

'I'm not bored,' Jack said.

'It's not that interesting—'

'Mrs Howell saw Bella was good with money and numbers,' said Summer, silencing Bella's protest with a loud, boozy outburst. 'So she fixed her up with a job with her brother or cousin or someone. Some guy who had a small local accountancy place. She qualified in five years, studying while working. There's all these courses and levels you have to do, but it was cool because the company sponsored her as long as she stayed there for like forever.'

'Three years after qualifying or I could leave earlier and pay them back some of the training costs,' said Bella, keen that Summer not deviate too far from the facts.

'But she stayed. Then left and went to uni!' Summer threw her hands up as if this was the craziest thing her sister had ever done.

'I was only twenty-six and I wanted to do a business qualification.' Bella's irritation at Summer's commentary faded quickly as she remembered her student days and smiled. She'd never be sorry she'd eventually made it to university. She'd met her best friend, Kate, on her first day. 'It was only two years and a higher education certificate. But Summer was at uni already—'

'History and French for the win!'

'And Dad was back on track and I wanted to broaden my skills set—'

'Pah! She wanted to know how to better run the businesses whose accounts she was keeping.' Summer snorted and let her head thump back against the seat. 'Always meddling. With the best intentions.' Her voice faded into a weak mutter as she added, 'And killer heels. Ethan would never have kept up. What a complete numpty he turned out to be. Have you told Jack about—'

'Oh, look!' In her eagerness to silence her sister, Bella screeched and pointed ahead as if she had seen a yeti at the side of the road rather than the humdrum Haileybrook sign. 'We're here!' She glanced at Jack who, though he only held her gaze for a moment, had a gleam in his eyes which made her spirits plummet. She knew that look: curiosity. Summer's comments about Ethan had intrigued him. Dammit.

Using her breezy 'nothing to see here' voice, Bella asked him, 'You said you're near the pub?'

'Yes, turn here, thanks. My place is on the right. I'll shout when we're there.'

Bella bit the inside of her cheek as she turned off the High Street, praying Summer wasn't so drunk she couldn't take a hint and would stay quiet until Jack was safely indoors. Following his directions, she pulled up to the curb in front of one of the two-storey houses in the cul-de-sac. The most recent additions to the village, they had been built in the 1960s with a similar Cotswolds stone to Haileybrook's older buildings, traditional slate roofs, and low stone walls surrounding their small front gardens.

Bella turned off the engine and she and Jack exchanged awkward smiles. 'Well, thanks,' said Jack, opening the door. 'I'll see you at work on Monday. Unless you were roped into helping with the village Christmas Fair tomorrow?'

For the first time, Bella was sorry she hadn't volunteered to run a stall. 'Actually, I managed to dodge that. Although I have a feeling I may still be called on to handle the money. And I'll definitely be coming to check it out. I don't think Lavender and her crew would ever forgive me if I didn't show my face. I take it you will be helping?'

Jack nodded. 'Lavender can be very persuasive. I thought my house move would be a good enough excuse for not getting too involved, but then she hit me with the cause they're raising money for.'

'Ah, of course. The children's hospice.'

'Exactly.'

'Well now you've made me feel bad for not running a stall,' said Bella.

'Don't worry,' said Jack. 'I'm sure Lavender will be mollified as long as you show up and spend generously.'

'Thanks for the life-saving tips.'

'You're welcome.'

Their smiles now relaxed and conspiratorial, Bella and Jack held each other's gaze. As she stared into his dark eyes, a kaleidoscope of butterflies fluttered around Bella's belly. How did she keep forgetting how gorgeous his eyes were? Soulful, with such long, dark lashes and—

'Right. Sorry.' Jack blinked as if emerging from a trance. 'I'm letting in the cold air.' He tilted his head towards the rear seats. 'Bye, Summer. I hope you feel OK tomorrow.'

'Thank you,' said Summer who, with her eyes closed, appeared to be on the verge of sleep once again.

'OK. Thanks again for the lift.'

'You're welcome,' said Bella to Jack's back as he got out of the car and shut the door.

The butterflies folded their wings and plummeted to the pit of Bella's stomach. Her smile dropped with them as Jack opened the gate in the garden fence and strolled up to the blue front door with its colourful stained-glass panel.

'Go after him.'

Bella twisted to stare at her sister. She was slumped against the back seat, staring at Bella with one unblinking eye. 'Go on, Bel. Go and say goodnight properly.' Summer waved a hand towards Jack's house. 'Quickly, before he's indoors.'

'Summer.' Bella huffed and returned her stare to Jack, who was searching his pockets, presumably for his keys. 'Why would I want to do that?' But even as she asked the question, her heart skipped, singing loudly that she did want to go after him. Her brain couldn't give her an explanation as to why, but—

Oh, sod it.

Bella grabbed the door handle, her fingers slipping in her first attempt to open the door. Stupid heart. Useless brain.

Bella scurried after Jack, her feet falling easily within the large prints he had left in the snow. Jack turned at the sound of her steps, his arm raised towards the lock, keys clasped between his fingers.

'I didn't say thank you properly,' Bella said, her words cascading out in a breathy rush. 'For taking care of Summer. I really appreciate it.'

A slow smile spread across Jack's face and, as the grin made his eyes shine, it also sent sparks of electricity all the way down to Bella's toes. Ah-ha! *That*. That had been why she had wanted to go after him. For a glimpse of his real smile.

'I'm glad I could help,' he said. 'Your sister's great, it was no trouble.'

Bella's lips curled as she dropped her gaze to the path and shoved her hands into her coat pockets. *You can leave now*, her inner voice instructed. *Stop staring at the man and let him get in out of the cold*. And yet her feet refused to budge. 'OK, well, I'll see you tomorrow. At the Christmas thing.'

Jack's smile flared a touch brighter. 'Looking forward to it.' He took a step closer to her, forcing Bella to tilt her head back to hold his gaze. She returned his smile and, as he dipped to brush a kiss against Bella's cheek, she swore her heart stopped. 'Goodnight, Bella.'

'Right, yes. Right.' Bella's heart had kicked back into life with a vengeance, booming with the shock of Jack's kiss and leaving her flustered as she retreated a few steps down the path. It took all her self-control not to lift her fingers to her cheek, which was tingling from brief contact with Jack's lips. 'Goodnight, Jack.'

She had turned and was opening the garden gate when Jack replied, 'Sleep well, Bella,' and the sound of her name in his rich, deep voice made the fine hairs on the back of her neck rise almost as quickly as the butterflies in her tummy, which decided it was the right moment to take flight once more.

Bella hurried back to the car. Jumping into the driver's seat, she glanced at the rear-view mirror and caught a glimpse of the enormous beaming smile taking over her face. Oops! She scrubbed a hand across her mouth. She didn't want Summer getting any ideas or she'd likely tell Dad that her big sister had a crush on a co-worker and then she'd never hear the end of it.

All was silent in the backseat as Bella pulled away and she relaxed, convinced that Summer—back in her drunken stupor—had witnessed nothing. Excellent.

But as she parked in front of her cottage, a smug voice from behind her said, 'See? Bet you're glad you listened to me now, aren't you?'

Chapter 34

The view from Bella's bedroom window the next morning could have inspired a holiday greetings card series. A pristine layer of powder cloaked the village green and the row of thatched cottages lining it, puffs of steam rising from their squat chimneys. The scarlet front of the postbox on the corner was one of the few bright splashes of colour in a glistening world of white. Bella grinned, her heart soaring with childlike delight as, for a moment, she was transported back to when she was a kid. Back to when waking to find snow would mean a day off school, snowball fights and sledging.

Bella slid her feet into her slippers and wriggled into the cosy embrace of her fluffy dressing gown. The previous night's events must have tired her more than she'd thought. Even though she had got Summer to bed at around 11 p.m. and gone to bed shortly afterwards, she had slept until ten.

But, as she padded down to the kitchen, she found herself looking forward to a lazy morning, perhaps luxuriating in a scalding bath. She flicked the kettle on and, hearing footsteps on the stairs, began to run her plan for a restful day past her sister.

'Summer? I thought we could go to the pub for lunch.' Bella took two mugs from the cupboard. 'Lucy recommended the macaroni cheese. Apparently the garlic bread is to die for. All made to Cath's recipes, of course. Because apparently no one else cooks round here.' She chuckled as she popped a teabag in the first mug. 'Then, once we're stuffed with pasta, we could pop over to the Christmas Fair to see J—' Bella winced. That had been close. Obviously it would be nice to see Jack at the Fair, but that wasn't her main reason for wanting to go. Of course not. Clearly not. 'To see how everything's going. And I wouldn't be surprised if Lavender has …'

Bella trailed off as she turned to the living room, where a grey-faced Summer was shuffling towards the sofa while hugging her dressing gown close to her tummy and making groaning noises that called to mind the undead.

'Summer?' Bella strode into the living room, spurred by worry. 'Are you OK?'

'I'll live.' Summer slumped onto the sofa, letting her head fall onto the cushioned arm rest. She lifted a hand to her head and closed her eyes. 'I'm never drinking again.'

Bella smiled, remembering the many times she had said the same. 'I can recommend it.'

Keeping her eyes closed, Summer extended her hand to grab Bella's. 'You are wise, o ancient one.'

'Hey!' Bella swatted Summer's hand away and crouched next to the sofa. 'Less of the ancient, thank you.'

'You can't be angry with me, Bel. I'm ill.'

'I've never been convinced that a hangover classes as illness.'

'You're heartless.'

'Oh dear. Ancient and heartless. Then I suppose it must be someone else who was about to offer to bring you some medicinal tea and toast?'

Summer opened one eye and the corner of her mouth twitched into the hint of a smile. 'For tea and toast, I would be prepared to take it all back.'

Bella squeezed Summer's shoulder gently. While they were growing up Summer had always been a good patient, taking medicine without a fuss and sitting quietly while Bella took her temperature. And though she had never enjoyed seeing her sister unwell, Bella had rather liked feeling wanted, with Summer insisting on curling up next to Bella on the sofa until she felt well enough to brush away her ancient big sister's attempts at nursing. 'I'll put the kettle on.'

Bella made to rise, but Summer grabbed her hand. 'I'm sorry about last night,' Summer said. 'I shouldn't have missed the nativity play.'

Bella smiled, pleased that Summer had said sorry without needing to be prompted. 'You missed the theatrical event of the year. It was hilarious and cute enough to make your teeth ache.' Bella squeezed Summer's hand. 'I missed you.'

'Sorry.' Summer swallowed. 'And thank you for coming to get me from the party.'

Bella gasped and clapped a hand to her chest. 'An apology *and* a thank you? You really are unwell.'

'Ha bloody ha.' Summer harrumphed. 'I would thump you, but I'm too weak.'

'Let me get you that toast—'

'Not so fast.' Summer's grip on Bella's hand turned vice-like. 'In return for my apology and thanks, I want to know everything about you and Jack.'

Bella shrugged. 'There's not much to tell,' she said, relieved Summer had closed her eyes again and couldn't see her reddening cheeks. 'We work together.'

'I'll say.' Summer's lips curved into a lopsided smirk. 'I was half out of it last night and I could still see a lot of things *working* between you two.'

'Oh I don't know,' said Bella, her pulse skipping. 'I doubt he's interested.'

'Are you being deliberately stupid about this?' Summer opened her eyes to glare at Bella. 'The man is clearly into you. You should go for it. He's nice. He held my hair back when I was being sick and he'd met me, like, fifteen minutes before. And he carried me to the car!' Summer shook her head, as if she found it hard to believe. 'Knights in shining armour are rare. If he's single, I'd make a move quick.'

Bella couldn't stop the smile creeping onto her lips, but it was quickly replaced by a frown. 'I'm not a hundred per cent certain about him being single. My sources seem to believe he is. But ...' Bella paused, suddenly struck by a vivid mental image of Jack and Dinah in matching skiwear, laughing as they sat cosied together on a ski lift. Dinah would be the better choice for Jack, wouldn't she? She was already part of his set.

'But what?'

'Oh, it's nothing.' Bella wasn't a fan of self-pity—it didn't solve many problems or get anything done—and she wasn't sure it was wise to share her worries with Summer.

'Come on.' Summer released Bella's hand and wriggled

so she was facing her. 'You can tell me anything, you know.' Summer batted her eyelashes and, as her stare turned wide and imploring, Bella's defences crumbled.

'OK. So … It's …' Bella growled at her sudden lack of fluency. 'Jack is great. I do like him. A lot. He's considerate. And kind. Hard-working. And—'

'Rather easy on the eye.'

'That doesn't hurt. But I don't know if I'd be good for him. I'd probably just make his life—'

'No! I'm going to stop you right there.' Summer waggled her index finger in front of Bella's nose. 'That rubbish you're spouting is Ethan's rubbish rattling around your head. And he has no business being in there because he's a total knob who didn't appreciate you.'

'He wasn't all bad. And it was a difficult situation.'

'Yes, both those things are true,' said Summer. 'But, in the end, he didn't side with you. And for that, I will never forgive him. If you want to, that's great. In fact, I encourage it. Good karma and all that.' Summer withdrew her hand, laying it on her forehead. 'But I will never let it go. I choose to remain pissed off with him forever, on your behalf.'

'Thanks,' said Bella, giving her sister a warm smile of gratitude. If Summer hadn't looked as if a squeeze might make her sick, she would have given her a hug.

'Does Jack have any brothers?'

'Three older ones.'

'Ugh!' Summer rubbed her brow and added, 'You might want to ask a few questions about that before you get involved with him.'

'They don't seem to get on. I'm not sure he has much to do with them, especially since he left the family business.'

263

'Good. That sounds promising.' Summer paused her massage of her temples and fixed Bella with her stare. 'You should tell him.'

'Tell him what?'

'You should tell Jack what happened with Ethan.'

Bella's stomach lurched. 'I don't think that's a good idea.'

'Why? I think he'd—'

'I haven't known him that long and—'

'And I'm sure he'll understand—'

'No, Summer, I don't—'

In Bella's dressing gown pocket, her phone jangled. A quick glance at the screen produced a frown so deep it made Bella's forehead ache. Lavender Williams. Drat. Why had she agreed to give the woman her number?

'Are you going to answer that?' asked Summer.

'It's Lavender Williams. The lady who's organising the Christmas Fair.'

'Well go on, it might be important.'

'Hmn.' Bella eyed the phone warily. She had a plan for a restful day with Summer and was loath to get pulled into any Brookfield drama. 'I thought we could have a nice pub lunch and then potter about in the afternoon. Perhaps nip over to the Fair as visitors, not stallholders.'

The phone continued to chirp. 'Please answer it,' said Summer, grabbing a cushion and pressing it over her face. 'The ringing is splitting my skull.'

Oh, dammit! Bella swiped to accept the call.

'Bella? What are you doing right now? Are you at home?'

Taken aback by the lack of a polite preamble and the high note of panic in Lavender's voice, Bella took a moment to answer. 'Yes, I'm at home.'

'Good. I need you to come to the community centre.'

'Well, I could maybe come in about an hour?' said Bella, glancing down at her dressing gown and fluffy slippers. 'My sister is visiting and—'

'No, that won't do at all—' Lavender broke off, her voice replaced by a series of muffled clangs and shouting. 'Bella? Are you there?'

'Y—es,' said Bella, increasingly fearful that she would be recounting the contents of this phone conversation to the police later that day.

'We need you here right now. It's an emergency.'

And with that, the line went dead.

Bella stared at the screen, open-mouthed. That had sounded urgent. But what if she scrambled over to the community centre only to find Lavender's great emergency was a disagreement over the ambient music selection or who got to draw the raffle? She glanced up at Summer. She'd been looking forward to some quality time with her sister and abandoning her while she was in a delicate state seemed unwise at best and mean at worst.

'Why are you still here, Bel?' Summer lifted the cushion enough to unmuffle her voice and continued, 'The woman said it was an emergency and that's your thing.'

'It's probably nothing important. I want to spend today with you.'

'But I won't be in a fit state to do anything for a while. You can go and sort Lavender and her friends out and be back in time for lunch.'

Bella bit her lip, a ball of tension tightening in her chest. Lavender had sounded distressed. And perhaps it was something that could be easily fixed. 'Are you sure you don't mind?'

'Not at all. Off you go, Bella to the rescue.'

'Right.' Bella jumped to her feet and made for the stairs, the squeeze in her chest loosening as she sprang into action.

'Bel?' Summer called from the sofa.

Bella paused at the foot of the stairs. 'Yes?'

'I know you're in a hurry, but I don't suppose there's any chance of that tea and toast before you go?'

Chapter 35

Bella scurried across the village green, her faithful black boots cutting a direct path through the snow coating the grass. Only fifteen minutes had passed since Lavender's SOS and, from how serene the outside of the community centre appeared, Bella might have believed the call to have been a prank.

The former school was a Victorian stone building with a slate roof. The windowsills beneath each of its tall rectangular windows held a shelf of snow and the iron entrance gates—set in the high walls which separated the small front playground from the pavement—were icy to the touch. Bella slowed as she reached the entrance and took a deep breath, preparing herself for what she would find inside before putting her shoulder to the door.

Crikey. She should have taken a few more breaths.

The hall seemed to be packed with the entire population of Brookfield. They were moving furniture, painting cardboard signs, balancing precariously from stepladders to hang paper chains, and talking. Talking very loudly. The white stone walls, oak floor and high roof only added to the cacophony. And some genius had thought, *'You know what this pandemonium is missing? Panpipe versions of carols!'* Bella winced at the irony, as she identified the ethereal strains blaring from the speakers as a haunting woodwind version of 'Silent Night'.

'Hello. Bella, wasn't it?'

Bella turned to find herself staring into the sharp, bird-like eyes of Grace Harman, who she had managed to avoid since first meeting her at Coopers' Farm almost two weeks previously. She was dressed in a sharply cut jacket and skirt in matching green tweed and not a hair in her tight bun was out of place. Her immaculate appearance and her penetrating stare made Bella's skin itch. Bella normally took great pride in how she presented herself, but in her rush to respond to Lavender's phone call, Bella had only managed to clean her teeth and face, apply dry shampoo and the absolute essentials in her make-up kit before leaping into the same beat-up jeans she had worn the previous evening and her only other Christmas jumper: a soft, long-sleeved sweater in pastel pink spotted with white stars and red candy canes.

'Yes,' Bella said, wishing she'd had time to apply some bronzer. 'Hello again.'

Grace nodded and turned her gaze away from Bella, a tight smile of satisfaction curling her lips as she surveyed the chaotic scene unfolding in front of them. 'You see? This is what I was talking about. The commune residents think they know how to organize an event like this, but look at this madness!' Her smile stretched a little wider. 'If they had only taken my advice.'

'Bella! At last!' Gripping a clipboard in her left hand, Lavender paused on her path towards Bella to issue some orders to a bickering group clustered around one of the stepladders. 'The grotto in the smallest classroom is practically finished and our Santa is trying on his costume. I need you to bring the sacks of presents from the Pavilion. Go!' she barked, sending the group scuttling away. As she neared Bella, she acknowledged Grace's presence with a curt nod. 'Grace.'

'Good morning, Lavender,' said Grace, her tone all honey. 'How is everything going?'

'All according to plan.' Lavender tapped a pen off her clipboard. 'Now, if you'll excuse Bella and me for a moment, we have important matters to discuss.'

'Of course.' Grace held up her hands. 'I know what it is to run an event like this. You go ahead.'

'Thank you,' said Lavender from between gritted teeth. 'Come along, Bella, dear.'

Lavender clamped her left hand around the top of Bella's arm and marched her across the corridor into the smallest classroom.

Though a fraction of the size of the hall, with a low ceiling and a series of tall, slender windows, the former classroom—now used for daytime and evening adult education sessions—felt far less claustrophobic than the bigger space. One corner of the room was occupied by a folding gazebo, which had been given walls made of large sheets of cardboard. The whole structure was smothered in tinsel and artificial snow and the painted door and windows on the flimsy brown walls reminded Bella of her gingerbread house. A large arrow pointing at the makeshift cabin and bearing the words *This way to the North Pole* confirmed Bella's suspicions that she was looking at Santa's grotto.

'What's going on?' asked Bella. What could possibly have Lavender so exercised? 'Has this got something to do with Iris's missing brooch?'

'What? No, no.' Lavender waved away Bella's concerns. 'That'll turn up. You'll see. No, I called you because that horrendous, tweedy'—Lavender cast a glance over her shoulder, presumably to check they were alone—'*hag* is doing her best to ruin the Christmas Fair.'

'Grace? What's she done?'

'Stolen our tree!'

Bella frowned as she stared at the dashes of fury in Lavender's pale cheeks. She had definitely missed a few steps leading up to this accusation of tree rustling. 'OK. How did she do that?'

'It's my fault for trying to make her feel included even though she tried to stymie our plans from the start.' Lavender planted her hands on her hips. 'I asked her to get involved and, after being initially reluctant, she said she'd be happy to put me in touch with a relative of hers who sells pine trees. Apparently they would give us a wonderful deal. And they did. But when I called them twenty minutes ago to ask when we could expect delivery—I'd been told ten o'clock—the girl I spoke to said she had no record of our order.'

'And you think Grace has something to do with that?'

'Of course she does. She's a witch.'

'Right.' Bella took in Lavender's increasingly red complexion, which was rapidly nearing the crimson shade of her jumper. Were her accusations a sign that the stress of running the Fair was getting to her? Or perhaps the village's tweed-clad busybody had called in some favours to tarnish the success of the event? But, whatever the truth of the matter, the most important question had yet to be asked. 'So why did you call me?'

'Isn't it obvious?' Lavender tutted and rolled her eyes. 'I called you because I need *you* to get a replacement tree.'

Chapter 36

Bella shook her head in the hope of fixing her ears. She could not have heard that right. 'You want *me* to source a tree—'

'Before two o'clock,' said Lavender in a breezy tone which in no way reflected the enormity of what she was demanding. 'Two thirty at the latest. The Fair opens at three thirty and we need time to install and decorate it.'

In a fog of disbelief, Bella asked, in a halting voice, 'You want me to find a tree and get it delivered here in the next three hours?'

'Yes, dear. I knew you'd be the person for the job. You're resourceful. And, to be perfectly frank, everyone else is busy.'

Bella nodded, her pride a little wounded. She was Lavender's last resort. Good to know. That said, she *was* resourceful. 'Why don't we borrow the tree from the entrance to the Pavilion at Brookfield?'

'That's a seven-footer. We need an eight-foot tree. Anything less will look paltry in the hall. And we mean to impress.' Lavender lowered her voice to a mutter. 'And wipe the smug smile off that hag's face.'

Her pulse accelerating, Bella tried again. 'Or how about the one at the barn at the farm? I'm sure Lucy and Seth would let us borrow it.'

'Only six feet. I noted as much yesterday at the nativity play. It won't do.'

'Oh. I guess I could call round all the shops to see if anyone has an eight-foot—'

'It can't be artificial. It must be natural. Pine or fir will be fine. And no sad, wizened, brown thing, either. It has to look healthy and splendid.'

Great, thought Bella, feeling less healthy and splendid by the second. Even if she could find an eight-foot, verdant, natural pine or fir tree, how was she supposed to get it to Haileybrook within the next three hours? And how was she supposed to fit lunch with Summer into a countryside Christmas tree hunt?

A crash followed by a series of bangs came from the hall. Lavender's head whipped towards the noise. 'Heavens above, what now?' Lavender returned her gaze to Bella. 'I have to go and look into that. Probably the Harman woman sabotaging something.' She glanced at her clipboard. 'And I haven't managed to locate Trevor. He was supposed to be here an hour ago. If you see him, let him know I'm looking for him.'

'Wait!' Bella scurried in front of Lavender, blocking her exit. 'I'm not sure I can find a tree that matches all your requirements in time.'

'Nonsense. I have every faith in you.'

Well, that makes one of us then, thought Bella, the bitter

taste of dread filling her mouth. 'But even the delivery would be almost impossible—'

'I can help.'

The grotto opened to reveal a figure dressed in black boots and a red velvet suit trimmed in white fur. Bella's heart had sped to a gallop at the sound of the deep voice and, though he had to stoop—dropping his face forwards out of view to avoid hitting his head on the low door frame—she knew Jack was the Christmas Fair's Santa. Of course he was.

And, for a moment, the crushing pressure of having to miraculously produce an enormous tree in the next three hours lifted as a rush of giggles rose in Bella's throat.

'That's marvellous, John,' said Lavender. 'Just make sure you're here for three o'clock. Right'—she nodded—'I'll leave you two to get on with it.'

Bella stared after Lavender, her jaw slack. She'd walked into a tree-shaped trap. And Jack … Well, he'd volunteered to join her in the trap. Perhaps all the good cheer and Christmas spirit had gone to his head? Bella turned her gaze to the head in question which, with its light dusting of dark stubble and thick wavy hair, was decidedly non-Santary. No, that didn't seem right. Santa-ish? Santa-esque?

'What?' Jack lifted a hand to his hair. 'Does my hair look weird or something?'

'*That's* what you think might look weird about you'—Bella signalled his crimson costume with her index finger—'when you're standing there in that get-up?'

Jack chuckled. 'It wouldn't be my first choice of outfit for going on a tree hunt, I must admit.'

274

'Good point. I'll wait while you change.'

'No can do.' Jack shook his head. 'I was handsewn into this thing by Wendy.'

Bella's eyes narrowed as a faint memory from the Christmas Fair committee meeting she'd attended on her first day at work resurfaced. 'Wendy was making the costume.' A smile crept onto her lips as she lifted her gaze from the shiny toes of Jack's boots up his long legs to the gold buckle on the belt. It was a great costume. Although it was rather baggy around the middle. Bella gestured towards Jack's midriff. 'Aren't you too slender to be Father Christmas?'

Jack smiled. 'I have a pillow to go in here. But the padding makes it quite hot, so I'm leaving it to the last minute. Same goes for the wig and beard. And I have some glasses too.'

Some of the giggles escaped from between Bella's lips. She couldn't help it. 'Small round wire glasses with no glass in the frames?'

'Obviously.'

'I will happily pay to see that.'

'Good.' Jack frowned, schooling his features into a mock-serious expression. 'Because we have strict instructions that we're to raise a record-breaking amount. And I hope you don't mind a wait. Lavender assures me there will be a queue to see Santa all afternoon.'

'I don't mind waiting.' A pleasant buzz of electricity sped through Bella as she held Jack's stare and watched a smile tug at the corner of his mouth. Such gorgeous eyes. Such a great mouth too. She sighed, wondering how it was possible to continue to find someone attractive when they were wearing such a ludicrous costume.

'Speaking of time'—Jack glanced in the direction of the corridor—'shouldn't we get on with our mission?'

Oh crap. The bloody tree. 'You're right. Let's go.'

Bella strode towards the exit, confident that Jack's long legs would make keeping up with her easy work. Where the heck were they going to get a giant tree at such short notice? Her mind spun, throwing up and rejecting possibilities in a fruitless whirl.

She was shouldering her way out the main door when Jack caught up. He slid his arms into the sleeves of a long black coat, fighting the resistance caused by the white fur trim on the cuffs of his suit. 'Do you already have a plan?'

'I have one idea.'

Jack drew level with her to walk by her side across the playground. 'Which is?'

Bella halted by the gates and, turning to face Jack, lowered her voice. 'We're going to liberate the tree from the church.'

Jack laughed, then stopped when Bella didn't mirror his smile. 'You're not serious?'

Bella lifted her arms in the biggest shrug she could manage. 'I had to pop in there the other day to collect some props for the nativity play. They've got another tree. It meets all Lavender's criteria. And anyway, I'm probably owed this after nearly being crushed by the darn thing—'

'That was a different tree—'

'Doesn't matter. Needs must.' Bella stalked off down the High Street in the direction of St Stephen's. She could hear Jack huffing, likely in disbelief, before scurrying to catch up with her.

He kept pace beside her and said, 'I'm not sure I can support a plan which involves theft—'

'Borrowing. We'll return it.'

'Borrowing from *a church*. At *Christmas*.'

Ignoring his raised eyebrows and incredulous tone, Bella said, 'There are no Christmas trees in the Bible though, are there? When you think about it, a tree is probably some kind of pagan fertility symbol and could even be seen as blasphemous.'

'So we'd be doing the church a favour. By stealing—'

'*Borrowing.*'

'Sorry, of course.' Jack's lips twitched but he kept a straight face. 'By borrowing the tree from St Stephen's we'd actually be doing the Lord's work.'

Bella held Jack's gaze, pleased she managed a whole second before laughing.

Jack grinned. 'While you may have a point about the whole pagan thing, I think I have an alternative which won't involve us getting into trouble with the law. Or the Almighty.'

'Spoilsport. Go on then, what's the alternative?'

'I have a friend who, well, he sort of … runs a Christmas tree farm.'

Bella halted so abruptly that Jack walked a couple of paces past her before turning back. 'You couldn't have mentioned this before I laid out my plan to get us both excommunicated?'

'Does the Anglican church excommunicate people?'

'I guess now we don't have to find out.' Bella opened her mouth to suggest Jack call his friend, but Jack was already removing his phone from his pocket.

'I'll call Ben. He owns me a favour.' He held the phone up to his ear. Bella took another breath, ready to tell him to ask if Ben had a spare van or could deliver the tree, when Jack said, 'I'll ask if he can lend us a flatbed or van to get the tree back here.'

Bella's lips remained parted as she watched Jack have an amiable, brisk conversation with his friend. Her heart thudded and her cheeks warmed, tingling in the crisp winter air. God, she loved efficiency. And initiative. Which, as turn-ons went, were probably pretty odd. Although, the sight of Jack running his hand absent-mindedly through his hair, mussing the thick dark waves into an alluring tangle, wasn't helping her stay cool either.

'OK. Thank you.' Jack ended the call. 'He can lend us a van. His place is about an hour from here. Do you want to drive the van back to Haileybrook or shall I?'

Bella had only driven a van a couple of times before. It had required making significant adjustments to the seat to allow her feet to reach the pedals and they didn't have that kind of spare time. 'If you could, that would be great. So we take my car to get there, then?' She pointed across the village green where her car was a crimson smudge under a thick layer of white powder.

Jack nodded. 'Great. Let's go.'

They crossed the High Street and followed Bella's straight row of footprints back towards her cottage. As they drew level with the bare cherry trees, the back of Jack's hand brushed against Bella's arm, setting off an explosion of sparks which skittered down her spine, making her shiver. Her heart—which had beat an untroubled rhythm throughout all her outlandish plotting to borrow the church's tree—skipped at the prospect of a car ride alone with Jack.

They paused outside Bella's garden gate and Bella was opening her mouth to ask Jack to wait while she went inside to fetch her car keys when the cottage door was whipped open to reveal a miraculously rosy-cheeked and bright-eyed Summer. The tea and toast must have worked wonders. Either that or Summer had been revived by the sight of Jack and the prospect of being able to meddle in Bella's non-existent love life. 'Hello, Jack!' Summer grinned and leant against the door frame. 'Are you and Bella saving the day together?'

'Nice to see you looking so well, Summer,' said Jack. 'And yes, we've been given a mission to get a Christmas tree.'

'Oo! Sounds like fun. Shame I can't come.' She gestured to her dressing gown and slippers. 'I'm still recovering from last night. But I'm sure you'll be safe in Bella's capable hands.'

Bella fired Summer her best 'shut up now' death stare but, on catching it, Summer's sly grin only widened.

'Jack,' said Bella through gritted teeth. 'If you don't mind waiting here a minute, I'll just pop inside and get my car keys.' She bustled down the path and shooed Summer inside. 'It's freezing out here. Get in before you catch your death.' She lowered her voice to a hiss, 'I wouldn't want the cold to kill you before I do.'

Summer chuckled as Bella ducked behind the front door and towards the key hooks. Keys in hand, Bella whirled back to the exit only to find it blocked by Summer. Her sister fixed Bella with a level stare. 'This is the perfect opportunity to tell Jack about Ethan.'

'Summer—'

'You're going to be stuck in a car together. What else are you going to talk about?'

'The weather? The Christmas Fair? How bloody annoying siblings are?' Bella made to swerve around Summer but her sister shifted to frustrate her escape again. Bella harrumphed and gave Summer another glare, but her little sister was unmoved.

'I'm not moving until you promise me you'll tell him.'

'That's blackmail!' Bella hissed, appalled and reluctantly impressed by Summer's tactics. 'And it's Christmas! How can you blackmail your own sister at Christmas?'

'I just think you've been given the perfect opportunity to tell Jack about Ethan. Get everything out in the open. It'll be good.' Summer dipped her chin and looked up at Bella through her lashes, blinking imploringly. 'Go on. Please?'

Bella sighed. She'd always found that look difficult to resist. But today the icy ball of dread in her chest spurred her to put up a fight. 'I don't think—'

'Fine. If you don't want to do it …' Summer twisted away from Bella to face the garden. 'Jack! I've got something to—'

'Fine! Fine!' Bella grabbed Summer's arm, holding back a violent urge to shake her. 'I'll tell him.'

'You promise?'

'Yes, OK? I promise.' Bella gave Summer a gentle shove as she released her arm and scurried towards the relative safety of her car and Jack's tall silhouette.

'Good luck!' called Summer, her bright tone edged with malevolent glee.

Bella glanced back and met her sister's cheery grin with a scowl. 'I can't believe I made you tea and toast.'

Chapter 37

Bella soon had to put the simmering irritation provoked by Summer's meddling on the back burner. The narrow local roads were treacherously icy and she had to channel all her energy towards steering a safe course. Fortunately, the tree farm was to the north of Oxford and it wasn't long before Bella was driving on wider, gritted routes. Possibly to allow her to concentrate, Jack had stayed quiet while Bella navigated the country lanes outside Haileybrook. The radio prevented the silence between them from becoming awkward and, as Bella turned onto the first main road, the folky strings of 'Fairytale of New York' drifted into the air and the tension in Bella's shoulders, arms and hands finally eased. The sky remained overcast, but thankfully the looming snow had not yet started to fall. Trying to further unwind, she took a deep breath and was struck by Jack's scent. The familiar light musky notes and something else. Something different and unusually Christmassy. Hints of clove, nutmeg and something sweeter …

'Jack?' Bella approached her question carefully. 'Is it possible that you smell of mince pies?'

Jack smiled. 'It's the Santa suit. Wendy made it and recently she's been batch baking mince pies to sell at the Christmas Fair. She likes to sew in her kitchen. The light is best there.'

Bella nodded and took another silent, slow inhale, her mouth watering at the thought of Wendy's mince pies. The ones she'd sampled on her first day at Brookfield had been tremendous. 'Speaking of good food, thank you again for the takeaway box from the party last night,' she said.

'You're welcome. Summer seems to be recovering quickly.'

Bella held in a harrumph of indignation. She still couldn't believe she'd worried about Summer only for her sister to bully her into making a painful promise. 'That's Summer. She tends to bounce back quickly. No doubt she'll be on the move again soon. She has plans for Christmas in Brazil.'

Jack's eyebrows sank into a frown. 'But, from what you said the other day, you're not planning on going anywhere any time soon, right?'

Bella did her best not to wince. The other day. When she was ranting at him before the nativity play. 'That's right. I'm here for the duration. Or at least until Ms Chan fires me for not being as good as the marvellous Harriet.'

'I doubt that'll happen. You seem to have everything under control.'

'Thanks.' Bella wasn't usually one to lack faith in her own competence, but the first couple of weeks at work had been more of a struggle than she'd expected and, until he spoke, she'd hadn't realized how much she'd needed a vote of confidence.

'If you don't mind me asking—'

'Uh-oh.'

Jack smiled. 'I was just going to ask why you decided to leave your job in London and move here? From what you told me at Ashley's wedding I got the impression you didn't exactly get along with your colleagues. But was the whole job that bad?'

'Yes.' Bella answered without hesitation. Her dad and Ethan had spent years telling her she must be exaggerating and, for a while, her conviction had wavered. Not any more.

'So did it get worse? What happened?'

Bella tightened her grip on the steering wheel. She had given this a lot of thought. Possibly too much. 'I never wanted the job in the first place. My boyfriend, he got a fantastic job in London and I wanted to go with him and I couldn't find the same kind of job I'd had before, so I ended up taking a position in a huge, faceless, soul-sucking number machine.'

'Wow. OK.' Jack nodded. 'And there was nothing good about it?'

Bella had been asked that before too. 'The pay was good.' Not that she'd had the time or energy to spend it. 'And the views from the offices were amazing,' she added, deciding not to mention that even the panoramic vistas over London from the glass-walled building had eventually lost their lustre. One day, while Bella was taking a break from her colleagues and staring out at the city below, the tightness in her chest had returned and she was struck by a mental image of a butterfly trapped in a glass case, its iridescent wings pinned ruthlessly to a piece of blank card.

'So what did you do before?' asked Jack.

Bella drew in a deep breath, glad to shift away from

thoughts of her former glass prison. 'I worked in a small firm in Birmingham and then, when I'd got my business qualifications, I went freelance, working with my clients on their books and how to develop their small businesses. It was great.' Bella smiled, remembering the buzz of seeing the people she'd built a relationship with thrive as their businesses grew. 'I knew their names, I knew about their families, their hopes and dreams. I knew there would be little to none of that working in an enormous firm in London.'

'But I'm guessing you did well anyway? I can't see you turning up for work and sitting on your hands or doing anything by halves, even if you didn't enjoy it.'

Bella smiled, feeling the warmth of Jack's compliment speed all the way down to her toes. 'You're right. I was promoted quickly, the salary kept increasing, there were bonuses and all of a sudden it was like I couldn't leave. Ethan'—Bella flinched but pressed on—'my boyfriend at the time, he quickly got sucked into the lifestyle of his high-flying firm and wanted to rent a bigger, better place, upgrade his wardrobe, get a more expensive car—which is ridiculous because no one living and working in London needs a car.'

What Bella didn't say was that, until recently, even thinking back to the crushing weight of her former work targets and the high expectations of her bosses, colleagues, Ethan and her dad would cause her ears to fill with a high-pitching drone and lights to flash before her eyes, the warning signs of an incoming migraine. Some days, the pressure had made it hard to breathe. And then there was Ethan. London brought out a new side to him. A grasping, competitive side.

'Soon the focus became saving up for a deposit to buy a place,' Bella continued. 'Not that I'm sure we would ever have found somewhere that was good enough.' Bella sighed. Ethan was an architect, one whose head had been turned by the amazingly expensive homes of his new colleagues, and house-hunting had been a never-ending stress which involved Bella compiling lists of places to view and Ethan shooting down every entry on them. And on the rare occasion anything came close to meeting his criteria, by the time he decided he'd like to view it, the place would already have been snapped up. 'And then there was all this socializing with his work friends which were supposedly dinner parties and theatre trips, but were actually pissing contests in disguise.'

'You're not a competitive person?' asked Jack, a note of incredulity in his question.

'When it comes to games, yes. But not money or houses or cars. How much money someone has or how much they spend on stuff isn't a measure of their worth.'

'So all people with a lot of money are awful?'

'No. I don't instantly dislike someone because they make a lot of money. If they've earned it honestly and paid their taxes they should be able to spend it how they want.' She paused, considering her love of a designer shoe. An occasional purchase which, to many, would seem an obscene extravagance. 'It's not that all people with pots of money are awful. It's the people who think having a lot of money—particularly if they haven't worked for it—makes them better than those with less who are awful. Especially those who then proceed to treat everyone with less than them like crap. They can all get in the bin.'

Jack pressed his lips together, considering her words.

'You think I'm talking rubbish?' asked Bella.

'Not at all. Actually I agree with you.' Jack nodded and tapped his fingertips on his knees. 'I'm guessing you're not a great monarchist.'

Bella cackled, her boisterous laughter drawing a grin from Jack. 'Don't get me started on the monarchy or the aristocracy,' she said, 'or you may end up being recruited to help me launch a people's revolution at dawn.'

'Noted. Although I would advocate for waiting for warmer weather if we're going to march on the capital and storm Buckingham Palace.'

'Excellent point. I'll consider it. Thank you for your contribution, comrade.'

Jack chuckled as they accelerated onto the motorway and, after Bella had merged with the traffic, he said, 'Why Haileybrook, though? You could have gone back to Birmingham. Why work at a retirement community in a small village in the Cotswolds?'

Bella bit her lip. Why indeed? Her dad had asked her the same question and she hadn't known how to tell him that she had endured years of suffocating stress in London. And when everything with Ethan blew up, she was knocked over by waves of self-doubt and loathing, guilt, disappointment, and eventually, rage. But then she had stumbled into a wedding in a tiny village in the middle of nowhere and experienced seven hours of happiness—during which even the trickier moments ended in laughter. It had been like relaxing at an oasis, peeking through a window at a better life.

How to say that without giving Jack reason to send her straight to a therapist? She took a deep breath. 'I suppose because after I left my job—I quit without anything else to go to—I spent a couple of months at my dad's place in Spain and I realized I wanted something completely different and while job-hunting I stumbled across an ad for the Brookfield job—' She drew another breath. Woah. She had to stop rambling. 'Long story short, I chose to move to Haileybrook because ... because I'm working on finding peace.'

Crap, that had sounded pompous. Her cheeks warming with embarrassment, Bella risked a glance at Jack. She wouldn't blame him if he opened the car door and threw himself out into the traffic.

But Jack remained in his seat, his brow furrowed in concentration. 'World peace?' he asked.

Bella laughed. Rather than pompous, she must have sounded like a beauty pageant contestant. 'God no. I mean, not that world peace wouldn't be amazing, but I'm a realist. Also—and you may not have picked this up from our interactions so far—but if faced with a choice between fight and flight, normally I will come out swinging.'

The corner of Jack's mouth twitched. 'So if you're backed into a corner, you'll choose violence. That ties in nicely with your aspirations to be a revolutionary leader.'

Bella grinned. 'No aspirations. I will lead the revolution if called upon. In the meantime, I'll keep looking for peace although'—Bella paused, considering how great a commitment to pacifism she could honestly make—'should anyone pick a fight with my family or friends, I can't promise to take it lying down. Which is why I barged into your family's party last night like, like—'

'An avenging angel?'

Bella caught Jack's gaze for a moment before he looked down at his knees, streaks of pink blooming along his cheekbones. Had he not meant to say that out loud? 'How about you?' Bella asked. 'Do you renounce violence in all its forms?'

'Usually.' Jack sighed. 'Although I think I'd taken it too far and turned into a doormat, especially for my family. I'm trying to be more assertive. Say "no" more often.'

'Sounds good,' Bella replied, while wondering how well Jack's assertiveness project could be going, given that he had attended his stepmother's Christmas party the previous evening rather that telling her he was too busy to make it. Although, he did walk out when he'd had enough. Baby steps. 'Are you going on that skiing trip this Christmas?' she asked. 'The annual one?'

'Yeah, I guess.'

Bella glanced at Jack. His expression was as sombre as his tone and Bella was struck by an urge to hug him, to wrap herself around him until his smile returned. Unfortunately she was driving. Drat. Why was he going on a trip if he wasn't looking forward to it? Was it habit? Obligation? Or, and a shiver trickled down her spine at the thought, could he be going because of Dinah?

'Are you not looking forward to it?' she asked. 'From those trophies and medals in your old room you're clearly a great skier.'

'It's not the skiing that's the issue. It sounds pathetic but, over the years, everyone on the trip has slowly paired off. It's getting to the point where soon I'll be the last unattached person. I had a bit of a panic the other day when I heard about Simon and Dinah getting together and—'

'Wait, wait. Stop. Hold it right there.' Bella lifted a finger from the steering wheel. 'Dinah and *Simon?*'

'Yep.'

'Simon the leery sexist arse?'

'That's the guy.'

'Wow.' Bella shook her head. 'I pray he knows how lucky he is.'

'I think he does. I only had a brief chat with him at the party last night but—'

'What? Sorry to interrupt again. This is a lot to take in. Simon was at the party?'

Jack shrugged. 'He's one of my youngest brother's friends. I bumped into him on one of my missions down to the wine cellar. He's buzzing about dating Dinah. He thinks his luck has come in and, thankfully, he's taking it very seriously. And I'm hopeful because I've never seen him like this about anyone before. You could feel the happiness radiating off him. He's on cloud nine.'

'Good.' Bella drummed her fingers off the steering wheel while she fought a sudden urge to break into song. It was difficult to hold back the smile that was stealing onto her lips. Jack had confirmed he was single. Dinah and he were definitely not a couple. Ha! Simon had better make space on that cloud.

She was basking in the revelations when Jack said, 'How about you? Are you going to stay with family or friends?'

Bella's fingers stilled as Jack's questions grabbed her by the ankles and dragged her back to earth. 'Uh, not this year. I spent last Christmas and a couple of months over the summer with my dad. That's a lot of family for one year. I fancy a quiet few days. Just me, the TV and possibly a tray of Wendy's mince pies.'

'Is this part of your quest to find peace?'

'Absolutely.' Bella nodded, hoping she was projecting confidence in her decision.

A loud growl came from Jack's midriff. Bella smiled. Jack might be a man of peace, but his stomach—like hers—was one for screaming and thumping until it got what it wanted.

He pressed a hand to his tummy. 'It must have been the thought of those mince pies. I don't suppose, if we get this tree quickly enough, you fancy stopping for lunch on the way back?'

At the suggestion, the initial rumblings of hunger in Bella's tummy shifted into something closer to a purr. 'Great idea,' she said. 'It's a date.'

The words had barely left her mouth when Bella wished she could swallow them and her stupid tongue along with them. This was what happened when she spoke without thinking first! And while lunch would be a perfectly nice first date and the idea of a date with Jack was certainly appealing, he probably wasn't asking like that.

Bella risked a glance at Jack. 'That is'—she said, taking a slower run at it—'that would be nice.'

Jack gave her one of his proper smiles, a wide grin that made his eyes shine. 'Great,' he said. 'As you said: it's a date.'

Chapter 38

The Christmas tree farm was well signed, with a large board—decorated with a cartoon of a jolly red-nosed reindeer—marking the entrance.

'Keep going,' said Jack. 'That's the public entrance. Ben told me to use the staff road.'

The second entrance was unpaved and, even though Bella inched the car along the rough path, the vehicle bounced and rocked, struggling with the uneven ground. By the time they stopped outside a small, low brick building, Bella felt as though her teeth had been rattled loose and was relieved to climb out of the car. She hissed quietly as the cold air struck her skin and the first fluffy white flakes of the day brushed against her eyelashes, causing her to blink.

'I'm going to pop into the office.' Jack motioned to the building behind him. 'See if Ben's there and how long it'll be till the tree is ready. Do you want to come?'

'I'll wait here,' said Bella. 'Stretch my legs before getting back in the car. Although if my toes start to freeze I might join you inside.'

'Glad to hear it.' Jack smiled and strode in the direction of the building, giving Bella a final glance over his shoulder before entering.

Crossing the unbroken sheet of snow with crunchy steps, Bella paused and let her gaze drift towards the deep green of the tree line in the distance. The last time she had stood outside quietly contemplating the snow had been at Ashley's wedding, huddled next to Jack in the gazebo. What she would give to revisit that moment! Closing her eyes, she took a deep breath and wished herself there. The glow of the barn lights in the darkness. The inquisitive robin. The mistletoe. Their fantastic kiss.

Bella sighed. The only thing missing from their encounter had been the opportunity to make snow angels, which was a pity. She had a feeling Jack would have enjoyed it and she would have loved hearing him laugh. But … perhaps it wasn't too late.

Bella opened her eyes and surveyed the deep layer of snow all around her. It put the dusting of flakes on the patio at the reception last year to shame. *This* snow here would be perfect for making snow angels. In fact—

'Bella!'

Bella spun round to face Jack as he jogged from the office building towards her and, as he drew nearer, her latest idea brought a mischievous smile to her lips.

'Hey.' Jack halted a few steps from her. 'The van will be ready in about five minutes. Ben's been brilliant. He wouldn't let me pay for the tree. I told him the Fair was raising money for the children's hospice and I think he may have taken pity on me when he saw this costume and— Are you all right?'

In reply, Bella stretched her arms out to her sides and threw herself backwards.

Whoompf! The thick carpet of snow caught her, cushioning her fall. She grinned up at Jack's wide eyes and open mouth. 'Hurry up or I'll be forced to begin making this angel without you.'

Jack shook his head, but his lips twitched into a smile as he paced a safe distance to Bella's side and, with straight legs and back, tipped back until he dropped into the snow like a felled tree.

Bella giggled as she closed her eyes and rowed her arms up and down to carve the angel's wings out of snow at her sides while flicking her legs together and apart to create the base of its gown. The muscles in her limbs soon tired, but her face ached more from smiling. She sighed and turned her head towards Jack, only for her gaze to collide with his as he rolled his face towards her. His grin was as big as hers, the sparkle in his dark eyes dancing.

'If anyone saw us now, they'd think we'd lost it,' Bella said.

'Probably.' Holding her stare, Jack moved his arm down from above his head, tracing the wide circle of his angel's wing until his outstretched fingers brushed against Bella's, causing her to startle at the sudden contact. And his warmth. She had forgotten how warm he was, even lying in snow.

Craving more of him—and not wanting him to read her surprise as dislike of his touch—Bella bent her fingers slowly and was thrilled when Jack did the same, leaving their fingers curled around each other.

She rolled her face back to the sky, closed her eyes and

released a deep sigh, her breath spiralling up in a coil of mist. And as she breathed in, she felt strangely weightless and rested, as though she had put down a heavy load she hadn't known she was carrying. Perhaps she was on the verge of achieving the sort of transcendent state mentioned in her meditation podcasts, a feeling of oneness with the universe. *Or perhaps*, her brain pointed out, *you're entering the early stages of hypothermia and should get up, you idiot.*

She opened her eyes and turned to Jack. His eyes were closed and his lips were curled in a quiet smile of contentment. 'Jack?' Bella's voice sounded muffled and, unsure she had spoken aloud, she squeezed Jack's fingers as she tried again. 'Jack?'

'Hmn?'

'I think we should get up. Before we freeze.'

Jack opened his eyes. 'Now you mention it, I may have lost some feeling in my toes.'

'Hand up?'

'Absolutely.'

They rolled towards each other and, gripping each other's elbows, slowly rose to standing. The process involved what may have been an unnecessary amount of giggling and grappling. Though, if asked, Bella would have sworn all the groping of Jack's forearms and biceps had been entirely justified to stop her falling.

'Why do I feel like I'm doing all the work here?' Jack asked between chuckles.

'What?' Bella feigned indignation. 'I'll have you know my low centre of gravity is probably the only thing preventing us from ending up on our backsides.'

'In that case I'd best hang on to you until we're back at the car,' said Jack, reaching down to wrap his hand around Bella's, her small fingers easily fitting against his large palm. 'For balance.'

'Exactly. Think of me like one of those penguin support aid things that they have for kids learning to ice-skate.'

Jack guffawed. 'I have to say I've never thought of you in that way before.'

'Really?' Bella pressed her lips together, struggling to school her features into a serious expression while her insides fizzed at the idea that Jack had potentially been thinking of her in other ways. 'Surely the resemblance is uncanny?'

'Hmn.' Jack made a show of inspecting Bella, running his gaze from the top of her head to her feet. 'I don't recall ever seeing one of those penguin aids in high heels.'

'Then I'm glad to have given you that mental image.' Bella's lips twitched before slipping into a smile, the effort at keeping a straight face too great. 'As the obviously far stronger person here, it's only right that I support you in all your six-foot-four daintiness.'

'Thanks. I appreciate it.'

'You're welcome.'

They trudged back to the car, Bella staring at their joined hands as sparks skipped along her arm, making her skin prickle pleasantly. She glanced up and met Jack's gaze, feeling the glow of his beaming smile shining on her, reminding her of the absent sun.

'We didn't take a picture of our angels,' Jack said.

'Never mind.' Bella shrugged. 'Although Summer would have loved to see a photo. She used to enjoy making

295

snow angels when she was little.' Bella glanced up at Jack and mirrored his smile, though there was a damp note in her happiness. Thoughts of Summer had reminded her of the promise she had made her sister. And, even though her sister had revealed herself to be a despicable bully, Bella always kept her promises.

Dammit. Their tree-finding mission was going so well, why should she ruin it by mentioning Ethan?

Because this is an ideal opportunity, her brain chimed in. *And the longer you don't tell him, the weirder it'll be when you do.*

'I hope the heater in Ben's van is decent.' Jack shivered and tightened his grip on Bella's fingers. 'This Santa costume looks great, but it definitely wasn't designed for lying in the snow.'

Bella gazed at Jack's relaxed, contented expression as he continued to ramble about his costume. The thought of doing or saying anything to wipe the smile from his face was not a happy one but, while her inner voice was always annoying, it wasn't often wrong. She should tell him.

'Wendy's done an amazing job,' Jack continued. 'I wasn't sure about the—'

'I wasn't entirely honest with you.' Bella blurted the words, knowing it was something she had to do quickly, like ripping off a sticking plaster. 'About why I was in the church, last year, at Ashley's wedding.'

Jack shifted so they were face to face and Bella's heart ached as a deep crease of concern appeared above the bridge of his nose. 'OK,' he said and gave Bella's hand an encouraging squeeze. 'Why were you really in Haileybrook that day?'

Chapter 39

Bella took a deep breath, aiming to get through what followed in one flurry of words. 'I told you a friend of mine was thinking of getting married there. But it wasn't a friend. It was me. I was going to get married there. Actually—fun fact—I should have got married there a few days after Ashley and, uh, Ethan—I've mentioned Ethan, my ex-boyfriend—well, he was my ex-fiancé.'

'Oh.' Jack's frown lifted. 'What happened? I mean'—his eyes widened, as if he was horrified he'd asked the obvious question—'it's none of my business if you don't want to—'

'No, it's OK.' Bella bit her lower lip, steeling herself. She'd only told the whole story twice before: once to Kate and once to Lucinda. And both times she'd ended up sobbing. That was *not* going to happen today. She'd stick to the facts and leave emotion out of it. 'We'd booked the church. It was Ethan's choice of venue and date. I'd have liked to have had the ceremony and reception in the same place, ideally somewhere with lots of outdoor space, and in summer so it would be warm.'

'Somewhere with room for that helter-skelter, bouncy castle and ice cream truck,' Jack said, his voice low and gentle.

'Exactly.' Bella smiled, pleased he had remembered her description of her dream wedding. 'But I was happy if he was happy. And life was so stressful, the wedding on the horizon was one of the few things keeping me going. But then ...'

It had all gone horribly wrong and her dreams of wedded bliss had crumbled to ash.

Bella didn't know if her thoughts had shown on her face, but Jack released her hand and slid his arm around her shoulders, drawing her close to him, sheltering her from the biting wind which was nipping her cheeks. Grateful for the gesture, Bella took a moment to rest her head against Jack's chest and breathe in his familiar scent, letting the sweet mince pie aroma from his costume revive her.

Leaving her cheek against the soft wool of his coat, she continued, 'Ethan was delighted when his big brother—Reece—agreed to be his best man. Reece is Ethan's only sibling and he'd always idolized him. I was happy too because Reece and I had got on from the first time we met. He was a nice guy, is a nice guy, it's not like he's dead or anything.' Although there were a few time she'd wished he was. Bella shuddered as she dismissed the memory. 'Then, in the spring before the wedding, Reece pulled out. Said he couldn't commit to the best man duties. Ethan was devastated and suspicious, but asked an old friend to replace his brother as best man—Paul, the man's a total arse, but that's another story. Anyway, Ethan wouldn't leave Reece alone about it. I think he suspected Reece didn't approve of the wedding because he hated me. And so he prodded and poked until Reece told him the truth.' Bella swallowed and raised her gaze to meet Jack's. 'Reece's problem was how he felt about me. But he didn't *hate* me.'

Jack's lips parted and he blinked as realization dawned. 'Oh,' he breathed, the single syllable containing both sympathy and horror.

'Yep. He'd fallen in love with me. The big idiot.' Bella sighed as she remembered the night almost two years ago when Ethan had told her. It had been while they'd been staying with Ethan's family for Christmas. Amid all the fun and festivities, Bella had been unable to wrap her head around what he was telling her and it had taken him a while to convince her she wasn't the victim of an elaborate prank. 'And I think we could have got past it. If Ethan and I had gone ahead with the wedding as planned, sure, Reece would have been upset, but eventually he'd have moved on, right? Met someone else, been happy, wondered what he'd ever seen in me. And, you know, maybe there was something I could have said to him to help him—' Bella paused and screwed her eyes shut, preparing herself for the worst part of the story.

Jack must have sensed it was coming because he began to draw slow calming circles on the top of her arm with his fingers. It was a small gesture and it helped. Jack cleared his throat and, in a gentle voice little more than a whisper, said, 'It wasn't your job to fix the situation. It wasn't your fault.'

Bella sighed. 'I wish Ethan had seen it that way. But he just couldn't get past it. We spent months circling back to the same argument and then, during our last fight, he said … he said *I* must have done something to Reece. That I must have been too friendly or too flirty with his brother. Basically, while he didn't say the exact words, he made it clear he didn't consider Reece's feelings to be his own responsibility, but that it had to be all my fault. At one point he even tried to blame the way I dress.'

Jack's hand had stilled and every line of his posture had snapped taut. With her ear pressed to his chest, Bella could hear his heart racing. He cleared his throat again. 'What did you say to that?'

'I asked him if he wanted me to dress in a nun's habit and Crocs every time I left the house.' Bella sniffed, confident she could blame the tears in her eyes on the cold air. 'I may have thrown in a few expletives as well.'

'Good. What did he say?'

'I think he realized pretty bloody quickly what he'd said was total nonsense and tried to back-pedal, but the damage was done. We stayed together for another couple of months, but he clearly couldn't get past it and I couldn't forgive him for having even thought that of me, let alone having voiced it.'

'The trust was gone.'

'Exactly.' Bella glanced up. Jack's comment had been delivered in the flat, certain tone of one who had lived a similar experience. Bella wondered if he would ever want to tell her about his and Ashley's break-up. If he did, she would be happy to listen. 'And, the worst of it was, I couldn't simply hate him. Reece had put him in a position where he felt he had to choose between loyalty to his brother or to me and I think about how I feel about Summer, how I'd do anything for her—'

'He could have handled it a lot better,' said Jack, giving Bella's arm a reassuring squeeze.

'Agreed. I think even he would agree with that. Like I said, he was genuinely sorry.' She sniffed again, but was pleased her eyes had dried. Though a faint trickle of regret slithered down her spine, it appeared the story of the demise of her and Ethan's almost seven-year relationship had finally lost its power to upset her.

A flutter of wings made Bella jump. She flinched away from Jack's arm as a robin swooped low over her head and landed on the roof of her car. Bella lifted a hand to her pounding heart. It was only a bird. A kamikaze dive-bombing avian menace of a bird, but just a bird nonetheless.

As if it were able to read her mind, the robin shook its feathers and puffed out its red breast, striking an indignant pose. It stared at Bella, and its black beady eyes reminded her of another reason she had wanted to tell Jack about Ethan, aside from her promise to Summer.

Keeping her voice low so as not to scare the robin away, she reached out for Jack's hand and, gripping the ends of his fingers, said, 'I wanted to tell you about what happened with Ethan because it partly explains why I left the wedding last Christmas. I had to run because Summer called asking me to send her money and she couldn't wait. But that wasn't the only reason.' Bella closed her eyes and took a steadying breath. 'I know me leaving made you believe that I didn't value our time together, that it didn't mean anything to me. But that's not true.' Bella held Jack's gaze, pleased to see the tiny curl at the edges of his mouth. 'It was wonderful. But I wasn't ready to be getting involved with anyone else. What had happened with

Ethan—though we'd been broken up for a few months—at the time of Ashley's wedding, it was still too ...' *Raw* was the word that immediately came to mind, but Bella dismissed it as sounding a tad melodramatic. 'I wasn't over it yet. I wouldn't have been good for anybody and I felt you deserved better. In fact, you deserve the best.'

Bella was encouraged as the suggestion of a smile at the corner of Jack's lips stretched a little wider. She shrugged, relieved she'd said what she needed to. She'd done her part. Now Jack had to decide what he wanted.

'So that's my sad story,' she said. 'Now you know I'm a total disaster and if you'd rather not have lunch with me or if you'd prefer to keep your distance at work, I get it.'

Jack blinked rapidly. 'I don't—' He paused, his forehead creasing in a deep frown. 'You're not a disaster. And I wanted to say—'

Bella's phone trilled, the noise sending the robin—who had been calmly observing their conversation—darting towards the trees. 'Sorry,' Bella said, fumbling in her pocket for her phone while mentally cursing the caller's terrible timing. She was tempted to silence the ringer and turn her phone off, but it might be Summer calling to say she'd let the bath overflow or started a fire in the kitchen or— Oh. *Great.* 'It's Lavender.'

'You'd better answer it,' said Jack. 'She'll keep calling until you do.'

'I'll put it on speaker.' Bella swiped to accept the call. 'Hi Lavender, how are—'

'Bella! Do you have a tree?'

'Don't worry,' Bella said in her best calming tone. 'Jack got us a tree and we'll be on our way back soon.'

'Now!' The shout was so shrill that Jack and Bella both instinctively recoiled from the phone. 'You must come back immediately.'

'But it's not even half past twelve,' said Jack, possibly hoping to do a better job than Bella at lowering Lavender's blood pressure. 'We should be back by half past one, which will mean there's lots of time—'

'No. Wendy and Iris have gone off in a tizzy because Wendy has mislaid her rainy day money or some nonsense, and there's still no sign of Trevor. We're short-handed. I'll need Bella to help decorate the tree!' This last statement was delivered in a tone that suggested Lavender regarded letting Bella anywhere near the tree as a sign of the End of Days. 'And Jack, there's so much to sort out for the grotto. Get back here.' There was a pause, during which Bella and Jack exchanged worried glances, then—perhaps having realized her tone was rather short—Lavender added, 'Thank you,' before hanging up.

Bella and Jack stared at each other, wearing similar unblinking, stunned expressions. Jack recovered first. 'OK then,' he said. 'I'll get the van and head straight back to Haileybrook. I wouldn't want to be responsible for Lavender having a heart attack.'

'Of course,' said Bella, her voice wobbling, betraying her uncertainty. For while, rationally, she knew Jack was right, an unpleasant heavy feeling had settled around her heart which was hard to ignore: disappointment. Lavender's call had put paid to their lunch plans and, although a quick bite at a motorway service station was hardly a romantic first date, Bella had been looking forward to it. Also, had Jack been a bit too quick to accept the urgency of Lavender's summons? Did he seem relieved? Was he using Lavender's call as an excuse to get out of their lunch date?

If you want to know, ask him! her heart urged.

No. Perhaps he needs some space to process all the Ethan stuff you dumped on him. And we're trying to be less impulsive, remember? chimed in her brain.

But he likes that we're straightforward, her heart countered, skipping at the memory of Jack's compliment. *Ask him!*

Jack laid a hand gently against the top of Bella's arm, jolting her out of her thoughts. 'See you back at the Fair,' he said and, as he strode across the snow towards the office, he added, 'I'll be the one in the white wig and red suit.'

With a cheerfulness as fake as her smile, Bella called, 'Wouldn't miss it!' and waited until he was safely inside to let her head thud against the side of her car. Ugh! Why couldn't she catch a break? She shuddered, a sudden chill racing into her bones, driving her to hurry inside her car and turn the heater to maximum. Frowning, she watched the windscreen wipers sweeping back and forth, batting ineffectually against the unrelenting snowfall. It was pathetic, she knew, but Bella identified with those wipers. She had never been superstitious but, given how many calamities the universe had been throwing her way lately— and they seemed to keep coming despite all her efforts to be a more calm, tolerant person—a small part of her was beginning to wonder if she was cursed.

Chapter 40

By the time Bella arrived back at the community centre, the tree had been unloaded and installed in a corner of the main hall. Jack had vanished, presumably to take up residence in the grotto, not that Bella had much time to wonder about his whereabouts. She had barely set foot in the building when Lavender ordered her to help decorate the tree. Any thoughts of a pub lunch with Summer swiftly became a distant dream.

When Bella finally got home, the hours she'd spent immersed in a nutmeg-scented riot of glitter and laughter, combined with a shortage of food and drink, had left her with a thumping headache. One which wasn't eased by Summer's inquisition, which began before she'd closed the front door.

'How did it go?' From her perch in the corner of the sofa, Summer jabbed at the remote control to mute the television and twisted to face Bella. 'Blimey! What's all that?'

Bella staggered over the threshold, straining not to drop the huge box sliding out of her weakening grip.

'Decorations,' she said as she parked the box by the foot of the stairs and shook her aching arms. 'There were tonnes left over after the Fair and Lavender insisted I take these.'

'Brilliant. This place could do with a bit of sparkle.' Summer skipped across the room and opened the box. 'But to return to my previous question: how did it go?'

'Really well. The Brookfield's ladies raised almost double the amount taken at the village Spring Fayre. Lavender is ecstatic. And, according to Trevor, when word got out of how much money they'd made, Grace Harman stormed out of the community centre looking like "she'd been slapped with a wet kipper", which made Lavender even happier.'

'That's great.' Summer looped a string of red tinsel around her neck like a festive boa. 'But I meant, how was the tree-finding mission?'

'Fine.' Bella turned to hang up her coat, pleased for the excuse to hide her face. Summer was angling for gossip about her relationship with Jack, but their visit to the tree farm had left Bella confused and she had nothing certain to tell her sister. She needed to ponder Jack's reactions to what she had told him about Ethan, a task made difficult by the throbbing ache at the back of her skull. Serious pain medication and a long bath would help. Having to regale her sister with the minute details of her and Jack's time together would not. 'We got a tree. Lavender was happy.' Bella shrugged. 'Job done.'

'Fine? Job done? Ugh!' Summer rolled her eyes. 'Don't hold out on me! How did it go with Jack? Did you tell him about Ethan?'

'Yes.'

'And?

Bella blew out her cheeks, exhaling slowly as she remembered Jack's sympathetic words and his warm, reassuring embrace. 'He was really understanding.'

But he may also have backed out of a date with me at top speed on discovering that I'm damaged goods, she added silently.

'You see? I knew it.' Summer grinned and wrapped another strand of tinsel around her neck. 'We can go to the pub for dinner and you can tell me all the— Are you OK?'

'My head's killing me.' Bella pressed her fingers to her temples and rubbed the pangs which had appeared there. No doubt stirred by guilt. She had failed to take Summer to lunch and now dinner. What sort of a host was she? 'I'm going to take some pills and head for the bath and then later we could—'

'Don't worry about me. I can take care of myself.' Summer knelt and took a green garland out of the box. 'Go ahead, I'll unpack all this.'

'Right.' A woozy sensation joined the pain in Bella's head as she imagined Summer randomly throwing clumps of decorations all over the living room in a chaotic festive mess like she had when she was a teenager. Back then Bella had waited until her sister was asleep and then swept in to straighten everything out. 'I'll see if I feel any better after a rest and we could put some decorations up later. Or tomorrow. Maybe order a pizza—'

'Bel! Go get your pills and have a bath. I'm fine. Oh, look!' Summer held up a sprig of mistletoe in front of a wide grin of delight.

Bella, who had one foot on the bottom stair, grabbed

the banister rail for support. 'Iris insisted I take that. I told her it would be a waste, but she wouldn't listen.'

'I like the sound of Iris. She's clearly a romantic.'

'She's great and less scary than Lavender. But'—Bella paused, glaring at the mistletoe which Iris must have smuggled into the box after her bout of suggestive eyebrow waggling—'she's also an interfering unreasonable optimist.'

Summer glanced up from the mistletoe and fixed Bella with a significant stare. 'And aren't those people just the worst?'

'Hey!' Bella would have been offended by what her sister was insinuating, but she was too unwell to summon the strength. 'I'm a benign interventionist realist.'

Summer snorted. 'Whatever. We can hang it tomorrow. Get up to the bath.'

Thirty minutes later and the industrial-strength painkillers Bella had dug out from what she thought of her 'London stash' had eased the pounding in her head. But the dim peace of the bathroom, the steam haze above the scalding water and the flickering glow of candlelight failed to soothe away all the lingering tension in her muscles. She would have to face Summer eventually and she already knew what her sister was going to ask her: what was her next move with Jack?

Maybe she should text him? Send him a light, witty message to check his time as Santa had left him unscathed. Something that said, *'I'm interested and I care, but I won't be crushed if you think I'm a liability you'd do well to avoid.'*

An insistent tapping sound drew Bella's gaze to the side of the bath, where she found her nails rapping against the porcelain. Ugh. Perhaps she should give controlled breathing for relaxation another try? What was it? Breathe in for four, hold for four—

A series of thuds from downstairs made Bella startle, sending a wave of water sloshing dangerously close to the rim of the tub.

'I'm OK!' Summer's yell carried up the stairs. 'I didn't break anything!'

Bella groaned and reached for her towel. What kind of havoc was Summer wreaking downstairs? And how much worse would any destruction get in the time it took Bella to get there?

Bella shuddered as she wrapped the towel around herself and stepped out of the bath. She loved her sister. More than anything. But a small part of her wondered how soon Summer might be setting off to Brazil and leaving her alone to relax in her quiet cottage haven.

Chapter 41

Bella's mood had significantly improved by Sunday afternoon. A blissful lie-in followed by a hearty roast lunch at the Cross Keys—during which Summer was too busy eating to ask her questions about Jack—had renewed Bella's festive zeal and all thoughts of a Christmas curse had long gone. Her headache had also vanished and, as she sang along to a playlist of Christmas classics while stringing tinsel along the living room curtain pole, Bella found herself so full of the joy of the season she decided she would go into work early on Monday and use the last of the decorations from Lavender to brighten up the office.

Bella moved the stepladder to below the archway between the living room and kitchen and set about rehanging the mistletoe. The previous evening Summer had slipped in her attempt to stick the sprig to the ceiling after clambering onto a wobbly kitchen chair.

Bella stepped down to the floor and smiled as she stared up at the cluster of white berries. Iris was a terrible meddler, but Bella had to admire her optimism in gifting her the mistletoe. Honestly, what was the likelihood of anyone Bella wanted to kiss visiting her cottage over Christmas? Especially now she'd told Jack about what happened between her and Ethan and—

Enough. Bella shook her head, making another futile effort to banish Jack from her thoughts. What she needed was a distraction. Perhaps a Christmas movie? With hot chocolate and marshmallows? Summer had always enjoyed that when she was younger—

'That looks good.'

Bella turned towards Summer's voice to find her sister at the bottom of the stairs, her backpack at her feet. She gestured in the direction of the bag. 'Going somewhere?'

'I told you. London, then Brazil.'

'Yes. You did tell me, but …' Bella pressed her lips together. Summer's defensive tone suggested she'd taken Bella's question as an accusation when it had only meant to express surprise. Summer's visit had been a shock and delivered more drama than Bella was looking for at this stage in her life, but today she'd felt her sister was finally settling in. The cottage would be very quiet without her. 'It's just … You only got here on Thursday.'

'Don't worry. I've been here long enough to be able to report back to Dad and tell him you definitely haven't gone crazy and everything's great. That should get him off both our backs.' Summer shrugged. 'And I've had loads of messages from the guys who are going to Brazil. They're already in London and want me to join them so we can plan flights. There's not much time if we're going to make it for Christmas. So …'

Summer's bags were packed. And Bella knew her well

311

enough to know her mind was made up. But couldn't she stay the rest of the day? 'It's dark out now. Why not stay until tomorrow? And how are you getting to London?'

'This will blow your mind, Bel, but there are these things called trains. And they run even when the sun has gone down.'

'Ha ha. The closest station is Norton which is a twenty-minute drive. Let me take you.'

'I'll book a taxi.'

'Please, I'd like to drive you.'

Summer chewed her lower lip. 'OK. If it's not a bother.'

'No bother. Are you sure you couldn't go tomorrow? It'd be safer travelling in daylight—'

'Bella, stop! I'm not a kid any more.' Summer raked a hand through her hair and muttered, 'You don't need to look after me. I don't want to be a burden.'

Bella opened and closed her mouth, lost for words. Summer was a globetrotting young woman, one who was clearly able to take care of herself. But right then— in Summer's slumped shoulders and scowl—Bella saw shadows of the devastated ten-year-old who missed her mum. Her heart twisting, Bella stepped forwards and placed a hand on Summer's shoulder. 'You have never been a burden. You're my sister.'

'You shouldn't have had to look after me.'

'True.' Bella nodded. 'But I didn't *have* to do anything. You know me. Do you think I would have plaited your hair if I didn't want to?'

Summer huffed a laugh. 'No. You'd have told me to tie the bloody stuff up in a ponytail and stop bothering you.'

'That sounds about right.' Bella smiled and, deciding to

risk it, wrapped her arms around Summer, marvelling for the umpteenth time at how such a little girl had managed to grow past her to the heady heights of five foot four.

'If I'm here, I'm just giving you more work to do,' Summer said, her voice muffled against Bella's neck.

Bella inhaled slowly, adding the vanilla scent of Summer's perfume to the mixture of sensations making her head light. Was that why Summer was always on the move? Was that why she had missed Dad's wedding and last Christmas?

'You are not work,' she said. 'I've had a few jobs in my time and being with you is nothing like work, I promise.' She pulled back to look Summer square in the eye. 'Dad and I, we want to spend time with you. We love you and we miss you. And Marion and Lucinda, and Lucinda's brother Michael—I've only met him a couple of times— they would all love to meet you in person. Video calling doesn't quite measure up.'

Summer's raised her head, revealing cornflower-blue eyes brimming with tears. 'I wouldn't want them to be disappointed.'

'Impossible.' Bella spoke with genuine conviction. 'You're amazing. And they're smart people.'

Summer laughed. 'That's good to know.'

Bella gave Summer another squeeze. Oh, she had missed her! It would have been so wonderful to have her around when she and Ethan had been crashing and burning in slow motion. But, as she clearly wanted Bella to acknowledge, Summer was a grown woman who didn't need her big sister holding her back.

'So when do you need a lift to the station?' asked Bella.

'There's a train in about forty minutes.'

'Wow.' Bella blinked, marvelling that she was surprised that Summer was leaving as swiftly as she had arrived. 'So do you want to go now?'

'If you don't mind.'

'No, that's fine. Let me get my boots.' Bella sat on the bottom step and slid her right foot into a boot. 'You know, if you change your mind and fancy a Christmas here in the middle of nowhere, you'd be very welcome.'

Summer pushed her left arm into her coat. 'Tempting, but I've given my word to these guys and I can't pull out now. You get it, right?'

Bella, who believed in showing up and detested those who went back on their word, had to admit defeat. 'OK. But if you change your mind about Brazil and want to come here for Christmas, you'd be very welcome.

'And if you suddenly decide you fancy Christmas in Brazil, call me.'

Though the idea of a warm Christmas, sunning herself on a Brazilian beach, had a certain appeal, it didn't fit with Bella's plan for self-renewal. 'I spent last Christmas in southern Spain and another two months there after I left London. Call me crazy, but I fancy a cold, snowy Christmas.' She shrugged, deciding not to tell Summer that she had also planned to spend it on her own. Another part of her new start. Which reminded her. 'I've been meaning to say, thanks for the meditation podcast recommendations.'

'I'm so glad you listened to them.' Summer crouched to tie her laces, bringing her gaze on a level with Bella's. She tilted her head to one side as she held Bella's stare and her smile turned sly. 'Hey, if you're going to be here in

Haileybrook this Christmas and Jack's going to be here too …' Summer trailed off, letting her one raised eyebrow do the talking.

Bella closed her eyes so Summer wouldn't see her rolling them. 'He won't be here. He has some skiing thing with his friends every year.'

'You could do that too.'

'Me?' Bella zipped up her second boot and let out a huff of incredulity. 'On skis?'

'Why not?'

'Can you buy heeled ski boots?'

'Don't be silly. Your height would be a strength. Your low centre of gravity would make you super stable.'

The sisters stood and Bella poked Summer in the ribs. 'Oi! That's enough of your cheek. Here.' Bella reached past Summer to retrieve her wool hat and scarf from the coat hooks. She looped the scarf around Summer's neck and pulled the hat down over her golden hair. 'You can leave them in London. But this way you won't freeze on your way there.'

Above the coil of scarlet wool, Summer's mouth formed an O of disbelief. 'But you love that scarf! And won't this leave you cold?'

Bella shrugged. 'I'll be fine. I have another hat upstairs somewhere and Kate got me a scarf a couple of Christmases ago so I'll—' Bella paused. Summer's bottom lip was wobbling and her eyes had filled with tears. Oh Lord, what had she said now? 'Summer? What's wrong?'

Summer used the heel of her hand to swipe a tear from her cheek. 'Nothing, I'm fine. Thank you again.' She sniffed. 'I … I don't think I've always been as grateful to you as I should.'

Oh. Bella's eyebrows rose. She had imagined, in the unlikely scenario that Summer should ever give her a sincere thank you, she would feel elated. But there was no joy to be had in watching her little sister cry.

'Come here,' said Bella, pulling Summer into another hug. 'You're welcome. And, if it'll make you feel better, you can buy me a fabulous new hat and scarf in Brazil.'

Summer sniffed again and nodded. Bella gave her an encouraging smile. 'Come on.' There was no point in lingering in the hallway until they were both blubbering wrecks. 'If you've got everything, let's go. Unless you'd like some gingerbread for the journey. Or there are definitely some of Wendy's mince pies around—'

'Um, actually,' said Summer, 'if it's not being incredibly cheeky ...'

Bella took her coat down from the hook and held her breath, certain that whatever Summer was about to say, it would be incredibly cheeky.

'As you've always been so supportive,' Summer continued, a wheedling note creeping into her voice, 'if I didn't have quite enough money for my ticket for Brazil, could you lend me—'

'No.'

Summer's brow shot upwards and her jaw dropped. An expression Bella understood as her reply had shocked herself as much as her sister. But, then again, Bella had been mulling over the wisdom of continually bailing her sister out for quite some time. And how could she expect Summer to change her behaviour if she didn't change hers?

'Sorry.' Bella winced. She hasn't meant to snap her reply. 'I love you, Summer. And I would do anything for you, but I can't keep giving you money.'

Summer's gaze narrowed. 'So you'd do anything for me except lend me a bit of cash every now and then?'

Bella sighed. Oh well. At least Summer's switch to sarcasm was going to make it easier for her to stick to her guns. 'If you've got a real emergency of course I'll send you money. And you have no right to be shirty with me. You're the one who said you didn't need looking after.'

Summer's scowl twisted into a pensive pout. 'But how am I supposed to know what qualifies as an emergency?'

'Easy.' Bella had given that a lot of thought too. 'Ask yourself: "Would I ask Dad for money for this?" I mean, would you call Dad right now and ask him to part-fund a plane ticket to Brazil?'

Summer snorted. 'No way. I'd never hear the end of it.'

'Exactly. All you have to do it apply the "Dad test" and you'll know. And if you want any advice on budgeting—'

'No, God, spare me. I get it. I'll try. I promise.'

'Great.' Bella reached past Summer, opened the front door and motioned for her sister to go first. 'After you.'

Summer stepped onto the front step and paused, turning back to meet Bella's gaze. 'I don't suppose, as it's Christmas, I could start trying out the Dad test thing after I get a ticket to Bra—'

'Out!' Bella bustled over the threshold, encouraging Summer to step into the light dusting of snow on the garden path. She kept her tone serious, but she struggled to stop a smile lifting the corners of her mouth as she said, 'Don't test the limits of my festive goodwill or you'll be getting a bus to the station. Let's go.'

Chapter 42

At five minutes to nine on Monday morning, Bella sank into her desk chair and leant back to admire her handiwork. Colourful paper chains hung above the window and door frames. Tinsel edged the countertop in the corner kitchen. A dwarf fir tree, draped in lights and baubles, brightened the corner behind the door. The office wasn't exactly a winter wonderland, but it was colourful and vibrant.

Bella spun her chair in a slow circle—the subtle silver thread running through her forest-green sweater catching the light—and decided she didn't care if Ms Chan ordered her to take down all the decorations before the morning was out. Come to think of it—she grabbed a pad of Post-its and pen and scribbled a note to herself—there were only five more days at work before the office closed until the new year. Plenty of time to organize a Secret Santa or a trip to the pub. If she made some suggestions to Ms Chan, Jack would probably back up her ideas, wouldn't he?

Jack. Bella sighed as she wrote his name on a new Post-it and underlined it. Despite having Summer to keep her busy, her thoughts had continued to circle back to him after their tree-finding mission. Her heart had urged her to message or call him or—at its most outrageous—go round to his house and ask him if he wanted to reschedule their lunch date. Summer would definitely have supported that suggestion. But her brain had reminded her that she should give him time. If he was still interested in dating her, he would let her know.

And while Bella—who was not a naturally patient person—had applied all the techniques she had recently learned to stop herself from contacting Jack, none of them had stopped her dwelling on memories of his brilliant smile, alluring scent, warm embrace—

'Morning.'

Jack stood in the doorway, looking devastatingly dashing in a perfectly fitted navy suit, powder-blue shirt and dark green tie which—extra points for subtle and stylish festiveness—was covered in rows of tiny silver snowflakes.

'Hi,' Bella managed to answer, her voice indecently breathy and her cheeks warming as her gaze roved over Jack's handsome face and strong, trim silhouette. 'You're looking sharp today.'

'You approve?' Jack undid the button of his jacket and did a slow spin, which he no doubt intended to be funny, but only made the blush in Bella's cheeks spread to the rest of her face. The back view was … well, it was pretty perfect and she wouldn't mind—

'Bella?'

Oh crap. She'd been ogling him. Not cool, Bella. She had to say something. Something friendly and fun and in no way lewd or inappropriate. 'I do approve,' she said, taking the opportunity to appreciate his appearance openly. 'You weren't tempted to stick with the red suit with the fur trim?'

Jack chuckled. 'I'm not sure our cleaning services supplier would appreciate me turning up to our contract review dressed as Santa. They might get the impression I'm not taking it seriously. Although'—he glanced about him, taking in Bella's changes to the office—'I think it would help me fit in here. Did you do this?'

Bella nodded. 'Lavender gave me a tonne of decorations from the Christmas Fair. I decorated my place and then it seemed a shame not to put up a few things in here.'

'It looks good.' Jack's smile slipped. 'Sorry I didn't see you after the Fair. I got swept up in helping dismantle the grotto. Some of the parts were heavy and I couldn't leave the ladies to struggle with them.'

'I know, it's fine. I was grabbed too. Lavender asked me to help her with all the money. Although I'm pleased to say, after what happened with the summer garden party funds, she is keeping hold of them until they can be safely banked.'

'Right.' Jack nodded. 'Bella, I wanted to talk to you about something.'

'Is it about Secret Santa? Or going on an office Christmas lunch or drink after work on Friday?'

'Uh, no. Actually I have to go straight to the airport from here on Friday.' Jack shrugged. 'Apparently they're expecting a lot of snow on the route to the ski resort, so it's important we head out early.'

'Of course,' Bella said as a cold shiver ran down her

spine. 'You can't miss your flight.' She grabbed her pen and dipped her head over her Post-its. With a flourish, she crossed the Friday drink idea from her list, grateful for the chance to hide her face which likely had disappointment written all over it.

'I wanted to talk to you about something else,' said Jack, approaching her desk.

Glancing up from her notes, Bella took in his furrowed brow and the muscles flexing in his jaw. Oh heck, he had more bad news for her, didn't he?

Jack tapped his fingers on the edge of the desk and said, 'Summer mentioned your house was cold. I could come and take a look at the boiler, see if it's something I can fix.'

What? *That* was what he was struggling to say? Bemused, Bella stuttered a reply, 'No, no. You don't have to do that.' She scratched her neck which was growing hot and itchy in response to a vivid mental image of Jack strutting about the cottage in a fitted black T-shirt, his tool belt slung about his hips ... Bella glanced down at the notepad on her desk and wondered if it would look weird if she used it to fan herself. 'It's a very kind offer, but the boiler seems to work and Cath did say I could call her if anything went wrong with it. So, thank you, but please don't worry.'

'Right.' Jack nodded and dropped his gaze to the floor. He balled his fingers into fists. 'Actually, I don't know why I said that. I mean, I do. I do want to help with your boiler, but that's not what I wanted to talk to you about.'

'It wasn't?'

Jack shook his head. 'The other day at the tree farm you were honest, admirably honest, about some very personal things ...'

Ah. Here it comes, thought Bella, her insides flip-flopping in a tumble of queasy somersaults. Here's the speech. Jack's moment to tell her she seemed like a nice person but was too damaged to get involved with.

Jack looked up, meeting Bella's eye to deliver the killer blow. 'And in return, I wanted to say—'

'Good morning, John,' Ms Chan marched into the office, her black skirt suit and expression appropriately grave for a Monday morning. 'I need to speak with you.' She turned to face Jack, giving her back to Bella.

Bella bristled at Ms Chan's interruption. How rude! She hadn't expected her manager to turn up and be full of effusive praise for Bella's office decorating skills, but surely a 'good morning' was a minimum? And blanking her and then turning her back on her was a new level of frosty, even for Ms Chan. Although, it was probably best the woman couldn't see the irritation and frustration beaming out of Bella's eyes.

'Of course,' said Jack, effortlessly polite in the face of Ms Chan's lack of polite preamble. How did he do that? Did he have politeness podcasts he could recommend?

Unable to demonstrate the same level of restraint, Bella cleared her throat. Twice.

Ms Chan turned towards the sound and blinked at Bella as if she was remembering she was there. 'Are you quite well, Bella?' Ms Chan took a small step back, her nose wrinkling in distaste. 'Your eyes look watery. You don't have a cold, do you?'

A part of Bella was tempted to fake sneeze. She was rather proud that she managed to only go as far as a pointed sniff. 'I'm fine, thank you,' she said, her gaze flicking to the paper chains above the window and tree in the corner. 'It's probably just dust from *the decorations*.'

'Good, good.' Ms Chan nodded, but her gaze was already on her office door, and Bella suspected her manager hadn't heard a word she'd said. 'In that case we'll leave you be. I'm sure you have plenty to be getting on with. John'—she turned and beckoned for Jack to follow her—'we'll use my office.'

Jack trailed Ms Chan into her office and gave Bella an apologetic smile before he closed the door. As the latch clicked into the frame, Bella's smile fell into a frown. Huh. Not a single comment on the decorations. Not even when she'd pointed them out. It was almost as if Ms Chan was distracted. But what could have knocked the laser-focused Ms Chan off balance?

Bella gazed down at her Post-its and tapped her pen against her list. Maybe she could invite Jack to an early Christmas lunch? Perhaps in a quiet corner of the pub he might feel able to tell her—

What was that?

Bella froze, holding her breath as she listened to the sounds on the other side of Ms Chan's office wall. She could have sworn Jack had raised his voice. But that was unlikely, wasn't it? What could he and Ms Chan be talking about which would make him— Hold on. That was definitely Ms Chan's voice and at a far higher volume than normal. What was going on in there?

Bella half rose from her chair and leant forwards, straining to see through the small window into the office. Both Jack's and Ms Chan's faces were hidden from her, but their voices rose and fell in urgent patterns and their gesticulations were fierce.

Bella's pulse skipped in response to the unfolding drama. Should she intervene and attempt to calm the conversation? She could always knock and claim to have been about to make tea or—

The office door flew open and Jack stood in the doorway, glaring back at Ms Chan. His neck and face were flushed and his lips were set in a grim line, his eyes shaded by a deep frown. 'Your position is ridiculous and you'll be hearing from my lawyers,' he growled at their manager, before striding towards Bella.

Bella rose to her feet as Jack marched across the office. Staring at his smouldering glower, she fumbled and dropped her pen, her hands suddenly clumsy. Blimey. Assertive Jack had tremendous, undeniable *power*. 'Jack? What's happened?'

Jack halted by her desk, his chest rising and falling quickly. He planted his hands on his hips and, when his gaze met Bella's, it burned with the heat evident in the rest of his face. 'I've been suspended. Effective immediately. I've been told to pack up and go home.'

Chapter 43

Bella laughed nervously. 'But, that's crazy. What possible reason could there be to suspend you? You're'—*wonderful* and *perfect* were the two words that came first to Bella's mind but, fortunately, having recently practised holding her tongue paid off and instead she said—'a model employee. Everyone loves you.'

'It's a confidential matter.' Ms Chan's voice made Bella whirl round. She had crept out of the office and was standing at Bella's shoulder.

Stuff that. Bella glanced at Jack, her own pulse accelerating in response to his shallow breathing and flushed cheeks. 'Have you signed anything to say you'll keep this matter confidential, Jack?'

Ms Chan stiffened. 'Bella, I'd like to ask you not to get involved—'

'No, I haven't.' Jack straightened and shot Ms Chan a glare which made her close her lips. 'Ms Chan just informed me that some of the residents have had some valuable items go missing. Ms Chan, on behalf of the board, is investigating and …'

Oh dear God Almighty. Bella's breath caught in her throat as she understood why Jack's words had failed him. How on earth could anyone accuse *Jack*—Jack, who didn't have a dishonest bone in his body—of anything criminal? It was preposterous, unjust and so enraging that—meditation, deep breathing and diplomacy be damned—she was going to go up to eleven and to hell with the consequences. Ms Chan didn't know how lucky she was. It was only thanks to some serious calming breaths that Bella resisted the urge to snatch up the string of tinsel draped along the back of her desk and wrap it around her boss's scrawny neck.

She rounded on Ms Chan and, pushing her shoulders back, injected a strand of quiet menace into her voice as she said, 'You've accused Mr Trentham-Whitley Smythe of *stealing?*'

'I, well, not as such.' Ms Chan's hand fluttered to her throat. 'After one of the residents reported a few items missing, I spoke with the board and they felt a swift, quiet resolution to the issue would be for the best.'

'Oh, did they now?' Bella narrowed her eyes, pretty sure her stare could have burned a line through the wall, let alone Ms Chan's conscience. 'Because no one has ever been falsely accused of something when the authorities are in a hurry to close a case, have they?'

'That's not, that is—' Ms Chan huffed, becoming more flustered by the second.

Bella crossed her arms. For the first time she was pleased she had been dragged into so many human resources procedures in her last job. A little employment law jargon could go a long way. 'Ms Chan, what evidence do you have to support your suspension of Mr Trentham-Whitley Smythe? I hope it's good, and by that I mean rock solid. Because if not, you are likely to be in breach of contract and he could claim for constructive dismissal. And, as you've all but accused him of being a thief, any lawyer worth their salt would encourage him to sue you blind for defamation of character.'

'Exactly what I plan to do,' said Jack, giving Bella a sharp nod of encouragement.

Bella returned the gesture, pausing for a moment to let Ms Chan—who was gulping as if trying to swallow a tennis ball—process her first volley, before she continued, 'I'll be more than happy to provide testimony regarding the considerable distress your unfounded accusations have caused him, surely grounds for seeking personal injury compensation. So, on what grounds do you base your suspicions of'—Bella paused, catching herself before she said, *'my client'*. Maybe she'd watched too many law and order dramas recently—'my colleague?'

Ms Chan stuttered, 'I, I don't think I'm at liberty to—'

'Wendy is missing some money and a necklace,' said Jack, who appeared to have found his cool, the colour in his face now a faint pink rather than fiery puce. 'Ms Chan asked her for a list of everyone who had been in her apartment and, of course, I was in there a few times for the costume fittings.'

'That's it?' Bella scoffed. 'Ms Chan, your evidence is entirely circumstantial. And how do you know this isn't a wider problem?'

'Whatever do you mean?'

'Have you asked other residents if anything of theirs

has gone missing?' Bella's mind whirled, remembering Iris's missing brooch. And it wasn't just the brooch. There was something else, wasn't there? 'This could be a pattern of behaviour, and if there are thefts in homes Jack hasn't entered or dating back to before he worked here—'

'The board demand immediate action,' Ms Chan snapped. 'I'm afraid—'

'If you suspend Jack,' said Bella, her heart hammering at her own audacity, 'then I walk. I quit. Right now. And you can explain that to the board.'

Ms Chan huffed a laugh. 'You wouldn't. You can't, you're under contract.'

'I'm on probation,' said Bella. 'I can quit any time without notice.'

'No.' Jack spoke softly, but his determination was clear in the set of his jaw and his calm, firm stare. He shook his head. 'Don't do that.'

'It's fine,' she said, ignoring the voice at the back of her head which was whispering that she'd really gone too far this time. 'I wouldn't want to work anywhere which would treat you, I mean, anyone, like this.'

'No.' Jack took a step closer to Bella and placed his fingertips on her shoulders. The featherlight touch made the skin at Bella's neck tingle pleasantly and was enough to stun her into silence. But Jack waited, holding her gaze steadily, patiently, as if waiting for a sign she was listening before he continued, 'I appreciate it. I do. But I don't want you to. I'm sure there's another solution.' He turned to Ms Chan. 'For example, I'm happy to go home and stay there for a few days, if that will give you some breathing space with the board.'

Bella opened her mouth to protest. He didn't owe anyone breathing space. Let them suffocate! A small squawk passed her lips, but Jack held up a hand and continued, 'On the condition that none of this appears on my employee record and you act swiftly to find the real culprit. And I mean swiftly. As I already said to you, I suggest you call the police.'

Bella smiled, the steel in Jack's tone stirring a warm tremor of admiration inside her. She could get used to this new, take-charge version of Jack. Oh yes.

Ms Chan fiddled with the top button of her high-necked jacket. 'I hoped to avoid the involvement of the authorities. To keep this quiet.'

'I don't see how you can,' said Jack.

'We find the thief ourselves. And we call the police and ask them to pop in for a cup of tea and make an arrest, rather than barge in with the sirens and battering rams,' said Bella, as a series of memories began to merge to form a picture, the start of a theory. She was going to have to call Kate to get her opinion. Her friend was something of an amateur sleuth and would absolutely love hearing about this case. 'I suspect this problem goes back some months, to before Jack came to work here. In fact, Ms Chan, I think this goes back to Harriet.'

Ms Chan's pale complexion took on a grey tinge. 'What? You don't think she had anything to do with this?'

'I think she may have been another victim.' Bella narrowed her eyes, willing her brain to do better. What would Kate have told her to do? 'Facts,' she said. 'We need to speak to the people who know about everything that goes on in this place.'

Ms Chan sniffed, probably put out that Bella didn't regard *her* as the person who knew everything about Brookfield. 'And who might that be?'

Bella and Jack exchanged a glance. A matching pair of conspiratorial smiles curled their lips as they turned back to Ms Chan and said, in unison, 'The Christmas Fair committee.'

Chapter 44

The inside of Iris's cottage was a reflection of her decorative tastes. The walls were painted in vibrant oranges and yellows, the carpet was deep green and the furnishings were in velvet, steel and glass. Sitting on the sofa, sandwiched between Wendy and Sanghita, Bella felt as if she were sitting in a modernist meadow, albeit one dotted with ceramic snowmen, angel-shaped candle holders and a series of crocheted baubles.

It was nearly four o'clock: the perfect time for afternoon tea. Always ready to cater, Wendy had laid on an abundance of mince pies, generous slices of fruit cake and a doily-covered plate piled with spiced biscuits iced in an assortment of pastel shades. The spread was enough to feed five times the eight ladies crammed onto Iris's slim sofas, armchairs and footstools. When Bella had arrived, she had been offered both a cup of tea and a glass of mulled wine, and she had gladly accepted the tea. Mulled wine was one of the few drinks which made her happy she had decided to give up alcohol.

'So, Bella.' Iris wafted in from the kitchen—a haze of teal and cerise in a flowing top and wide-legged trousers—and tugged the curtains closed, shutting out the gathering gloom outside. 'Is it time for the big reveal yet?'

Wendy shuddered, jogging Bella's arm and sending the tea swirling around the cup in her hand. 'I'm so sorry if I got John into trouble,' Wendy said, the corners of her mouth drawing downwards. 'Do you think he's all right? I haven't been able to eat a thing since yesterday when you told me Ms Chan had been going to suspend him.' She clasped a hand to her stomach. 'I imagine it's the same for him. Maybe we should pop round to his place later with some more food?'

Wendy had visited Jack on Wednesday afternoon bearing tins of mince pies and profuse apologies. From what Bella had gleaned from his brief messages, it had taken him an hour to reassure her and he feared it might take him several weeks to get through the sweet peace offerings. 'I think he's fine,' said Bella. 'And I'm sure he appreciated your visit, but hopefully we can get this sorted today and then he can come back.' Bella smiled at Wendy, while stifling a pinch of envy: she would have loved to 'pop round' and see Jack. In fact, a couple of times since Monday, she had got as far as wandering across the village green and approaching the end of his road before thinking better of it and marching herself home. Kate—whose stern amateur detective voice had emerged the second Bella had filled her in on the possible thefts—had told her to stay away from Jack and any other suspects while the investigation was ongoing. Bella was doing her best to heed her advice.

'But how is it getting sorted?' Sanghita asked. 'You've been incredibly tight-lipped.'

'Quite,' Iris said, sinking onto the armchair on the other side of the coffee table. 'You've hardly told us anything. Surely you can spill the beans now?'

Bella sighed. She wasn't a natural at all this Poirot stuff. What would Kate say if she were here? Facts. She'd tell her to start with the facts. 'Ms Chan got involved when Wendy discovered some money and jewellery had gone missing—'

'My mother's pearls,' said Wendy, 'and a few hundred pounds I have at home in case of emergencies. I might have thought I was mistaken about the pearls, but I keep a close eye on the money and I knew I hadn't spent any of it. But I never would have said anything if I'd thought for a second it would get John into trouble, I—'

'It's fine,' said Bella, cutting Wendy off before she got into her stride. 'He knows.' Jack was staying remarkably calm throughout the whole episode. Bella admired his ability to remain so zen and trusting of the process. 'I realized that Wendy wasn't the only person who had "mislaid" something precious. There was Iris's brooch—'

'I knew I hadn't lost it!' Iris thumped the arm of her chair in indignation. 'And Lavender making me feel like I was going dotty.'

'Having spoken to each of you over the past few days,' continued Bella, 'almost all of you have had at least one item of jewellery go astray. And, having asked you about your visitors, there is a common thread. And then there's the incident of Harriet and the summer garden party money. Although she was never officially blamed for anything, given how meticulous she was, suspicions arose that she must have taken, rather than miscounted, some of the cash. And the real culprit has been happy to foster those suspicions.'

'But if that's the thief's game, why didn't they take any of the money we raised at the nativity? Or from the Christmas Fair?'

'I suspect the nativity money was a close thing, but stayed safe because there were too many eyes on the collection box. And the Christmas Fair ...' Bella glanced at the clock on her phone. 'Well, that's yet to be seen.'

'I don't understand why you've been so cloak and dagger about this,' said Iris. 'When you visited us over the last few days, all your questions were roundabout and vague. Why didn't you tell us what was going on? And why did you let us think that John was really in trouble?'

'Sorry. I couldn't be sure it wouldn't get back to the thief that we were on to them. And I hoped that if they thought Jack, sorry, John, was in the frame, they'd think they'd got away with it and relax. But, don't worry, if everything goes to plan'—Bella glanced at the time again—'the real culprit should be turning up here any moment—'

A loud knock was followed by the sound of the front door opening and closing. Footsteps approached.

Her pulse kicking up a notch, Bella set her cup on the table and rose to meet the new arrival, who paused on the threshold to the room while adjusting the knot in their silvery silk scarf.

Iris gasped as her jaw fell. 'Lavender?'

Chapter 45

'I don't believe it!' Wendy exclaimed.

The room erupted into a general cacophony of disbelief, although, down on the sofa next to Bella, Sanghita muttered, 'I'm not surprised.'

'Everyone, everyone!' Bella held up her hands for quiet. 'Lavender isn't the culprit. *Obviously*,' she added, shooting an admonishing glare at Sanghita. 'Did it work?' she asked Lavender.

'I believe so.' Lavender grinned, her eyes shining. Gone were the signs of fatigue and stress which had weighed on her during the Christmas Fair. A central role in uncovering a criminal enterprise seemed to have had a similar effect to a week at a luxury spa. 'You know, Bella, I owe you an apology. I was so sceptical when you first told me.' She seized Bella's hands and held her gaze, the gleam in her eyes joined by sadness. 'No one wants to believe they've been a fool.'

'Don't be daft. You've been brilliant. We couldn't have done it without you.'

'Done what?' Iris all but shrieked as she sprang to her feet, the movement making the coffee table vibrate and the mulled wine slosh about in its pitcher. 'What is going on?'

'All will be revealed, Iris,' said Lavender, reverting to her usual bossy tone. 'Patience is a—'

There was another knock at the door. Every stare snapped in its direction. Lavender raised her index finger to her lips and passed a significant look around the ladies before shuffling out of the room.

A collective breath seemed to be held as the door latch and hinges squealed. Bella swore she could hear pulses racing, although that was probably just her own heartbeat, which was booming in her ears.

Out in the hallway, Lavender's voice was muffled as she welcomed their unseen guest. 'We've been expecting you. Go on through.'

The lounge door swung open and the ladies in the room leant forwards as one, straining to get a look at the latest arrival.

A pair of brown brogues swished over the carpet, their progress halting abruptly, as their owner noticed the stunned faces of their hosts.

'Good afternoon, ladies,' said Trevor, flashing his broad white smile, which only faltered slightly as he took in the open mouths and wide eyes around him. His gaze roved from Iris to Bella and back to Lavender, the white bobble at the tip of his red Santa hat swinging. 'How are you all?' He snatched the hat from his head. 'Well, I hope?'

Trevor's polite greeting was met with a buzz of whispering as the women put their heads together to express their shock. Bella nodded at Lavender, who had

336

closed the door and positioned herself in front of it, then cut across the noise to say, 'Please take a seat, Trevor. Here, have mine.'

Bella rose and gestured to the sofa, but Trevor replied, 'I couldn't possibly take your seat.'

'No, no, I insist,' said Bella, manoeuvring Trevor into position and giving him an encouraging push.

Not expecting Bella's forceful shove, Trevor half fell onto his rear, huffing in surprise as his backside hit the cushions. It took him a moment to shuffle to the edge of the seat and compose himself, straightening his trousers and unbuttoning his blazer. 'It's lovely to see so many familiar faces here. And a new one.' Trevor turned the full power of his Clooney-like smile on the lady sitting in the middle of the sofa opposite him. In her late fifties, she was dressed in a faun shade trouser suit which complemented her light brown skin and eyes. She gave Trevor a tight-lipped smile which emphasized her delicate pointed chin and high rounded cheeks.

'Trevor, this is Aparna. She's our special guest.'

'Wonderful!' Trevor slapped his hands against his knees. 'The more the merrier. I hope I haven't kept you waiting to start the carol rehearsal?'

'Don't worry, you're right on time,' said Bella. 'In fact, you're exactly the man to help us with a dilemma.'

'Oh?' Trevor grinned, a charming twinkle in his eye. 'I'd be delighted to help.'

'Excellent. It's nothing too complicated. We just need you to tell us whether you've kept Iris's brooch or sold it?'

The echo of Bella's words faded, leaving behind a silence so thick it was as if the room had been buried by an avalanche of snow.

Trevor's smile froze in place, but a muscle at the corner of his eye twitched. 'I'm sorry?' he said. 'I'm not sure—'

'Or maybe,' said Bella, 'you could tell us what you've done with the four hundred pounds of the Christmas Fair money you took from Lavender's apartment earlier this afternoon?'

Trevor stuttered and glanced about him, wearing the wide-eyed mask of a confounded innocent. But, when he found his silent appeal for support was met with nothing but frosty glares, he dropped his gaze to the hat in his hands, which he was gripping tightly enough to turn his knuckles white. When he lifted his gaze again, a timid smile played on his lips. Bella narrowed her eyes. He thought he could get out of this, didn't he?

'Bella, dear,' said Trevor. 'We all know you're keen to clear John's name. But it's rather irresponsible to be running around pointing the finger at innocent parties.' He chuckled, as if the idea itself was ridiculous. 'I honestly don't know what could have put the idea into your pretty head.'

Bella ground her teeth. Violence was never the answer, she reminded herself. Never. Not even when it was deserved, tempting and no one else in the room would stop her.

She tilted her head and flashed Trevor a cold smile which she hoped was terrifying. 'What put the idea in my pretty, daft little head?' she said. 'Actually, it was your sketchy behaviour at the nativity play. I thought I'd surprised you at the donation table by being stealthy, but you jumped out of your skin because I'd interrupted you assessing how difficult it would be to take money from the collection box.'

'That's absurd!'

'Really? Because you told me you were impressed with how much money I'd managed to collect. I didn't think anything of it at the time, but how did you know how much money was in the box? It was cardboard, the top and sides were opaque. How could you know how much money was in it unless you'd been handling it and, I suspect, lifting the lid to take a look?'

Trevor's lips parted again but this time the only sound which emerged was a strangled croak. Finding she had zero sympathy for his predicament, Bella rolled on, 'And then the way you were so keen to blame Harriet was odd when you were such a good friend to her. Did you enjoy making her doubt her sanity? Was that part of the game for you?'

'Bella—' Trevor's panicked gaze roved the room and settled on Iris. 'Iris, you don't believe any of—'

'You made me believe you cared for me,' said Iris, wrinkling her nose in disgust. 'I invited you into my home and you stole from me.'

'And from me,' said Lavender. 'From all of us. Not to mention the charities the monies from the summer garden party and now the Christmas Fair were for.'

'That money was for the local children's hospice, Trevor,' said Bella, unable to keep her revulsion out of her voice. 'You make Ebenezer Scrooge look like a saint.'

'I didn't take anything!' Trevor threw his hands up and Wendy and Sanghita, who had already inched as far to the edges of the sofa as they could, almost leapt over the armrests. 'All right then,' he said, 'if I'm this master thief you're making me out to be, where's your proof?'

'I thought you'd never ask,' said Bella. 'Aparna, if you wouldn't mind.'

Aparna rose and rounded the coffee table, taking what looked like a small black tube from her jacket pocket. She paused in front of Trevor. 'If you could turn out the main light, please,' she said.

'Of course.' Bella nodded. 'Lavender, would you do the honours?'

'Gladly,' said Lavender, flicking the switch by the door with a vicious snap.

The soft illuminations on the Christmas tree in the far corner of the room were joined by a stream of violet light coming from the black tube in Aparna's hand. All eyes followed the eerie dark light down to its target, Trevor's hands, which were covered in glowing red smudges.

Gasps of horror shuddered around the group. Bella grinned. *Got you*, she thrilled silently. Got you, you thieving toerag.

Bella glanced at Aparna and, noticing her stony expression, schooled her own features. This was serious business. 'Aparna or, to use her full title, Detective Inspector Mitra,' said Bella, 'has been incredibly helpful over the past few days. A member of her team applied the invisible powder to the Christmas Fair money. Then Lavender simply had to leave it lying around in her house and invite you over to lunch. Anyone who touched the money would get covered in the powder. It leaves a stain on skin and clothes which is only visible under an ultraviolet light, like the one DI Mitra is shining on you right now, Trevor, *dear*.'

Aparna switched off her flashlight and Lavender flicked on the overhead lights, leaving everyone blinking in the glare, but no one more so than Trevor. The muscles at the sides of his eyes twitched, as if he'd suddenly developed a nervous tic. 'This … this …' He stammered as dashes of red appeared in his cheeks. 'This will never stand up in court. It's entrapment!'

Bella sighed. 'I'm not an expert on these things. But DI Mitra's team are currently searching your apartment and I imagine their findings, in addition to the obvious fact you've had your nasty hands all over the Christmas Fair money, are unlikely to help your defence.'

Trevor's face slackened and his complexion took on a waxy sheen. 'You have no right to enter my house! You'd need a warrant!'

'Yes, that's why they have one.' Bella shrugged. She had wanted to ransack Trevor's place on Monday, the moment she had suspected him of being guilty. But DI Mitra had ordered her to hold off until a warrant could be obtained. 'I'm sure DI Mitra will be happy to show you a copy after she's arrested you.'

While Bella was speaking, Lavender had slipped out into the hall. Now she returned, followed by two uniformed police officers. They helped Trevor to his feet as Aparna informed Trevor he was under arrest and didn't have to say anything. As Trevor was escorted out of the apartment, Bella hoped he kept talking the whole way to the station and every word dug him ever deeper into a cold, muddy pit.

Iris pushed to standing, keeping one hand on the back of the armchair to steady herself. 'Do you think I'll get my brooch back?'

'I hope so,' said Bella. 'If they've found it in his apartment it may be evidence for a while, but they can give it back eventually.'

'I can't believe it.' Iris shook her head. 'I mean, I do. But, I don't think I would have believed it if you hadn't caught him literally red-handed.'

'He's a convincing charmer,' said Bella. 'That's his entire thing.' Bella took in the tears welling in Iris's eyes and decided it wasn't the time to tell her that DI Mitra had had Trevor in her sights for a while. He was her number one suspect for a series of crimes at two previous retirement communities which involved a string of besotted ladies being robbed of jewellery and cash. 'He took everyone in.'

Lavender patted Bella on the shoulder. 'You did very well, Bella. Elegantly done too.'

'Thank you.' Bella smiled. She was doing her best not to be smug, but she was rather proud of herself. She had managed to get through the whole process of confronting Trevor without swearing or shouting. Which, for her, was a major achievement. Particularly when Trevor deserved to be hit hard with every expletive under the sun. The smarmy swine had made the grave error of upsetting the committee ladies and, most importantly, Jack. Bella's stomach clenched whenever she remembered his wounded expression when Ms Chan had suspended him. And, as Wendy began to sob and was comforted by a visibly shaken Sanghita, a familiar ball of anger tightened in Bella's chest. Trevor would never know how lucky he'd been to escape the room without her throwing a shoe at his head.

But though it would have been wonderfully cathartic to pepper Trevor with a barrage of X-rated insults or thumps with her stiletto heels, Bella was on a quest to become a calmer, more thoughtful person.

'Have you ever thought about joining the police, Bella?'

asked Lavender. 'I think you could be good at catching criminals.'

'Oh no,' said Bella. 'I'm a committed armchair detective only.'

'I'm partial to a Poirot,' said Iris. 'Wendy likes that modern one. *Napier*, is it?'

Wendy managed to hold in her tears long enough to nod before breaking into another bout of sobbing. Oh dear. Much more of that and the whole room would be in floods. There had to be a way to lighten the mood. And, as a fellow *Napier* fan, one idea did come to mind …

Bella frowned, Lucinda would probably kill her for what she was about to do, but she wasn't about to leave poor Wendy in a state. 'You know, my stepsister,' said Bella, 'her boyfriend is Alex Fraser. He plays Dexter Hartford in *Napier*.'

Wendy's blubbing halted, Bella pushed on. 'He arranged for me and my friend to visit the set last year. We got to appear in the background in a café scene. If you like, Wendy, I could ask him if he could do the same for you?'

Wendy blinked at Bella, stunned. At her side, Lavender nudged Bella and made a pointed cough.

'Oh!' said Bella. 'Maybe I could ask if all of you could visit? A group trip?'

A chorus of happy murmurs greeted Bella's suggestion. Oh Lord, thought Bella. She was going to have to think of a spectacular Christmas gift for Lucinda and Alex this year.

'That's wonderful, Bella,' said Lavender. 'But I really do think you should consider a career in the force.'

'I appreciate your confidence, but I think working for

the police would be rather stressful and I'm hoping for a quiet life.' Bella sighed and gazed at the Christmas tree in the corner. 'But, with how things have been going recently, I'd settle just for a quiet Christmas.'

Chapter 46

'I'm sorry to bother you at home, Bella. Particularly when you're on holiday.'

'No, it's fine, Ms Chan. I'm pleased you called. I won't spend the holidays worrying about it now.' Bella smiled as she opened the fridge, her lips only drooping slightly when she noticed how empty it was. Ms Chan had warmed up to her considerably since Monday morning's drama and, while in her previous job she would have regarded a call from her boss on a Friday evening as a huge intrusion, perhaps this was a sign that one day she might be allowed to call Ms Chan by her first name.

But even if her manager had been terrifyingly frosty, Bella would have happily taken her call to hear that Trevor had been charged and was being kept in custody until his bail hearing.

'Did the police tell you anything about the stolen jewellery?' asked Bella as she wandered into the front room.

'They found a few items in Mr Webster's apartment.' Ms Chan's voice dripped with disgust, as if Trevor's name left a foul taste in her mouth. 'Iris's brooch and I believe Lavender's pearl earrings and gold necklace were also recovered.'

Bella punched the air. 'That's amazing. They'll be so happy.'

'Indeed. An early Christmas present. And, speaking of Christmas, I'd better let you get back to your holidays. I'm sure you have a lot planned.'

'Yes, lots. Loads. Non-stop,' said Bella, wincing as her stomach twisted. She hated lying. 'Do you have plans?'

'I'm going to Thailand. I'm off to the airport tonight. I imagine I won't be too far behind John.' Ms Chan chuckled, unaware that her words had wiped the smile off Bella's face. 'Well, enjoy your break. Thank you again for everything you've done this week, and for being so discreet. I know the board appreciate it.'

'You're welcome. Merry Christmas.'

Bella ended the call, threw the phone onto the sofa and slouched down after it. Lying on her back, she stared up at the ceiling and sighed. The white plaster made her think of snow, which sent her thoughts back—once again—to skiing and, inevitably, to Jack. She glanced at the clock on the mantlepiece. Seven p.m. Jack was probably sitting down to dinner and managing to smile and chat politely though surrounded by happy couples.

Bella's tummy rumbled. It had been a long time since Wendy had dropped by the office and insisted Bella finish off the chocolates from the Christmas Fair committee's afternoon meeting. Food—something actually nutritious—was probably a good idea.

Bella glanced at the clock again and thought back to the

message Cath had sent her that morning. Her landlady had wanted to check in on Bella and invite her round to dinner at seven. Bella had politely declined. She didn't want to be a nuisance and was looking forward to some quality sofa and TV time after a stressful week. But now the thought of Cath's chicken pie—succulent morsels of perfectly cooked chicken in a smooth creamy sauce, topped with fluffy mashed potato—made her tummy growl. Hmn. If she was incredibly apologetic, maybe Cath wouldn't mind her arriving a few minutes late?

Bella snatched up her phone and was composing a message to Cath when the doorbell rang. She frowned. Who could that be? She glanced down at her outfit. Not expecting any callers, she had changed into her grey leggings, fluffy yellow slipper socks and oversized, fleece-lined hoodie in midnight black, complete with a hand-warmer front pocket. It was one of her comfiest ensembles, but not the sort of thing she would normally wear in public.

The doorbell rang again. Oh well, thought Bella as she scooped up her phone, strode to the door and grabbed the latch. If their urgency was as great as their persistent ringing suggested, her mystery caller probably wouldn't notice what she was wearing.

On the doorstep, bathed in the blue haze cast by the lights in the wisteria, Cath was bouncing from foot to foot. Bella took her fidgeting as a sign of how freezing the night air was and opened her mouth to ask her to come inside, but Cath jumped in first.

'Bella, hello. Sorry, can't stop. We've had wonderful news. Elle, our daughter—I think I mentioned she was travelling—well she just called to tell us she's back in the country. She was trying to get back to Haileybrook on her own steam to surprise us, but she and her boyfriend have got stuck outside Oxford. The trains are up the creek because of snow or the wrong leaves or something, so we're off now to collect them.' She gestured behind her to the end of the path where Bella could make out the shadow of Malcolm, Cath's partner. He was standing by their car and raised a hand in greeting. Bella waved in response as Cath charged on, 'Obviously this means we won't be home for dinner and I thought I should tell you in case you changed your mind.'

'That's very kind of you,' said Bella, pressing her hand to her mutinous stomach and hoping Cath couldn't hear its wails of despair. 'And that's such exciting news. Is Elle home for long?'

Cath's grin stretched. 'Until the new year. It's the best present we could have had.' She paused, her gaze roving over Bella's loungewear, and her smile slipped. 'But if you need us at any time—'

'Oh no,' Bella rushed to say, dismayed that Cath clearly saw her as some sort of charity case, 'please don't worry about me—'

'You must pop round. Elle would love to meet you.'

'And I would like to meet her.'

'Cath!' Malcolm's voice boomed down the path. 'They're waiting for us.'

'Don't let me hold you back,' said Bella. 'Happy Christmas.'

'Happy Christmas,' said Cath, who was already halfway down the path. 'Oo!' She paused. 'I could bring round some chicken pie for you later.'

'No, honestly. It's fine.'

'Well, if you're sure,' said Cath, slipping through the garden gate. 'See you soon!'

'Bye!' called Bella, keeping a wide smile on her face until she had closed the door and slumped against it. Well. That was another plan scotched.

Pulling up her favourite delivery app, Bella had ordered a large pepperoni pizza before she got back to the sofa. As if it knew food was on its way, the rumbling in her stomach eased but, as she flopped down onto the seat, it was replaced by a tightness behind her ribs. Ugh. What was wrong with her? It was lovely that Elle was coming home for Christmas and to see Cath radiant with joy. So why couldn't Bella fully share in that happiness? Why had her landlady's delight at her imminent family reunion stirred a heaviness in Bella's heart?

Bella rolled her eyes. Lord, she was ridiculous. Here she was, sitting alone in a beautiful cottage in a chocolate box village. No fights with housemates over who had used all the milk or left dishes in the sink. After a bumpy start, she had settled into her new job and things promised to be even better after the holidays. She had everything she'd wanted, including plenty of peace and quiet. So why couldn't she shake the hollowness settling over her like a leaden fog?

She should do something. Wallowing, while tempting, was unlikely to help and was often a one-way ticket to a migraine. When she had mentioned her recurring stress headaches to her sister, Summer had recommended one of her own favourite ways to combat negative thoughts and emotions: visualising herself in a safe place. Bella had always struggled to manage it, but it was worth another try.

Wriggling down the sofa until she was reclining with her head propped on a cushion, Bella closed her eyes and, following Summer's instructions, told herself to imagine she was somewhere she felt calm, happy and safe. Rather than attempt to create a complete picture immediately, she approached her imaginary surroundings cautiously, building up the image through small details, starting with what she could see.

A pristine white blanket of snow stretched into the distance. On the horizon, a line of deep green trees squatted below a sky filled with puffy clouds tinged with grey. Somewhere nearby, a robin trilled and whistled, the sound joined by muffled crunching noises and her own giggling which formed the melody over a bass line of deep, genuine chuckles.

Bella took a deep breath and smelled damp earth, spice and sugar and, under these scents, tantalising notes of wood and musk.

At her back, the ground was solid and sent a nip of cold into her limbs, a contrast to the warmth in her hand which was held in a firm, but gentle grip. As she rubbed her thumb over the back of the strong fingers clasping hers, a soothing sensation raced through her, making her nerves sing and tingle, her lips part as her muscles loosened and her heartbeat slow to a regular rhythm. It was as if the hand holding hers was an anchor, steadying her in a stormy sea.

Bella's eyes snapped open. Oh, wow. Finally, *finally*, she'd found the clarity all the podcasts had been promising for months! And she had got it wrong. She had thought she wanted a break from the noise, crowds and bustle of the city. To find some quiet and solitude where she would have room to breathe and think. But what she had really been searching for was inner peace: the sort of warm, soothing feeling she had experienced when holding Jack's hand as they traced angels in the snow. The sort of contentment she had felt when surrounded by friends in the hubbub of the nativity play or the chaos of the Christmas Fair. The sort of satisfaction that came when sending a thieving scumbag to prison while clearing an innocent man's name.

Bella sat up, her heart thrumming with renewed energy. What should she do now? What was the point of an epiphany if you couldn't *do* anything with it?

Jack. She should talk to Jack. Even if he was probably halfway up an exclusive Swiss mountain pass or, if he was sensible, snuggled under a blanket in the lodge with a mug of hot chocolate and marshmallows. Bella smiled, a vivid image of Jack coming to mind: hair tousled, dark eyes shining, a small smile of contentment curling the corners of his lovely lips, wearing a tight-fitting, roll-neck sweater, while lounging by a large open fireplace holding a steaming mug.

Right. She was going to send him a message. Her fingers trembling with a rush of adrenalin, she grabbed her phone and tapped it against her top lip. Would it be weird to message him out of the blue? Perhaps she could use telling him about Trevor's detention as an excuse? Ms Chan said she'd update Jack, but what if she forgot?

Oh sod it. Do first, apologize later.

Hi,

I hope you had a good flight and are safely at the lodge. I hope someone brought hot chocolate and marshmallows!

In case Ms Chan hasn't already told you

The doorbell rang and Bella glanced up from the screen, a deep frown creasing her brow. The pizza delivery was usually quick, but not this quick. Bella dropped her phone on the coffee table and snatched up her purse. She rifled through it for a tip as she padded over to the door, her cheeks heating in shame. The pizza place must have started expecting her order and have prepared her a pizza just in case. Blimey, she needed to make time to cook for herself.

She reached for the latch. What was the delivery guy's name again? Mark? Marcel? It definitely began with *M*. Perhaps it was—

Oh.

Jack's black wool coat only partially covered the dark blue roll-neck jumper beneath it. His clothes, combined with his rumpled hair, were so similar to Bella's recent vision of him, it was as though thinking about Jack had manifested him. Blimey, thought Bella as she ran a smoothing hand over her own hair. Maybe those visualization gurus were on to something after all.

However, the real Jack standing on her path was decidedly less relaxed than the fireside version she had imagined. Streaks of red flamed in his cheeks and his chest heaved as if he'd jogged to her door. He dropped a backpack on the ground by his feet and, as Bella opened her mouth to greet him, he raised a hand to stop her. 'Just, wait a minute. Sorry, but I need to say this, so if you could let me, I'd appreciate it.'

Bella pressed her lips together. Her heart thundered, pattering a rapid tattoo against her ribs. *Well hello there, assertive Jack.*

Though she had many things she would have liked to say to him, she held her tongue and nodded, silently willing him to continue.

Chapter 47

'OK.' Jack ran a hand across his mouth. 'I wanted to say thank you in person. Thank you for never believing I was stealing from the residents and for working so hard to clear my name. I really appreciate it.' He exhaled, his breath leaving a trail of mist in the chill night air. 'But, while that's important, what I really want to say is: you were right. I should have asked you what your name was, back at Ashley's wedding. I was rude and inconsiderate.' He shook his head. Apparently, even after a year, he still found his own behaviour unbelievable. 'But you were wrong about something else.'

Oh? Ready for a challenge, Bella crossed her arms as she held Jack's stare. Now *this* should be interesting.

'You said I didn't ask you anything about you at the wedding because I didn't want to know.' Jack took a deep breath, his gaze flicking upwards, as if he were struggling to remember the next part of his prepared speech. 'But that's not true because ... because I felt I knew *so much* about you. I knew you're funny and great with kids. I knew you have excellent taste in films. I knew you were kind—I mean, you jumped in to save a stranger from a difficult situation. And I know that you did that, in part, because you didn't want to go back and socialize with the people from your job you hated'—Bella nodded, she couldn't argue with his analysis—'but you didn't have to help me or stay for the reception. And I knew you were smart and unafraid to start scandalous rumours to boost a guy's reputation. Thanks again for that.' He smiled and Bella chuckled, recalling the stunned faces of the ladies in the loos when she'd hit them with stories of Jack's sexting prowess.

As he continued to hold her gaze, Jack's smile faded and his expression turned earnest. 'I should have guessed your name because I knew you were beautiful. And sexy. And an amazing kisser.' His stare dropped to Bella's lips and her heart boomed in response, sending a rush of heat up her neck. 'I knew I wanted to spend more time with you and I was devastated I didn't get it. Mostly because it was my own fault for not asking your name, not getting your phone number and not getting my arse back outside quickly like I promised. I'm sorry I took my annoyance with myself out on you when I saw you again.'

He closed his eyes and sighed. Dazed by his words, and a little light-headed, Bella raised a hand to the door frame to steady herself and waited for him to continue.

Jack opened his eyes. 'You suggested, a couple of weeks ago, that we start again, and I, like an idiot, didn't take you up on that offer. But I'm hoping it's not too late.' He extended his right hand to Bella and smiled. 'Hi, I'm Jack. I live here in Haileybrook and work at the local retirement community. And, though it may not be much of a character reference, I've recently been cleared of all suspicion of being a thief.'

Bella laughed and grasped Jack's hand. The brush of his warm skin against hers sent sparks speeding up her arm. She grinned. 'Nice to meet you, Jack. I'm Bella. I live here in Haileybrook and work at the local retirement community. And I'm delighted to hear you're not in the habit of robbing elderly ladies because that would put a serious dent in my plan to invite you into my house.'

'Thank the Lord, it's freezing out here!' Jack sucked in air through his teeth and scooped up his bag. He ducked—almost bending double to pass safely through the low cottage door—and shuffled past Bella into the lounge.

Chapter 48

'So,' said Bella, as she took Jack's coat. 'While I liked everything you had to say out there, I have some questions.'

'Pleased to hear it. Fire away.'

As Bella turned to hang Jack's coat by the door, she shot a sneaky glance back at him. He was taking in the lounge which, even with Christmas decorations to study, took him mere seconds. But it was long enough for Bella to admire his broad chest and shoulders, which the navy sweater showcased to perfection. Somewhere in Switzerland there were a bunch of skiers who didn't know what they were missing.

'Why aren't you on the slopes?' she asked. 'Did your flight get cancelled?'

'Uh, no.' Jack slipped his hands into his pockets. 'I got to the airport and everywhere I looked there were people who were so happy and excited about getting away. And I thought, "What am I doing?" I didn't feel any of that excitement. I don't get on that well with any of the other people going and being surrounded by loved-up couples makes me feel like a ridiculous third wheel. To be honest, I've been dreading it and I should have said no when Ashley sent the invite. I've only been going out of habit.' He shrugged. 'So I messaged Ashley and told her I wasn't going.'

Bella nodded, impressed. 'And she took that well?'

'Not exactly. She called me and told me not to be daft, that she wanted me there and I had to get on the plane. She kept insisting and so I told her the truth: that I didn't enjoy the ski trip, I had someone— uh, I mean, some*where* I'd rather be and if she didn't like it then … tough.'

Bella beamed, her insides fizzing with delight at Jack's Freudian slip. 'OK,' she said, trying not to get too excited. She didn't want to jinx the moment and bring the Christmas curse down on her head at the exact moment it appeared to be lifting. 'And you came here, to my place, because …'

'To say what I said out there—'

'About me being right, I got that.'

Jack's lips curled into a lopsided smile. 'And the whole part about you being *wrong*. Did you get that too?'

Bella scrunched up her nose and pretended to consider her answer. 'Actually, I think that was my favourite part. I mean, it's so rare that I'm wrong. It's important we learn to savour such extraordinary moments.'

Jack's smile stretched. 'I'm also here because I wanted to ask if you're busy over the next couple of weeks. Because I don't have any plans any more and I was hoping you'd help me use our holiday fortnight to work through the stacks of food that the Brookfield's ladies have given me. Oh, and in the meantime—' Jack grabbed the bag at his feet and opened it. 'I brought some initial supplies I thought you might appreciate.' He held up a tub of hot chocolate powder, wait—Bella tilted her head to read the label—make that some seriously good chocolate powder. Jack certainly had taste. 'And these too,' he said, reaching into the bag and pulling out a huge bag of mini marshmallows.

'Thank you, that's very thoughtful,' said Bella, her insides turning as gooey as the marshmallows. He'd brought supplies! And wanted to spend time with her over the next couple of weeks!

'You're welcome,' he said, passing the gifts to Bella. 'It's not like I could rock up here empty-handed. That would have been rude.'

'Hmn.' Bella's smile turned dreamy. She did love good manners.

Yes, but it's probably not a great idea to stand goggling at him, slack-jawed, her brain chimed in. And, for once, Bella had to agree.

She gave herself a shake. 'I'll pop these in the kitchen.' She shuffled towards the archway between the two downstairs rooms, deftly sidestepping the dip in the floor. 'But hot chocolate and marshmallows, while delicious, aren't really a meal. How do you feel about pepperoni pizza?' Bella set Jack's gifts on the countertop and spun round to face him. 'I've ordered far too much and it's on its way.'

'Sounds great, thanks.' Jack strolled after Bella and, as he neared the hidden hollow in the floor, Bella's lips parted to warn him—

But she was too late.

Jack's foot landed awkwardly on the uneven surface and he staggered, tipping into a fall.

Bella darted forwards, throwing herself into him to halt his slide. She collided with his chest, her low centre of gravity paying off, both for Jack—who got to remain upright—and herself—as she found herself wrapped tightly in Jack's embrace, her cheek pressed against the soft wool of his jumper.

Jack shuffled his feet to right his posture and take weight off Bella, but kept his arms around her. 'Is it just me, or is this a little familiar?'

Bella smiled as she also recalled the first time they'd met. At least this time there wasn't a giant fir tree between them. 'A little. But you're far less spiky than that tree.' She pulled back to look up at Jack's face, her gaze travelling up and up, until it snagged on Iris's late addition to her decoration haul which was hanging from the kitchen archway above them. Bella huffed a small laugh. She must remember to thank Iris for her optimism.

'What?' Jack followed her stare and his smile slowly grew into a grin. He lowered his gaze until it met Bella's. His eyes contained a glimmer of amusement and—Bella hoped she was right about this—something darker and wolfish. She ran the tip of her tongue over her lower lip and felt a thrill of satisfaction as Jack's gaze followed it. 'Now this,' he said, 'seems *very* familiar. So, what do we do now?'

'Well, given that you referred to our previous kiss as "fantastic"—'

'I actually said *you* were fantastic,' said Jack, lowering his head closer to Bella's, leaving only a few tantalising inches between them.

'Thank you. You're not so bad yourself.' Bella's lips twitched. It was increasingly difficult to keep a straight face. And not to grab Jack by his sweater and climb into his arms. She took a deep breath. God, he smelled amazing.

'And given that the mistletoe thing is a longstanding festive tradition, I think we should do our bit to uphold ancient customs.'

She glanced up at the mistletoe and the rest of her body followed, bringing her to her tiptoes and her face closer to Jack's.

'Sounds wise. We wouldn't want to anger any ancient spirits by ignoring custom, would we?'

'Of course not,' said Bella, sliding her hand up to Jack's shoulder, his sweater soft and smooth over the hard planes of muscle beneath.

Jack ran a thumb along the side of her face, his touch warm and gentle. 'Good,' he murmured as he closed the space between them and, when their lips touched, Bella could still feel the smile on his.

Her skin quickly began to heat and, when Jack slid a hand into the hair at the back of her neck and applied the lightest pressure to tilt her head and deepen the kiss— she'd forgotten that trick of his, honestly the man was a *magician*— she soon felt thoroughly boneless.

Jack pulled away and Bella let out a small whimper of disappointment, which quickly turned into a hum of pleasure as he dipped his head lower to brush his lips over the sensitive skin beneath her ear.

'I have a question,' said Jack, his voice a deep rumble against Bella's neck.

'Hmn?' Bella managed. Words. She'd had so many words a minute ago. Where had they gone?

'I know you made the comparison yourself the other day—'

'Mm-hmn?'

360

'When you mentioned your low centre of gravity. But are you intentionally dressed like a penguin?'

Bella gasped and shoved Jack away. She glared at the amusement in his eyes and glanced down, taking in her yellow socks, grey leggings and black top. A top whose hand warmer was a white rectangular patch of fluff. Dammit. The man had a point.

Bella laughed and swatted Jack playfully. 'Cheeky! These aren't exactly my best going-out clothes.'

'I like them.' Jack grinned and pulled her back against him. He hooked his thumb into the neckline of her top, teased it to one side and lowered his lips to the tender skin along her collarbone. 'You'd look good in anything.'

Bella shivered as a zap of electricity shot down her spine. Mmn, that was so good. Why had she swatted him again? Oh, yes. 'It's still a ruddy cheek,' said Bella, making a half-hearted effort to push Jack away. 'I like assertive Jack, but this impudent character—'

'You don't like him?'

'I'm not sure,' said Bella, her eyes drifting shut as Jack stroked a hand lazily along her spine, making her thoughts turn hazy. 'I'd have to see more of him to be sure.'

'And when you say see *more* of him—and he is *me*, I'd like us to remember—'

Bella laughed and batted Jack lightly on the shoulder, thrilled to discover his mind was going to salacious places. 'Let's wait and see, shall we?'

She rose to her tiptoes again and Jack stooped to meet her. His soft lips brushed hers but, before she could get carried away, she sighed and placed a hand on his chest to halt his advance. Without her high heels, their height difference was daft and they should sit down before he developed a bad back and she got neck strain. 'We should take this to the sofa,' she said, her voice a breathy whisper.

Jack raised his eyebrows. 'But I thought you wanted to wait before seeing more of—'

'Oh, shut up!' Bella thumped Jack again, her light blow bouncing off his broad chest. 'I meant, maybe we should sit down and *watch some TV* while we wait for the pizza.' Bella gave Jack a coy smile. 'And maybe carry on the fantastic kissing a bit too. If you don't object.'

Jack held up his hands in surrender. 'No argument from me.' He grinned. 'Sounds like a plan. Anyway, you're always right.'

'I'll get that in writing later. And, in the meantime, as you've been such a model guest'—she gestured to the hot chocolate and marshmallows on the counter behind her— 'let me be a decent host and offer you a drink. Tea?'

'Tea would be great, thank you.' He gestured towards the television. 'Shall I see what's on?'

Bella ran a hand over her hair, attempting to appear cool. Calm. Not at all like the prospect of cuddling up with Jack on the sofa was filling her with a jittery, sparkling sensation which made her feel like dancing. 'Sure,' she said in what she prayed was a nonchalant tone. 'Help yourself to the remote.'

Bella spun towards the kitchen and, as soon as she could be certain there was no chance of Jack seeing her face, she let her lips stretch into a broad beaming smile. She floated over to the countertop and, humming the melody of 'Hark! The Herald Angels Sing', flicked on the kettle and retrieved two mugs.

As she waited for the water to boil, Bella's gaze wandered to the window. Outside the snow had returned, drifting down over the garden, glistening in the cottage's warm light.

Bella grinned as she grabbed the kettle. Let it snow! For all she cared, Haileybrook could become cut off from the rest of the world for the next two weeks. She would be curled up on the sofa with Jack and enough mince pies in the cupboard to see them through a blizzard.

A lightness in her step, Bella glided back into the lounge and placed the mugs on the coffee table in front of Jack who was browsing the channel guide. Bella settled down on the sofa and took a breath, ready to begin a debate with Jack about their viewing options, but all thoughts about the relative merits of the various Christmas specials on offer were wiped from her mind when Jack wrapped his arm around her shoulders and pulled her to his side. Doing her best not to purr with pleasure, Bella lifted her legs up onto the seat and wriggled until she was tucked neatly against him, her head resting on his arm. *Ahhh.* She released a deep sigh which failed to come close to expressing how extremely comfortable she was, snuggled up against the soft fabric of Jack's jumper, breathing in his gorgeous clean, spicy scent.

Bella's eyes drifted shut. Her pulse slowed to a regular rhythm and gradually the last traces of tension in her body disappeared, replaced by soothing waves of peace and contentment which settled over her like the silent snow slowly enrobing the village.

Bella's lips curled into a small, satisfied smile. 'Merry Christmas, Jack,' she said.

Jack placed a tender kiss on the top of her head. 'Merry Christmas, Bella.'

Also by Claire Huston

If you enjoyed Bella's story and reading about her new village home, you can return to Haileybrook and meet Lucy's best friend Elle …

Elle's A to Z of Love

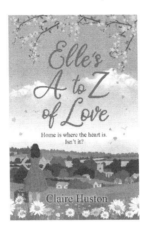

Haileybrook, a beautiful village in the peaceful Cotswolds countryside, is most people's idea of heaven on earth.

Born and raised in this small slice of paradise, Elle Bea can't wait to leave.

It should be easy, but every time she packs her bags for exotic adventures, old loves and loyalties pull her back.

Will Elle be forced to forget her dreams of far-flung places and epic romance, or can she grab one last chance to have it all?

An uplifting, romantic story about friends, family and the relationships that make a place a home.

Or perhaps you'd like to know more about Bella's stepsister, Lucinda? Or her best friend Kate? You can read their stories in the Love in the Comptons collection of standalone romcoms that can be read in any order.

The Love in the Comptons collection

♥ *Art and Soul* (Becky and Charlie's story)
♥ *The Only Exception* (Lucinda and Alex's story)
♥ *Clues to You* (Kate and Max's story)

Acknowledgements

Thank you for reading *Bella's Countryside Christmas*. If you can, please leave a short review on Amazon as this will help other readers to find the book.

Thank you, as ever, to my publishing dream team: my editor, Alison May; my proofreader, Imogen Howson; my cover designer, Gail Bradley; and Sarah Houldcroft at Goldcrest Books for all the hard work involved in transforming a manuscript into a book.

Thank you to Rachel Gilbey at Rachel's Random Resources for organizing my cover reveal and blog tour. A massive thank you to the bloggers who took part and to all the other bloggers and readers who have generously used their time and platforms to feature and review *Bella's Countryside Christmas*.

Thank you to the Romantic Novelists' Association and particularly the members of the Birmingham Chapter for their support and encouragement.

Thank you to my husband for his continued optimistic belief that I will one day sell enough books for him to take early retirement. And finally, thank you to my mum for giving the book a final proofread in record time.

About the author

Claire Huston lives in Warwickshire, UK, with her husband and two children. She writes uplifting modern love stories about characters who are meant for each other but sometimes need a little help to realise it.

A keen amateur baker, she enjoys making cakes, biscuits and brownies almost as much as eating them. You can find recipes for all the cakes mentioned in her first novel, *Art and Soul*, at www.clairehuston.co.uk along with over 150 other recipes. This is also where she talks about and reviews books.

You can also find her on lots of social media platforms. Find your favourite here: linktr.ee/clairehuston_author

Printed in Great Britain
by Amazon

50326163R00207